Also by Bronwyn Parry

Storm Clouds

BRONWYN PARRY

hachette
AUSTRALIA

 hachette
AUSTRALIA

Published in Australia and New Zealand in 2015
by Hachette Australia
(an imprint of Hachette Australia Pty Limited)
Level 17, 207 Kent Street, Sydney NSW 2000
www.hachette.com.au

10 9 8 7 6 5 4 3 2 1

National Library of Australia
Cataloguing-in-Publication data

Parry, Bronwyn, 1962– author.
Storm clouds/Bronwyn Parry.

ISBN 978 0 7336 3329 4 (paperback)

Deception – Fiction.
Murder – Investigation – Fiction.
Suspense fiction.

A823.4

Cover design by Hannah Janzen
Cover photographs courtesy of Getty Images, thinkstock.photo.com.au and bigstockphoto.com
Text design by Bookhouse, Sydney
Typeset in 12.75/19.75 pt Adobe Garamond Pro by Bookhouse, Sydney
Printed and bound in Australia by Griffin Press, Adelaide, an Accredited ISO AS/NZS 14001:2009
Environmental Management System printer

MIX
Paper from
responsible sources
FSC
www.fsc.org   FSC® C009448

The paper this book is printed on is certified against the
Forest Stewardship Council® Standards. Griffin Press holds
FSC chain of custody certification SGS-COC-005088. FSC
promotes environmentally responsible, socially beneficial
and economically viable management of the world's forests.

Storm Clouds
is dedicated to the memory of three
inspirational friends, lost far too soon:

Kerry Hawkins,
with whom I shared many visits to national parks, a love of
sewing and textiles, and a rich and wonderful friendship;

Deborah Anderson,
influential friend of my youth, who encouraged me – and
so many others – not to let uncertainty stop me from
trying something new and reaching for my dreams;

Matt Richell,
CEO of Hachette Australia, who believed in
my books right from the beginning.

CHAPTER 1

The late afternoon sun shone straight at the dusty windscreen, semi-blinding Erin so that she didn't see the small landslide of rocks and dirt across the rough fire trail in time to avoid it. The four-wheel-drive Hilux utility tilted as one wheel mounted the edge of a rock, and then dropped suddenly as the rock spun off to the side. Metal scraped on stone, the steering wheel dragged to one side and the right front wheel went *thunk, thunk, thunk* before the vehicle stopped.

She swore as she switched off the ignition. A flat tyre. The last thing she needed at the end of a twelve-hour workday. She swung out of the ute, knowing exactly what she'd see. Sure enough, the Hilux had thrown a tyre off the rim.

Changing a tyre? No worries. As a National Parks ranger

working in rugged country, she'd changed a fair few, and she methodically chocked the other wheels securely and gathered what she'd need – the jack, the wrench and the spare tyre from beneath the truck.

But changing a tyre on an isolated bush track miles from anywhere when the wheel nuts were so frigging tight she had to battle for minutes to loosen them? Despite her strength and fitness, Erin ran through her entire vocabulary of swear words twice before she'd removed the first one. She brushed hair that had escaped her ponytail out of her eyes.

'Where the bloody hell are you when I need you, Kennedy?' she muttered into the silence.

Simon Kennedy. Fellow National Parks ranger. Friend. And army reserve soldier who'd been gone on deployment for close on two months. Maybe in Afghanistan. Or Iraq or some other war-torn hellhole. He had to be overseas somewhere, because in the two months since he'd been abruptly called up for army reserve service there'd been no word from him. Two months without an email, a text. Nothing.

She used her pent-up frustration as well as her boot on the wrench and the third wheel nut finally loosened. Hallelujah. She might get this tyre off sometime before nightfall.

She wouldn't make it home before dark, though. Twenty kilometres back to the Goodabri National Parks office to leave keys and swap the work truck for her own ute. Seventy kilometres back to Strathnairn. She *should* go into the National Parks district office there and return some borrowed equipment, but no one would need it before morning. And she just wanted to go home to the cottage she rented on the edge of Strathnairn, pig out on some comfort food – she'd done more than enough physical work this week to justify a dozen cheese-laden pizzas – watch some mindless TV, and have an early night.

Assuming she could get this tyre changed.

A stick cracked in the undergrowth and she stilled, gripping the handle of the wrench. She spent most of her days out in the bush alone and had never scared easily – until three months ago, when her colleague Jo had stumbled across a body, and a drug lord's minions had terrorised the park. They'd all since been arrested, but Erin still responded warily to any sudden sound. Now she scanned the bushland around her for the source of the noise.

Ten metres away among the trees, a six-foot, well-muscled male watched her. Fortunately not a human one. A full-grown red kangaroo, powerful and dangerous if threatened. But this one only studied her, his upright posture showcasing his height and strong shoulders, until he decided she was no threat and resumed grazing the native grasses in the scrub.

'Good decision, big boy,' she murmured. 'You stay over there, and I'll stay over here.' Unlike the time a few months ago when she'd inadvertently disturbed one and Simon had stepped between her and the kangaroo to protect her. No Simon to step in this time, but she could always jump into her utility in the unlikely event that the roo changed its mind about her. Very unlikely. She had far more chance of being bitten by a venomous snake than being attacked by a kangaroo.

The fifth wheel nut defied all her strength and curses for a good five minutes. Giving in wasn't an option – she was going nowhere until she changed the tyre. They were so short-staffed she had no colleagues closer than an hour away, and they'd both be finished for the day anyway, so she'd just damn well have to manage by herself.

By the time she'd removed the last nut her shoulders and back ached from the exertion. She replaced the wheel, fastened the damaged tyre in place of the spare, put away the jack and the wrench and removed the rocks she'd used to chock the other wheels. Climbing into the driver's seat, she stretched her neck and rubbed her shoulders before turning the key in the ignition. There'd been way too many long, lonely days with too much work.

No point whingeing and moaning. She put the truck into gear and eased her way over the loose rough ground. Home, a hot shower, and pizza. Definitely a good plan.

In the small town of Goodabri – population barely three hundred – she parked in the yard behind the National Parks office, closed and silent after hours. It took her only a few minutes to leave the work ute keys, collect the paperwork she'd need for a meeting tomorrow, and lock up again. In her own ute, she reversed out into the back lane, on her way home at last.

Only one other vehicle moved on Goodabri's main street – a white LandCruiser, a block ahead as she turned into the street.

She caught her breath. A white LandCruiser with two spare tyres on the back, and indicating a left turn.

Simon. Simon Kennedy driving back into Goodabri as unexpectedly as he'd left two months ago.

The rush of pleasure at his return dragged with it the undercurrent of uncertainty that had plagued her during those two months of silence. She'd regarded him as a friend – a good friend. But what good friend didn't happen to mention in almost a year of working together that he still served in the army reserve? Dammit, she'd liked him. More than liked him, although – for reasons that had nothing to do with him – she'd quashed any errant fantasies of anything happening between them. And she still couldn't quite believe that she'd never known, that he'd never told her, and worse, that she'd never suspected he hid something so important. So much for being able to read people.

And there she was again, on that round-and-round-and-roundabout of emotions and second-guessing and trying to work out how to make sense of her feelings.

She shook her head, as if she could shake the confusion out of it. Her hang-ups, not his. Plain and simple, they were friends, and he'd been away, serving the country. So she'd do the friendly thing and go welcome him home.

Goodabri had only a few streets, and she followed Simon's route left off the main street then right into the next, and pulled up five houses down in front of the weatherboard house he rented.

He stood at the back of his LandCruiser in the driveway, a kit bag resting on the tray. Old Snowy McDermott, his neighbour, leaned on the fence post between them, settling in for a good long yarn. Snowy could talk the hind leg off a horse and usually missed most social cues, but Simon saw Erin and excused himself to Snowy as she got out of the ute.

As they walked the fifteen paces towards each other, the light cheeky comments she might normally have made turned to dust on her tongue. For months they'd worked side by side in the relaxed way of equals, trusting and relying on each other in their physically demanding duties for both their National Parks jobs and volunteer SES service.

He wasn't in uniform now. Not the army uniform she'd never seen him wear. Not the National Parks uniform, nor the SES uniform they both wore often enough outside work. Just faded jeans and a white t-shirt that stretched over his fine physique and highlighted the deep hazel of his eyes. Eyes that reflected the warmth of his easy grin and gave little hint that he'd been anywhere but a relaxed holiday away.

The early autumn sun had started to set, casting a golden outline around him, almost as if nature wanted to make a gilded statue of the soldier hero. Whereas she . . . she was no hero.

They stopped half a metre from each other, within touching distance, but neither of them made a move to touch. He was out of her reach in too many other ways. Maybe the caution that had stopped her making a fool of herself in the months before he'd left had been good sense, rather than cowardice.

She resisted wiping suddenly sweaty hands on her uniform trousers and summoned up a grin, aware of Snowy watering his garden close by. Keep it simple, keep it light. Just the warm, familiar teasing she'd missed in his absence.

'If I'd known you were coming back today, I would have volunteered you for the regional planning meeting in Moree tomorrow.'

His eyes sparkled. 'Phew. I've had a lucky escape then. Who drew the short straw?'

'Well, since Jo's on light duties and not allowed to drive, I got the long straw, the middle straw *and* the short straw.'

'Jo's back at work?'

'Yes, working half-days. But it's not quite three months since her craniotomy so she's not allowed to drive yet.'

'So you've been doing all three of our jobs, all this time.'

'Yeah. You owe me. Although I suppose if you've been off saving the world, that might cancel the debt, soldier.'

His cheerful, relaxed expression slipped and the light in his eyes dimmed for a moment before he gestured with a jerk of his thumb towards the house. 'Come on in and tell me the news while I dump my gear, and then I'll shout you dinner at the pub.'

Back at his LandCruiser, he grabbed his kit bag with one hand and then slid a metal case out. His rifle. Invaluable in feral animal campaigns. She'd usually managed to put out of her mind that in the army, his targets didn't have four legs. His past army service had been abstract in her head, something she rarely considered in detail, because on the few occasions he'd spoken of his experiences he'd sounded carefree, as if his deployments, even in Iraq and Afghanistan, were barely more adventurous than an outback camping trip. But then he'd gone again, between one shift and the next, with scarcely a word of explanation to her. Nods and murmurs from senior National Parks staff who'd known him longer suggested there was more to his role than he'd ever let on, leaving her with the distinct impression that he'd been – was still – a commando with significant experience in covert operations.

No wonder he was such a valuable member of the volunteer SES squad and a capable National Parks ranger, especially in dealing with the law-enforcement aspect of their roles. Maybe the signs had always been there, and she just hadn't recognised them.

But the fact that he was still in the army – that changed things, changed how she felt, although she'd spent the past few weeks trying fruitlessly to put a finger on how and why. Not that there was any point in trying to understand it, since she mattered so little to him that he'd not contacted her once since his abrupt departure. They were friendly colleagues in a small community, nothing more. So she'd keep things at that level.

She grinned with a good imitation of her usual cheekiness. 'Well, since you apparently couldn't remember my email address all this time, I'll let you shout me dinner.'

She'd not often seen him discomfited, but now he grimaced. 'Sorry. Not much internet access where I've been.'

Obviously not a local army base, then. But he headed towards the house without any further explanation. He set down his bag and the rifle case to unlock the front door and from behind she saw the sudden wariness tensing his spine as he pushed it open.

The odour hit her. Pungent, nauseating, *dead*. 'Sheesh, Simon, did you leave dead fish in your —'

'No.' His hand moved towards his hip, reaching instinctively for a sidearm that wasn't there. 'Keep back, Erin.'

She stayed on the doorstep while he entered, as alert and cautious as if walking into a terrorist's hideout instead of a typical Australian colonial cottage. There were four doors off the short central passageway, two on each side. In the dimmer light inside she watched as he approached the second on the right, the only door not closed. Although he had no gun to hold ready, he used the partially open door as cover to glance into and check the room.

Whatever he saw startled him with a visible jolt. He swore and dropped his guard, striding into the room.

In a few steps Erin covered the length of the passage and followed him through the door. His study had been ransacked, computer equipment smashed, books and DVD cases torn apart and thrown on the floor. But she stopped hard when she saw what Simon had discovered, and nausea rolled in her stomach so violently that she barely resisted the urge to turn and run.

He knelt by a woman sprawled on the floor, his hand on her wrist to check her pulse. But there could be no pulse. There had been no pulse for hours, maybe days. Numerous wounds on her torso had stained her white dress dark red, and blood from her slit throat had dried in splatters all around her on the polished wood floor. Her eyes stared blankly at the ceiling.

'How . . . ? What . . . ?' Erin's throat wouldn't make a full sentence.

Simon turned his head slowly to look up at her, eyes shadowed, his mouth a hard line. 'I don't know how she got here, Erin, or why. I haven't seen her for years.' But he didn't move away from the woman, and there was an intimacy of sorts in the way his fingers rested loosely on her wrist.

The closeness of the room, the stench, the buzz of flies filled Erin's head, almost suffocating rational thought. 'Who . . . ?'

'She's . . .' His voice came out as ragged as a storm-ripped tree. 'She's my wife.'

CHAPTER 2

'Your *wife?*'

The disbelief and hurt in Erin's voice cut him like a whip. Pain he deserved, for betraying the trust and friendship they'd built. But the slim hope he'd held on to for months – that a relationship with Erin might eventually be possible – had already shattered the moment he saw Hayley's body on the floor.

That Hayley could be *here*, after all these years, made no sense. That she could be here, and dead . . . he couldn't even begin to process it in his mind. Logic eluded him, and grief, anger and shame boiled together, caustic in his gut. Anger with Hayley, for being absent so long, denying him the chance to make things right between them. Anger with the bastard or bastards who'd murdered her. Anger with himself, for failing his wife yet again, in the worst way possible. And for failing Erin.

But he couldn't disintegrate, couldn't give in to the emotion and sit there on his knees and howl like a wounded animal. He was a soldier and he needed to send Erin out of there. So she'd be safe.

'Get out,' he rasped. He didn't dare look at her, couldn't bear to see her stricken eyes again. 'Go to Snowy's. Call the cops.'

'No.' Her hand closed over his shoulder, her fingers warm through his shirt. 'Simon, you have to come outside with me.' A hitch in her breathing unsteadied her voice but she continued, more in control than he was. 'We'll call the police from outside.'

'I can't . . .' *Leave Hayley like this. Leave her alone.* Because he'd left her alone far too many times, despite her pleas, despite her need of him.

'We can't contaminate the scene. Simon, I'm sorry, I know this is a shock, but we have to *think*. The best thing we can do for her now is leave the room as it is for the police.'

Erin's strength – considering *him*, when she had every right to be angry – hammered logic into his brain. She didn't know, and would never know, that his grief was as much for her and for his dreams of them as it was for Hayley. But she was right. He couldn't do a damn thing for Hayley now except help find her killer.

As he rose to his feet he scanned the room again, alert, wary. Soldier, not husband. Protector, not friend.

'They're probably long gone,' he said to Erin. 'But keep close behind me.'

Nothing stirred in the house as Simon listened briefly at the closed door of each room on their way out. He didn't touch the front door handle but instead hooked the door with his foot to draw it partly closed, a small barrier against the prying eyes that would doubtless start to gather once the police cars arrived. In the way of small towns, word would spread faster than a bushfire on a hot gusty day.

But right now the sun had sunk below the horizon, Snowy must have finished his watering and gone inside, and the street was as quiet and lifeless as the house. Simon's training nagged at him to do a circuit of the house, check for anyone lurking, or evidence of who, when and how, but Hayley's death must have occurred hours ago and the perpetrator was unlikely to still be around. He'd stay by Erin's side and let the police scour the house and surrounds for evidence.

Erin had her phone out before he did. Her usually lively face pale and drawn, she flicked rapidly through her contacts. 'I'll call Tess. She can be here in just a few minutes, and she'll know how to set things in motion.'

His thoughts still reeling, he didn't object or insist on making the call himself. The new police officer had arrived in Goodabri only days before his abrupt departure, so he scarcely knew her. Better for Erin to talk with her.

He leaned two hands on the roof of his vehicle, dropping his head down while she made the call beside him. Professional, not panicking. Capable in a crisis. Unlike Hayley's doe-eyed dependence.

'Tess? It's Erin Taylor. We've got a situation at Simon's place in Grey Street . . . Yes, he only just got back, about ten minutes ago. I went inside with him. We found a . . . a homicide. Hours, maybe a day or so gone. A woman. Simon's . . .' Her breath caught and she didn't say the word 'wife'. 'Simon knows her.'

Did he know her? Know Hayley? He might have once. Fourteen years ago. Perhaps not even then, despite three years of marriage. They'd married too young, too inexperienced to make the marriage last. And his career – he'd always put it first. Before her. Before anything. He could make sense of himself as a soldier, but a husband? Jesus, he'd made a mess of that.

And after all this time she'd come to him, out of the blue, and now she was dead because he hadn't been there to look after her as he'd vowed on their wedding day.

Someone had killed her. A random attack? Someone she'd brought with her? Or had a killer come for him, and found her?

•

Erin finished the call and slipped her phone back into her pocket. 'Tess is on her way,' she told Simon. 'She won't be long.'

She had no idea what else to say, and her mind raced with questions she didn't want to ask. Simon stared at the ground, his face tight. Hands thrust into her pockets, Erin leaned back against the LandCruiser, huffing out a breath, and the silence hung between them.

Simon had a wife. One he'd never mentioned in her hearing in ten months of working side by side. His wife, his army reserve membership . . . come to think of it, she couldn't recall him talking about family either, or where he'd grown up, or any of the other aspects of his past that people usually talked about, at least *mentioned*. Not that she'd told him anything about her family. Her family wasn't relevant to her, hadn't been for almost twenty years.

But Simon had a *wife*. A pretty woman, from Erin's glimpse of the body. Long brown hair, delicate, girlish features, slim build. Murdered. The multiple injuries meant it had to be murder. Despite the warmth still in the air, Erin's skin prickled. Sometime in the past day or so, a killer had entered Simon's home and attacked the woman with a knife or something similar. The injuries, the amount of blood – she hadn't died instantly, she must have been terrified and in pain in those last minutes. *She.* Simon's wife, lying dead in his house, and Erin didn't know what to call her.

'What is her name?' she asked him, the words stilted in the silence.

He lifted his head slowly, and his eyes took a moment to focus on hers. 'Hayley. Hayley Munro.'

Hayley. A pretty name for an attractive woman.

A police car rounded the corner into the street. No time

to ask Simon more, even if she could untangle her thoughts enough to frame questions beyond the most basic.

The police car parked across the road. Erin knew the day shift usually finished at seven, but Tess was still in uniform. Still in uniform, and alone, because she was the only officer stationed in Goodabri, with the rest of her colleagues fifty minutes' drive away in Strathnairn.

'What have we got?' Tess asked without preamble as she strode down the driveway. Brusque, focused, not a woman who easily relaxed – but Erin respected her, her commitment and her skills.

Simon straightened up, and although he didn't quite snap to attention his unguarded moments were over. He answered the policewoman's question in short, clear sentences. 'A murder. In the bedroom I use as a study, on the right. I've been away for weeks, only just arrived home. The victim is my wife, Hayley.'

Tess raised an eyebrow. 'You have a wife? Ex?'

'Separated. For fourteen years. I haven't seen her in almost that long.'

Fourteen years? Fourteen years he'd not seen her? Erin had never read him as a man who'd just up and leave, ignore his responsibilities. But that was a hell of a long time to be apart and not divorced.

'So what was she doing —' Tess broke off, her interrupted question echoing Erin's thoughts. 'Time for questions later. I'll go take a look.' She rested her hand on the weapon at her side. 'Any signs the perpetrators are still around?'

'I didn't check the back of the house, but I think not. I'll come in with you, just in case.'

Tess considered for a moment before nodding. 'Okay. Only as backup. Don't touch a thing. Erin, stay out here and make sure no one else comes onto the property.'

Erin waited beside her own ute as the blue of the sky deepened and Venus glowed, the first star low on the horizon. No cars or people came along the street. The sounds of a television drifted from Snowy's front room, the canned-laughter decibels louder than the actors' dialogue. Tess would likely ask him if he'd seen or heard anything next door, but given his propensity to leave his hearing aids turned off, Erin doubted he would have.

Just a quiet street in a small town, twenty or so houses on large blocks that once would have boasted well-tended gardens, a couple of dogs in the backyard, chook sheds and veggie patches. Some of them undoubtedly still did. But Goodabri's population was ageing, many of the younger generation leaving for jobs and opportunities in larger towns, and a number of these houses were empty, or their residents were elderly, like Snowy, and not up to as much outside work as they'd once been. Had anyone seen Hayley arrive? Or her killer? Or heard her cries when she was stabbed?

Erin rubbed the goosebumps on her bare forearms. If Snowy had seen or heard anything, he would have mentioned it to Simon. That was Snowy, full of friendly curiosity. If he'd seen anything, he wouldn't have been able to resist saying something about it.

A white sedan came around the corner and slowed. In the dimming light, Erin couldn't clearly see the driver, but she knew the car. The detectives' car, from the Strathnairn police station. Aaron or Nick . . . ?

She breathed a little easier when Nick Matheson stepped out of the car. Aaron would make a good detective one day but Nick had years of experience, senior rank, and well-honed investigative instincts. In the past few months, since he'd fallen hard for her colleague Jo, he'd also become a good friend. She wasn't used to seeing him in uniform, but he'd been appointed acting inspector for the district recently, and he wore it with natural authority.

'You got here quickly,' she said. Even if Tess had called him before she'd arrived, he couldn't have made the seventy kilometres from Strathnairn so fast.

His smile was brief, distracted. 'I was on my way back from Tenterfield. Tess is inside?'

'Yes. With Simon. I'm staying out here to keep the crowds under control.' Erin waved her hand at the deserted street. 'Would you like me to phone Jo, tell her you'll be late?'

'That bad, is it?'

Of course he hadn't seen yet, presumably only received a coded message from Tess over the police radio about a death. The image of the dead woman floated into Erin's memory again. Because this wasn't the first murder in the district in recent times, she had a fair idea what it would entail for a local detective with few resources nearby. Additional officers from Strathnairn were at least fifty minutes away. Forensics from Inverell an hour, minimum. More likely two. As acting inspector, Nick would be heavily involved, overseeing operations and allocating and approving resources.

'Yes,' she told him. 'You're definitely going to be late.'

'Shit. Okay, yes, phone her. Thanks.'

Erin had the number dialled before he'd reached the door of the house, but when her friend answered she realised she hadn't thought about what to say. She couldn't discuss a murder, even with the discreet Jo, in the middle of the street and before official announcements were made.

'Simon's back but there's been some trouble at his place,' she said quickly. 'Nick asked me to phone you.' As Jo asked an anxious question, Erin hastened to reassure her. 'No, no, they're both fine. But Nick wanted me to tell you that he'll be here for a while.'

'Somebody's hurt?' Jo asked. 'Or . . . ?'

'Nobody we know,' Erin said. 'Not a local.'

Jo must have heard the brittle edge to her composure. 'Are you okay? Do you need to talk about it?'

Yes. Erin bit back the plea. She let few people close, but if she could lean on anyone, it would be Jo. *Simon's come back and his wife has been murdered here in Goodabri and did you know he had a wife? Because I sure as hell didn't.*

No, she'd deal with this alone. She made herself smile so her voice didn't come out tight. 'No. I'm okay. I'll see you tomorrow.'

Another police car turned into the street, and Erin set her shoulders back and walked forward to meet it. As a National Parks ranger she worked closely with the police, knew everyone in the district command, and her responsibilities in the SES also involved helping out in emergencies. In a small community like Goodabri, a murdered woman was an emergency. There'd be an influx tonight of police, forensic officers and the coroner's deputy. They'd need the crime scene secured, they'd need food, a place to work other than the tiny, cramped police station, and some of them would need accommodation overnight.

She shoved aside her personal confusion, all the questions going through her mind. Later she could deal with the emotional chaos. Right now, she had work to do.

•

Hayley lay dead in his house, murdered with one of his kitchen knives, which doubtless had his fingerprints all over it, and he probably had no alibi for the last seventy-two hours.

Simon waited in the claustrophobically small interview room of the Goodabri police cottage and steeled himself for the interrogation to come. A husband was always the first suspect. An unsuccessful marriage and a soldier husband who had reason to want his wife out of his life? That made means, motive and opportunity. He could almost feel the handcuffs closing around his wrists.

The hands of the clock on the wall crawled slowly around the dial. Nick Matheson must have called in the homicide specialists from Sydney. Standard practice with a crime like this. He'd heard the thud-thud of the police chopper flying in to land at the showground half an hour ago, although it seemed longer. He'd checked the time against his watch several times, in case the clock batteries were dying.

Eventually cars pulled up outside, doors slammed, footsteps and voices entered the station.

'You've got the husband in here? Have you cautioned him?' A woman's voice, clipped, brisk, authoritative.

'He's come voluntarily, Leah, to tell us what he knows about the deceased.' Nick's tone packed just as much firm authority into his reply. Simon hadn't known him for long, but he liked and respected what he'd seen in those few weeks. Their nascent friendship wouldn't cloud Nick's judgement, and the detective could well suspect him, but at least he'd get a fair hearing.

Nick opened the door and showed in the woman and another plainclothes cop. There was no sign of the man he'd shared a couple of drinks with in the Strathnairn pub in Nick's unsmiling face and formal introductions. 'This is Detective Senior Sergeant Leah Haddad from Homicide in Sydney, and Detective Sergeant Steve Fraser. They will be leading the investigation.'

Simon recognised Haddad from the murder investigation at the beginning of summer when Jo had found a body in the park and all hell had broken loose. In their brief encounters back then he'd pegged Haddad as a career cop, capable and hard and determined.

Although he stood and offered his hand, she ignored it.

Fraser he found harder to size up. Around his own age, with enough experience to put a sharpness behind the brown eyes. Suit, white shirt, dark tie, and a handshake firm enough to challenge his own. Although Fraser played it relaxed, straddling a chair and loosening his tie as though they were sitting down for a friendly drink in a bar, Simon's instincts heightened to alert. He'd be a fool to think of Fraser as some kind of devil-may-care detective. The rigid formality of the senior woman detective contrasted with Fraser's relaxation, but he'd bet they were running the good cop/bad cop routine. Either that, or they were trying to piss each other off.

Haddad fixed Simon with a cool, dark-eyed stare that might have intimidated a less hardened man. 'Mr Kennedy, I understand that you have identified the deceased as your wife?'

'Yes. Her name is Hayley Elizabeth Munro.'

'Munro?'

'She took her grandmother's maiden name when she was eighteen and kept it when we married.'

'Did that bother you?'

'Bother?' What was she trying to suggest, that he was some Neanderthal prick who wanted total control over a woman?

'It's the twenty-first century, for chrissakes. Of course it didn't bother me.'

'How long have you been estranged?'

'Separated,' he emphasised. 'Estranged' implied hostility and resentment, and he wanted to correct that impression. 'Hayley needed some space, needed some time to herself. She was only nineteen when we married, I was barely twenty-one. I was in the army, and often away on exercises or deployments. That's a hard life for a young woman. After about three years she left to go on some kind of alternative-lifestyle healing retreat when I was deployed to East Timor. Other than one brief visit, she didn't come back.'

'When was that?'

'We separated fourteen years ago.'

Haddad raised a defined eyebrow. 'Fourteen years? And you never divorced?'

'There was no pressing reason to. I cared about my wife, Detective. I had a responsibility towards her. Her life had not been easy and she was . . .' He struggled for words. *Not like Erin.* Yeah, that'd go down like a lead balloon. He shoved thoughts of Erin away. 'Hayley wasn't emotionally strong.'

Despite the late hour, the room was stiflingly hot, and while Haddad was distracted by a text message on her phone, Fraser rose and filled three plastic cups from the water cooler just outside the door.

Passing a cup across to him, Fraser asked, 'When was the last time you saw Hayley?'

Simon let the water cool his throat before he answered. 'About eighteen months after she left. She'd been travelling with a girlfriend. I'd had sporadic postcards from her, the occasional phone call. I wasn't in the country myself a whole lot at the time. She came back to Sydney once, to collect some things. She was heading back to the north coast for a job as a nanny at some kind of retreat place. She was excited about it – she'd always loved being with little kids. She gave me a phone number and a post office box address before she went.' And a kiss. She'd given him an affectionate, casual kiss before she'd hurried off to catch her train. A kiss on the cheek. Like a sister. 'She said there wasn't anyone else, but she needed some more time to become stronger before she came back. That she still couldn't cope with being an army wife with me so often away overseas. But she said she was happy and peaceful within herself.'

'You're telling me you haven't seen your wife since then?' Haddad, finished with her text message, glanced at her notes. 'For over *twelve years?*'

Simon kept his gaze steady. 'Yes.'

'But you never divorced,' she said again.

'No.'

Haddad clearly couldn't comprehend it. Perhaps a woman like her wouldn't tolerate anyone lingering in her life if she didn't have a use for them.

He searched for words to explain. 'Look, I was – am – a soldier. I've almost lost count of the number of tours of Iraq and Afghanistan and other places I've done in that time. I stayed in the reserves after I left the full-time army and I'm still sent on active service. In between studying for a science degree, earning a living and my army service, getting a divorce I didn't need hasn't been a high priority. Until —' He broke off. *Until Erin walked into the National Parks office.* He had to keep her right out of this. 'About five months ago, I wrote to her, with the divorce papers and a settlement offer. I sent my new contact details when I moved here to Goodabri. But I didn't hear anything from her before I was called back to service again.'

'Not even an email or phone call?'

'No. I'm not even sure she has an email address. She's only ever contacted me by mail or phone. But I only got back to town tonight. I haven't had time to see if there's a letter.' He'd shoved the small pile of mail Snowy had collected for him into the pocket of his kit bag without flicking through it. 'I had no idea she was coming here. Last I heard, she was living in a community on the north coast and loving it. I don't know where she's been since then, what she's been doing, who her friends are. And I don't know who killed her, or why. Maybe it was someone she knew. Maybe it was someone trying to get at me.'

'I'm not interested in conjecture,' Haddad said curtly. 'Can you account for your whereabouts for the past few days?'

'I arrived back in Australia on the weekend. I left the regiment's headquarters on Monday morning. I called in to see my stepfather in the Hunter Valley for coffee. And then I drove north and camped in an isolated valley in the Oxley Wild Rivers National Park for three nights. I left there earlier this afternoon and drove back here.'

'Can anyone vouch for your presence there?'

'I doubt it.'

She zeroed in on that. 'So you have no alibi for the past three days.'

Fraser leaned forward, ignoring Haddad's scowl. 'Come on, surely someone knows you were there. You're a park ranger, right? You didn't meet up with the local rangers at all? Have a yarn at your campsite?'

'I'd just come home after seven weeks in Iraq. I wanted a few days alone to . . . readjust.' To stop being Sergeant Kennedy, with responsibility for a small group of highly trained men and a near-impossible mission deep in extremist territory, and become easygoing Simon, with a new national park to develop and a team of colleagues who weren't trained to kill anything other than feral animals.

He always needed at least a few days alone to reset his equilibrium. It took time to strip himself of the discipline, the harshness of war, to bridge the chasm between one half of his life and the other. This time he'd wished for a month but had to make do with three too-short days and nights of solitude in the wilderness.

'There's a locked gate on the road into the area. I collected the key from the depot at Walcha late on Monday afternoon.

I spoke briefly with the local ranger then. But the area I camped in is almost two hours from there. And I just dropped the key in the lockbox at the gate when I left.'

'But surely the local rangers would have been out there during that time?' Fraser persisted.

'It's wild country that few people go to, so they don't make the trip out often. The only person I saw was an old army mate. Gabe McCallum. Must have been Tuesday morning. He lives up on the tablelands but sometimes musters brumbies down in the gorge country. I met him by the river and we talked for a short while. But he left to track a mob of horses. He stayed in the area – I saw the horses a few times and signs of him – but a couple of hikers came down the river and neither of us was looking for company. I'm a commando, Detective, and he used to be one. Even a raw recruit could be invisible for days.'

'You're a commando?' Fraser asked. 'I grew up near the Holsworthy base. All the girls had their sights set on the 4 RAR commandos. Damn tough competition for us ordinary mortals.'

'Yeah, I was 4 RAR,' Simon conceded. Not that he'd had much to do with the local girls. Even then, he'd understood that the job put pressures on any decent relationship. 'I'm in the 1st Commando Regiment now. It's a mix of full-time and reserve soldiers.' When he'd agreed to stay on in the reserves, he'd envisaged more of a training role. It hadn't worked out that way.

'So can your friend verify your presence in the national park yesterday and this morning?' Haddad demanded.

'On Tuesday, yes. Whether he saw me after that, I don't know. I'll give you his contact details but he's usually out of mobile range.'

Fraser passed a notepad and pen across the table and Simon noted down Gabe's name and phone number. Maybe Gabe could give him an alibi. If they could get hold of him. Cutting promising foals out of the herds of brumbies in the gorge country gave him a reason to avoid civilisation. Since a mission had gone badly wrong a few years ago – no fault of Gabe's – he preferred the company of horses to people.

'Thanks,' Fraser said. 'We'll get on to him asap.'

Despite Fraser's matey routine, Simon didn't relax. Nor did Haddad. If it wasn't for the fine worry lines on her forehead he'd have judged her a cold-hearted woman, but she clearly took her work seriously and that suggested at least some emotional commitment. Her phone vibrated again and she glanced at the message.

'Forensics have finally arrived,' she said. 'I'll go meet them. Steve, you check on the incident room set-up. We can't work in here. Mr Kennedy, I may have some more questions for you after I've spoken with the forensic officers. Please wait here.'

'Am I under arrest?'

'Not at the moment. But your wife is dead in your house and by your own admission you probably have no alibi.' She stood, looking down at him, exuding suspicion and determination.

'As you'd expect, we need to ascertain your whereabouts for the last few days and investigate all the possibilities.'

Hands flat on the table, Simon rose to his feet. With the table between them he didn't tower over her, his intention assertion, not intimidation. 'I expect that you *will* investigate all the possibilities, Detective Haddad. I expect you to establish whether this was a targeted crime or a random one. I expect you to find out where Hayley has been, who with, and whether anyone she knows would have a reason to follow her here and kill her. And I expect you to contact army intelligence and ask them if anyone I may have pissed off in Afghanistan, Iraq, or East Timor could possibly have identified and found me.'

He deliberately, neatly, put his chair in place under the table. 'Now, if your forensic officers are searching my home I believe I have a right to be present. And since I remember what state I left the place in two months ago, I should be able to show them what, if anything, has been disturbed. So, that's where I'm going.'

He held the door open for her before he followed her out.

•

The empty half of the old double-shopfront building National Parks leased in Goodabri's main street had seen use in emergency operations before – for a joint emergency services training exercise not long after Erin came to the district, and three months ago as a police critical incident room when Jo's discovery of a body in the park had revealed a violent criminal gang operating in the area. So when Erin phoned her boss in Strathnairn to report the evening's events, Malcolm didn't hesitate for a moment in approving the cooperation between services.

'I'll call Nick now and formally offer use of the building,' he said. 'Do you need me to come out there tonight?'

Drive seventy kilometres each way to open up a building when she was already on the spot? 'No, I'll deal with it, Mal. I'll see you tomorrow.'

Yet when she parked behind the deserted building she wished she had asked Mal to come. Walking into a dark, empty building at night when a murderer was out there, somewhere . . . She glanced back at the shed where the folding tables and chairs were stored. The shed she hadn't been into for over a week. The main building itself should be safe enough – the other staff had been in and out of there all day, and she'd been in an hour or two ago to drop off the keys – but she'd wait until someone else came before she went to get the tables.

She unlocked the back door of the empty side of the building first, and without going in, called out, 'If anyone's lurking in here, you've got five minutes to escape before I come in. The police are on their way, so be quick.'

Silly, perhaps, but it couldn't hurt and at least there were no neighbours around to hear her being paranoid. Inside the National Parks office, she collected the basic essentials for people working late into the night – mugs, coffee, milk and sugar.

She didn't spook easily, but she'd far rather be out in the bush alone than walking into the empty rooms of the office next door, especially with her hands full. The mugs clutched in her fingers clunked against each other as she reached to thumb the light switch inside the rear door. The bare bulb flared to life, and her pulse skipped a beat as she caught movement out of the corner of her eye. A huge huntsman spider scuttling up the wall. It stopped at eye level, watching her. Harmless enough, but she gave it a wide berth, dumped the mugs on the table in the kitchenette, and found a broom to encourage it out the door.

The mirror image of the National Parks side of the building, this side likewise had a tiny bathroom, a windowless storeroom, and a small office tucked in behind the large front room that had for over a century housed a general store. Now it waited, echoing and empty, dust coating the wooden floor, for the few times it came to life when space was needed to coordinate emergency responses: fires, readiness exercises, murder investigations. An old ice-cream poster on the wall watched over it all, a reminder of normality.

Mal must have got on to Nick and the police authorities quickly, for Erin had only just opened the blinds on the large front windows when a police car pulled up outside. Matt Carruthers, one of the constables from Strathnairn. In his early thirties, Matt had plenty of country policing experience, handling the job with dedication and a sense of humour, and reliable in a crisis.

'Nick sent me over to start getting things sorted,' he told her when she unlocked the front door to let him in.

Erin handed him the broom. 'If you can sweep up the dust, I'll bring over the urn from our office and get it heating for coffee. Then you can give me a hand getting the tables from the shed.'

Matt grinned. 'Caffeine first. I like your priorities. It's going to be a long night. Homicide in Sydney have sent DS Haddad here again. Do you remember her?'

'I saw her in action last time. She's very . . .' Erin sought a polite word, '. . . determined, isn't she?'

Matt didn't bother with polite. 'Hard-ass Haddad. Rumour has it she can bust balls with a telekinetic glare.'

'I wouldn't let her hear you say that, if I were you,' a male voice drawled at the doorway. 'Or you might find out if it's true.'

Matt straightened to attention, the broom still clasped in one hand. 'Sorry, sir.'

The guy strolled in, his suit jacket slung over one shoulder and a laptop bag in his other hand. He glanced at Matt's nametag. 'Relax, Carruthers. I won't tell her. I'm DS Steve Fraser.' He turned a hundred-watt grin on Erin. 'Did I hear someone mention coffee?'

'Coming soon, courtesy of interagency cooperation.' Erin indicated the National Parks and Wildlife Service badge on her uniform sleeve. 'I'm Erin Taylor, one of the rangers. Our office and visitor centre is in the other half of this building.' She matched the firmness of Fraser's handshake. Despite the boyish grin, he had a few years on her – she'd place him in his late thirties, perhaps even early forties.

'You're a colleague of Simon Kennedy's?' he asked.

'Yes. Our district office is in Strathnairn. We manage four parks and three conservation areas, most of them closer to Strathnairn. But we have this office for the new Goodabri Rivers park nearby. I've been overseeing the park and its development while Simon was away.'

The cheerful grin had softened, replaced with a relaxed but professional regard. 'Inspector Matheson – Nick – said you were with Simon when he found the victim.'

'Yes. I'm happy to answer any questions you or your colleagues have.' She'd gone over those few minutes in Simon's house with Nick already, but once the preliminaries were established he'd said he wouldn't be running the investigation, because of Jo's friendship with Simon, and because as acting inspector he was overseeing all police operations in the district. So she'd tell the little she knew again, to Fraser or the other detective, however many times it took.

'Thanks, Erin, I appreciate it. We'll have a chat as soon as things are set up here.' Fraser turned to Matt, systematically wielding the broom along the length of the main room. 'Any idea of the arrangements for comms, Carruthers?'

'Techs are coming from Tamworth but they'll be a while yet.'

'Data coverage is fairly patchy out here on the mobile network,' Erin told Fraser. 'And even satellite broadband won't be anywhere near what you're used to in Sydney.'

'Sydney? Oh, I'm not from Homicide. I'm just a country detective. I work mostly out of Birraga these days. But I happened to be at the same meeting in Tenterfield as Nick today, and he's roped me in to this one.'

Birraga, a couple of hours south – she knew the name, had seen it in the news not so long ago, with a series of violent crimes. Fraser had described himself as 'just a country detective', but if he'd been in Birraga this past year or so, he'd have notched up plenty of experience in murder investigations.

He didn't seem to mind turning his hand to anything, though. When she returned from next door with the urn, he and Matt had fetched the first of the large folding tables from the shed and were wiping off the dust with damp handtowels from the bathroom.

'We have a whiteboard you can borrow if you need it,' she offered. 'I'll need a hand moving it, though.'

Fraser volunteered before she finished speaking. As they manoeuvred the large, awkward whiteboard out of the Parks office via the front door, he asked casually, 'How long have you and Simon worked together?'

The very casualness of the question put her on alert. 'I joined the Strathnairn office about ten, eleven months ago. I'd met him a few times before that, though, at meetings and training sessions – I worked out of Armidale before here.'

'Did you ever meet his wife?'

A trick question? Trying to find holes in whatever Simon might have said in their interview? She could only assume he'd told the police what he'd told her. She kept her answer simple and honest. 'No.'

He waited until they'd angled the whiteboard in through the next door before he asked, 'Do you know him well?'

'We work together in a demanding job. We're also volunteers with the SES. We're friends as well as colleagues, but there's nothing more to it than that.'

'You're both in the SES? So you'll have seen him in some stressful situations?'

No mistaking the direction of his questions now. The friendly help in lugging things around was just an excuse for an off-the-record interview. All the questions about Simon meant he had to have some suspicions. Suspicions she planned on dispelling, fast.

'Yes, I've seen him in plenty of stressful situations.' She shoved her end of the whiteboard against the wall harder than she'd intended and locked the wheels with a stamp of her boot before she faced him. 'I don't know what you think we do, but National Parks work isn't all about picnics and possums. As well as project planning and park management, we deal with illegal shooters, bushfires, search and rescue, floods, the works. Sometimes,' she gave him a sardonic smile, 'all on the same day. And I can assure you that if I'm going to be abseiling down a cliff to reach a kid stranded by a bushfire, then the person I'd most want to have with me is Simon, because he's damned calm and cool-headed in a crisis. I have never, ever seen him lose his temper.'

Unlike herself. She'd barely kept hers from exploding. Tiredness and the emotional toll of the last couple of hours were undermining her self-control. Shit. She had to get on top of it, concentrate on answering Fraser's questions without being snarky. For Simon's sake – and for Hayley's.

'He's a soldier, seen a lot of active service. What about PTSD?' Fraser must have noticed her over-reaction, but he kept his manner casual, curious, as if he wasn't grilling her about a murder suspect. 'Any signs of that?'

Post-traumatic stress disorder? Erin couldn't think of any occasion when she'd had cause to doubt Simon's emotional or mental stability. 'I know he's served in war zones. He doesn't talk about it much, other than in passing. But he's a very together person. Very . . .' How could she say what she meant? Explain her sense of the solidity of Simon's character? 'Very . . . grounded. Level-headed. Look, talk to Nick. He's become friends with Simon. They're both martial-arts types. Nick's done years of undercover work and I guess that's not so different from the military. I'm sure you'll trust his judgement more than —'

A sharp, loud crack sounded behind her and she spun around, heart stalling.

'It's okay,' Fraser said, his hand steadying on her shoulder for a moment. 'It's just Carruthers.'

Adrenaline flooding her body, Erin tried to breathe slowly. Just Matt, carrying in a stack of chairs from the shed, letting the flyscreen door at the back thwack hard against the frame as he came through. Just Matt, and she'd jumped almost to the ceiling, in front of the detective.

'I'm sorry,' she said to Fraser, embarrassment making her laugh thin and strained. 'I'm edgy, I guess. Knowing there's a murderer lurking around, somewhere out there. I'm going to be wary of every sound, every dark place, every stranger until you arrest the bastard, Detective.'

His brown eyes watched her, not unkindly, but not softly, either. 'Stranger? Be careful, yes, but be aware, too. Far more often than not, murder victims are killed by people they know.'

She stared back at him. 'You can't seriously believe Simon killed her. It's impossible. He wouldn't kill any —'

Fraser raised an eyebrow and her voice trailed away as reality hit.

Simon was a soldier. A commando. Had been for years. Her easygoing, reliable friend was very capable of killing a person, in any number of ways.

She swallowed against a dry throat and turned away from the detective, unexpected tears burning her eyes.

CHAPTER 3

A few neighbours and other townspeople had gathered at a curious but respectful distance from his house, beyond the police tape and the growing collection of official vehicles.

Simon walked down the driveway beside Nick and Haddad, aware of the eyes watching him. Conjecture would be running wild, transforming quickly into rumour and gossip. After all, they barely knew him. He'd moved here from Strathnairn only a month before his latest call-up, and although some of them already knew him through his National Parks and SES work in the wider district, he was still a newcomer, a stranger in their midst. Unless someone had seen Hayley, or her killer, they had no reason to trust him or believe in his innocence.

The senior forensic officer who met them at the door wasted few words on polite sympathy. 'Can you tell me exactly what you did when you arrived earlier?' he asked. 'How you came in, where you walked, what you touched?'

No longer on alert for danger, as he entered his house this time Simon immediately began looking for anything out of place. Not easy, with detectives on either side of him, and forensic officers already moving methodically through the rooms. He described his earlier movements, answered questions, all the while fighting the urge to drag the officers standing around Hayley's body away from her, to protect her from their impersonal scrutiny.

Small, fragile and defenceless, but he hadn't been there to protect her from the killer who'd stabbed her multiple times. He couldn't even protect her from the man who photographed the wounds and described her condition into a voice recorder.

He'd caused her so much grief, when he'd only wanted to keep her safe from harm. If it turned out someone had come here looking for him and found her . . . He pushed past Nick and walked out of the room, hardly able to draw air into his lungs.

In the kitchen, one of the forensic officers lifted out the plastic bag lining the swing-top rubbish bin beside the sink. A bag hanging straight, lightly weighted with rubbish.

Simon reached out a hand to take it but the woman held it back. Of course. They weren't going to allow him to touch anything. 'I emptied that before I left,' he told her. 'I put in a clean bag.'

There was a soft metallic clink as the officer lowered the bag to the floor and opened the top to peer inside.

Nick must have followed him and overheard. 'What's in there?' he asked from behind Simon.

Her glance darted to Simon before she answered the detective. 'Cans. An empty packet or two.' She reached in with a gloved hand, carefully shifting the contents. 'One tin was sliced peaches. There's a salmon can, too. And . . .' She pulled out three plastic wrappers, uncrinkled them to see the labels. 'Skim milk powder. Nuts. And a muesli bar.'

Long-life food. Nothing perishable. 'I had all those things in the pantry,' Simon said. 'I emptied the fridge before I left and switched it off.' His thoughts racing to process the possibilities, he turned to Nick. 'Hayley must have needed food. You saw how skinny she is. And her clothes . . .' That simple white dress, the scuffed and worn leather sandals. 'She can't have had much money.'

Haddad crossed the passage from the study to join them. 'Is there any drug paraphernalia?'

Simon's anger flared as the forensic officer started to go through the rubbish again. 'Hayley didn't do drugs,' he insisted.

'You have no idea what she did or didn't do in the last twelve years,' Haddad retorted.

The truth of it stung, but Simon didn't let Haddad see it. 'No. But I knew her for years before that. Her mother was an addict. Hayley was determined not to be like her and avoided all drugs. She wouldn't even take a painkiller.'

'People change. Make sure you collect the bathroom bin contents, too,' she instructed the officer.

'Do you always believe the worst of people?' he grilled Haddad as he followed her out.

'Yes. It's quicker and easier. I'm rarely pleasantly surprised.'

Easier? Haddad possibly didn't realise how much she'd revealed with her use of the word and with the almost inaudible sigh that followed it. Not as hard as the persona she projected. That gave Simon more hope. If Haddad genuinely cared about victims, then she'd care about truth, too, and about justice.

In his bedroom, his bed was as neatly made as he'd left it, the light summer blanket unrumpled. The clean jeans and t-shirts that he'd hurriedly brought in from the washing line and dumped on the end of the bed had been neatly folded. A lump formed in his throat. But then he caught sight of an orange blanket and a pillow on a beanbag in the corner and it almost undid him, the shock a sledgehammer to his gut, making him grip the doorframe for stability while the room wavered in front of him.

'What is it?' he heard Haddad ask.

A memory. A memory of a rushed marriage, a hurried move from barracks to an apartment, a delivery van that failed to arrive with a new bedroom suite and bedding . . . His wedding night he'd just been able to afford the honeymoon suite in a Parramatta hotel, but the second night of their married life they'd curled up together on the beanbag on the floor of the empty bedroom of their new apartment, cuddling under the orange blanket they'd found at an op shop minutes before it closed.

Whenever he'd come back from deployments, Hayley always had that blanket on the bed, a bright splash of colour against the subdued blues in the room. He'd kept both the blanket and the beanbag, all these years, because it never seemed right to get rid of them.

'Kennedy? Are you okay?'

'Yeah,' he lied. He cleared his throat. 'Hayley loved that blanket. She must have found it in the wardrobe. The beanbag was over there, under the window, so she's moved it.' To the corner between the bed and the wall. Tucked in where no one could see her from the window, and barely from the door. 'She could have used my bed, or the bed in the other room. So why huddle down there?'

Haddad folded her arms and studied him coolly. 'Some men treat their wives like dogs,' she said.

He silently counted to three before he answered, crushing his anger for a more reasoned response. 'You must have seen some atrocious things in your career, Detective. But most men respect and do their best to care for the people they love.'

'Did you love her?' Haddad challenged.

No clear answer sprang to his mind. His gaze drifted back to the orange blanket, the memories of the first days of his marriage vivid. He made an attempt to answer the question honestly. 'I thought I did,' he said. 'But I'm not sure anyone really understands about love in their early twenties. And the army demands a lot from any marriage. I meant my vows, though, and honouring them was important to me.' And he'd kept them, all of the formal ones of the marriage service. It was his own vow to protect her that he'd failed in, too many times. He'd protected her from her father, in those early years. But that hadn't been enough.

'You should contact her father,' he said to Haddad. 'He is . . . at least he was . . . involved in drug dealing. He served a few years in prison in Victoria. Hayley's evidence – she was only fifteen – helped put him there. He never forgave her, and when he got out he threatened to kill her.' That's why she'd run to Simon, terrified, catching an overnight bus from Melbourne to Sydney to find him at Holsworthy army base. Only his own threats, backed up by four of his army mates who joined him in a desperate drive to Melbourne on a few days off, had made the bastard keep his distance from Hayley.

Haddad looked doubtful, as though she still wanted him in the frame. 'I'll need a name, address, whatever you know about him.'

'I kept a file for a while. He was convicted of a series of aggravated assaults about ten years ago, and went back to prison. He might be out by now.'

'You kept a file? What kind of file?'

'Just a few records, mostly media reports of the second conviction. I had a private investigator check on him, years ago, to make sure he was still in Victoria, away from Hayley. It's all on my computer.' The one smashed on the floor of his study. 'The hard drive is backed up online. I can get the file for you.'

'Hmm. Forensics may be able to get it off your hard drive.'

Shit, she was trying his patience. He blew a long breath out through his nose to try to keep his anger in check. 'Detective Haddad, examining the scene of a murder is one thing. But I believe searching my computer files requires a warrant.'

A quick gleam in her eyes almost made it to a smile. 'Do you have something to hide, Kennedy?'

He briefly considered handing her the drive there and then. If she expected gigabytes of porn and other suspect activity then the actual contents would disappoint her. But principle and procedure mattered.

'Private doesn't equate with criminal, Detective,' he reminded her. 'My personal correspondence, papers and journals are private, and not relevant to this. Except . . .' Yes, except one. 'I can give you a copy of the letter and the settlement offer I sent five months ago to the last address I had for Hayley, from years ago. I assumed she hadn't received it because she didn't respond.'

Until now. She'd come to him and he'd not been there for her. So she'd clung to the orange blanket with its reminders of youthful love and optimism, just as she'd clung to it through his long absences during their marriage, and as usual he'd returned too late.

44

He'd never be able to sleep in this room again without the bright image of that blanket haunting his dreams. But then he'd likely never be able to sleep in this room again at all.

'Your computer is part of a crime scene, Kennedy,' Haddad said bluntly. 'I have every right to take it into evidence and search it.'

He shrugged and didn't object further. His privacy didn't matter that much in the circumstances.

Out in the passage, he hesitated, undecided which way to go. Not back into his study, where Hayley lay. Nor the kitchen, where she'd fed herself meagrely from his cupboards. Needing space and air, he headed for the front door. After one last glance around the bedroom, Haddad followed him, until a voice calling his name halted them both.

He turned. The senior forensic officer – Simon couldn't recall his name – apologised for interrupting. 'I'm going to need your fingerprints, Mr Kennedy. It's just routine. We need to be able to determine which prints are yours and which prints . . . aren't.'

'No worries,' he answered without thinking. Stupid thing to say, when of course he had worries.

He followed the man outside to the forensic van.

'My fingerprints will be all over the knife,' he said, while the officer – Cunningham, his nametag read – pulled out a case from the back. 'It's one I use regularly.'

Cunningham made no comment, but Haddad, Simon noticed, hovered nearby, listening and watching.

'It's your favourite, is it?' she asked.

If she was trying to trip him up, she wouldn't succeed. In eighteen years as a commando, he'd been through advanced interrogation training and exercises multiple times. Nothing she did or said could approach the treatment he'd received from the trainers. He could stick to name, rank and number through days of the harshest handling. But they were supposed to be on the same side, so he'd give her more than that. 'I do a lot of cooking,' he answered.

As he laid out his equipment on a folding table from the van, Cunningham asked, 'Would Hayley have had a house key? Or would the house have been left unlocked?'

'No. I definitely locked all the doors before I left. And Hayley doesn't have a key to this house. I only moved in ten weeks ago.'

Haddad stepped closer, hemming him in between Cunningham and the van door. 'There's no sign of forced entry, Kennedy. Can you explain how your wife got inside?'

'Not for certain.' He held her gaze while the forensic officer pressed his finger against the scanner. 'But there's a spare key on a magnet under the table on the back veranda. We had a different table in Sydney, but that's where we kept the spare key then.'

'Mr Kennedy . . .' Cunningham began, but although he maintained his courteous manner, he gripped Simon's hand more firmly and didn't press the next finger onto the scanner. 'Is that blood around your fingernails?'

Blood? Simon looked down at his hand, at the traces of a dark substance around the edges of the nail and under the blunt, work-short tips. How the hell had blood . . . ? The memory of his journey back this afternoon re-formed, although hazily, as though it was days rather than hours ago. 'I found a wallaby on my way out of the national park. A wild dog had got it, started ripping into it. It was dead, but only just, so I checked its pouch for a joey. I didn't have a lot of water left to wash my hands thoroughly afterwards.'

Haddad snorted. 'Oh, nice story, Kennedy. Quite original. I just don't happen to believe it.' She drew herself up straighter, and although she still had to look up at him, her face hardened and the solidity of her stance became a warning. 'I'm arresting you on suspicion of murder. You do not have to say anything. However, anything you say or do may be noted and used in evidence. Do you understand that?'

He could have protested, but he remained silent and allowed her to snap the handcuffs on his wrists. Clearly she wanted to secure the evidence on his fingernails before he could scrub it off. They would find the truth of the blood soon enough – assuming their analysis could tell the difference between macropod and human blood. But as for all the other evidence . . . yeah, not surprising she'd focused on him.

He'd just have to clear his name, somehow, and fast. Because whoever had killed Hayley was still out there, and if they were targeting him, it might not take them long to discover his close friendship with Erin.

•

Erin waited in the Parks office, half-heartedly attempting to work while all the time her attention was split between the activity next door and keeping watch for Simon. Even if he didn't call her to check on her – and she expected her phone to ring any moment – he'd see the lights on and come in. He'd have to. He had nowhere else to go, with his house a crime scene and Goodabri's small hotel booked out with detectives and forensic officers.

When a car pulled up outside, she hurried to unlock the door . . . but it wasn't Simon. It was Bruce Lockyer, one of the National Parks staff who'd worked a few days a week in the Goodabri office since an injury took him off fieldwork. A colleague she regarded as a friend. In his sixties, he had a gentle way about him and a respect for women that might have had something to do with his long and devoted marriage and the two adult daughters of whom he was immensely proud. Although she didn't think of him as a paternal figure, Erin sometimes wished her own father had been more like him.

'What's going on, Erin?' Bruce asked as soon as she let him in. 'I was at a Lions Club meeting at the pub and rumours are flying. The police have blocked off Simon's street. I saw the lights here. Tell me he's all right?'

'Simon's not hurt,' she assured him. 'It's . . .' She didn't know how much she could, or should, say. Or how to say it.

'The police are setting up next door. It's something bad, isn't it?'

In a small community like Goodabri, everyone knew the police would only come in numbers for a major crime. And if the mortuary van hadn't driven through town yet, it would soon. News would fly that there'd been a murder, and where.

Erin nodded. She led Bruce into the office kitchen, and dragged out a couple of chairs from the rickety table. The fatigue draining her body made her grateful to sit.

'Simon just got back tonight. I was with him when he went into his house, and we found . . . a murder victim. A woman. Simon's . . .' She might as well say it. 'Simon's wife.'

'His wife? Simon's not —' Bruce shook his head. 'He's never mentioned being married.'

'Yes, well, he is, apparently. I didn't know either.'

'You didn't know? But you two are —' He broke off, his cheeks flushing.

The warmth in her own face might have just been from the stuffiness of the kitchen. 'We're friends, Bruce. That's all.' Maybe if she kept repeating it, she and everyone else might believe it. 'He said they've been separated for a long time.'

'And she was murdered? In his house?'

'Yes.'

'No. No. I don't . . .' His face paled to grey, his hand shaking as he rubbed his head, and he suddenly seemed much older than his years. 'Listen, you said you saw her. Was she . . . was she a skinny woman, doll-like? Young? Maybe thirties? Long hair? Hippy-type dress?'

'Yes. All that.' Concerned about his stress, Erin laid her hand gently on his across the table. 'Bruce, did you see her?'

He dropped his head and nodded. 'It was on Monday afternoon, not long before I closed up here. She came in, looking for Simon. I told her he was away and we weren't sure when he'd be back. She was a little thing, quite shy, just said he was an old friend and she was passing through town. I didn't think anything more of it, assumed she'd just gone on her way. But it must have been her.'

He'd gripped her hand almost painfully tight, but Erin didn't move it. The chance of the woman he'd seen being someone else? Close to zilch. On Monday afternoon, Hayley had been here. Today was Thursday. And she'd been killed maybe yesterday or this morning.

'If I'd only done something . . .' Bruce muttered.

'Bruce, you couldn't have known.' Who was she trying to convince – him or herself? She thought it through, aloud. 'She didn't tell you who she was. Simon had never told us she existed. If she'd asked for help you would have found a way to help her.' He'd have taken her home to his wife and they'd have looked after her as though she were their own. 'If she was in town for a few days, surely other people must have seen her or spoken with her.'

Restless, driven to do *something*, she went to the sink, filled the electric kettle with water and dumped a couple of tea bags into mugs. Tea. A good strong cup of tea might give Bruce enough composure for his drive home on dirt roads to his wife. Eventually. And she could do with one herself. 'I'll go next door, tell the detective you saw her. Are you okay to talk with him?'

'Yes.' He cleared his throat and repeated it more strongly. 'Yes. I'll just phone Mary-Rose. She'll worry if I'm late.'

Lucky Bruce, to have someone like Mary-Rose to worry about him. She shoved aside the thought and left the room to do something useful.

Next door, someone from the pub had delivered the platters of hearty sandwiches and pizzas that Erin had arranged earlier. Matt was still there, setting up a computer with the IT guy from the Strathnairn station. Steve Fraser munched on a slice of pizza held in one hand while he typed rapidly on his laptop with the other.

Hearing Matt greet her, Steve glanced up, and that rakish, all-charm grin dissolved the frown he'd been wearing. He waved the slice of pizza. 'I gather we have you to thank for organising this. Caffeine *and* food. You're a goddess.'

Erin disguised the swift rush of pleasure at the unaccustomed compliment with an indelicate snort. 'Definitely not a domestic one. But if you've got a feral goat problem, or you need a firebreak burned, that's my realm.'

He laughed outright, but when she told him why she'd come, he was all detective again, the frivolity swiftly erased. 'He saw her on Monday? Is he sure of the day?'

'Yes. He's only working Mondays and Fridays at the moment.'

'Right. I'll need to talk with him. Is he still around?'

'Next door. He's a bit shaken.'

'Grab some pizza and sambos and we'll go and have a chat with him.'

Erin glanced at the food, too keyed up to feel hungry, although she hadn't eaten much all day.

'Take some while you can,' he urged. 'Forensics and the rest of the horde will be here shortly and there won't be anything left after that.'

She wrapped a couple of sandwiches in paper serviettes. She might be hungry once she stopped. Simon might be hungry, too. Not quite the pub meal he'd suggested hours ago, but there'd be nowhere open to get food later, either here or in Strathnairn, and her own fridge was pretty bare.

Bruce had filled in the time she was gone making some notes on a writing pad and drinking his industrial-strength tea.

'I wrote everything down,' he told the detective, tearing the sheet off the pad and passing it to him. 'It's not a lot. What she looked like, what she said, as best as I can remember. There were a couple of other people here when she came in, so I didn't have a lot of time to talk with her.'

Fraser pulled out a chair and sat down at the table, genial and approachable. Erin watched him from where she leaned against the kitchen bench, trying to gauge if his manner was genuine or calculated.

'Did you see her around town after that?' he asked. 'At the pub, maybe, or even in the distance?'

'No. No, I'm sure I would have noticed. But I live out of town on the Strathnairn road, and I've hardly been in Goodabri since Monday.'

Fraser glanced between Bruce and Erin, including them both. 'So, if we want to find out if anyone else saw her, what's the best way of getting the message around town? Is there a local radio station or newspaper?'

Erin gave him points for asking advice, consulting community members, but it still could have been a practised performance rather than genuine interest. Her once well-developed bullshit detector had been idle for a while, and she no longer knew if she could rely on it.

'Tomorrow's newspaper has already gone to print,' she said. 'They could probably put something online in the morning, but posters around town would be more effective. In the pub, in the bakery, at the service station. That would get people talking.'

'Good. I'll get some posters made, and we'll try that.' His phone buzzed and he pulled it from his pocket and glanced at it in a smooth, quick move. And then he swore.

He muttered an apology, but she wasn't sure if that was for swearing, for the loud scrape of his chair as he pushed it back, or for his abrupt departure from the room, already thumbing a number on his phone and putting it to his ear. Before the front door closed behind him she heard, 'Why the hell did you arrest him?'

Arrest? Erin's brain raced. Whose arrest, so early in the investigation, would Fraser be shocked by? She went to the window to try to hear his side of the conversation, both desperate for and afraid of the answer. Only one answer made sense – but it didn't make sense. How could they have arrested Simon? *Why* would they?

Through a gap in the blinds, she could see Fraser pacing up and down under the streetlight, the road deserted. She stopped short of going outside, but he spoke loudly enough that she heard his words, and the vain hope that he might have been discussing an entirely different case – or man – dissolved.

'*Shit.* Yeah, well, you'll have to bring him here for now until we can take him to Strathnairn. The local station doesn't have holding facilities.'

The old wooden floorboards creaked behind her and she spun around, but it was only Bruce, entirely harmless in his checked shirt, his hand around the stoneware mug.

'I think they've arrested Simon,' she said, keeping her voice low.

Bruce's frown creased his face. 'Simon? But he couldn't have . . .'

'That's what I want to think, too.'

Bruce gave her a sharp glance, but she didn't say any more. She wanted to believe in Simon, to believe in the friendship they'd shared, in the trust she'd placed in him again and again in multiple dangerous situations. But fingers of doubt clawed at that belief, scraping away certainty. He might not have lied to her, but he'd lied by omission. Despite their friendship, he'd kept secrets. His wife, his active army service, his commando expertise.

How could she trust, how could she believe in a man who hid that much of himself? And how could she know what else he hid, and what he was capable of?

●

To be arrested and cuffed in full view of his neighbours was bad enough, but walking from the police car to the makeshift incident room with Erin watching . . . that was a humiliation Simon found hard to bear.

He met her gaze, tried to convey with an attempt at a smile that it would all be okay, but the pain in her eyes gouged him and he feared that even if proof of his innocence came quickly, nothing would be the same between them again. Shame ate at him – not so much for the cuffs on his wrists, but for the hurt he'd caused her, when he'd only wanted to do the right thing. He'd been so determined not to betray Hayley, he'd betrayed Erin instead.

He saw Bruce standing behind Erin in the open doorway of the National Parks building, and despite Haddad's firm grip on his arm he stopped on the pathway. 'Erin, can you stay with Bruce tonight? It might be safer if you don't go home alone.'

She glanced back at Bruce, who nodded, before she demanded, 'What the hell's going on, Simon?'

Simon shook his head. 'I don't know. But this —' he raised his cuffed hands slightly, 'will be sorted by morning. I'll come into the Strathnairn office then.'

Haddad huffed an irritated breath and he succumbed to the pressure on his arm to go inside. He didn't look back at Erin. She hadn't rejected out of hand the idea of going to Bruce's, and he had to hope she'd agree to it. But after Haddad had instructed him to sit at one of the tables while they arranged transport to the larger station, he considered enlisting help in persuading Erin.

Matt Carruthers and three other officers from Strathnairn – cops he'd worked alongside on various rescues and incidents in the parks – carefully avoided looking at him, concentrating on results from a doorknock around town. Cunningham and his crime scene offsider were occupied with preparing to take samples from the blood around his fingernails. Haddad entered data on a laptop, presumably logging details of his arrest.

Only Fraser acknowledged his presence. 'Can I get you a coffee? Or some not-quite-congealed pizza?'

'Just coffee, thanks.' The burger he'd bought at the Macca's drive-through in Glen Innes hours ago still sat heavily in his gut.

They'd handcuffed his wrists in front, not behind his back, and he took the large mug Fraser brought him in both hands and breathed in the caffeine fumes.

The detective propped himself against the table. 'We've got this whole procedure we have to do when someone's arrested.

The custody sergeant at Strathnairn will go through it with you, but since that's a little while off, is there anything we should know now? Medications? Allergies? Other medical conditions?'

More of the good-cop routine. Perhaps hoping he'd relax and let something slip. Or perhaps not.

'No medical conditions.'

'Good. Won't be long before they take you to Strathnairn – just waiting on a car from there. The custody sarge will allow you to contact a lawyer. Nothing else worrying you?'

On a hunch, Simon decided to take the good-cop persona at face value. 'Have you met Erin?'

'Your colleague next door? Yes.'

'Can you persuade her to stay with friends tonight? It may not be safe for her to go home alone.'

'Not safe? Why?'

Simon looked him straight in the eye. 'Because Hayley was brutally murdered in my house, and I'm not the killer. Erin lives alone, and this whole district knows that we're workmates and friends. If someone's trying to get to me, they might target her.'

Fraser appeared to be considering the request, but before he could respond a car pulled up outside, a door slammed, and Nick strode in, his face troubled.

'We need to get a team together quickly,' he announced to the room in general. 'Campers in the Goodabri Rivers park have phoned in an emergency call – they saw a woman go over the falls at the Niland Gorge about an hour ago, and they think she might have been pushed.'

Simon's mind raced through implications and possibilities. Three waterfalls in the park, and it had to be Angel Falls – the least accessible. 'It's very rocky at the base and there's not much deep water,' he told them, 'but there's a chance she survived the fall. There's no vehicle access, though – it's a four-kilometre walk in. You'll need a guide. I'll —'

Haddad didn't let him finish. 'I'll take Kennedy into Strathnairn and keep things going on the case, as we can only hold him for a limited time. Steve, you lead the team into the gorge. Get one of the other park rangers to go with you.'

Simon clenched his hands around the mug. With Jo on restricted duties, there were no 'other' rangers familiar with that park, except for Erin.

As if reading his mind, Nick asked quietly, 'Does Erin know the area, Simon? Or one of the field staff?'

'Yes, she does. We surveyed for a new track there a little while ago.' The day before his call-up came. A day of sunshine, rewarding work and companionship, and he'd held on to the memory through long nights in frigid, barren mountains in northern Iraq. 'But I probably know the river access better, and you'll need to search all along the gorge. Nick, let me take them out there. Please.'

Despite his senior status as acting inspector, Nick turned to Haddad. 'Detective?' The formality of his address when he'd known Haddad for years signalled that he wouldn't use his rank to override her. At least, not in public, and perhaps not so early in an investigation he'd put her in charge of. In the short time Simon had known Nick, he'd seen that fairness and respect again and again.

Haddad glared at Nick as if daring him to challenge her. 'No, Nick. I'm not releasing him now. The evidence we have so far points to him, and I need what's on his hands. Plus out there, where he knows the land, he's too much of a flight risk.'

Nick gave no indication as to whether he agreed or disagreed. 'Steve, if Erin's still next door, ask her if she's willing to go. She's SES as well as Parks, so she'll know the drill.'

Simon considered arguing, even momentarily imagined leaping to his feet and fighting his way out the door. But no matter how easily he could do it, even with the handcuffs, it would be stupid. Haddad wore a handgun on her hip – they all wore them, but Haddad wouldn't hesitate to fire at him.

His injury or death wouldn't protect Erin, out there in the wilderness in the dark night. She was capable and professional and he had to let her go and do her job, no matter that the access down the gorge was narrow, steep and dangerous in daylight, let alone darkness; no matter that at least one killer still roamed free, and perhaps another had pushed a woman over a cliff.

CHAPTER 4

Urgency and its accompanying rush of adrenaline stifled, at least for now, the tiredness that had been dragging at Erin's mind and body.

'The falls are only about forty metres high,' she explained to Steve Fraser as she hastily pulled equipment from the storeroom shelves and handed it to him to stack. 'But they're at the top of a narrow and rocky gorge. The river's flowing reasonably well at the moment. If she fell into the waterhole at the base, she might be okay. But if she hit the rocks, we'll be carrying her out. Or winching her.' She passed him a couple of bags of abseiling gear. 'Have you done much hanging off cliffs?'

His mouth quirked in a quick grin. 'Yep. Did a stint in search and rescue. I have all the certificates somewhere in a drawer.'

'Good. But you aren't going to be abseiling in those clothes.' She nodded at his grey suit trousers and leather shoes as she hoisted a bag of ropes onto her shoulder.

'I've got overalls in my car,' he said. 'We'll load this and I'll change while you're briefing the others.'

A few minutes later, the small group gathered around the map spread on the information counter. Bruce, Matt, Tess, Nick, a couple of other constables from Strathnairn, and Fraser at the back, stripped to his jocks and t-shirt without inhibition and dragging on overalls while she talked. She didn't officially have charge of this operation – that responsibility lay with Nick – but they all looked to her for her knowledge of the area.

'The Niland River campground is the closest vehicle access. That's the best place for a staging ground. Nick, I suggest the officers you've called in and the SES from Strathnairn meet us there.'

He nodded agreement. 'I'll coordinate things from there. What's the access like to the river?'

'There's a walking track up to the falls lookout here —' she followed the line of the track on the map with her finger, 'but we've really tried to discourage people from going to the falls themselves, so the old track beyond the lookout is closed.'

'The witnesses said they'd just got to the lookout when they saw her at the edge,' Nick said. 'Just before she fell.'

'It's dark,' Fraser commented, buckling a police equipment vest over his overalls. 'How can they be sure of what they saw?'

'There's a full moon. They're not sure if they saw one or two people at the edge, but they're agreed that they saw a woman fall.' Nick paused for a moment before he added, 'A woman in a white dress.'

A woman in a white dress . . . Erin swallowed. Two in one day? It had to be just coincidence – but she hadn't noticed white dresses suddenly becoming super fashionable.

Fraser raised an eyebrow at Nick, evidently also noting the coincidence, but he asked nothing more and she silenced her own questions. Her job was finding the woman; the police investigation could make the connections if any existed. She reached for a photo she'd taken off the display board. 'This is the view of the falls from the lookout. You can see there's a fairly wide, flat area at the top – when it's not high, the river breaks into numerous channels through the rocks. You can often rock-hop across it. But a few of the channels are deep, and can be fast flowing. If she fell from this area, here, she may have hit the water below, where it's deepest. But if she fell from either side of that . . . it's rocks below. There's some water in places, but not enough to break a fall from that height.'

She didn't have to spell out the rest for them. Unless the woman had been very lucky, they'd be carrying a body bag out of the gorge. And if by chance she had survived the fall, her injuries were likely to be severe and time-critical.

'There's a walking track from the campground that goes about two kilometres along the river bank,' Erin continued. 'Not up as far as the gorge, though. Nick, if you send the SES team along there, they can check that downstream section. Just in case she's made it that far.'

'What's on the other side of the gorge?' Fraser asked. 'Is there easier access from that side?'

'Up here near the falls,' Erin circled the area on the map, 'the national park boundary is only about two hundred metres away. Beyond that is private property, a few thousand hectares, but a lot of it is scrub and there are no access tracks to the falls that I'm aware of. I gather the property was sold some months ago, but I haven't had any contact with the new owners.'

Nick considered the map. 'The campers said they hadn't seen anyone at the campsite, and no vehicles. So the woman could have come from that property to the north.'

'Possibly,' Erin agreed. 'Or from the state forest next to it, here. There's an old fire trail that runs parallel with the gorge on that side, but it hasn't been cleared for years.'

If someone *had* pushed the woman, Erin couldn't help hoping that person had gone north, rather than back towards the camping area. Even with armed police in the team, she didn't want to encounter a killer in the dark on a rough bush track.

•

'Detective Haddad, you have already asked my client these questions at least twice, and he has answered them. By my calculation, you have less than three hours remaining before you must either release or charge him. May I respectfully suggest that you are wasting everyone's time going over the same ground.'

Simon watched the silent battle of wills between the two women facing each other across the interview table. His lawyer was at least ten years older than Haddad, and her assertive, no-nonsense manner gave the impression of decades of experience in a demanding profession.

Despite the detective's obvious confidence and determination, they all knew she had little solid evidence against him. Haddad had continued with her earlier tactics: trying to wear him down, find inconsistencies or contradictions in his story. Those tactics might even work – on a guilty man. Simon simply repeated the truth, again and again, and could keep doing it as long as she wanted to. But he battled not to let his frustration show. While she persisted here, grilling him, Hayley's killer remained free, and Erin was out searching rugged, isolated country through the night to try to save a life.

'We'll take a short break,' Haddad conceded abruptly. 'I'll have the custody sergeant bring you some refreshments. Interview terminated at eleven-fifteen p.m.,' she added, and switched off the recorder before walking out without another word.

Aware that the custody sergeant was keeping an eye on him through the observation window and would be noting his behaviour, Simon channelled his pent-up energy into standing and stretching tense neck muscles, rather than pacing the floor of the small room and pounding his fists into the wall as he wanted to. Control, patience and focus. He didn't intend to give Haddad any justification for her evident belief that he'd murdered Hayley in a fit of anger.

Massaging an obstinate muscle in his neck, he watched his lawyer write up the last of her notes. 'What happens now?' he asked.

'She can apply to hold you for another eight hours while investigations continue. She won't be able to get the blood analysis back in that time frame, though. That will take around twenty-four hours, by the time they get it to the lab in Sydney and run the tests. She could well argue that because that could potentially be very strong evidence, you are likely to be a flight risk and she should be given the extended time to find additional evidence that puts you at the scene at the time of the murder so that you can be formally charged.'

'Will the extension be granted?' The prospect of being detained until well into the morning concerned him. The confinement itself didn't particularly worry him, and under normal circumstances he'd be patient because it was only a matter of time before they cleared him of having Hayley's blood on his hands. But in normal circumstances Erin wouldn't be out in the bush in the middle of the night, already exhausted from doing his job on top of her own for weeks, risking her life when he should be the one guiding the search.

'I'll argue against the extension, of course,' his lawyer said. 'But yes, I think in the circumstances it's likely that it will be approved.'

Simon dragged out his chair and sat down again. He needed to think, needed to go through everything so that he could find some way to *prove* he hadn't murdered Hayley. Because with Fraser caught up in the search at the gorge, and Haddad focused on him, no one was looking for the killer.

•

The full moon almost directly overhead lit their way as Erin led the first search team along the walking track cut through the scrub, the path just wide enough for two to walk side by side. Steve Fraser kept an even pace beside her, with Matt and Tess following behind.

They scarcely spoke. Erin's thoughts buzzed with questions she wished she could ask the detective, but even if he had answers, she doubted he'd share them. And there were questions she could scarcely dare to ask, even in her own mind. Questions about Simon; questions about her own feelings and her knowledge of him. She couldn't believe him guilty of murder, but with every trudge of her boot on the ground, a small voice of doubt taunted, *What if . . . ?* What if he was guilty?

They'd walked in the moonlight most of the way, but as they neared the lookout platform the tree cover became thicker and the breeze picked up, dancing eerie shadows across the dim path. Erin flicked on her head torch. Time to concentrate on the questions she might have a chance of finding answers for soon.

The clunking of four pairs of boots on the steel base of the lookout platform echoed in the darkness, briefly drowning out the background sound of the waterfall. The rocky gorge fell away beneath the struts of the platform, moonlight catching on the water below.

Erin swung her backpack off and took out a powerful spotlight. 'Let's see what we can see from here. With any luck we'll spot her quickly.'

Fraser paused with his water bottle half raised. 'And without luck?'

'Without luck it will be a very long night.' Even longer for the woman, if she was still alive. And if she was, Erin just hoped she'd see the searchlights and know that help wasn't far away. 'Okay, we'll just use two of the searchlights for now, to preserve the batteries. So pair up. Two sets of eyes per light. We'll start directly below here and sweep the area methodically, from one side of the gorge to the other. Matt, you work downstream, I'll work upstream. She's wearing white, so that should make her easier to spot.' Unless she was under the scrubby trees or rocky ledges, or had become wedged in among the boulders. If they had to search every inch of the river gorge on foot, they'd have to wait until daylight.

Matt went to the opposite side of the lookout, and his searchlight flicked on, glinting on the water below. While Tess tightened a bootlace, Fraser stepped to Erin's side.

She'd said to pair up, and he'd picked her. She'd have preferred Tess with her. She liked Tess's resolute focus and dependability; she knew where she stood with Tess. With Steve Fraser, she wasn't so sure. When he'd shed his suit earlier to change into his dark blue police overalls, it seemed that he'd also cast aside the suave, smooth persona for an altogether more rugged, down-to-earth practicality. His air of competence should have been reassuring, but she couldn't forget that he was actively investigating, and his colleague had arrested Simon.

Erin turned on her searchlight, resting both arms on the railing of the lookout to steady it. With her light beam beside Matt's, she began the first sweep from directly below them, down across the rocky river and up the steep side of the gorge opposite. The river wound among boulders and straggling scrub, the water low and sluggish now, but the evidence of the last flood was still tangled in the branches of the trees.

'The water can come up high,' she commented to Fraser as she began the next slow sweep with her searchlight, grasping at anything easy and straightforward to say. 'If it rains heavily in the district, or on the hills to the east, the river can rise quickly, and the gorge acts as a choke. You don't want to be down there if it's raining anywhere nearby.'

'They're not forecasting any rain, are they?'

Erin kept her eyes on the illuminated patch of river. 'Chance of storms at the weekend.' The weather forecast she'd checked before leaving town had only heightened her sense of urgency. All the more reason to find the woman and get her out of there as soon as they could.

They fell silent, but within moments Matt muttered something and Tess drew in a sharp breath.

'What . . . ?' Her own breath catching, Erin swung her searchlight around to join Matt's, hovering on a patch of something pale-coloured near a rock. Hope died as soon as she saw the shape. 'It's a goat,' she said. 'Just a dead goat. That's one less feral animal I'll have to worry about.' That probably sounded more callous than she'd intended. She hated to see any animal suffer, but feral goats did huge damage to the environment, competing with native species for water and feed. The surefooted animals didn't often fall into gorges, but like every other animal, sometimes they had a run-in with a venomous snake, or were injured in a fight, or simply died of old age.

'Errgh.' Matt flicked his light away. 'Let's hope we don't have to wade in goat soup downstream of it.'

Erin turned her spotlight back to where it had been to resume the search. 'Nope. It won't be there long. A fox or dingo will likely drag it out tonight.' And might have a go at the woman, if they didn't find her soon. Yet another reason to hurry.

Within minutes, Erin's spotlight caught a patch of white just visible through some scrubby foliage not far from the base of the waterfall.

'I think that's her.' She thrust the light at Fraser so she could focus her binoculars with both hands. 'But I can't see if she's in the water or not.' Matt's spotlight joined hers, brightening the area, but with the shadows of the scrubby trees in the gorge she still couldn't see clearly enough. 'We'll have to walk up along the edge of the gorge. See if we can get a better view further along.'

'Is there a track along the edge?' Fraser asked.

With no time to waste, Erin hoisted her pack onto her shoulders again. 'There's an old track that we closed because there were some landslides. It's fairly rough in places. Not easy in the dark, but we'll just take it slowly and carefully.'

'I assume,' Tess said drily, as Erin unlocked the steel gate across the old, overgrown track, 'that as we're about to start clambering around the edge of a gorge at night-time, no one saw the assistant commissioner's email this morning about occ health and safety procedures.'

Even as she spoke, Tess helped Erin swing the heavy gate open. Whatever the police boss's email had said, it obviously wasn't going to keep her from the search, whether it contravened health and safety regulations or not. But Erin caught the edge of a challenge in the glance Tess tossed Fraser.

'I didn't happen to see it, Constable,' he said, with the air of a cheeky schoolboy pretending innocence. As Erin moved off down the track, he followed, walking beside Tess. 'Anything in the email I should be aware of?'

'The usual, sir. A stern reminder to undertake risk assessments and follow procedures. And a note about disciplinary processes for those who fail to do so.'

As far as Erin knew, the two of them had only met tonight, but the touch of amusement in the detective's voice and Tess's manner suggested an undercurrent of . . . well, she didn't have a clue what, but since neither of them seemed to have any inclination to stop the search, it didn't concern her right now.

'Well, let's agree, Constable,' she heard Fraser say, 'that an informal risk assessment has taken place. We're searching a specific location for a woman who may be seriously injured.

We have radios and emergency equipment, an experienced guide, and there's backup at the campground. But I'm not ordering you, so if you consider it too dangerous . . .'

He deliberately trailed off, and Tess snorted. 'Oh, don't worry, sarge. I make my own decisions and take responsibility for them. If I thought this was beyond average crazy, I'd definitely let you know.'

He laughed. 'Oh, I can assure you that if it all goes pear-shaped, AC Fraser will be certain to make sure it's my head that rolls.'

Erin half turned as she held back an overgrown branch for them. 'AC Fraser?' she asked. 'Family?'

'Only genetically.' He made light of it, as if he didn't care.

Oh yeah, she knew about that kind of family. But the detective's family was none of her business, and sure as hell not her priority right now.

'We're coming up to the area where the landslide was,' she told them. 'The track's pretty dangerous – part of it's gone and there's a sheer drop – so we'll have to bush-bash around that section.'

The overgrown track had been easy walking compared to the rough ground and dense scrub she led them through now. In the darkness, she moved slowly to reduce the risk of any of them losing their footing on the rocky ground. But fine branches she could barely see whipped her cheek more than once, and when she walked face-first into a spider's web, she swore and stopped so suddenly that Fraser collided with her from behind.

Strong hands, warm on her shoulders, steadied her. *Male hands*, her body noted, with a flicker of longing. *But not Simon's*, another small voice quickly said.

'You okay?' Fraser asked.

No. I hate this confusion. She stepped out of his touch, scrubbed at her face to remove the clinging sticky web and concentrated on the here and now. 'As long as I've got no spiders crawling in my hair, yes.'

'A ranger afraid of spiders?' he teased, although he did quickly check over her ponytail. 'You must be in the wrong job.'

Grateful for his friendly manner, she responded, 'Oh, I'm not afraid of them. Fascinating creatures, spiders. And vital to the ecosystem. I just hate the creepy-crawling feeling in my hair.'

'I'm glad it's you out front clearing the webs, and not me,' Tess commented, and Matt made a clucking noise at her, imitating a chicken.

They all kept up the banter while they made their way through the scrub, Erin ensuring she contributed light-hearted comments now and then. Better to keep the darkness at bay and avoid thinking too much about the task awaiting them. She'd worked with Matt often enough, and with Tess once or twice, and Fraser's relaxed friendliness boded well for an efficient team. They might indeed have to work seamlessly together very soon, depending on what they found.

When they joined the track again, not far beyond the landslide, she signalled the others to stay put and climbed nimbly over the old fence that had never kept curious walkers away from the edge. Here a large flat rock overlooked the gorge, with a more direct view of the waterfall than they'd had from the lookout. Fraser followed her over the fence – that didn't surprise her – and joined her as she aimed the beam of the searchlight at the rock pools to the right of the base of the falls.

The woman floated in water fed by a rivulet, away from the deeper pool carved by the main channel of the river. A low-growing bush clinging to the rocks entangled her, keeping her from the flow of the water.

'I think she's . . .' Erin lifted her binoculars for a closer look. 'Yes. She's face up.'

Fraser echoed her thoughts. 'So she could still be alive.'

'Yes.' Perhaps she'd fallen into the deep water and managed to make her way out of it. Perhaps. 'It's a slim chance,' she added, 'but . . .'

'But we're going down there to find out.'

'Yes. I am, anyway.'

'We are. Two is safer than one. So, what's the best way down there?'

'We could go back along the top and work our way down, but the slope is steep and there are no tracks. Or we could abseil down the cliff here. I think that's safer, and it's sure as hell quicker. It's a fairly even rock wall, and with Matt and Tess at the top, they can help light our way down.'

It took very little time to unpack the equipment, find suitable anchor points and gear up. She'd been half worried that Fraser had been boasting when he'd said earlier that he was experienced, but as he quickly and calmly prepared she quit doubting his proficiency. She was beginning to suspect that the laid-back, devil-may-care image Steve Fraser cultivated didn't, in reality, go deep.

But as she checked her radio and the torch on her helmet and positioned herself at the edge of the cliff, she wished for the comfortable familiarity of Simon beside her instead of the detective who – despite his easygoing persona – might yet charge Simon with murder.

She pushed off from the edge before Fraser did. Tess and Matt held the searchlights steady as she descended, illuminating the rock shelf she was aiming for, devoid of scrub and a few metres above the water level. But the contrast between the dark and the light from the searchlights messed with her depth perception and she landed unevenly, the shelf not as smooth as the searchlight had made it appear. She almost fell, swearing as she regained her balance just before her knees hit the ground. Stupid, so stupid, to let other matters distract her.

'Careful! It's uneven,' she called to Fraser as he followed her down. Teamwork. Looking out for each other. That's where her head had to be. There was nothing either of them could do about Simon's predicament for now.

Fraser landed easily, unclipping from the rope within seconds and divesting himself of his harness as quickly as she did. They were still thirty metres from the woman, over boulders and rocky ground held together by straggling casuarinas and acacias.

'Take it slowly,' she warned Fraser as she set off, looking for what might be the safest way down off the ledge onto the boulders below. 'Believe me, you don't want to break an ankle down here.'

'Might be the only way I get any time off,' he quipped behind her. 'We're too short-staffed to take rec leave.'

'Yep, same with us. But if you're going to break a limb, do me a favour and do it back at the campground. 'Cos I don't want to carry you out of here.'

The beam from her head torch caught the white of the woman's dress and their idle chat dried up. Erin clambered down off the ledge and skirted around pools of stagnant water, remnants from the previous week's rains which had temporarily swelled the river. A few more rocks to scramble across, and then . . . then she'd just have to deal with whatever they found.

The main channel of the falls splashed a steady flow into the larger pool nearby, sending a light spray metres around and making all the rocks slippery. The woman floated in the pool below the trickling secondary falls, tangled in the branches of a dead casuarina that had toppled into the water, its roots still embedded in a rock crevice. Face up, eyes closed, pale, and still but for the gentle drifting of her long hair on the surface. Face up, but more than a metre from the edge of the pool. Beyond easy reach, and no way, from here, to tell if she still breathed.

'We have to get her out. Hell knows how.' Erin slid her pack off aching shoulders and began to tug open the fastenings on her SES jacket. The thin branches of the straggling casuarina wouldn't hold her weight. She'd have to go in to the water to reach her.

Fraser's hand closed on her arm. 'Hold on for a tick. Crime scene. I'll get a couple of photos for the record before we plunge in there.'

Her thoughts circling the problem, she shrugged off her jacket and started unlacing her boots while he snapped a few shots with his phone. 'No need for both of us to get wet. I can take her weight in the water, but I'll need you to pull her up here.'

He opened his mouth to object, but must have realised she was right. Smart man. 'How deep is it in there?' he asked instead.

'Less than two metres. I think.' In the stark contrast between torchlight and moon shadow, she couldn't see the bottom. 'The main pool's much deeper. Complete with whirlpools when it's flooding. This one's fine.'

She stripped down to shirt and underwear. Although the autumn night wasn't cold, she'd appreciate dry clothes to put on afterwards. If Fraser noticed the totally impractical red lace G-string, he used his brain again and didn't comment. Dammit, she could almost like this guy. Except for the whole investigating-Simon issue.

Simon wouldn't have commented on a lace G-string either.

Shit, why the hell was she thinking that now? She tucked her hair under her helmet and slid from the rock into the water. Cold water. Cold enough to suck her errant thoughts away. She didn't touch the bottom, taking the few strokes necessary to swim to the woman. She found a footing on an underwater rock and, chest deep in water, took the woman's outstretched hand to feel for a pulse.

Nothing. Nothing but the gentle lapping of the disturbed water, the sound of the falls, and the scrape of Fraser's boot against rock as he moved to shine the light more directly for her. No moaning from the woman. No breathing. From here, Erin could see the jagged, broad gash on the side of her head, and the way her neck twisted, broken.

'You can radio Nick.' The cold had seeped into her throat, making her vocal cords stiff. 'Tell him we won't be needing the rescue helicopter.'

By the time she'd disentangled the body from the branches, she almost had her leaking eyes under control. Fraser leaned well over the water to lift the body up and onto the rocks, and then his two strong hands gripped hers and he helped her out. He handed her an unfolded space blanket. 'Wrap this around yourself. Are you okay?'

The night air chilled her wet skin and her teeth threatened to chatter so she just nodded, clutching the blanket close around her. She'd find her dry clothes in a minute, dig out the sweatshirt from her pack. When she stopped dripping.

Fraser knelt beside the woman on the cold stone, his fingers against her neck, confirming the death. A youngish woman. Perhaps thirty, thirty-five, her skin lightly tanned and her face devoid of makeup. But it was her dress that drew Erin's attention away from her face. Plain white cotton, a simple short-sleeved wraparound shift, tied at the waist with thin ties.

The damp fabric clung to her body but the top had skewed, exposing one breast. In an act of respect, Fraser drew the edge of the bodice closed and as he did so, Erin saw the stitching edging the fabric, and the delicate line of decorative flowers.

'Steve,' she said, making her tight throat work. 'Her dress – it's the same as Hayley's.'

'Yeah, that's what I thought.'

'No, I mean . . . not just the same style.' She knelt beside him, dropping the blanket enough to point at the edge of the bodice he'd just closed, keeping her eyes on that small detail. 'It's hand-stitched and embroidered. It's a home-made dress. I didn't see it for long, but I think Hayley's was, too.' She remembered spots of blood on Hayley's dress, like red flowers on the stitched leaves. 'They're both wearing embroidered dresses, and believe me, this isn't the latest fashion.'

'You think they knew each other.'

'Yes. They must have. The chances of two women making the same dress from the same fabric in the same area are pretty slim.' *And then being murdered . . .* The chill seeped into her bones. This woman's death *might* have been accident or suicide, but the timing, the circumstances, the report of someone else there with her . . . something was very wrong.

Erin reached for her own clothes, dragged on socks and trousers, then stripped off her wet shirt and rummaged in her pack for her sweatshirt. Fraser kept his back to her, taking a few more photographs of the woman. When she pulled her sweatshirt over her head, he was holding his phone in the air.

'You won't get a signal here. You'll need a sat phone.'

'I don't suppose you happen to have one?'

'Mal – our boss – insists we always carry one now, since we're usually out of mobile range.' She took it from its pocket on her pack and keyed in the passcode before handing it to him. 'I presume you're reporting in to Detective Hard-ass.'

'Thanks. Yes.' As he copied the number from his mobile into the sat phone, he said, 'Leah's a good detective. I worked with her a few months back in Birraga, just before she came here for that other case. She's tough but she's thorough and fair.'

A sudden clatter of falling stones startled Erin, and she spun around towards the sound, hearing the multiple soft plops as they hit the water in the pool below the falls. Not from the top of the cliff where Tess and Matt waited; no, they'd fallen down the steep slope on the other side of the falls.

Fraser grabbed the spotlight with his free hand and directed the beam at the slope. 'I suppose it's one of the goats,' he said.

It could have been a goat. Or a fox or a dingo or a wallaby. Except the silhouette she'd briefly glimpsed on the cliff edge against the night sky stood tall and didn't have four legs.

CHAPTER 5

Hours dragged by. Simon lay on the mattress, hands clasped behind his head, and stared at the white ceiling of the holding cell. Despite his fatigue – he'd slept rough the last three nights – he didn't plan on sleeping now. Custody procedure didn't allow him a pen and paper, so he worked mentally through possibilities, unanswered questions, and ways to find those answers.

But his thoughts kept circling back to Hayley, hiding in his house for days, sleeping on the beanbag, wrapped in the old orange blanket, and relying on his pantry for food. She'd been in the National Parks office on Monday afternoon but not said anything to Bruce about needing help. Going by the food she'd eaten, she'd probably been in his house since sometime not long after that, waiting for him.

The harsh truth knotted his gut. If he'd come straight back to Goodabri after leaving Sydney, if he hadn't taken those three days in the wilderness, he'd have arrived home around the same time she came looking for him.

If, if, if . . . All the years of his marriage were littered with ifs and regrets, guilt and remorse.

She must have received his last letter, because she'd known where to find him in Goodabri. But why had she hidden like that? He'd seen no sign of a bag or purse, nothing belonging to her in his house, and no evidence of food other than his. He'd check thoroughly when they let him back into the house, but everything pointed to her having no money. No money, no clothes, no belongings. Had some hardship befallen her? Had she run in fear from something? If so, why hadn't she asked anyone in town for help? Bruce would have helped her. Snowy would have helped her, and Tess at the police station. Hell, at least half this town knew what it was like to fall on hard times and would have bent over backwards to do what they could for her.

She must have found the key to enter the house, but how had the killer got in? The absence of any evidence of forced entry indicated three potential explanations: that she'd let her killer in; that she'd left a door unlocked; or that her killer had been with her all along. The possibility remained that someone had come looking for him and found her instead, but the more Simon considered it, the less likely it seemed. He didn't rule it out, but given all the other questions around Hayley's sudden reappearance, his instinct leaned towards the killer being someone connected with her, not him. And if that was the case, then who or what had she become involved with that had cost Hayley her life?

Voices came from further down the corridor. He didn't catch many words, but he recognised the custody sergeant's broad ocker accent and Haddad's clipped tones. And then he *did* hear Haddad's sharp, 'I am well aware of the time.'

Because his watch had been taken from him for safekeeping in the custody office, along with his phone, wallet and belt, Simon couldn't be sure of the time, but it had to be close on three in the morning. Hours since Erin had left on the search, and he'd heard no news.

Restless, he got off the bed and dropped to the floor to begin a round of one-armed push-ups. He'd hardly done ten when footsteps stopping outside the door and the beep of the electronic lock alerted him to roll out of the way of the person entering. He rose from the floor and sat on the edge of the bed, making no moves to the door.

Not Haddad but Aaron Georgiou, the detective constable who usually worked with Nick, stopped just inside the door, leaving it wide open. A sign of trust? Caution? Procedure? Simon knew him, as he knew most of the police in the district. Although young, Aaron had the makings of a good cop; he was dedicated, hard-working and honest. Too honest to play power games. Whether that would help or hinder his career, only time would tell. But Simon trusted him.

They must have called him in at short notice, for instead of his usual business shirt and trousers he wore jeans and a light sweatshirt.

'You okay?' Aaron asked. 'For a moment there I thought you were writhing on the floor.'

'Push-ups. I can't sleep, might as well do something. Is there any news from the search?'

Aaron hesitated, glancing away as if unsure whether he should share information with a man under arrest, before he said, 'I heard they found her.'

'Alive?'

Aaron gave the smallest shake of his head.

Simon swore. 'Accident or . . . ?'

'Too early to tell,' Aaron said, his voice low. 'They'll bring her out once it's daylight. Forensics are heading there now.'

Simon wanted to ask about Erin. He didn't. He was still under arrest for murder, and he had to keep her right out of it. A lot of people knew they were friends – good friends – but he was glad, now, that he'd made no moves towards anything more. No one knew what she meant to him. None of this shadow over him would fall on her.

Aaron thrust his hands in his pockets and leaned against the doorframe, informal and unthreatening. 'Look, Simon, I'm not here for any official interview. The custody sergeant won't permit it at this hour. But since you're awake, he says it's okay to ask a question about Ms Munro that might help us. But you don't have to answer anything.'

'Ask.'

'Do you know of any other names your wife used?'

'I told you her maiden name. I guess she may have used my name, but I never heard her do so. Why?'

'Did she have a driver's licence?'

'Yes. I taught her to drive. She got her licence the first year we were married. Why do you want to know?'

Aaron gnawed on his lip for a moment. Things were definitely awkward. 'We need to find out where she was living, and who with. We need to establish her next of kin.'

Simon swallowed and nodded. He probably wasn't her next of kin. He couldn't be, after all this time. If Hayley had a de facto partner, that person would take precedence over a long-separated spouse. And Hayley was pretty and loving, with a warm heart and generous spirit – surely someone had valued that, and loved her?

'I gave Detective Haddad the PO box address in Lismore. That's the only address I have. She went to an alternative lifestyle retreat up that way. That's all I know.' Simon gripped the edge of the mattress. He couldn't pace in the small cell. Couldn't move much, couldn't walk out and try to assuage this helplessness with action. 'You should ask her father. I doubt she kept in touch with him, but perhaps he knew where she was. I've already told Detective Haddad about his previous threats of violence to Hayley.'

'Yeah, we're trying to locate him. The thing is . . . there's no record of Hayley that I've been able to find. Not under Munro, or Kennedy, or her birth name. No licence, car rego or electoral roll. No police record. Nothing I can find on the web either, or on social media. I'll get onto the post office in Lismore in the morning, check who rents the box. But for the moment, I've got no clues at all.' He dragged a hand through his hair. 'Did you know any of her friends? Girlfriends from when you were together? Maybe other army wives? Even old school friends?'

'Not really. She was always shy, didn't make friends easily. Her father was physically abusive. They moved to the town I grew up in when she was sixteen. She'd left school by then, and I don't think she had many friends other than me. After we were married and she'd moved to Holsworthy . . .'

He dredged through his memory, trying to recall what Hayley had been doing when he'd been absorbed in training. 'She was so shy we didn't have much of a social life. She studied for her childcare certificate. She did have a friend in the course.' He could picture the woman from the couple of times he'd briefly met her, when she'd come to pick up Hayley for a girls' night out. Hayley had spoken of her fairly often. 'Her name . . . it was something old-fashioned. Celia . . . no, Sybilla. Sybilla Braithwaite. When Hayley went on the trip around Australia, she went with Sybilla. But I don't know . . .' There was too much he didn't know. 'Look, I don't know if they stayed friends, if Hayley went to the north coast with her or alone. She might not have seen her for years.'

'It's worth asking her. Sybilla Braithwaite isn't a common name. That might make it easier to find her. If you think of anyone else, let me know.'

After Aaron left, Simon remained sitting on the mattress, dropping his head back against the wall, his eyes closed. He'd lived with Hayley for three years, and he could barely remember the name of even one of her friends. There must have been more, although other than the occasional mention of an acquaintance he couldn't recall her having friends. He'd encouraged her to go out, join groups, meet people and get involved in activities outside her studies, but she always found some reason not to. And although they'd socialised sometimes with the guys in his unit and their girlfriends and wives, she never seemed to feel comfortable with them.

Shyness, lack of confidence, her constant feelings of not fitting in – they were a big part of the reason why he'd not objected when she'd left to go travelling, why he'd given her space to spread her wings and find her own way. She'd had a shit of a life until he'd married her. He wasn't sure if he'd given her a better one, even if she'd been safer with him than with her parents or on the streets.

When it came down to it, he'd hardly known her. He'd given her money, safety, a place to live, gentleness and affection. They'd shared some good times – movies, picnics, renovating their apartment, quiet evenings together – but he'd always felt . . . yeah, he'd always felt as though he had to look after her. She'd deferred decisions to him, always asked for his guidance, initiated little herself.

She'd needed him in so many ways. Until she didn't, and she'd left. Even the withdrawals from their joint bank account had become fewer and further between, then they'd stopped.

Shit, he was just going around and around it all, and getting nowhere. Some sleep, if he could get it, might give his brain some clarity. Or at least get him through these interminable hours of uselessness in the cell.

He stretched out on the narrow mattress and punched the pillow into a semi-comfortable shape. He must have slept, because he dreamed, a jumbled, scattered jigsaw of memories and imaginings, experiences and fears; of Hayley and Erin, of his father, of war and shattered houses and a refugee child, crying and crying and crying.

He jerked awake, the child's cries still echoing in his mind. No stranger to bad dreams, usually he'd get up, walk around, drink a glass of water, and maybe read for a while to clear his mind of the clinging, spider-web strands of the dream. He swung his legs around to sit on the edge of the bed, but here he had nowhere to walk to.

The beep of the keypad sounded, loud in the stillness, and the door opened. Aaron again, tiredness beginning to show in the shadows under his eyes. He carried a cardboard coffee cup and Simon caught the scent immediately.

'I'm glad you're awake,' Aaron said, passing the cup to him. 'I've got some good news and some bad news.'

Simon wrapped his hands around the cup and inhaled the rich, steaming aroma. 'Coffee is good news.'

'I thought it might be. But even better is that your friend Gabe responded to my messages and confirmed your whereabouts yesterday morning. He saw you leave your camping spot. So we're releasing you without charge. You're free to go.'

Free. The word meant far more to him now after less than twelve hours in a cell than it had a day ago. 'The bad news?'

Aaron glanced out into the corridor as if checking for listeners. He dropped his voice. 'Hayley's friend Sybilla. We can't find her. No one can find her. The thing is, she was reported as a missing person eleven years ago. There's been no sign of her at all since then.'

•

Time moved slowly with nothing to do but wait for daylight. With the forensic officers deciding against rappelling down the cliff in the dark, Erin stayed at the bottom with Steve to protect the woman's body until they could lift her out of the gorge in daylight. Although Matt and Tess hadn't found anyone in their search for the figure Erin had seen, they stayed and kept an eye on things from the top of the gorge.

Her SES jacket provided little cushioning against the rock Erin sat on beside Steve, but at least it was a barrier between her butt and the chill of the stone. And the two episodes of

Doctor Who they'd watched on Steve's phone had helped them pass a couple of hours. The debate about which Doctor was best absorbed another half an hour. They both carefully avoided discussing Simon, or Hayley, or the corpse lying a metre away.

The full moon dropped gradually towards the west, beyond the walls of the gorge and out of their sight now, although the silvery light reflected on the top half of the falls. Most of the time they left the torch switched off to discourage mosquitoes and other insects, their eyes accustomed now to the moonlit night.

The bush around them rustled with small sounds – the grumbling hiss of a possum, the quiet whoosh of an owl overhead, the low, pulsing hoot of a frogmouth somewhere in the distance. And always the steady, soporific splattering of the waterfall nearby.

Steve yawned, and checked his watch for the second time in as many minutes. 'Sunrise is around seven, isn't it?'

'Yes.' An hour to go. Longer before the team up above carried a stretcher in and got it down to them. Erin delved in the side pockets of her pack, feeling for the two muesli bars she'd been saving. 'Here. Have some breakfast. Is there any coffee left in the thermos?'

He took the muesli bar and gave the thermos an assessing shake. 'About half a cup each. I'll ask them to send down some more. Preferably with bacon, eggs, and hot buttered toast.'

'I'm hankering after French toast. But fat chance of either, out here. You should get some sleep. I guess you'll still be working most of the day.'

'I'll be fine.' The plastic wrapper on the muesli bar crackled as he ripped it open. 'Wouldn't be the first all-nighter I've pulled. But why don't you take a nap?'

'I'll wait until I get home. The bedding's not exactly comfortable here.' Home, fresh coffee and her own bed – beautiful thoughts, but still hours away. An hour until daylight, probably another hour or more before they had the body strapped into a stretcher and ready to lift up the rock face. Then they'd be carrying her through the bush, back to the camping ground and the police team. Then another hour or so to Strathnairn and home.

Except she had to see Simon first, find out what had happened. If he was still in custody . . . No, surely he couldn't be.

She'd overheard parts of Steve's conversation with Leah Haddad on the satellite phone, hours ago. He'd wandered a short distance away to make the call, yet made no real attempt to hide his side of the conversation from her. But because it was police business, and she respected that, she'd said nothing about it since.

Now, after hours sitting side by side on the flat rock surrounded by the dark stillness of the bush and the gentle splashing of the falls, they'd established, if not a friendship, at least a working partnership, so when she finished eating the muesli bar she broached the subject hanging unspoken between them.

'Would you have arrested Simon? Do you really believe there's evidence against him?'

In the dim light she saw him turn his face to her. 'Would I have arrested Simon?' he repeated thoughtfully. 'I'm not sure I can answer that, or whether my answer would mean anything. I wasn't there at the house with him, Erin. I don't know what Leah saw, or thought she saw, or what was said to make her suspect him. But I do know that she's a good detective. She's thorough and dedicated and she wants to find the truth.'

Not what Erin wanted to hear, but she couldn't fault his honesty, or the way he spoke of his colleague. 'What does your instinct say?'

'Instinct? Instinct is highly overrated.' He leaned forward with his elbows on his knees and stared straight ahead. She assumed it was a dismissive comment, until he took a deep breath and continued, 'A couple of years ago I let "instinct" guide my judgement. I believed a man was guilty of murdering a child, and when his life was threatened I didn't rush to save him. He died at the hands of a mob, and a colleague – someone I care about – was seriously injured trying to protect him. But it turned out the man was innocent. My "instinct" in that case was nothing more than prejudice and anger.'

And he carried the scars, apparently. A man with a conscience, even if it hadn't always been uppermost. But he'd bared a painful part of his past candidly, and she unsuccessfully sought words to respond.

Again he turned his face towards her, and the starlight reflecting off the water danced silver across the angled lines of his profile. 'Erin, I'm much more cautious these days. We don't have enough evidence yet. I don't believe anything in particular about Simon at this stage. I'd *like* to think that the killer is just some random madman Hayley opened the door to rather than a dedicated soldier, but they've got a history, and it isn't a happy one. I have to consider all the possibilities. Including . . .' His slight pause alerted her. 'Including the possibility that a woman who cares about him may have been incensed when his wife arrived in town.'

The fact that he'd guessed – read? – the feelings for Simon she'd tried to hide shocked her almost as much as his implication. 'You think *I* could have murdered her?'

'I said I had to consider all the possibilities.' His voice in the darkness was even, and although it wasn't harsh it wasn't light and teasing either. 'You work in town, and it's a small town. You could easily have met her since she arrived. You knew the house was empty and you're strong enough to have overpowered her. So it's a possibility.'

Put like that, she could see the logic. The decidedly uncomfortable logic. So much for professional friendliness and the good working relationship she thought they'd established. He'd probably been watching and assessing her the whole night.

'Should I be grateful that you haven't arrested me yet?' she asked, without much in the way of humour.

Five minutes ago, she would have seen the smile he threw her as simply light-hearted and friendly. She wouldn't make that mistake again. 'Theoretical scenarios aren't evidence,' he said. 'I've got a dozen or more of them. They give me options for the directions to start making enquiries. But I'll start pruning them when we have forensic data, post-mortem evidence, and witness and alibi statements.'

She kept her mouth shut. No use in protesting her innocence when she didn't have much of an alibi, whatever the time of Hayley's death. She mentally ran through her own movements. Wednesday afternoon and evening working alone in the park, before she'd gone to her home on the edge of Strathnairn – still alone. Yesterday morning she'd been up at the crack of dawn and out to check campsites and refill toilet-paper stocks before arriving at the Goodabri office around lunchtime.

If Hayley had been murdered on Wednesday night or Thursday morning, it would be impossible to prove to Fraser that she'd been somewhere else at the time.

•

The first rays of sunlight glinted on the tops of the trees outside the police station. Simon paused on the footpath and breathed in the fresh air. A light breeze fluttered the sun-gold leaves, bringing with it a few degrees of autumn chill.

With his vehicle in Goodabri and probably still being examined, he checked his wallet for his access card to the Strathnairn National Parks depot. Yep, he had it on him. He could take a work truck out to the search site.

He'd just started walking towards the depot when the police station door swung open again. Dee, one of the constables, called after him, 'We're heading out to the park now if you want a lift.'

Dee wore her search and rescue overalls, and introduced a new, very young probationary constable as they finished loading some gear into a four-wheel-drive police vehicle. He knew Dee from around town and from his work in Parks and the SES. She didn't seem perturbed by the fact that he'd been arrested and might still be under suspicion of murder. Her attention was on explaining procedure and the task to the new recruit, and Simon sat in the back, largely forgotten for most of the trip.

At the staging ground, Nick gave him an apologetic smile but made no comment about his arrest or release, launching straight into instructions for the morning-shift team of Dee and her offsider and a couple of cops from another station.

'The SES crew are up there with Matt and Tess, setting up the tripod to bring the victim out. Simon, can you take the basket stretcher and help them? Dee, take a couple of the relief crew and have a look at the top of the falls, now that it's light. Look for any evidence and for any signs of the person Erin and Fraser saw last night. Then relieve Matt and Tess. They've been out there all night.'

Erin had seen someone in the bush during the night? Simon interrupted to ask, 'Is Erin still there?' She had to be – her ute was parked near the walking track beside the Strathnairn SES truck.

'Yes,' said Nick. 'She and Fraser found the victim at the base of the falls. They're still there.'

She'd been at the base of the falls all night? The temperature hadn't been frigid, but it hadn't been warm either, and here at the campground a light morning mist hovered around the river. It would be denser – and cooler – in the gorge.

Simon went to the SES truck, unlocked as he expected, and found a spare helmet and a discarded jacket in the back. He dragged out the basket stretcher, ran a quick check over it. Designed to be used in difficult terrain, it separated into two easily-carried parts.

Dee and her offsider were still consulting the map with Nick, so he set off without them, both halves of the unloaded stretcher a fraction of the weight of a full military pack and weapons.

After the night in confinement both his body and his mind welcomed the jog along the track. The early sunlight, rising above the treetops, burned away the river mist and the chill. Somewhere in the vicinity, a group of kookaburras cackled raucously, proclaiming their territory, and as he rounded a bend near the lookout platform a couple of rock wallabies scattered into the bush. He had no time now to stop and enjoy it, but he never failed to appreciate the beauty and peace of the bush – and the fact that here, in a landscape unscarred by war, he had no need to be watchful for mines, snipers or ambushes.

The overgrown track from the lookout to the waterfall had been well trodden during the night by the police and SES teams, and he had no difficulty following where they'd left the path to skirt around the collapsed part. He heard voices well before he emerged from the tree cover, and fortunately caught sight of a guy rope before he jogged into it.

At the top of the cliff they'd made good progress setting up the tripod and rigging for the high-angle recovery. He received a couple of surprised glances from the police officers present, and grins from several of the SES crew, but nobody made an outright comment on his release.

'Hey, Kennedy,' one of the SES guys called. 'Whaddaya reckon about anchor points for this belay? The ground's as crumbly as a biscuit.'

There were enough cops around to protect Erin if last night's figure in the dark still lurked nearby, so for the next twenty minutes Simon turned all his attention to practical matters while they finished setting up the gear. Although the volunteer crew had trained for such rescues, most of the district consisted of flat plains so they rarely needed the skills for vertical extractions. He had more experience, gained mostly in a park in the high country further east rather than in the army.

He didn't mention Erin, and although Tess coordinated communication with her and Fraser in the gorge – via both radio and more informal shouts – he took no part in it. She might not have known he was there. But while others lowered the stretcher, he grabbed a harness and a helmet and clipped on to one of the ropes.

'What do you think you're doing, Kennedy?' Tess demanded.

'I'll go down there to bring the body up. The other two must be exhausted and chilled. It's safer for me to do it.'

'And you haven't been up all night?'

'I've been warm, dry and well fed, not sitting on cold rocks in the middle of nowhere.'

She could have ordered him to stay – the police had charge of the operation – but she didn't. Maybe she trusted him. Or maybe she trusted the judgement of her colleagues: Haddad, who'd let him go, and Nick, who'd sent him here. Or maybe she just figured that down in the gorge he had nowhere to run to, and there were plenty of police around to ensure he didn't do anything stupid.

He descended swiftly and easily, the rock wall sheer and without dangerous protrusions. Fraser met him at the bottom, having just finished unhooking the stretcher from the ropes used to lower it, and they carried it between them over the rocks to where Erin waited with the victim.

He didn't realise how much he'd wanted to see Erin's quick grin until he didn't see it. She just nodded a greeting and turned away from him, but not before he saw the dark shadows under her eyes. It should have been him down here all night. She'd worked her butt off for months, carrying the load of three staff, and although he'd always admired her fitness and strength, that kind of workload was too much for anyone.

They'd laid a first aid blanket over the dead woman. He hadn't given her a great deal of thought, except to curse the circumstances that necessitated Erin having to be out here. But when he and Fraser set the basket stretcher beside her, and Erin gently lifted the blanket away, he saw the similarities to Hayley's dress immediately. A mate's alibi couldn't count for much, so was this why they'd let him go? Because the two women – and their deaths – might be connected, and he'd been in the company of the police when this woman had fallen?

Strands of her long dark hair, dry now, fluttered across her face. A memory from long ago stirred, an image, hazy in remembrance. His focus had been on Hayley, the day they'd laughed over drinks on the balcony of their apartment. Hayley, laughing and relaxed, as he'd rarely seen her.

The woman's head was tilted to the side, away from him. He leaned over her to get a better view of her face. And then he rose and stepped away from her, his thoughts reeling.

For all she'd barely acknowledged him moments ago, Erin came to stand beside him. 'What is it, Simon? What's wrong?'

The water falling into the pool seemed louder, joined by the thudding in his ears. What the frigging hell was going on? First Hayley, now . . .

Both Erin and Fraser waited for his answer, Erin with worry creasing her forehead, Fraser in a ready stance, hands on his hips, watching him carefully.

'I think I know who she is,' Simon said. 'I can't be sure – it's years since I've seen her. But I think she's Hayley's friend, Sybilla Braithwaite. Aaron told me she's been missing for eleven years.'

CHAPTER 6

Her brain foggy with tiredness, Erin struggled to think through the implications. Hayley and Sybilla were friends. Simon knew both of them. The police already suspected Simon . . .

Simon's brain must have been functioning faster than hers, because he said to Steve, 'I was going to take the body up. But I guess you don't want me anywhere near her now.'

'Yeah, that's probably best,' Steve said. 'I know you've got a pretty solid alibi for when she fell, but you're the only link between them so far. I can take her. You look after Erin. It's been a long night and she's exhausted.'

Leave before the job was done? Erin shot Steve a glare. '*She* can both look after and speak for herself. Besides, unless you've got a Superman cloak hidden somewhere, you're going to need help carrying her to the cliff base.'

'Tess could come down. Or some of the others.'

'Tess has been out all night too.' Impatience and chill made her stamp her feet on the spot. 'Come on, let's get this woman onto the stretcher and out of here.'

Simon didn't touch the victim, but Erin and Steve transferred her to the stretcher without difficulty, strapping her in securely. Erin didn't let her gaze linger on the woman's face. Experience had taught her to keep things impersonal when dealing with the deceased. Respectful, careful, distanced. Emotions were too distracting, so she focused her attention on the mechanics of the task. Straps, ropes, clasps to keep the remains safe for the investigators and for her loved ones.

Steve didn't object when Simon stepped forward to help them carry the stretcher over the rocks to the base of the cliff. And although the woman was slightly built, they needed Simon's strength; even with it Erin's arm ached by the time they'd covered the short distance.

While Steve harnessed up and attached the stretcher to the ropes, she slid off her backpack and rubbed the painful muscles of her shoulder.

'Are you okay?' Simon asked quietly.

'Ratshit tired,' she admitted, because he was a friend and he'd never belittled her, 'but it's nothing a hot shower and a sleep won't fix.' And maybe a cry. A cry for two dead women, and for the mess of her own emotions that had only become more tangled since Simon's long-awaited return. So much for thinking that everything would be easier once he came back.

'What about you?' she asked. 'You've had a hell of a night.'

'I'm fine. I —' He broke off, changing his mind about whatever he'd been about to say. 'Come on, let's get geared up. We've still got to get back to the campground. But I'll drive you home from there. If . . .' He paused, and his voice thickened as if with discomfort. 'If you're okay with that.'

Was he ashamed about being arrested? Did he think she didn't trust him? She might be uncertain and confused about a heap of things, but she no longer had any doubts about his innocence. 'Let's get back to the vehicles. We can argue then about who's driving.'

She didn't argue, though, when he swung her backpack over his own shoulder. By the time she reached the top, she was glad she didn't have the weight dragging on her. She hadn't exactly been on the go for all of the past twenty-four hours — she'd just been waiting around half the night — but none of that had been particularly comfortable or restful.

'Between the SES and us, there's plenty of people here to carry the stretcher out,' Tess said as Erin divested herself of her harness. 'No point staying around. You and Simon should go home. I'm sure Fraser will be in touch later if he needs anything more from either of you.'

The walk from the campground had seemed long enough at night, although it was only a few kilometres. The return trip in daylight should have seemed shorter, but although Simon still carried her pack, weariness weighed her down. She had to concentrate on her feet to avoid stumbling.

Neither she nor Simon spoke much. They passed a few people on the track: the forensic officers returning to search the waterfall in daylight, and a couple of their SES colleagues heading up to relieve the crew who'd worked overnight.

When they emerged from the bush at the campground, they saw Nick and his detective offsider, Aaron, deep in discussion at the picnic table scattered with maps, radios and other equipment. Steve had returned her satellite phone, so unless Tess or anyone in the police team had one, he couldn't have reported the victim's possible identity yet.

'We have to tell them who the woman might be,' Erin said. 'Steve won't have mentioned names over the radio.'

'I'll go do it. Do you want to wait at your ute?'

Wait out of earshot? She shook her head. The only way she'd have any chance of working out what was going on was by staying informed. As informed as the police would allow, anyway. And since Steve had his suspicions of *her* – suspicions that Haddad would undoubtedly share – police information would likely dry up as soon as she was off the immediate scene.

'She's *Sybilla*?' Aaron exclaimed when he heard the news. 'She's been alive all this time?'

'You'll need to get her family or someone who knows her better to identify her. I only met her a couple of times. I could be wrong.'

'She has family,' Aaron said. 'Parents, and two sisters.' He turned to Nick. 'How do you recommend we contact them?'

Erin bit her lip to keep her composure as the mental blocks she'd held in place against thinking of the victim as an individual with a life and a history crumbled. Sybilla had a family, people who loved her. People who had worried and searched and hoped every day for the past eleven years for some news of her. And now they would hear this worst of outcomes.

Nick's grim face reflected how they all felt. 'It's Leah's case and her decision, but she'll probably first want to liaise with the detectives who investigated her disappearance. They may have fingerprints on file. That'll be the quickest way to confirm if it's her. When Fraser gets here, Aaron, you can go back to Goodabri with him to brief Leah.'

'Make sure the forensic people look at her dress and Hayley's,' Erin said. 'I think they're home-made, and they're very similar. Maybe they got them from a market stall or shared a pattern or something. If you can find who made the dresses, you might find out more about where they've been.'

All three men looked at her, evidently not entirely compre-hending the significance of the dresses. Practical guys whose most taxing fashion decision was whether to wear a blue shirt or a white one. They'd probably never sewn a seam in their lives.

'Do people share sewing patterns?' Nick asked. 'Or maybe the design is some kind of internet trend?'

'Yes, people do share, and you can buy patterns online,' she said. 'But the odds of two women coincidentally making the same pattern out of the same type of fabric are very long. It's not even a particularly fashionable style, unless you're into alternative stuff. So, if you ask me, they've either bought them from the same place, or they've been living together somewhere and shared the pattern.'

'Thank you for that, Erin,' Nick said, grave and formal, befitting his acting inspector role. 'Thank you for all of your help in this.' He glanced from her to Simon. 'Both of you.'

She'd worked long enough in predominantly male environments to interpret the silent communication between the two men. Nick couldn't apologise outright or say anything implying criticism of Haddad, but it was there in his eyes. For professional reasons he gave Haddad the respect due, but Erin suspected that in private his conversation with the detective might well be blunt.

Simon gave a slight shrug. 'No worries,' he said, as if being locked up half the night was of no importance. 'I guess someone will let me know when I can access my house and vehicle again?'

'Yeah. I'm afraid it may be a day or so yet. Aaron, check with Forensics about their time frame for releasing the scene.' Nick considered Simon and Erin again. 'I guess I don't need to remind you not to talk to others about the case. Leah or I will be releasing a statement later today.'

Erin found a reassuring smile. 'Don't worry, Nick. We know the drill.' Don't compromise a police investigation – especially in a small town. And especially when the murderer might still be around.

Nick's face relaxed a fraction, and for a moment he wasn't a senior cop in uniform but a fast-becoming-friend, the man with the good sense to fall for her friend Jo. Lucky Jo. Lucky Jo to have found someone she loved and to be building a strong relationship with him.

Whereas Erin . . . yep, the one she'd found had turned out to be not quite who she'd thought him to be, and she still didn't know how she felt about that. Just as well they were only friends and she'd never made too much of a fool of herself. Just friends. She could keep doing that.

'Do you need a ride?' she asked Simon as they left Nick and Aaron. 'I'm heading home to Strath, but I can go via Goodabri if that's where you want to go.'

'No, Strath is good. I'll need to get a few things in town.'

'You know how I said we could argue later about who was driving?' She tossed him her keys. 'I'm so damned tired that I won't argue.'

Her limbs and head felt heavy as she climbed wearily into the passenger seat of her ute. It occurred to her that Leah Haddad might think she was stupid to get into a car with a man who'd been arrested for murder. But Leah didn't know Simon at all. Erin did – at least some aspects of him. So did Nick, and if Nick had held the slightest doubt about her safety he'd have done something about it, instead of raising a casual hand in farewell as they drove past him on their way out of the campground.

She had no concerns about her physical safety. But as she stole a glance at the man beside her, his mouth tight and eyes straight ahead as he negotiated the winding dirt track, she knew that her emotional safety had been in jeopardy for months. The things she hadn't known – his *wife*, his army reserve service – raised a stack of questions about what else she didn't know. She wanted to shake him, push for answers, give him hell for not being straight with her and for going off without a word. Fortunately, before she gave in to the temptation, she remembered that in the last sixteen or so hours he'd found and lost his wife, spent a night in a cell, and helped retrieve the body of another woman he'd known.

So what if someone being less than truthful pushed a few buttons in her psyche? She was a mature, intelligent adult, and it wasn't all about her.

•

He'd had no real time alone with Erin since those first few minutes after they'd discovered Hayley's body. Now they had at least forty minutes, just the two of them in the ute, and he had no idea where to begin, what to say. *I'm sorry* was easy enough. But before he could decide which of several apologies should come first, Erin broke the silence.

'I'm sorry,' she said. 'I can't remember if I said it earlier, Simon, but I'm sorry about Hayley. It must have been one hell of a shock for you.'

'Yes.' A shock, definitely. A sorrow? Oh, he had plenty of regrets, for sure, and sadness for Hayley, as well as anger that someone had murdered her and cut her life short. But grief? The raw truth was that she'd been out of his life so long that her absence would change little in his day-to-day life. Except . . .

'Erin . . .' He spared a glance from the road to look at her. '*I'm* sorry. I should have told you about Hayley. It's just that . . .' Damn, he had to pull together some coherent words. Honest, coherent words. 'I wanted to finalise things with her, make sure she was looked after properly, before I —' *Just say it.* 'Before I started anything with . . . anyone else.'

'Oh.' Silence for several seconds. He heard her slight intake of breath before she asked, 'Is there a particular "anyone" you have in mind?'

'Yes.' Would she understand what he meant? For a man who'd looked death squarely in the face plenty of times, he found he didn't have the courage to be completely upfront and face the possibility of rejection right at this moment. 'Yes, there is. But just now . . . well, I've got to sort this out. Hayley's death. The police investigation, finding out where she's been, funeral arrangements.'

'Of course that's your first priority now,' she said quickly. 'Anyone,' she put a very slight emphasis on the word, 'would understand that.'

Hope flared and he might have smiled at the tacit message, but as he slowed to turn at a T-junction, he had to give way on the narrow dirt road to the mortuary van, heading out to collect Sybilla's body, and the sombre sight made them both fall silent.

Had the van already collected Hayley from his house? It was likely. The idea of them moving her disturbed him more than he expected. Sweet Hayley, more helpless now than ever. He owed it to her to ensure that her killer was found and stopped.

Hayley murdered, Sybilla dead – how could those things be unconnected? The idea that Sybilla had murdered her friend and then thrown herself from the waterfall had occurred to him. Probably to the police, too. But that theory didn't explain the person seen with Sybilla at the top of the falls, or the figure Erin had seen in the night – likely the same person. That person had to know what had happened, at least to Sybilla.

'The figure you saw out at the falls – anything that might give a clue as to who it was?'

'No. Just a silhouette. Definitely human, not a goat or a kangaroo. But I couldn't say if it was male or female, old or young. It was dark, and from a distance.'

'Any campers in the area that you know of?'

'Only the couple who saw Sybilla fall. They arrived yesterday afternoon. The police and SES searched around the gorge last night and this morning but didn't find anything. Including any sign of how she got there. If there's a car, it's on a fire trail, or on the other side of the gorge, in the state forest or on one of the properties.'

'Unless she walked through the park from one of the other campgrounds,' he mused.

'She was only wearing sandals, and I didn't see any indication of rough walking. The police checked the picnic area at Casuarina Falls and the SES are doing the fire trail between there and Niland Falls. But that's almost ten kilometres.'

And only a fraction of the huge area of the park. 'The north of the gorge is more likely, isn't it?' he asked, thinking aloud. 'The state forest access tracks come in closer.'

'That's what I think. I suggested to Steve Fraser that they look around out there, speak with the landholders.'

'Will he?'

'I don't know. He's not easy to read.' She shifted in her seat, turning slightly towards him. 'You should know – he thinks I might have murdered Hayley.'

'He accused you of that?' Simon hadn't seen any signs of major tension between the two of them down in the gorge, but they hadn't been overly friendly either.

'Not as such. Just said it was one of the possibilities he's considering. And I don't have an alibi.'

'He doesn't know you very well, does he?'

'You don't think I'm capable of killing someone?'

He'd seen enough in war zones to know that given enough reason, everyone was capable of killing. But Erin murdering Hayley? No, that didn't add up at all. So far from possible, in fact, that he answered with a touch of lightness. 'You're far more likely to have taken her home and given her a good feed. Besides, you don't leave a job half-finished, Erin. If you had murdered her, you'd have taken her somewhere out in the bush where no one would find her. And you'd have cleaned up my place so there was no evidence at all.'

The corners of her mouth turned up in a wry smile. 'Thanks for the vote of confidence. I'm glad you're not doubting me, on top of everything else you have to worry about.'

He turned onto the main road from Goodabri to Strathnairn, still a minor road but sealed and smoother than the potholed sandy dirt of the road to the park. Easier on the tension in his neck. He took one hand from the steering wheel to massage the tight muscles.

'I'm sorry you've been dragged into this. Hell, I'm sorry about so many things, Erin. You've got more than enough reason to be angry with me already.'

She didn't say anything straightaway. He stared at the black ribbon of road and replayed their conversation in his head. She'd been more subdued this morning than usual. All her comments had been brief, factual. He'd put that down to fatigue, but maybe . . . maybe he'd misread her earlier statement about 'anyone' understanding.

They'd gone a kilometre or so before she spoke. 'The two weeks you went camping with your old army mates in November – you were really on reserve service, right?'

He'd not actively lied back then – he *had* been camping with army mates, on a training exercise. But that wasn't any excuse. 'Yes, I was.'

'Why the secrecy?' He heard curiosity rather than censure in her voice. 'Heaps of people are in the reserves and go off training a couple of times a year.'

'It's complicated.' But he had to find some way to uncomplicate it, fast, so he could explain and keep her trust. 'Erin, I'm a commando. It's not your everyday reserve service. Much of what I do, even as a reserve, I can't talk about. So when I started in Strathnairn it seemed easier to say nothing, other than to Malcolm, rather than have all the questions and conjecture from everyone.'

'So I guess you can't even say whether you were just training these past two months, or on some kind of operation. Active service. Whatever you call it.'

'Sometimes I'm sent overseas. We're often involved in training local teams, or joint ops, and occasionally special ops. Not as often as the movies suggest, though. And usually for me, now, not for as long as it was this time.'

'But you can't say where you were this time, or for what purpose.'

'No.' He could tell immediate family the general details of which theatre of operation he was being sent to, but Erin wasn't his family. He'd added his stepfather to his official army record of next of kin when Hayley didn't come back. He'd maintained a close relationship with Ray even after his mother's passing, and valued the older man's friendship. Ray didn't panic. Ray understood the risks and had a fair idea of the challenges in most of the places the army sent him, but he kept his worries to himself, and welcomed Simon back after each tour with a few perceptive questions that didn't require answers he couldn't give. In his quiet, undemanding way, Ray provided more support than Simon's wife had ever been able to give.

'That must have been tough on Hayley,' Erin said. 'But even tougher on you, I imagine. I hope they give you good support over there – wherever "there" is – and when you come back. Because I'm guessing it must be pretty damned lonely sometimes, if you're not able to talk about what you've been doing and what you've seen.'

The sunlit road in front of him became less distinct and he had to blink to clear his vision. If he hadn't already been head over heels for her, he'd have tumbled the last distance there and then. Lonely? Hell, yes. More so since he'd left the full-time army and the company of mates with whom he'd shared the adrenaline-pumping months and years. Achingly lonely since the day Erin had walked into the Strathnairn office with a cheeky grin, an intelligent, down-to-earth attitude and an easy way with people. And all the months since then, during SES training and jobs and the inevitable drinks at the pub afterwards. When he'd spoken of his previous army experience, lightly, as if it had scarcely impacted on him, she'd listened more closely than the guys had, and he'd brushed off her questions with simple answers that stopped a long way short of complete. Keeping the two halves of his life separate had been relatively uncomplicated – until Erin.

He slowed for the speed limit change as they drove into the tiny community of Derringvale. Smaller even than Goodabri, just a scattering of houses, a shop, a pub and a school. A few little girls played inside the fence of the school playground, skipping and laughing and unconcerned for their safety, racing each other as the bell rang for morning classes. So different from the little girls he'd seen in faraway places, kidnapped and executed for their 'crime' of seeking an education.

He gripped the steering wheel. Memories like that . . . yeah, exactly the kind of thing he couldn't talk about easily to anyone. Exactly the reason why he restricted himself to incidental, unimportant tales of army life and kept quiet about his continuing service. Shock a pub full of half-plastered emergency services guys with the brutal realities of a dozen murdered kids he'd been too late to save? See the light drain out of Erin's eyes to be replaced with horror? Hayley had had nightmares for weeks the one time he'd told her about an atrocity. Never again.

'Simon? Are you okay?' Erin asked, and he realised he'd not responded to her, not talked about not talking.

'Yes. Sorry.'

Neither of them came up with anything else to say while they covered the last fifteen kilometres to the outskirts of Strathnairn. He thought maybe she'd dozed off, but when he glanced across she was looking out the window, her face turned away from him.

When they turned into the lane to her cottage, she asked, 'Have you got somewhere to stay, since you can't go back to your place yet? You're welcome to my spare room, if you want it.'

Her spare room? In a cottage smaller than his? They'd shared huts sometimes, out in one of the parks, and the staff bunkroom at the Riverbank depot, but always there'd been at least one other person with them, usually more. Staying at her place when his wife had just died and they'd both already been tagged by the police as suspects would only complicate matters further.

'Thanks, but I'll just camp out in one of the park huts. Until we know what's going on – until the police make some progress – it's better if I keep to myself.'

'I understand,' she said, and he thought she did recognise what he hadn't said. 'Let me know if you need anything.' A deep yawn caught her, scrunching her face. She shook her head, adding when she could talk again, 'I'm going to sleep for hours. Do nothing today but . . . Oh, shit. It's Friday. The Goodabri rescue helicopter ball is tonight.'

A major community fundraiser for the vital service. He'd gone to it the last few years, not because he enjoyed formal social events but because if it wasn't for the regional rescue helicopter, people injured or taken seriously ill this far from major hospitals might not survive. Just a few months ago, he'd helped load Jo into the chopper when she'd been critically injured. And so a few weeks later, the day before his unexpected call-up, he'd happily handed over his hundred dollars for a ticket to the charity ball.

He turned into her driveway and stopped beside her cottage. 'Sleep all day. Then you'll be fine to dance all night.'

'Can't sleep all day.' Her grin flashed, and even though it didn't quite light her eyes, he'd missed it so much it served as an electric jolt to his failing spirits. 'I've been making a dress for months. It's stunning, but I've still got some sewing to do.'

He was already out of the ute and reached into the back seat for her pack. 'I didn't know you sewed. That's how come you saw the similarities between the dresses?'

'Yes. I made most of my own clothes, growing up.' For a moment her mouth tightened, but then she smiled again, although not as naturally as usual. 'I don't do much anymore, but this one's a special project. I've got nowhere else to wear it, so dammit I'm going to finish it and wear it tonight. Even if I yawn all through the speeches.'

He came around to her side of the ute and handed over her backpack and car keys. 'I'm going to hire a car for the next day or two. Would you like me to drive you?' So much for keeping to himself.

'You're going? But surely . . . You certainly don't have to go, Simon, under the circumstances. And there's no need for you to drive all the way back out here to give me a lift – I'll be perfectly fine to drive after a bit of a sleep. And you know me – I probably won't even have any wine tonight.'

Yes, he'd been at the pub with her and the SES crew often enough to know she seldom drank, and then only a glass. 'I bought my ticket months ago. And I need to be there tonight. Most of Goodabri and the district will be there. If anyone saw Hayley – if anyone knows anything – my presence will make sure it's talked about. Some useful information might come out of it.'

'Good point. But if you decide not to go after all, I'll be keeping my ears tuned for any clues, and I'm sure Nick will be, too.' She held out the keys. 'How are you getting into town now? Do you want to take my ute?'

'It's only a couple of k's. The walk will clear my head. I'll see you tonight.'

He waited until she was inside, and even then he paused at the end of her driveway, on the pretext of checking his phone, to make sure she'd encountered nothing untoward. He heard the water pump kick in – her old farm cottage was just outside the town boundary and water supply – and relaxed. She was either going for a cup of coffee, or a shower.

Thinking of Erin in the shower did absolutely nothing to clear his head.

He set off at a punishing pace towards Strathnairn's small business district. Practicalities. He had to keep his mind on practicalities. He currently had only the clothes he wore, his wallet and phone. His house and vehicle might be out of reach for a couple of days. He could buy a change or two of clothes from Dylan's, the men's clothing store in Strathnairn. He could probably even hire a dinner suit there for the ball, if they had one left in his size. Or he'd hire a standard suit, or a kilt if he had to. Being a rural ball in Goodabri, it wouldn't matter much what he wore. Some of the locals considered new jeans or moleskins to be formal wear.

He could shower and change at the Strathnairn National Parks office. There he'd also have computer access, and he'd start searching for any information he could find. Hayley hadn't had an online presence, but at the very least there'd have to be something in old news reports about Sybilla Braithwaite's disappearance. He only had the PO box address for Hayley, but he'd start scouring maps and records and calling in favours from contacts to try to locate any alternative lifestyle communities in the area.

He had to be able to find something, somewhere.

•

A long hot shower and five hours of sleep made Erin feel semi-human. A strong coffee almost completed the process. But the fragments of dreams still clung to her mind, catching her unawares and sending her mood spiralling down. Erotic dreams were one thing. Erotic dreams about a guy whose wife had just been murdered? Yeah, so not the right time. His comment about wanting to make things right with Hayley before starting something new with 'anyone' still applied, even though 'right' was no longer an equal, amicable divorce.

She had to give him time. She had to give herself time. Time to get to know him better than she did. And right now, this afternoon, she had a more urgent task to accomplish than worrying about a relationship that might or might not ever evolve.

She carried her coffee mug into the spare room, where her nearly finished dress hung on the back of the door. Little evidence remained of the bridesmaid's dress she had found in an op shop a year ago. A wealthy bride of the 1980s with more money than fashion sense had obviously decreed for her bridesmaid an ostentatious flummery of puffy sleeves and full gathered skirts in pale blue pure-silk lace. A travesty, really. But Erin knew quality fabric when she saw it, and over the last year she'd patiently unpicked the seams, rescued the yards and yards of lace, and overdyed and totally refashioned it into a dress as unlike its original form as it could possibly be.

And as unlike the simple white dresses of the two dead women as it could be.

The memory dulled her mood. Under the circumstances, she wasn't looking forward to tonight's ball with the same anticipation she'd felt a couple of months ago when she'd decided to finish the dress in time for it. But Simon was right – with many people from Goodabri and the district attending, Hayley's murder would be on everyone's mind, and likely a topic of hushed discussion. The woman had been in town for several days before her death. Surely someone had seen her. Or her killer.

Erin drank the last couple of mouthfuls of rapidly cooling coffee and set the mug down well away from the sewing table before she took the dress from its hanger. If work hadn't been so mad these past few weeks, it would have been finished already. But she had only another metre or so of scalloped lace edging to hand-stitch on, and a hook and eye closure at the top of the zip. Easy. Half an hour, max. Plenty of time to finish it and then spend some relaxing time pampering herself before she got dressed.

She deserved to pamper herself. She worked hard at a respectable career and served her community and she'd made it on her own. And this dress was no designer knock-off for her father to sell as the real thing. Nor was it one of the countless formal dresses for wealthy students that she'd made to support herself through university. She rarely sewed these days, because years of sewing for money had burned her pleasure in it, and because she preferred being outdoors rather than inside, but when she'd seen the silk lace in the op-shop window her old love of textiles had resurfaced and she'd vowed to make something special, purely for herself.

Pity, now that she was finally going to wear it, that she wasn't in the frame of mind to really do it justice. Pity that the one man she'd fantasised about impressing had so many other things on his mind that he probably wouldn't even notice she wasn't in uniform and boots. But she'd wear it with pride anyway, because this was part of who she was, alongside the practical, unfeminine career she'd chosen. It wasn't a part she showed her male workmates, because although they were great guys it was easier if she didn't remind them too often that she was female. But tonight, in this dress, they'd notice.

She sewed the last stitch, snipped the thread and returned the dress to its hanger, taking it through to her bedroom to hang on the front of the rickety old wardrobe. Done. Finished. She couldn't help grinning. Still a couple of hours before she was actually going to wear it, but she twirled on the spot anyway, as if she was already clothed in lace and silk instead of cotton yoga pants and a t-shirt.

Now she just had to do her nails, maybe a facial, decide how to do her hair . . . girly things she hadn't done for months. She kept her fingernails short and unpainted because the physical nature of much of her work would have wreaked havoc on a manicure, and her toes were usually invisible, encased in socks and boots.

In the bathroom, she found the solitary bottle of polish she owned, a deep crimson she'd last worn – when was it? Almost twelve months ago? Yep, the farewell party from her old job, before she'd transferred to the Strathnairn division of National Parks.

The lid of the bottle took some effort to open. Not a good sign. The brush was stiff, the remains of the polish clumpy, unusable. Either she needed to give up the stuff entirely, or wear it more often. A quick check of her makeup bag revealed a similar problem with her mascara.

She checked her watch. Not quite five o'clock. Still enough time to dash into town and do a quick restock. The chemist shop carried makeup, and it didn't close until five-thirty. Within five minutes she'd changed into jeans and a shirt and was reversing the ute out of the drive.

Like most regional towns, Strathnairn's main street had more than its share of empty shopfronts. Sometimes pop-up shops took temporary leases for a few days or a week. When she nabbed a parking spot right outside the chemist, she noticed that an empty shop nearby had a rack of clothes hanging out the front. Strath didn't have much in the way of clothes shops – it barely supported two boutiques and a small department store – so someone selling clothes was worth a look. After she'd bought her makeup.

She dithered for all of a minute over nail polish colours, and ended up choosing three – a rich blue, a crimson and a clear top coat. She could decide at home which one went better with the dress. She even remembered to get a fresh bottle of remover. Not a total failure in womanly things. Foundation, eyeliner, mascara and lipstick. Just as well yesterday was payday.

She turned left out of the chemist to check out the pop-up shop. It had about the same amount of stock as a market stall – a rack of clothes out front, a couple more racks inside the open double doors. A decorative timber sign hung in the window. Hand-painted in blues and greens, with a stylised earth in one corner, it read: *Simple Bliss*.

Erin paused to glance over the pamphlets and books on the table beside the rack of clothes out the front. Two piles of books had a twenty-dollar price tag. The cover of one matched the words on the sign – *Simple Bliss: Finding Beauty, Balance and Bliss* – and the other used a similar style and font to proclaim *The Path to Bliss*. The author's name took up a good third of each cover: Joshua Kristos.

Erin's scepticism meter swung straight into the red zone. Joshua, Yeshua, Isaiah, Jesus. Okay, so it was a common enough name, and Kristos wasn't uncommon either, but Joshua Kristos publishing books about bliss? Her father would probably wish he'd thought of it.

An advertising flyer caught her eye and she picked it up. *Discover Bliss*. An invitation to visit a community and enjoy a get-back-to-nature retreat, with the promise that visitors would discover the 'bliss of simplicity' for 'bodily and spiritual renewal'. All for a mere hundred and fifty dollars a day, with three days recommended for spiritual renewal. Erin dropped the flyer back on the pile. She got back to nature every day, and could offer visitors to the park a three-day stay for a whole lot less than four hundred and fifty dollars.

A young woman in a light blue top over loose dark blue trousers came out of the shop with a friendly smile. 'Hello.' She indicated the flyer. 'Are you interested in revitalising your spirit? We'd love to welcome you for a visit.'

'Thanks, but I'm a bit too busy at the moment.' About to turn away, Erin stopped and took a little more notice of the woman. Maybe in her early twenties, her long, light-brown hair was caught back in a plait and she wore no makeup or jewellery, but it was her wrap top that really caught Erin's attention. Similar in construction to the dresses Hayley and Sybilla had worn, it had a narrow decorative woven band on the edge of the bodice where the others had been embroidered.

'Maybe that's all the more reason,' the young woman said gently. 'The stress treadmill damages us so much. My name's Willow, by the way.'

'Hi, Willow. I'm Erin.' She didn't want the young woman to notice her staring, so she browsed through the clothes on the rack as an excuse to linger. Mostly plain colours, cotton or linen or some mix; dresses, tops, jackets and trousers with embroidery and decorative woven bands. Practical, comfortable clothes.

'Everything is made in Australia, from locally grown organic hemp and linen,' Willow said. 'We're a cooperative of artisans. Nothing is factory-made.'

'Locally grown hemp?' Erin put on her best innocent blonde expression. 'I didn't think it was legal.' She knew very well what was legal and illegal. She'd lost count of the number of marijuana crops she'd found in national parks and reported to the police. Industrial hemp required a special permit, and as far as she was aware, not many had been issued in the district.

Willow laughed lightly. 'Don't worry, this is quite legitimate. We have a supplier who is growing experimental crops of low-THC cannabis. Did you know it's a wonderful, ecologically sustainable crop? It uses much less water than cotton, and it's great for fibre, paper and many other uses.'

'Is that so?' Erin lifted a crimson dress from the rack. A lightly fitted A-line style, with a round neck, short sleeves, and buttoned down the front with small polished wooden buttons. But it was the lines of cream embroidery running around the neckline that interested her. Trailing stem-stitch vines with satin-stitch flowers. Not complex, but effective. 'I like this one. The leaves and buds are pretty.'

'We believe in making things that are both practical and beautiful. Would you like to try it on?'

'It's not really my colour.' She flicked through a few more dresses. Yes. There was one. At least one. She held up the mid-blue wrap dress. V-neck, with decorative stitching alongside a narrow band that became the ties around the fitted bodice. She hadn't had time to study Hayley's dress, but Sybilla's dress definitely had the same shape and details. 'This is great. It looks so comfortable and cool. So, do you guys sell over towards the coast? I'm pretty sure a friend of mine had a dress just like this. I think she bought it at a market somewhere.'

'Yes, we mostly sell at markets. We're only new in this area, though, and there aren't a lot of markets here.'

'Yep, Strathnairn is too small for a regular one. But the autumn festival is coming up, and there are always a fair few stalls at that.' Erin didn't have much time to spare, and no clue how to – or even whether she should – ask any questions about Hayley and Sybilla. Gut instinct told her not to mention names or details. Gut instinct and her promise to Nick. She checked the size of the dress, and the price on the recycled cardboard tag. Sixty dollars. 'How long will you be here?' she asked. 'Will you be open tomorrow?'

'No. I'm just waiting for my friend to get back, then we're packing up. We won't be here tomorrow.'

Sixty dollars for a dress she'd never wear but which might provide clues to where Hayley and Sybilla had been? 'Okay,

I'll grab this one now. Do you have a website or contact phone number if I decide I want something else?'

'Yes, we're on the internet,' Willow said as she carried the dress to the table inside. 'But it's so much better to make personal connections, isn't it? I'm sure we'll be back here fairly often. Our new place isn't far away.'

Erin feigned only casual interest. 'Really? Where is it?'

'North of here. Off Millers Road. There's a great set-up for our work, and the main house is beautiful. Very peaceful.'

Off Millers Road. Off Millers Road, which ran to the north of the park, a couple of kilometres from the falls where Sybilla had died.

The table inside had more copies of the retreat flyer and the two books by Joshua Kristos. While Willow carefully folded the dress with unbleached paper to protect it from creases, Erin picked up the flyer again. Three days, four hundred and fifty dollars, and a promise of rediscovering simplicity and finding bliss. When Willow slipped the folded dress into a paper bag, Erin popped the flyer in, too. 'I'm due for some time off. Maybe I'll think about visiting. Things have been a bit tough lately.'

'Oh, I'm sorry.' Willow touched her lightly on the arm. 'Do consider coming. We'd love to have you. There'll be massages and meditation, and when your mind and your body are awakened you'll feel so much better, so much lighter. So blissful.'

We. Always 'we', not 'I'. Just what kind of group of artisans also hosted visitors for awakening retreats? Her gaze fell on the books again. Bliss. Joshua Kristos preached simplicity and bliss. 'This guy – Joshua Kristos – is he some American preacher or something?'

Willow's smile became radiant, her eyes shining. 'Joshua is Australian. He's so wise. So gentle and caring. He changed my life. I would have been lost – probably dead by now – but look at me. I've never been so healthy or so blissful in my life. Oh, please do come to us. Joshua will be there from Sunday. He will show you the way to bliss.'

Alarm bells rang so loudly in Erin's mind that she could hardly summon up an answering smile. Either Willow was a great actress or she believed everything she said. Maybe this Joshua did have all the answers to life's problems. Erin had met a couple of truly wise people in her life. But far more likely his 'answers' related to how to scam money from gullible people. Erin understood too well some of the numerous ways that could be done.

She handed over cash for the dress, murmured something about running late when Willow seemed to want to prolong the conversation, and left the shop with the bag in hand.

Once back in her ute with the door closed, she pulled out her phone. Filling in time last night, she'd entered Steve Fraser's contact details, and she phoned his mobile now.

'I've got something for you,' she said when he answered. 'A dress that's probably made by the same people who made Sybilla's dress and maybe Hayley's. If you'll still be in Goodabri in two hours, I can bring it when I come for the ball.'

'I'm in Strathnairn now,' he said. 'Can you meet me at the police station in five minutes?'

As Erin reversed out of the parking space to drive the two blocks to the station, a woman dressed in loose trousers and a kimono-style top hurried along the footpath with a couple of calico grocery bags. Willow emerged from the shop and greeted her with a beaming smile that faded rapidly to concern. She took the bags from her, placed a hand on her arm as if the woman was unwell, or worried about something.

Erin didn't get much of a look at her but her impression was that the woman was older than Willow, maybe around her own age, mid-thirties. Another one of the 'artisans'? Another follower of Joshua? Maybe both. But certainly not blissful, just now.

Steve was approaching the station on foot when she parked in front of it. He carried a suit bag over one shoulder and a large bag from Dylan's Menswear. Shoving open the door with one shoulder, he waved her through. He shone one of his friendly, not-to-be-trusted grins at Dee at the reception counter. 'Have you got a meeting room we can use, Dee? I need a quick chat with Erin.'

Yet another young female officer he was already on first-name terms with, Erin noted. He probably made a habit of it. Not that there was anything improper in his manner, and Dee – and Tess last night – was well able to handle all types of men. That came with the job, just as it did in the National Parks and Wildlife Service.

Dee buzzed them through to a small room just inside, with a table and four chairs. Steve draped the suit bag over the back of one of the chairs. 'I got the last tuxedo for hire in Strathnairn. It's a tad loose, but if I stick my chest out it will be fine.'

'You're going to the ball tonight?'

'Yeah. Good cause, good opportunity to meet the locals informally. You said you're going, too?'

She nodded. 'And we don't have much time.' So much for doing her nails and pampering herself. She'd be lucky to be ready by seven at this rate. 'Look, there's a pop-up shop just down the road, selling clothes. I think you need to compare this —' she drew the blue dress out of the bag, 'with the dresses the women were wearing. This one's made by some sort of cooperative. See, the tag's got a webside address on it.'

'"Simple Bliss"? My knowledge of women's fashion would fill a pinhead, but that's not a well-known brand, is it?'

'No. But the thing is, the woman at the shop said this group have a place just north of the national park. You know how I mentioned that one of the properties bordering the park changed hands last year? I think that may be where they are.'

Steve whistled. 'You ever considered the police force as a career? You've got further than I have this afternoon.'

Definitely not the police for her. Not with her background. She shrugged off his compliment. 'It was just a piece of luck. The real estate agent should be able to tell you what places have been sold on Millers Road in the past twelve months.'

'I can probably find it online easily enough. I'll go and see this group in the morning. Simon said that Hayley had been involved with some sort of hippy mob up on the north coast.'

Hayley had been into alternative groups? Erin closed her eyes, leaned her forehead on her hands, trying to arrange all the pieces together. A hazy picture emerged, shadowy in places, with plenty of holes but maybe . . .

She reached back into the bag for the flyer. 'Okay. There's something else. There's a guy by the name of Joshua Kristos. I'm not sure of his connection with these "Simple Bliss" people, but I get the impression he's some kind of self-help guru. He's written books all about finding yourself through simplicity and bliss – they had them for sale in the shop. It sounded as though Willow had met him.' She passed the flyer across the table. 'They invite people to visit the community on retreat, and he's supposed to be there this weekend. It might be nothing, but . . . well, if he comes up in your investigation at all, my gut says he could be worth a second look.'

Steve quickly read the flyer before giving it back to her. 'Thanks. Haven't heard of him at all but if the name comes up, I'll remember it.'

As Erin drove home her thoughts gnawed at the issue. There were plenty of communes, communities and other groups around that shared similar alternative philosophies to the Simple Bliss group. Ecological awareness, self-sufficiency, paganism, earth-worshippers, all types of non-mainstream thinking, and most weren't anarchists, rebels or drugged-out dropouts. Hayley could have been connected with any one of those. However, her clothes – and her presence in Goodabri – possibly linked her to this group.

But no matter which way she looked at it, Erin kept coming up against the one question: how could being involved with a group that embraced simplicity and bliss have led to Hayley's death? It didn't make sense. There had to be something else, some other reason why she'd been murdered.

CHAPTER 7

When Erin had described her dress as 'stunning', she'd used exactly the right word. Simon stopped dead in the doorway of the Goodabri ex-servicemen's club function room and stared. He might have been standing there a few seconds before a lady behind him apologised as she squeezed past him. Gathering together a few dazed brain cells, he entered the room, nodding at some people he knew, tugging at the unaccustomed pressure of his shirt collar and bow tie as if it was the cloth that was stifling his breathing and making his chest tight. But instead of banging his head against the wall to knock some sense into it, he stood at the edge of the room near the door and watched Erin.

He found her hard enough to resist at work, in the practical masculine cut of her park ranger uniform. But in that long, rich blue dress that he had a good view of as she chatted with their boss on the other side of the dance floor . . . The style might have been demure, were it not for the fact that the fabric covering her shoulders, throat and arms and dipping low on her back was merely lace. The allure of bare skin behind the strands of blue lace and the panels of lace at the sides of the skirt that every now and then gave him a glimpse of long, naked leg made his brain cells fuse.

It had to be the sexiest, most erotic damn dress he'd ever seen.

It was going to drive him raving mad. All of his efforts these past months to avoid thinking of her in sensual terms shattered. The evening ahead was going to be a slow torture requiring all his strength to avoid making a total fool of himself.

She hadn't seen him yet. He could turn around and walk out and she wouldn't even know he'd arrived. Except what would that achieve, other than to prove him weak and a coward? Besides, others had already seen him. Leaving wouldn't just be cowardly, it would be stupid. Although he'd experienced plenty of heart-stopping fear on the battlefield, he'd always known the gunfire and grenades were aimed at the nameless soldier, not Simon, not him personally. Here, though, reputation, respect and friendships were on the line.

He needed a drink. He needed a dozen drinks, but one would have to do because he had to keep a clear head. There were only a few people at the bar so he joined them, waiting his turn, his back to the room and the mesmerising sight of the woman he'd fallen for months ago, standing with Mal Stewart and laughing as she talked with him. The fact that their boss was happily married and one of the politest, most respectful men he'd ever met did little to assuage his irrational envy.

The dinner-suited guy next to him swivelled on his bar stool, a middy of soft drink in hand, one elbow comfortably on the bar. Steve Fraser. At least with the detective he didn't have to make polite conversation, as if nothing was wrong. Or face awkward conversational silences from people who had heard about Hayley and didn't know what to say.

'Didn't think I'd see you here tonight,' Fraser said.

'It's a good cause. Are you here working or socialising?' The guy must have gone to the trouble of hiring a tuxedo, because he couldn't have made it to Birraga and back for his own suit since this morning. Although he looked as at ease in it as James Bond, Simon doubted he carried formal wear in the back of his car along with his police search and rescue gear.

'Like you said, the rescue helicopter service is a worthwhile cause. Plus this is a good opportunity to meet the locals. Did you get my message?'

'I've been out of phone range. Only heard the beep when I came into town.'

'Order your drink. Then I'll update you outside where it's quieter.'

This early in the evening, people were still greeting friends and no one had yet wandered out onto the small terrace overlooking the rear car park and looking down towards the river behind the club. Simon ignored the tables and chairs and instead leaned on the railing, watching the reflections of the moonlight flicker on the slow flow of the river, drinking the mineral water he'd bought. Whatever it was Fraser had to tell him, he preferred not to be sitting. Or drinking alcohol.

The detective propped himself at the railing beside Simon. He kept his voice low, even though no one was nearby. 'Leah's on her way to Newcastle for the post-mortem examinations. They'll do both women's tomorrow. If you have any objections about Hayley's, for religious or cultural reasons, you'll need to lodge them by first thing in the morning.'

Simon took a sip of his water but it didn't dislodge the hard lump in his throat. Post mortem. The forensic pathologist would go over every inch of Hayley's body, remove her organs, take samples of her blood. Was that the ultimate intrusion? No doubt it would be done with respect, for the sole purpose of finding answers, but he hated, hated the thought of it.

'No objections,' he muttered.

Fraser nodded. Maybe he understood something of the horror. He'd been a policeman long enough.

'Forensics have finished with your place,' he said after a moment. 'You can go back anytime. You may want to get a crime scene cleaner in, though. Insurance might cover that. Assuming there's someone in the region that does it.'

He could go back to his house. Where Hayley had died. The spartan accommodation of the old stockman's hut on one of the trails in the park seemed far preferable. 'Thanks. I'll go over and collect some things in the morning.' And search the place himself to see what he could learn about Hayley's time there. 'Have you found out anything yet? About where Hayley had been living?'

'Not yet. But Erin found a lead that might be promising. I'll check it out first thing in the morning.'

'Somewhere local?'

'Local-ish. It might not amount to anything, but it's all we have so far.'

Fraser wasn't going to tell him where. Not yet, anyway. Understandable, until they'd confirmed it. The police wouldn't want him going there himself until they knew the situation. But he could ask Erin later. Instead of pressing Fraser on the point, he changed the subject. 'You told Erin that you thought she could have killed Hayley.'

Amusement curved the detective's mouth. 'I said I hadn't discounted the possibility.'

Simon felt no amusement at all. 'You should discount it,' he said bluntly. 'Erin isn't stupid. Or vindictive.'

'Oh, she definitely isn't stupid. Very smart woman, your Erin.'

Simon much preferred Haddad's straightforward interrogation to Fraser's matey, good-humoured routine that could trip him up if he wasn't careful. 'She's not "my" Erin,' he said. 'There's nothing between us.'

'Nothing?'

'Friendship. Respect.'

'That's all?'

'Yes.' He wanted to leave it at that but Fraser wasn't stupid either. The cop wasn't the first to assume that something was going on between him and Erin. Before he'd gone away, plenty of people had made teasing comments linking them. Yet no one had teased him about Jo, in the days before Nick's arrival, despite their friendship. Maybe you just couldn't hide the kind of attraction that drew him to Erin. 'She's smart and funny,' he said. 'Gutsy and down to earth and she throws her all into everything. But I was married.'

'Ah. That mattered to you, did it?'

'Yes.'

'That's very honourable of you.'

A car drove into the car park below and swung into a parking space. Tess stepped out, the light catching the satiny, moonlight-coloured gown she wore.

'Don't all decent men try to be honourable, do the right thing? Don't you?' Simon glanced at Fraser, curious about his response, but the man watched Tess as she hurried towards the entrance.

'Me? Honourable?' He gave a short, humourless laugh without taking his gaze off the policewoman. 'No, I can be a right royal bastard sometimes.'

Someone tapped the microphone inside and the MC began her welcome.

'We'd better go in,' Fraser said. 'Which table are you on?'

'Seven, I think it is. Mostly National Parks people.' Including Erin. At least with a table of ten there was a good chance he wouldn't be sitting next to her.

'Someone cancelled so I got a ticket at the last minute. I guess I'm on their table. Let's hope they're interesting people and that the speeches won't be too long or boring. I'd much rather dance with beautiful women. Speaking of which, did you see Erin? That dress – serious wow factor.'

The man was teasing him. Or trying to provoke him. Simon kept his mouth shut and his fists clenched by his side as they went back into the brightly lit function room.

At table seven, Malcolm Stewart had already claimed one of the seats beside Erin. Bruce Lockyer sat on the other side of her, with his wife Mary-Rose beside him. Then there was Rob, one of the field staff, and his wife, Camille; Nick sat between Mal's wife, Susan, and Jo. They'd alternated men and women and, whether by accident or design, the only vacant chair was on the opposite side of the round table from Erin.

Friends, all of them, but none had known he was married until last night. Their greetings were subdued, not the usual cheerful banter, but he didn't read any censure in their faces and the tightness in his chest eased a little. Erin gave him a shadow of her normal smile, her gaze concerned and direct, and he had to tear his eyes away from her as Mary-Rose came around and stood on tiptoe to give him a kiss on the cheek.

'I'm so sorry about Hayley, Simon. Such a tragedy, such difficult circumstances. You know you're very welcome to come and stay with us, if that would make things easier for you.'

'Thank you. And thank you, Bruce. That's very kind of you. But I'm just going to stay out at one of the huts for a day or so. It's beautiful and peaceful in the bush.'

He took his seat between Jo and Camille as the waitstaff – students from the hospitality course at Strathnairn – began serving the first course. He'd scarcely thought about food all day, but the aromas jumpstarted his appetite.

Jo rested her hand lightly on his forearm while they waited to be served. 'If there's anything at all we can do, Simon, just ask any of us. Nick has to be all official and distant because he's acting inspector, but the rest of us don't.'

He wasn't used to seeing his colleague in makeup and a gown, but she was still the Jo he liked, with her practical, no-fuss manner and sharp, logical way of thinking. Her new, shorter hairstyle – a legacy of the surgery after her head injury – suited her. But as much as he liked her and enjoyed working with her, he'd never been at risk of falling for her. Just as well, since Nick had come on the scene and he'd have made formidable competition, for all he seemed civilised and gentlemanly in his tuxedo. Never underestimate Nick: that was the lesson Simon had learned the first time they'd trained together on the dojo mats at the Strathnairn Police Youth Club, when Nick had floored him in seconds despite a leg injury.

'Thanks, Jo. I appreciate it. I understand Nick's position.' And he did, and respected the man all the more for his commitment to his work and to his colleagues.

He let the conversation flow around him as they ate dinner. Light topics. Easy topics. Bruce and Mary-Rose's grandchildren. Nick and Jo's planned trip to Japan. Susan's quilting taking over the house. Erin's dress.

'It is beautiful,' he said in his first contribution to the conversation, after someone else complimented her on it. *You're beautiful*, he didn't say. 'You're very skilled at sewing.'

'You *made* it?' Susan exclaimed. 'I didn't know you sewed. I always imagined you were more into fixing cars and building fences and things.'

A faint blush rose on Erin's cheeks. 'I got the bug when I helped my grandfather restore an old treadle machine. It was a natural progression to learn how to use it. I still have that machine – it's a fantastic piece of engineering and is still going strong, a hundred years after it was made.'

He could imagine her tinkering with the machine, keeping it clean, oiled and rust-free with the same attention to detail she applied to work equipment, the same frown of concentration as when she sharpened a chainsaw. He already loved her for her practicality – she was beautiful to him even in a dusty uniform and with a smear of grease on her cheek and her hair windswept. But after tonight he would always picture her as she sat across the table from him in the sensual elegance of that rich lace, with her long hair twisted loosely into a soft, elegant arrangement at the nape of her neck.

The MC announced the first round of auctions, and all attention turned to the stage as one of the local auctioneers ran through the process and began his spiel about the first of the donated items. Simon watched and listened as the people of Goodabri and the surrounding district rallied to support the vital helicopter service, the bidding lively on item after item. There wasn't a lot of money in Goodabri – employment options were limited and a large proportion of the population were either retired or seasonal workers – but people gave what they could, and many of the items had been donated by locals rather than by big business. Warmth, humour and generosity of spirit flowed, and the dollars raised mounted.

This, *this* was a big part of why he'd stayed in the army and continued to serve. Because less fortunate towns and villages threatened by violence deserved the chance to maintain or rebuild that spirit of community, to be active citizens shaping their own futures. Although he'd confronted terrorists and warlords and people willing to kill and maim for power or money or politics or religion, it hadn't changed his belief, rock solid at the core of him, that most people were good at heart. The bastard who had plunged a knife repeatedly into Hayley was an aberration, a twisted specimen of humanity, not the norm.

When the first round of auctions finished and the music started up again, people began to leave their tables to dance or mingle. Simon made his way to a group of the younger guys from his SES unit, who were carefully avoiding dancing by loitering at the back of the room.

'Jesus, Kennedy, didn't expect to see you here tonight,' one of them said. 'I heard the vic at your place was —' He stopped abruptly when one of the other men jabbed him in the side with an elbow, none too subtly.

'Yeah, she was my wife,' Simon acknowledged. 'But we've been separated for a long time. I can't say I'm really in a party mood, but I came tonight to ask people if they knew anything. We know Hayley arrived in town on Monday. People must have seen her. People may have seen her killer. I'd be grateful if you guys could help spread the word, encourage anyone who may know something to contact the police.'

For the next half-hour, while the band played a range of 1940s and 1950s covers, he moved from group to group, asking for information, pointing out Steve Fraser, urging them to contact him if they'd seen or heard anything. He didn't get to talk to everyone, but he spoke with a fair proportion of the guests, and from the serious expressions and the whispers he heard around him he could tell he'd succeeded in making Hayley's murder a topic of conversation. There'd be plenty of speculation about him and his relationship with Hayley, but between his efforts and those of the police, word would ripple out into the community faster than even the Strathnairn newspaper or radio station could spread it.

He kept his distance from Erin. She danced with a few men – a gentle swing with Bruce, a more laughter-filled attempt to jive with one of the SES guys who seemed to have two left feet, and rather more success dancing to 'Blue Suede Shoes' with Fraser, who apparently didn't step on her strappy blue shoes. Not that Simon was watching her . . . well, he tried not to. There were whole minutes when he didn't look for her at all.

When the bandleader announced the last dance before dessert and the next round of auctions, Erin appeared by his side. 'Come, dance with me,' she said.

He almost refused, but she gave a tiny shake of her head, and although he didn't understand the warning, he took the hand she held out and followed her onto the dance floor.

Slow music – he could manage to move vaguely in time to that. The whole get-close-and-touch-her ballroom hold? He could do that, too. Possibly even without grinding his teeth entirely to dust in frustration. He kept inches between them and didn't dare relax his arms. If he just focused on the top of her head, and not on blue eyes he could drown in, or the texture of lace and the curve of her waist under his right hand, or the fresh, floral smell of her perfume, he might be able to function intelligently.

'Everybody's talking,' Erin said softly. 'There are a few rumours flying, lots of speculation. But no one other than Bruce so far who saw Hayley.'

'What are the rumours?' he asked.

'That you murdered her. That I murdered her. That the guys who ran rampant last year are back and no one in Goodabri is safe in their beds.'

'They're in jail.'

'Yes. I did try to assure Nancy Maguire and the hospital volunteer ladies of that. But hosing down rumours can be harder than fighting bushfires on a windy day.'

'Is that why we're dancing? To hose down rumours?'

'It's not the only reason. But yes, most people think I'm sane enough not to dance with you if I thought you were a murderer. And you'd be unlikely to dance with me if you suspected me. Although that might be more convincing if you weren't scowling so much.'

'Sorry.' Now that she mentioned it, he became aware of his facial muscles aching from the tension. If he tried to smile, it'd likely crack his face. He made a conscious attempt to relax his face, with little success. If only he could hold Erin close, very close, and bury his face in her hair. No. Impossible. That would set the rumours flying at warp speed and place her in a difficult position.

But the longing blazed through all the other discordant, demanding questions in his head and he had to fight his instincts and dig deep for some semblance of control. He needed Erin. He needed her strength, her common sense, her laughter, her friendship, her touch. But Hayley lay dead in the Newcastle morgue and until he had answers, he wasn't free.

The music continued thrumming but he dropped his hands, took a step away from her. 'I can't do this, Erin. I'm sorry. I can't.'

The image of the hurt in her eyes stayed with him as he walked out through the main door, through the foyer of the club, down the steps and into the coolness of the night.

•

He couldn't do what? Dance with her? Bear to be near her? Erin paused in the foyer, uncertain whether to follow him or not.

Among the handful of people chatting in the quieter space away from the music, she spotted Steve deep in conversation with an older woman, someone she didn't know. Despite his focus on the woman, Steve caught sight of her.

'Are you looking for Simon?' he interrupted his conversation to ask. 'He went outside. Tell him not to go far. This could be important.'

She found Simon sitting on a bench in the small war memorial park next to the club. The water jets in the centre of the low, round memorial fountain bubbled gently, the moonlight shimmering on the constantly shifting surface of the pool.

He must have heard the tap of her heels on the paved pathway because he stood up as she approached. 'I owe you an apology,' he said, the tension around his eyes even tighter than before. 'That was appallingly rude of me.'

'There's no need to apologise, Simon. You've got a lot on your mind just now. If you want company, I'm offering it. If you'd prefer to be alone, I'll leave you in peace.'

Despite the shadows, she saw a hint of his normal smile. 'Truth is, I always want your company, Erin. Please, sit with me for a few minutes.' In a quietly gallant gesture, he unfolded a large handkerchief from his pocket and wiped the dust off a section of the bench before she sat down.

She didn't know what to say, what he needed from her at this moment. The camaraderie and light teasing that had characterised their relationship before he went away fell far short of the circumstances now. She'd told him earlier that 'anyone' – that *she* – understood that he needed time to deal with Hayley's death. But the tacit admission of their . . . their what? Interest? Attraction? Affection? She couldn't put a word to that, either, and therefore had no guide to what he wanted from her, now.

He sat near her without touching, leaning forward with his elbows on his knees, hands clasped. He seemed to be staring at the wall of the fountain, where the names of Goodabri's sons and daughters who had served in world wars and other conflicts were inscribed, a small cross carved beside the names of those who had never returned home.

He'd been away, overseas somewhere, in an operation that had taken the best part of two months. She'd tuned in to the morning news on the radio every day of those weeks, dreading hearing of Australian soldiers killed or injured in Afghanistan or Iraq. She hadn't even known for sure if he was overseas, but from the murmured comments of senior Parks staff it had seemed most likely. But he *had* been overseas – he'd confirmed that earlier. And he was still in the army reserve, still a commando, and they could call him up again at any moment.

Every time he went away, there'd be a chance he wouldn't return home. She would have to get used to that. Somehow.

The band had finished playing and the hum of many voices drifted out from the hall. The light breeze brushed her skin through the lace, cool but not cold.

Simon broke the silence. 'My head's so full, I'm not sure where to start. But I want you to know – you're beautiful tonight, Erin. You are anyway, but in that dress you're . . . you look like a goddess. You're breathtaking. Literally. And you have every right to be proud of your skills and accomplishment.'

Of all the compliments she'd received during the evening, his meant the most. He'd said *she* was beautiful and breathtaking. Not the dress. Not that she 'scrubbed up okay' or that he 'almost didn't recognise her' or that the dress 'must have cost a fortune'. And he'd complimented her skills in a way that *did* make her proud.

'Thank you. Dressmaking makes a change from wrangling fencing wire or building walking tracks. Underneath the tomboy me is another side that likes playing with pretty fabrics.'

'I've never thought of you as a tomboy,' Simon said. 'Never. A capable and practical woman, yes. Capable and practical and beautiful and sensual and I wish . . . I wish things had been different tonight.'

Sensual. Every second man tonight had called her pretty or beautiful, and the cheekier ones had called her sexy, but they'd just been light-heartedly flirting. Simon wasn't flirting. He'd spoken aloud what they'd left unspoken, unacknowledged for months. Her libido had started weaving a whole new set of fantasies when she'd first seen him tonight, the black dinner jacket and bow tie a radical change from his work clothes but somehow accentuating his height and muscular power. If she could have taken him somewhere private, stripped off those clothes, let the heat between them build, unconstrained . . .

Her skin flushed, every nerve begging, just imagining the touch of his naked skin. Reality blew a chill wind over the brief flight of fantasy. Not possible. Not now. Not tonight. 'I wish things were different, too,' she said. 'Maybe they will be, sometime in the future.'

'Yes. I hope so.'

She didn't add anything more, because what else was there to say? She'd wait, and see what happened once he'd had time to come to terms with Hayley's death. She closed her eyes against the wave of sorrow. Her determination to be adult, mature and considerate didn't help to fill the ache in her heart, the cold empty place in her bed, or the loneliness in her soul.

The auction restarted inside and the auctioneer's smooth, fast-paced patter created a new rhythm, accompanied outside by the burbling of the fountain.

Simon shifted on the seat to face her, still keeping that small distance between them. 'Fraser said you'd found out something. About where Hayley might have been.'

Glad to have something solid to concentrate on, she told him briefly what she'd learned.

'Simple Bliss? They're called that?'

When she nodded, he said, 'I think you might be on to something. For years, Hayley used to send me Christmas and birthday cards, although they weren't always on time. No letters, but sometimes she included a note – just a couple of sentences. The thing is, she often mentioned bliss, or being blissful. And loving the simple life.'

The instinct that had suggested a connection between Hayley and the woman in the pop-up shop firmed into belief. 'We have to tell Steve. Do you still have the cards?'

'Yes. In a box at the house. If the police haven't taken them already, I'll go look for them.'

'Let's see Steve first. He was talking with a woman, said there might be something relevant.'

Simon's phone buzzed in his jacket pocket and he drew it out, glancing at the number before answering. He paused, listening. 'Yes. We're just outside. Okay, will do.' He stood as he put his phone away. 'Fraser's in the club committee room. He wants us in there.'

The committee room, just off the foyer, was empty save for Steve, Tess, and the woman Steve had been speaking with in the foyer. The woman clutched a handkerchief in her hand, her eyes red, and Tess sat beside her at the table, holding her other hand. Someone had brought in a tray of cups and saucers, as well as coffee and tea pots, and Steve poured out tea.

Erin closed the door behind them, shutting out some of the noise from the ball and the curious onlookers.

'Simon, Erin,' Steve began, passing a cup of tea to the woman, 'this is Catherine. Catherine's the new community nurse at Strathnairn.'

Erin smiled and nodded at the woman as she sat down at the table beside Simon. In her fifties or so, Catherine had silver strands in her hair, a round, kindly face, and a string of mauve glass pearls around her neck that matched the satin of her gown. She wiped another tear from her eye as she said hello to them both. Whatever she'd told Steve, or been told by the police, it had clearly upset her.

'Now, if this was Sydney or Newcastle or even Tamworth,' Steve continued, 'I'd be following procedure and wouldn't be telling you this.' He cast a quick glance at Tess, who met it with her cool, unflinching gaze. 'But it's not. It's a small community in a sparsely populated region and we have to do things differently out here. The thing is, Catherine visited a patient out at Page Hill on Monday morning and picked up a hitchhiker on the way back to Strathnairn.'

Page Hill. Erin knew the locality. About forty kilometres north-east of Goodabri, east of the area of the park where Sybilla had died. And the shortest route between Page Hill and Strathnairn – dirt roads mostly, but reasonable – passed through Goodabri.

'Catherine's description of the woman matches Hayley. Catherine, perhaps you could tell Simon, in your own words, what you told me?'

'I went to Sydney on Tuesday and only got back today. I just heard. About . . . about the murder.' Catherine paused to breathe in, clearly trying to suppress her emotion. 'My condolences, Simon. It must have been a shock to you.'

He acknowledged her sympathy with courtesy. 'Thank you. Please go on. I appreciate your help in this.'

'The woman I gave the lift to,' she began, 'she wasn't actually hitchhiking, but she was a couple of kilometres past where Millers Road meets the Goodabri Road, and she was limping, so I stopped. There's nothing out there. The properties are few and far between, and there's hardly any traffic on the road. She said a friend had given her a ride to the junction and she thought she could walk the rest of the way. But she had some bad blisters and I couldn't leave her there, with such a long way to go She seemed polite and harmless, no sign of drugs, so I offered her a lift.'

Not unusual, out in the bush. You had to be careful, but Erin sometimes offered a ride to hikers or people stranded by a car breakdown.

Catherine took a sip of her tea. 'I didn't quite believe her about getting a ride to the junction – the blisters were bad, like she'd walked a fair way – and it seemed odd her being out there alone, without a car. I tried to get her to talk but she was very reluctant. Nervous, in fact. I thought maybe she was afraid of something or in some kind of trouble, so I pressed her a little. She finally said she had to get to her friend in Goodabri. That she needed his help. She said her daughter was caught up in a cult, and she needed his help to get her out of it.'

Simon started, as though the words had whipped him. His voice harsh, guttural, he repeated, 'Her *daughter*? Hayley has a *daughter*?'

CHAPTER 8

He'd almost shouted the words, when Catherine had told him all she knew. Hayley had a daughter. A dozen more questions joined the hundreds of unanswered ones already drumming in his head, and he had to fight to stop anger overwhelming him. Anger with Hayley. With himself. With this whole damn situation that left him powerless and uncertain.

Ashamed of his outburst, he gritted his teeth and tried to soften his voice for the sake of the woman who had only wanted to help. 'Did she say anything about the girl?'

'No, not much. We were almost at Goodabri, so there wasn't much time. I asked about the cult, what kind it was, and she said she'd never have thought it was a cult, but "he" had changed, she said that he'd lied to them for years, and that he scared her now. I offered to take her to the Strathnairn police station, but she said she wanted to see her friend first. That he'd know what to do.'

He'd know what to do? What bitter irony. He had no clue what to do, where to start, even what to ask next. The question that drummed loudest in his mind, over all the others, was: *Whose daughter?* Who had fathered Hayley's child?

As if she'd read his thoughts, Erin asked, 'Did she give you any indication of the girl's age? Or why she didn't have her daughter with her?'

Catherine shook her head. 'No. I didn't have time to find out. I should have. I shouldn't have just left her in Goodabri. If I'd just done something more . . . But she was so adamant her friend would help her and she said he was a good man. I was already running late for another appointment so I dropped her on the edge of town.'

After everything, Hayley had still believed in him, and again he hadn't been there. The knife in his chest twisted a few more times.

'Did she have anything with her?' Tess asked. 'A bag or a case or anything?'

'Just a little cloth bag. A bag with a drawstring – like a kid's library bag. It was red. I don't think there was much in it – it looked very light.'

A small bag with something light in it that she'd taken the trouble to carry with her when she'd fled. He had no doubt now that she *had* fled – that she'd run away from someone or some situation that frightened her. Why else would she have hidden in his house for days?

He looked at Fraser across the table. 'Was the bag found at the house?'

'Not that I'm aware of. Leah didn't mention it.' Fraser had his phone in his hand, as though he itched to call or send a message immediately. Or perhaps he was only checking the time. He placed the phone back on the table and stood up. 'Catherine, thank you for your time. You've helped us a great deal. Did you come with friends tonight? Or would you like someone to drive you home?'

'No. Thank you. I'm here with friends.' Catherine nervously smoothed the skirt of her gown as she got to her feet. 'I hope you find the person who did this, Detective. That poor woman. And I hope you find the girl, too. She was so worried about her.'

'We'll find her,' Simon assured her, as much a vow to himself as a promise to her. 'I won't stop looking until we find her and make sure she's safe.'

He waited only until Fraser had seen the woman out and closed the door behind her. 'I'm going over to my house to find that bag.'

Fraser didn't object. 'Good. I want to know what was in it. Tess, do you live somewhere nearby? Can you get into uniform quickly?'

'Yes. Just give me ten minutes. But isn't it a bit late to go knocking on doors?'

'We're only knocking on one door. A place out on Millers Road. Your local real estate agent in there,' he waved a hand towards the function room, 'told me he sold it last year. All done through lawyers on behalf of a private company and he didn't meet the new owners. We need to go there and find out if Hayley or Sybilla came from there, and if so, inform whoever lived with them of their deaths.'

'Would you call me afterwards?' Simon asked. 'I don't care what time it is.'

'Will do. I'll also want to know what, if anything, you find.'

If Simon could have gone with them to the property, he would have, but that was a police job. Fraser was already allowing him to return to his place to search for the bag, a concession that Haddad probably wouldn't have permitted. It was a more effective use of his knowledge and time than driving out to Millers Road on what could be a wild goose chase. But if Hayley had been living there . . . Fraser would tell him within the next couple of hours. The detective seemed to be driven by pragmatism rather than procedure, and committed to finding out the truth.

'I'll go find Nick and update him,' Fraser said, already moving towards the door. 'Tess, I'll pick you up at the station in ten minutes. Erin, are you going with Simon?'

'Yes,' she said. 'Two sets of eyes are better than one.'

'There's no need, Erin,' Simon argued. 'You were up all last night. Have a couple more dances to enjoy the ball, and then go home and sleep.'

She gave him the raised eyebrow she usually reserved for the young guys in the SES squad when they were being particularly macho and dense. 'Dance when I could be helping? Sleep without knowing what you and Steve have found out? Not likely, Kennedy.'

He didn't argue any further.

After she'd collected her purse and shawl from the main room, they drove in his hire car the couple of blocks to his house. His LandCruiser was still in the driveway, where he'd pulled up yesterday evening. No one had yet removed the police tape from across the front of the house and the driveway, so he parked the hire car on the road. The houses in the street were darkened. His mostly elderly neighbours usually went to bed early, although a few of the more socially active were still at the ball.

Goodabri didn't run to streetlights anywhere other than the main road, but the moon lit their way as they crossed the front yard and he unlocked the door. The breeze was picking up, blowing a few wisps of cloud across the sky, swaying the branches of the grevilleas under the front windows so that they tapped softly against the glass.

Simon paused in the passageway, just inside the door. He'd liked this old house, the few weeks he'd lived in it. He'd even considered buying it. A crazy idea, investing in real estate in a tiny town like Goodabri, but the place could be done up, and the block of land was large, with plenty of room for a decent shed, a vegetable garden, an outdoor entertainment area. All the things he'd wanted to do for years and never done in any of the places he'd bought.

But as he walked into the house tonight, the memory of Hayley's body lying on the study floor erased that former enthusiasm, and the rooms and passageway seemed small and cramped rather than cosy, as if the very walls were huddling down in despair. If it hadn't been for Erin by his side he might have huddled down against the wall himself.

His phone beeped with a message – Fraser confirming that the forensic officers hadn't found the bag. He showed it to Erin. 'Where would you put a small bag?' he asked.

She drew her light shawl a little tighter around her shoulders, as if she, too, felt the coolness of the house. 'We're assuming it's still here. Whoever killed her and trashed your spare room was looking for something. Maybe they found it and took it. But maybe they didn't. That's what we'll hope for. Do you know which room she slept in? Because if I go and stay in someone's house, I leave my things in the room I sleep in.'

That made sense. Hayley had always been tidy, not left things lying around. A habit belted into her by her abusive father. 'I'm pretty sure she slept in my bedroom. Not in the bed,' he added. 'On a beanbag on the floor.'

'You look in there. I'll start in the living room.'

A reluctance to enter the bedroom made him go to the study door. He flicked the light on. They'd taken Hayley, of course, and only the bloodstains on the polished floorboards remained. He dragged his gaze away from the floor to scan the rest of the room. The drawers in the computer desk had been pulled out and emptied. He couldn't see his flash drives and camera cards in the pile of files and books on the floor. Had the forensic officers taken them? Or the person who'd trashed the place?

His smashed computer was gone, too, and the hard drives. But he'd seen them earlier, so the police must have them now. The fact that the killer had taken so much interest in the computers and drives suggested it was some kind of data they were looking for. Or hoping to destroy. Hayley hadn't carried much in her red bag, but a whole lot of data could fit on a thumb drive or an SD card. Or perhaps they were concerned that she'd left something on his computer – emails? Letters? Images?

The sofa bed in the corner seemed almost undisturbed, although the two small cushions he often propped behind his back when reading had been shifted from their customary spot at one end. He couldn't remember noticing them earlier, but then he'd been too focused on Hayley. No way to know whether they'd been moved before the police went through. No way to know if Hayley had settled down on the sofa with a book, lying on her side, using a cushion to support the book in a comfortable position as she'd often done, or if her killer had searched behind them.

'What did they think you were hiding, Hayley?' he murmured. 'Where did you put it?'

Nothing obvious leapt out at him in this room. Erin's suggestion of the bedroom made sense and he went back into it. First things first before he forgot about them: he needed to get the cards Hayley had sent him. He'd kept all of them, close to thirty of them. A cottage this age didn't come with built-in wardrobes, but the old art-deco one he'd picked up from a clearance sale was a good tall piece with shelf space above the hanging rack. If the police had searched here, they'd left no sign of it, and taken nothing.

He reached up for one of the boxes he stored there. *Paperwork*, according to his own scrawl on the packaging tape that he'd sealed it with when he'd packed up to move to this house. The cards were all in there, along with papers relating to his parents and his own army service.

He didn't open it, just left it on the bed so he wouldn't forget to take it.

Moving around the bed, he picked up the orange blanket and folded it, then stood for a long moment with it over his arm, remembering. He thought they'd been happy, those first few months. Perhaps they had been. Perhaps Hayley had been. But maybe he'd just been happy to have a pretty woman in his home, to have regular sex. He'd only been twenty-one, after all. And part of his contentment might have been his sense of doing the right thing, of being a man and looking after her as a decent man should. His grandfather had certainly thundered at him often enough about responsibility.

All these years later, the only thing Simon was sure of was that he hadn't felt as alive with Hayley as he did with Erin.

He could hear her in the kitchen, opening cupboard doors, her heels clicking lightly on the lino floor. Doing the job that needed doing, thoroughly and without complaint or chatter.

He laid the folded blanket on the bed and lifted the beanbag out of the way. Nothing underneath it. He pictured Hayley curled up there, tucked in between the wall and the bed, hiding, and he got down on his knees and ran his hand along the space under the bed. The police had probably already searched there and he wasn't surprised to find nothing. But as he pushed the beanbag back to search further under the bed, his fingers touched something firm under the faux velvet of its cover. He unzipped the beanbag and thrust his hand between the inner and outer covers, reaching until he felt a twisted cord, a different texture from the other fabrics. He grasped it, pulling it out. The red bag.

Erin came down the hall, stopped in the doorway. 'You found it.'

'Yes. Hidden inside the beanbag.'

'Good.' She frowned, and bit her lip. 'I think there's someone outside.'

He rose to his feet instantly. 'You saw them?'

'No. I heard some noises when I was in the living room. I thought it was just the wind in the bushes outside. But when I was in the kitchen I heard more noises. Footsteps, I'm sure. The blinds are closed so I couldn't see out.'

A sound came from the back of the house – a hiss, a whoosh.

The moment he reached the hallway he saw the reflection of the light flickering against the polished wood of the open kitchen door. Glass shattered, and his single glance into the kitchen before he slammed the door closed showed the back wall of the weatherboard house alight, a window broken and the blinds burning.

Erin, just behind him, had seen it too. Simon thrust the red bag into her hand.

'Go out the front,' he told her. 'I'll grab the box of letters.'

But before she'd made it to the front door, the same fiery whoosh of sound came from that direction, and light danced through the leadlight windows on either side of the door.

Both doors, impassable.

Bastards.

Simon switched into battle mode and moved instinctively. 'Out the study window,' he ordered. He was only three steps from the bed and he grabbed the orange blanket and the box of papers before following Erin. Smoke was creeping out from under the kitchen door and the loud crackling and roar of the flames told him the fire had taken hold. The old timber house wouldn't last long.

He slammed the study door shut behind him for the little extra time it would give them. The window overlooked Snowy's house with the driveway to the old garage at the back. Erin had already tugged at the stiff latch, but he knew it wouldn't allow the window to open wide enough anyway. He nudged her aside and with his arm padded by the blanket, smashed the glass with a few quick blows.

He could see no one outside, nor smell fuel in the immediate vicinity. Only the smoke blown by the wind. He laid the folded blanket over the jagged glass in the window frame.

'Out you go,' he said to Erin, giving her a hand up through the window. She moved quickly, despite the awkwardness of the long dress, the cloth bag slung over her shoulder. His hand held her steady as she balanced for a moment in her heeled sandals on the ledge before gathering up her skirt and jumping nimbly down to the gravel below. He passed the box out to her before he climbed through himself, then grabbed the blanket.

He could hear the fire catching in the roof above the kitchen, the heat hitting the corrugated iron. At the front, the fire hadn't caught so strongly yet, and his LandCruiser in the driveway was still some distance from the flames. He couldn't see anyone in the open front yard, or in the street. But from the lane behind the long backyard he heard the roar of a car engine and tyres spinning in gravel.

'See if you can rouse Snow,' he said to Erin. If she couldn't wake the old man within a minute or two, he'd smash the door down. 'I'll just back the LandCruiser out.'

'And call Nick,' she said. 'At least half the RFS crew are at the ball. He'll alert them quicker than triple-0 will.'

They'd be ten minutes yet, getting their gear and the truck. His cottage would be well alight by then, and there might be a battle to save Snowy's place and the vacant house on the other side of his own – but with the low pressure from his own water tank and no street water, he couldn't fight it, just try to protect people and salvage the little he could. It only took him a few moments to reverse his LandCruiser down the driveway and swing out onto the road, parking behind the hire car in front of Snowy's place to leave space for the fire truck. Erin was still pounding on the front door.

He dialled Nick's number as he jogged across Snowy's lawn, and passed Erin the phone just as Nick answered. While she spoke rapidly to Nick, Simon trod on some of his neighbour's precious flowers to bang on his bedroom window.

He'd never been so pleased to hear the old man's garrulous complaints.

'Fire, Snowy!' he yelled. 'Unlock the door!'

'I'm coming. Hold on, I'm coming.'

Simon could hear him shuffling around in his room, but it took over a minute before the latch on the front door clicked, and Snowy opened it, dragging a dressing gown on over his pyjamas.

Simon stepped inside and took his arm. 'You've got to get out, Snow. My place is on fire. You need to get some distance, to be on the safe side.'

For once Snowy heard okay, and his inherent good sense kicked in. 'Jesus, lad. Have I got time to get my wallet from the bedroom?'

'Super quick, Snow. Super quick.'

The old man moved pretty fast in spite of his gammy leg, grabbing his wallet from the bedside table and a wooden box from beneath it. 'Always dreaded fire,' he said as Simon ushered him out the door. 'Got all the important things in me box.'

'Good on you.' Grateful for the old man's pragmatic cooperation, Simon steered him across the lawn to Erin.

She immediately wrapped the orange blanket around Snowy. 'I'll take him down the road. I don't have my protective gear, dammit. I left it at home tonight.'

She usually carried her SES uniform in case of callouts, just as he did. He shook his head. 'Don't worry. The RFS will be here in minutes. Just keep Snow somewhere safe.'

He unreeled Snowy's garden hose and started damping down the side of the house to protect it, but it wasn't long before the heat from his burning house made him retreat. A siren wailed on the main street, just a few hundred yards away. There was nothing more he could do. The fire truck had powerful hoses, plenty of water, and the crew had all the right protective gear.

For a brief moment he considered going to look for the arsonist, but it had been quite some minutes since he'd heard a car drive away at speed. They'd easily be well out of town by now. Better to wait until the police arrived and they could look for any evidence in the back lane.

So he stood out on the road, in his dinner suit and bow tie, beside Erin in her beautiful dress and Snowy in his grey pyjamas and maroon dressing gown, and watched his house burn. The adrenaline rush of the desperate moments in the house showed little sign of fading; his heart raced, his senses were heightened, and every muscle was tensed, primed to fight.

•

Erin had battled enough fires out in the bush to recognise that the house was already beyond saving. Part of the roof had collapsed, and some internal walls, and flames billowed out the windows. The RFS crew had leapt to work, their strategy to extinguish the flames and prevent them from spreading to the houses on either side. The direction of the breeze reduced the risk to Snowy's house, but the vacant house on the other side remained in danger.

Simon had given her his jacket and she pulled its warmth close around her. When Snowy accepted an invitation from the neighbour across the road to go inside for a rum, he shrugged off the orange blanket and draped it around her, over the jacket, before waving a cheery farewell and wandering off with his friend.

'Are you warm enough?' Simon asked, breaking his silence. 'I can drive you back to the club if you like.'

'I'm perfectly fine. I don't really need the blanket. Didn't want to hurt Snow's feelings, though.' She'd already wished more than once for her practical SES uniform and boots. Somehow, seeing the dress, all the guys forgot she had certificates in firefighting, search and rescue, truck driving and other heavy-duty jobs, and thought she was a delicate flower, needing looking after.

She and Simon hadn't said much with Snowy there, but once he'd gone she quietly voiced the thoughts occupying her mind. 'One of the noises I heard was probably fuel splashing on the back door. Whoever did it knew we were in there.' They'd only just arrived, they'd turned on lights – there was no way the arsonist couldn't have realised they were inside.

'Yes.'

He'd already thought of that, obviously. Not surprising, for a man used to war and fighting.

'But the timing was quick,' she continued, laying out the logic because logic was far preferable to considering what type of person would try to burn them to death. 'Unless someone followed us from the club, they were either waiting for you or they weren't targeting you specifically. Just your house.'

'Fraser only told me tonight that I could come back here. No one could have known that I would. So the primary aim had to be to destroy the place. But when we showed up – well, me, anyway – they must have seen the chance to get rid of me, too.'

She still had Hayley's cloth bag over her shoulder, so she reached under the blanket for it. 'Here. I guess you'd better see what Hayley was hiding.'

He took the bag and then hesitated, fingering the drawstring cord but not opening it straightaway.

The headlights of a car turned into the road and it pulled up behind the LandCruiser. Nick's car, she saw, when he dimmed the lights. Nick and Jo hurried over.

'You're both okay?' Jo asked, giving them the once-over, checking for injuries.

'We're fine. Honestly.' Erin removed the blanket from her shoulders to demonstrate that she wasn't the walking wounded.

Jo never fussed, and now she accepted the assurance as given – one of the things Erin appreciated about her. They'd been friends ever since Jo joined the Strathnairn team, and although Jo had a stack more letters after her name than Erin's Bachelor of Natural Resources, and gave scientific papers at international conferences, she was warm, perceptive, and easy to get along with. In the largely male environment they worked in, Erin valued having someone like Jo around.

'What happened?' Nick asked. 'You said arson on the phone.'

Simon gave a succinct report. No emotions, just facts arranged in precise order.

'A can of fuel and a couple of matches and it's all too easy to torch a place,' Nick said, with the grimness of experience. 'But why didn't the person do it when the murder was committed? That would have slowed down our investigation and destroyed most of the evidence.'

'The murder may have been unplanned,' Simon commented, still with that same emotionless, objective distance. Erin almost envied his military detachment, and yet his abrupt departure from the dance floor earlier this evening, his words to her afterwards and his reluctance to open Hayley's bag all suggested strong emotions that couldn't always be rigidly contained. During the last twenty-eight hours he'd been through hell, on top of whatever horrors he'd experienced in the previous two months. But he wouldn't show any weakness or vulnerability in front of Nick and the RFS crew. Probably not even in front of Jo.

'Do you need us to wait here, Nick?' Erin asked. 'It's going to be a little while before they get the fire out.'

'No. No sense breathing any more smoke than necessary. Steve will want to talk with you, but he won't be back for at least an hour. Can you wait for him? Maybe at the Parks office, if you don't want to go back to the ball?'

'I'll wait in the office,' Simon said. 'Fraser can find me there. Erin, you might as well go home. Fraser can speak with you tomorrow.'

He mustn't be thinking clearly if he thought she'd meekly go home and leave him to deal with this alone. 'I'll wait for Steve with you.'

Jo decided to return to the ball, in a move that Erin suspected was more about leaving her alone with Simon than a desire to socialise. With Steve and Tess still out, Haddad travelling to Newcastle, and the couple of night-duty officers working out of the Strathnairn station on a call elsewhere, Nick had no officers to call on and would be at the scene for a while.

While Simon drove his LandCruiser around to the National Parks office in the main street, Erin gave Jo a lift in his hire car to the ex-servicemen's club, where she planned to pick up her ute and leave the hire car in the relative security of the club's parking area.

'Is everything okay between you and Simon?' Jo asked on the short drive. 'You hardly spoke two words to each other over dinner. And you didn't dance for long.'

He just walked out and left her there, right in the middle of the dance floor . . . Yep, that would be the current hot topic of conversation at the ball. Soon to be replaced with: *Burned to the ground. Heard a rumour it might have been arson . . .* At least with Jo going back in there, she'd put paid to any of the wilder speculation.

Erin turned into the club's driveway and headed for a vacant parking space near her own ute. 'He only arrived back last night, Jo. The wife he never mentioned was murdered, in his house. That's enough complications as it is, without another death, an attempt on our lives, and a bucketload of unanswered questions. So there isn't anything between us, other than our existing friendship.'

'I'm glad that's still intact. I've missed working with you guys. Not much longer now, though – I'm expecting the all-clear on Monday for driving and for resuming full-time work.'

Would it be the same as it had been, the once close-knit team of Jo, Erin, Simon and Mal back together again? It would be good but no, not exactly the same. The events that had led to Jo's injuries, and now Hayley's murder – those shadows would lurk always.

Erin made herself smile. They'd need to keep positive and to celebrate the small victories to get through. 'Yay on the full-time return. Although you might not be so pleased when you see the backlog of paperwork I've left for you.'

Jo snorted indelicately as she got out of the car. 'What do you think I've spent the last two weeks doing while I've been stuck in the office?'

'Avoiding Mal's attempts to cocoon you in bubblewrap?' Erin wasn't entirely joking about their boss's overprotectiveness, and Jo rolled her eyes in agreement. 'Speaking of Mal, can you make sure he knows both Simon and I are unhurt? I don't want him worrying any more than he undoubtedly will.' Or coming straight around to the office tonight to check on them. She could rely on Jo to dissuade him from that.

By now, she thought, Simon would have opened up Hayley's bag. She knew from its weight that it contained more than a toothbrush and a change of underwear. Perhaps she was being overprotective of *him*, but despite his undoubted ability to physically protect himself, she suspected he needed space tonight.

As she got into her own ute and arranged the skirt of her dress so it wouldn't impede her driving, a wave of tiredness and emotion made her want to rest her head on the steering wheel. She resisted the urge. Stay strong, keep moving, keep going – the words became a silent chant.

Steve would be back soon. Simon might have discovered what Hayley was hiding. They might have some answers about who killed her, and why, whether Sybilla's death was connected, and why someone had tried to kill Erin and Simon tonight.

She still wore Simon's jacket over her dress and she pulled it a little closer around her body as she drove. A purely imaginary source of strength, but she needed all the strength she could muster.

•

Simon untied his bow tie, folded it and tucked it in his shirt pocket. He washed the ash and smoke from his face and hands, and made a pot of strong coffee, all the while knowing these were avoidance tactics. He'd put Hayley's bag and the box containing her cards on the desk in the small office behind the main room. The office Erin had been using in his absence. If he looked in the top drawer of the desk there'd be a stash of black jelly beans.

And there he was, thinking of Erin again, instead of confronting whatever it was Hayley had left him.

He carried his coffee mug into the office and sat at the desk. Before he opened the bag, he pulled out the desk drawer. More delaying tactics, but sure enough, the half-full packet of jelly beans sat in the corner. He almost took one, for a form of Dutch courage, but closed the drawer instead, leaving them untouched.

The twisted white cord that loosely knotted the drawstring bag closed came undone easily enough. He opened up the bag and removed the few objects, one by one, placing them on the desk. A small book with an embossed cover. A pencil stub. A pair of folding scissors. A square of cotton with a half-completed embroidery of butterflies, wrapped around a little fabric book with pins and needles neatly lined up in the felt pages. And an envelope with his own handwriting on it – the letter he'd sent her just after he'd moved to Goodabri, ten weeks ago.

He picked up the book. An unlined notebook, like one of the many he'd bought Hayley for her sketches. She'd always carried one, and he encouraged her drawing, because it was one of the few ways she had of expressing herself.

In fact, maybe this was actually one of the blank journal books he'd bought her for her birthday – the Celtic design of the decorative cover seemed familiar. And it was well worn, the gold embossing faded away in places, the page edges thickened through repeated turning.

He opened it to the first page. A pencil sketch of a baby wrapped in a blanket. A tiny baby, all crinkles and frown and yawn.

He turned the page. Another sketch. An older baby, maybe a few months, a beaming smile directed right at him. The next page showed a baby standing, little hands grasping the seat of a wooden chair for support. He kept turning pages. The baby – and it was the same baby – as a toddler, in a simple dress with a bow in her hair. The toddler hugging a small dog. A little girl, maybe three years old, bright-eyed in a short top and baggy trousers. On and on through the pencil sketches he went, page after page, more than fifty drawings, watching the little girl grow up. Some of the sketches were detailed, layered;

others might have been quickly done. But nonetheless it was a loving record of the child's life.

The last drawing showed the girl with her long hair loose around her shoulders, smiling directly at the artist, a small knife in her hand, apparently about to cut a cake decorated with candles. Candles arranged in a semicircle around the number thirteen, iced crookedly on the cake.

Thirteen. The girl had turned thirteen years old.

Hayley had left just on fourteen years ago. He'd last made love to Hayley the night before he'd shipped out, fourteen years ago. They'd been trying – again – to conceive.

Her daughter had already turned thirteen. The daughter she'd come to him to get help for. And she'd brought this little album of drawings, a record of her daughter's life.

He stared at the girl's face, its shape and her features, elfin, dainty and girlish. More like the Hayley he remembered than the lifeless woman on his floor last night. But definitely her child.

Numbness protected him from feeling. A paralysing numbness that radiated out from the large, frozen weight in his chest.

CHAPTER 9

Erin parked at the back of the building, beside Simon's truck. A light burned in the office; other than that, both halves of the building were in darkness. Not enough police in the district to have many people on duty for a second night running – although Steve and Tess should be back soon, and she wouldn't be surprised if Nick was calling Aaron in again. She doubted any of them had slept much since last night.

Her own eyes gritty from lack of sleep and from the smoke, she fumbled with her key at the back door, calling out, 'Just me,' as she managed to unlock it and push the door open.

Simon lifted his head from his hands when she entered the small office. There was no light in the hazel of his eyes. Hadn't been since those first moments yesterday before they'd found Hayley. Only pain, unguarded now, deep and dark.

She pulled out the chair opposite him and asked, 'What is it?'

'She's thirteen.' His voice was rough, hoarse, as though the words hurt him to speak. 'Hayley's daughter is thirteen.'

Thirteen. And Hayley had left him fourteen years ago.

'Did she say if . . . ?'

'She didn't say anything.' He passed across a small notebook.

Drawings. She flicked through the pages. Fifty or more drawings of a girl, from babyhood through childhood and into early adolescence.

Simon stood abruptly and paced to the window, staring out into the night. 'She could be my daughter. Or she could be someone else's.' He set out the statements as facts, as if he'd been repeating them in his head, time and again. 'For all I know, Hayley could have been having an affair before she left. Maybe that's *why* she left.'

If so, she was a fool, Erin thought. No, that was uncharitable and unkind. She hadn't known Hayley. She had no right to make any judgements.

'Did she give any indications of having an affair? Did she have any male friends you knew of?'

'No. She had very few friends. And the last time I saw her she said there was no one else.' He frowned, shaking his head in bewilderment. 'But that would have been after this girl was born. She came back to our place to get some things, but she didn't tell me about the baby.'

'Did you . . .' Hell, she wasn't sure how to ask this. She could almost understand a woman hiding a baby if her husband didn't want children. 'Did you want kids? Was it something you'd talked about?'

'Yes. We wanted a family. Hayley especially, but yes, me too.' He paced the small room, restless, and paused to face her, his back against a filing cabinet. 'I wanted to be a decent man. I thought I'd probably make a good father. But in three years, she only fell pregnant once. And she had a miscarriage. While I was deployed overseas and couldn't be there for her. We didn't have any luck conceiving again. I had to go away again, but when I came back we were going to do all the tests, find out why.'

'But then she left?'

'Yes. She left while I was gone. If she was pregnant again, I never knew.' He gave a long, slow exhalation. 'So there you go. I'm a spectacular failure as a husband.' He gave her a wry smile that attempted to make light of things and only succeeded in making her want to cry for him. 'I hope she found someone who made her happier than I did.'

Words eluded Erin. Words she could speak aloud, anyway. What kind of woman treated a man the way Hayley had treated Simon, who had only wanted to do right by her? A heartless, manipulative bitch? A selfish, self-absorbed one? A woman incapable of caring? Or a woman too damaged or afraid to make the emotional commitment a relationship required?

Whatever kind of woman Hayley had been, she'd done Simon an injustice, and hurt him deeply. Erin wasn't sure she'd be able to forgive her for that. But Hayley was gone and Simon was here, and he'd endured more in the last two days than anyone should ever have to.

'Marriages founder for a lot of reasons,' she said gently. 'It doesn't have to be anyone's fault. You're not a failure.'

He acknowledged her words with another small smile but the sorrow in his face didn't ease. So she went to him, to give him the kind of hug she'd give any good friend in need.

The initial stiffness in his body dissolved after a moment, and his arms closed around her. She'd only meant to give him a quick hug but she didn't step back to end it. Her head barely reached his shoulder, and when he didn't let her go she rested her cheek against his shirt and felt his arms tighten around her, and the light pressure of his face on her hair.

It felt right, holding him, and although she meant to give support, she drew strength from him, too. With one arm around him and her other hand on his chest, she closed her eyes and focused on him, on the warmth of his skin through the cotton shirt, on the rhythmic pulse through her palm, on the intimacy of their bodies close together, touching in trust.

There was heat, too, and desire that could flare in an instant, but neither of them took it anywhere, or said anything. Just that long, motionless embrace, the unspoken need to hold and be held overriding physical desire and all the other concerns and complications. And she was grateful for those moments, for the closeness shared with him.

The sound of a car engine slowing impinged on her awareness, and headlights flashed outside the window. Simon instantly tensed again, letting her go rapidly and striding out of the room, all protective soldier on alert. She followed more slowly, the loss of his warmth leaving her feeling cold and alone.

But it was only Steve's car, and he climbed out wearily, and knocked on the door of their building while Tess opened the police rooms.

'Any news?' Simon asked as he yanked open the door.

'Not much. Come through to our office and I'll update you.'

Tess had the lights on and a kettle boiling in the kitchen of the police incident rooms. Steve collapsed into a chair with his feet up on another one. Erin's feet ached from unaccustomed hours in high heels, and she sat on the edge of a table beside Tess. Simon propped a shoulder against a wall, hands in pockets, his face shuttered. He didn't look at her, as distant now as just a few moments ago he'd been close.

'I heard about the fire,' Steve began, his gaze moving between her and Simon. 'Jeez, sounds like you both had a lucky escape. I'm glad you're okay. Sorry about your place, though, Kennedy. I gather everything's gone.'

Simon shrugged, as if it didn't matter. 'I'm insured. And I lived in a high-bushfire-risk area for a few years, so I scanned important photos and documents. My stepfather has copies. The rest is just stuff. Plenty of people lose far more than I have.' He changed the subject without mentioning Hayley's bag. 'Did you find out anything?'

Steve noted the redirection of the conversation with a slightly raised eyebrow but went along with it without comment. 'I spoke to a woman at the homestead who said she didn't know either woman,' he said. 'She claimed to know nothing about Hayley, or about a child, or about Sybilla. I'm not entirely convinced.'

'Neither am I,' Tess said. 'It was as though she expected us, had rehearsed her response. She didn't show any of the classic signs of lying, but I doubt she was genuine.'

Steve nodded. 'Unfortunately, without something more to go on, we couldn't press her.'

Erin had to concentrate to shift her brain back into analytical mode. 'Did you ask about the dresses?'

'Yes. She just said she and her friends make clothing and sell it at markets from the north coast up into southern Queensland and online. They've apparently sold hundreds – anyone could have bought the dresses.'

All perfectly reasonable, on the surface. But it didn't explain why both Sybilla and Hayley, wearing those dresses, had died in this district. 'Did you see the others?' Erin asked. 'Did you see Willow, the young woman I spoke to?'

'It was close on midnight when we got there. The woman we spoke to – Mary – said her friends were sleeping. I didn't have enough reason to ask her to wake them.' Steve yawned, his eyes screwed tightly shut. He had to be exhausted. They all were. 'I've spoken with Aaron and he's researching a few things. If we can come up with something else, a reason to go back out there and ask more questions, we'll do it in the morning. I don't suppose you found Hayley's bag, by any miraculous chance?'

Erin looked to Simon, letting him answer the question.

'Yes,' he said. 'I found it.' He breathed in, then out, slowly and deliberately before he continued. 'There's a sketchbook with drawings of her daughter. She's turned thirteen already. There's a drawing of her with a birthday cake. I'll go get the book.'

Steve waited until Simon had left the room before he asked Erin, 'Thirteen? Does he know if the girl is his?'

'No. There's nothing in the sketchbook except images. But . . . she could be.'

'Shit. What a way to find out.'

Erin could only agree. He'd wanted children, he'd said. And with his gentleness, his steadiness and his respect for others, he would have made a good father. If this girl was his, then he'd missed out on all those years of her life. That had to be going through his mind. For a man like Simon, it would be hard knowledge to bear. Yet he'd not said one word in anger against Hayley.

•

Simon took a few moments in the silence to reinforce his mental control before he went back into the room with Hayley's things. Too many concerns whirled in his thoughts. He would have to go through them, one after another, when he had time and space to think straight. Right now he would show Fraser the sketches, and then take Erin home to Strathnairn. Tomorrow – no, later today, since it was after midnight – he could do the practical things, like notifying his insurance company and getting the basics he'd need. In the days to come, he'd deal with the rest. Even if the girl wasn't his child, he had to find her, ensure her safety and welfare. He owed that to Hayley. Finding her was the urgent task. Working through all the emotions? He had a lifetime to do that.

But one thing was clear in his mind: if she *was* his daughter, she would have to come first in his life from now on. She'd lost her mother, had no other family. Except him. Wherever she'd been, whatever her personality, her history, her state of mind, if she was his daughter she was his responsibility, now and for the future.

His life would be changed, irrevocably. And because of that, the perfect moment of that soul-soaring hug with Erin would have to stay in the past. Even if he cleared his head about Hayley and dealt with the ramifications of her murder, it wouldn't be fair to Erin to contemplate a future with her if he had a teenage daughter he had to put first.

And he had a lifetime to work through the emotions of that, too.

The bright fluorescent lights in the police rooms stung his tired eyes when he took Hayley's book and the rest of the bag's contents through to Fraser and the others. Someone had made coffee and he accepted a mug from Erin. One brief glance at her and his mental discipline took a hard hit. If not for all of his resilience and emotional endurance training he might have fallen to his knees and howled.

'I've just spoken with Nick,' Fraser said while he flicked through the sketches. 'They've found the fuel can in the back lane. Let's hope Forensics can get some prints off it.'

'Speaking of prints,' Tess interjected, 'shouldn't that book be evidence? Gloves would be a good idea, sarge.'

Simon cursed himself for not considering the bag as material evidence in Hayley's murder. 'Erin and I have already handled it,' he admitted.

'Don't stress over it,' Fraser said, although he took gloves from the box Tess proffered. 'This book is years old. There'll be prints all over it, mostly Hayley's. Listen, the forensic mob won't be back until morning. I'm going to photograph a couple of these images, but if you want to take this tonight, have a bit more time with it, you can.' He shot a conciliatory glance at Tess. 'Take some gloves, though. Just in case we need to dust it later.'

His throat tight, Simon muttered a thank you, grateful for the detective's thoughtfulness. If they had to dust the book, some of those drawings might be ruined. And they might be the only images he'd ever have of the girl – his daughter? – growing up.

Fraser snapped a few photos on his phone from the last pages of the book, and took a quick glance at the other items in the bag. 'I doubt they trashed your office looking for her stitchery,' he said. 'So there has to have been something else. Dammit.'

Something else they'd either found, or which was lying in the rubble of the house.

This time it was Tess who stifled a yawn, and Erin caught it, yawning too. Slumped in a chair with her hands wrapped around a coffee mug, she looked exhausted.

'Right,' Fraser said, pushing himself to his feet. 'Nothing else we can do here tonight. Tess, you're dead on your feet. You're off duty as of now. Nick's ordered a briefing here at eight in the morning so I'll see you then. Simon, if you can drop those things back before lunchtime, I'd appreciate it. Have you got somewhere to stay tonight?'

'You're both welcome to crash at my place if you like,' Tess offered, looking at Erin and Simon. 'There's a spare bedroom and a sofa bed in the living room.'

Simon waited for Erin's answer.

'Thanks, but I'll go home.' Her grin was crooked with fatigue. 'It's about time Cinderella changed out of her dress, and I don't have working clothes with me.'

'I'll drive you,' Simon said, and after only a slight hesitation she nodded.

They took his LandCruiser rather than her ute, since he had to bring Hayley's things back in the morning.

'You can give me a lift back when you come,' Erin said, as they turned onto the road to Strathnairn. 'I'll do the weekend rounds of the camping areas out here tomorrow morning.'

Collecting money, cleaning toilets, taking out rubbish and generally keeping an eye on things. Regular visits that took time because of the distances involved. 'Can't Rob do it?' Simon asked. 'You surely must be due some days off.'

'Rob's doing the three other parks. Besides, I was thinking . . .' In the dim light inside the vehicle he saw her turn to him. 'I was thinking that the fences out near Angel Falls need checking. The fences on the north side of the river that adjoin the private properties up there. We could do that tomorrow afternoon.'

And take a look at the property the Simple Bliss women lived on, if only from the boundary. Simon liked her thinking. 'If the police don't turn up anything new in the morning, you're on.'

'Good,' she said. When she didn't say anything else for a while, he glanced across and saw that she'd fallen asleep. She slept the rest of the way, and he drove through the quiet night with only his thoughts for company. Tiredness dragged at him, too, but his brain was too busy to doze and he kept the vent blowing cool air on his face to stay alert.

She woke as he turned into the dirt track to the farm cottage she rented, the LandCruiser bouncing over the potholes.

'I'm sorry,' she said. 'I meant to help keep you awake.'

'No need,' he told her. He pulled in to park in her driveway, and flicked on the internal light before turning to look at Erin. Strands of her hair drifted around her face, loosened from the soft arrangement, her eyes still heavy-lidded from sleep, his jacket swamping her . . . Desire and need hit him hard.

'You are going to stay, aren't you?' she asked, and then she blushed slightly. 'The bed in the spare room is made up. No sense you driving back out to the park or trying to find a hotel at this hour.'

On long nights in the mountains in northern Iraq he'd allowed himself to imagine driving to Erin's place after SES training or work, going inside with her, closing the door on the world and being with her, just the two of them. With her confidence and self-assurance she'd be no shy lover, and his imagination had revelled in that knowledge. But that was before he'd come home and found Hayley's body. And before he'd heard about her daughter.

He had too many regrets to count, and there'd be no point going over them anyway. And both he and Erin were bone-tired, and sunrise would be here soon enough, with all the demands of the new day.

'Thanks, Erin. I appreciate it.' He'd had plenty of experience at controlling his longing for her. Mental discipline had got him through war and grief and loneliness. Unsatisfied desire wouldn't kill him. It might send him to hell, but a different one than his grandfather had preached about.

However, his resolve and discipline took a nosedive when he followed her into the living room of her cottage and she shrugged out of his jacket and handed it back to him. The warmth of her body lingered in the cloth, and standing close to her he could smell the light floral highlights of her perfume above the smoky undertones. The skin of her shoulders, pale and smooth beneath the blue lace, tempted his fingers, her pulse fluttered at her throat, and her blue eyes, deep and direct, held questions and promises.

He only meant to brush her cheek with his hand, to acknowledge his feelings for her with one small caress, before he stepped away. Instantly, though, she turned her face and kissed his palm, and the bolt of desire speared right through his veins to his heart and his groin and his brain. He might still have been able to resist the craving to pull her to him, but she stepped into his arms and he instinctively drew her in further, body to body. But he just held her, he didn't kiss her, and she understood and cuddled in close, resting her head against his shoulder.

He'd always believed that the notion that a man couldn't control himself was a hideous, deceitful and misogynistic myth. He still believed that, without reserve. But with Erin in his arms he needed all his fortitude to ignore the whispers urging him to put aside his resolve. The devil's whispers, his grandfather would have said. Another one of the old man's beliefs he'd rejected, long ago. He'd seen evil, and it had nothing to do with the relationship between him and Erin.

Erin shifted just enough to lightly touch his cheek with her fingertips. 'I know what we said earlier. So, you tell me.' Her voice sounded calm and sure and husky. 'You tell me what you need. What you want.'

Her understanding and her empathy almost undid him. He couldn't let her think he didn't care. 'I want . . .' He wanted honesty between them. Honesty and openness and trust. His throat gravelly with need, he said, 'I want to kiss your mouth until we're both gasping for breath. I want to taste your mouth and feel your skin, and unzip your dress and slide it off your shoulders. I want to discover every inch of you with my mouth and my hands and my body.' Giving his imagination that much rein fired the heat in his body. Hell was here and now and he was burning in it, and although he could have ended it he didn't. He didn't move his hands. He didn't move them to caress her, he didn't move them away. But he kept hold of her as if he clung to a life raft, and he continued to murmur into her hair, 'I want to make you cry out in pleasure and to bury myself in you and find peace and sleep with you in my arms.'

Her shiver vibrated through his body and her fingers dug into his back. She drew in her breath in a small gasp. 'So tell me why we aren't following through on that, Kennedy. Because I'm aching for you and I want to make love with you here and now, no matter what the future brings.'

He groaned in frustration, hating that it had become about him, rather than her, when she deserved to be cherished and loved and satisfied. 'Because there's so much in my head I can't get straight. When – if – we make love, I want you to be able to believe that it's totally about you and me and *us*, not just some adrenaline reaction or me trying to bury myself in you to forget what's going on.'

She didn't say anything for a long moment. She gradually withdrew from his arms, took a step back, but one hand remained gently touching his shoulder. A last connection she seemed hesitant to break. He didn't want her to break it.

'You have more honour than I have.' Her regretful smile cut straight into his heart. 'As if I didn't know that already. Go to bed, Simon. Get some sleep. Help yourself to anything you need. I'll see you sometime after sunrise.'

She stepped forward again, lifted her head to his and kissed him on the mouth, no fleeting brush of the lips but a promise, brief and hungry and passionate, that almost demolished his resolve. And then she turned and walked into her bedroom, closing the door behind her.

He'd done the right thing. If he told himself that often enough he might begin to believe it. But among all the confusion and unknowns that Hayley's death had brought, the one thing that shone clear and certain was that he cared for Erin more deeply than he'd ever cared for his wife.

And he wished that doing the right thing didn't make him feel so much of a bastard for hurting her.

•

In the quiet of her bedroom, Erin tugged down the zipper of her dress and stepped out of it, her eyes tightly closed, holding back tears.

She wouldn't cry. She wouldn't cry, because who cried when a good man acted with honour and respect? Who cried when they'd been sensible and not complicated matters any more than they already were? But her heart just wasn't listening to all the sensible, rational reasons to hold off from starting anything with Simon.

She draped the dress over a chair and pulled on her yoga pants and a soft, well-worn sweatshirt. Comfort clothes, nothing even slightly sensual about them. She crawled into bed and hugged the spare pillow. Her brain whirred, her feet throbbed from the hours in heels, her body buzzed with unsated need, and her heart ached. Not a good recipe for sleep.

Hayley had been murdered, her friend Sybilla was dead, and her daughter was with a group that might be a cult. And the Simple Bliss group, who'd denied knowing Hayley or Sybilla, invited visitors to experience their life.

Erin rolled onto her back and stared up at the ceiling, still clutching the pillow to her chest. Joshua would be there at the community on Sunday. Surely they'd find the girl before then. But it was already Saturday and tomorrow was Sunday and that didn't give them much time.

Hayley had believed her daughter to be in danger. Whether the girl was Simon's daughter or not, she was just thirteen years old. And someone had murdered her mother.

Erin rolled onto her side again, pulling the pillow close. She had too many accrued days off and needed to use some. She'd do whatever she had to do.

•

Machine-gun fire swept the village square, children and women screamed and died, and old men laughed and laughed . . .

Simon jerked awake, half out of bed before he recognised the raucous cackling of kookaburras outside the window.

He fell back against the pillow, sweat dampening the twisted sheets. He hated waking up like this, the nightmares so fresh and vivid that it took time and conscious effort to disentangle the real from the remembered and from the fears his subconscious tormented him with.

Erin's house. The bed in Erin's spare room. Sunrise, going by the glimpse of light through the gap in the curtains. Daylight, and a mob of kookaburras proclaiming their territory to all and sundry.

And Hayley was dead and Erin could have died last night in the fire and Hayley needed his help to rescue her daughter from . . . from what?

He swung his legs to the floor and reached for Hayley's bag, laying out the contents beside him on the bed. He traced the spiral design on the book cover with his fingers. *What did you want to tell me, Hayley? What do I need to know?*

He leafed through the pages again, looking for something, any clue. Once again, the child's likeness to Hayley struck him. She was clearly Hayley's biological child, not a child she'd adopted. But still he could see nothing of himself in the girl.

His response swung between relief and sadness, back and forth. The relief he understood – a daughter would complicate his life no end. Yet he also discovered that the old, buried grief of Hayley's miscarriage still had the power to hurt, even after all these years. The shattered hopes and dreams they'd shared, for the child, for the family they'd build, still haunted him with questions of what might have been.

But she'd left him and had a child, and excluded him from her life. Except for the birthday and Christmas cards she'd sent each year, he could have believed she'd forgotten him altogether.

So why had she come to him for help? And what threatened her and the girl? Damn, he was going over and over the same ground and getting nowhere.

He dragged on the trousers he'd worn last night but left the shirt draped on a chair, as it reeked of smoke. Trying to be quiet and not wake Erin, he went out the back door and around to his vehicle to get the clothes he'd bought from Dylan's yesterday, and the box with Hayley's cards.

Despite his efforts to make no noise, the water pump kicked in, which meant Erin had to be up. After the dreams he'd had of her last night, he almost lacked the courage to face her, but he went back inside, anyway. The kettle was boiling in the kitchen and the sound of briefly running water came from the bathroom. He found coffee mugs and coffee and had a pot made before she emerged.

'A semi-naked man in my kitchen making coffee? Now I know I'm still asleep and dreaming,' she joked, almost as easily as their usual teasing but for the way she averted her gaze from his bare chest. He should have put the shirt on, smoke and all.

As for her . . . somehow her tousled ponytail, baggy sweat-shirt and yoga pants were sexier than her ball gown. And that was a train of thought he needed to derail, fast.

'I'll go wash and put some clothes on, if it's okay to use your shower.'

She took her cup of coffee and waved him towards the bathroom. 'Go. Don't use all the hot water. I may be awake enough to function when you're done.'

He showered, shaved and dressed in army-fast time, and his coffee was still reasonably hot when he carried Hayley's bag into the kitchen. Erin worked at her laptop on the kitchen table, a half-eaten slice of toast on a plate beside her.

'Help yourself to toast,' she said. 'Sorry I don't have anything much else to offer. Grocery shopping is on my to-do list.'

She seemed absorbed in what she was doing, so he put a slice of bread in the toaster and opened the box of cards while he waited. The earliest cards were bought ones: landscape or wildlife photos on the front, blank inside other than Hayley's handwriting wishing him a happy birthday, or a joyful Christmas, in the neat, small letters that had always seemed to him to represent her timidity, her fear of being noticed.

It is beautiful here and I love the simple life, she'd written in one. In another: *It is peaceful being so close to nature.* And in later cards: *I am blissful and happy*; *My work is joyful and rewarding.*

He'd kept the cards roughly in order of receipt; after the first few years, most of them were home-made, evolving from plain pieces of cardstock decorated with cut-outs of coloured paper to rustic handmade paper illustrated with her own drawings. And still those brief, one-sentence notes assuring him of her contentment, and each one signed from her 'with love'.

He went back through the pile, this time looking closely at the drawings on the cards she'd made, each of them in her simple, naturalistic style. A kangaroo and her joey. A magpie pair and their young one, more fluff than feathers. A possum on a tree branch with her baby on her back. Now he saw it: mothers and babies, time and again. And then there was a drawing of a little girl, hair in short pigtails, hands outstretched, reaching for a butterfly. Another of a little girl bending down, offering something to a pair of ducks. A young girl reading in the fork of a tree, long hair falling forward across her face. The young girl playing a flute, again with her hair concealing her face.

Until now he'd never looked too closely at the pictures. Only enough to notice and be glad that Hayley was still drawing, a positive sign for her. She'd often drawn children, but in the midst of her depression after the miscarriage she'd been unable to pick up a pencil.

His coffee and toast were both cold. He passed the pile of cards across the table to Erin. 'Tell me what you think,' he said.

He'd barely poured another cup of coffee when she said, 'It's the same girl, isn't it? Her daughter.'

Hayley's daughter, who'd chased butterflies, fed ducks, climbed trees and played the flute. A happy childhood. Simple. Peaceful. *Blissful.*

'Hmm,' Erin said, after she'd read the cards. 'I think you need to look at this.' She handed him a sheet of paper she'd had next to her laptop – an advertising flyer, but not a glossy one. Blue and green ink on textured cream paper. The heading read: *Discover Bliss.* 'The woman I spoke to yesterday in the shop gave it to me. She was also selling a couple of books by a Joshua Kristos – apparently he's a "blissful-living guru" who's going to be visiting them tomorrow. So I've been looking him up.'

'And?'

Erin stretched back in her chair and combed her fingers through her sleep-mussed hair. 'There's not a lot. A website, with some extracts from the books, and links to buy them. They're self-published, but available through the major retailers as e-books and as paperbacks. And if the rankings are anything to go by, they're doing fairly well. They're both in the top one hundred in self-help books. I don't know if that means much, money-wise.'

'When were they published?' he asked. 'Because Hayley's been talking about this stuff for years.'

'The first of these books was two years ago, the latest about a year. But there are references to his writings going back longer than that. And you can download some of his earlier stuff from the website. "Letters", he calls them.'

'Letters to?'

'His followers, I guess. He starts most of them with "Dear friends".'

'Does he use a capital for "friends"?'

'No. Not on the ones I've seen. Why?'

'My stepfather is a Quaker – you know, the Religious Society of Friends. My mother became one, too.'

Erin closed her laptop, giving him all her attention. 'Is that why you're so honourable?' she asked, with a wry smile. 'A religious upbringing? You don't talk about your family.'

He hadn't talked about his wife, either. Which probably didn't make him honourable at all. So maybe it was time to let Erin know a little of the background that had shaped him.

'Not exactly religious. My father was a Vietnam vet, and the war turned him into an avowed atheist. Which didn't go down well with my maternal grandfather, who was a strident old-school hellfire-and-brimstone minister.' He could have added 'and hate-filled bastard' but he didn't. 'After my dad died, my mother and I lived with Grandad for seven years or so. It was . . .' He tried to think of an adequate descriptor. 'Volatile, you could say. He and I didn't agree on pretty much anything. But we needed a roof over our heads and he needed a carer after a stroke. So we stayed. He died when I was eighteen. Mum married Ray about the same time I joined the army. Her beliefs were always much closer to his than to her father's.'

Elbow on the table, chin on her hand, Erin asked, 'But aren't Quakers pacifists? How did your mother . . . I mean, did your army career create problems between you?'

'Quakers are very good at respecting differences between people. Ray and I have had some good discussions over the years.' He rubbed his thumb over the geometric pattern on the pottery coffee mug and sought for words to give shape to his thoughts. 'But what it comes down to for me is that it's not an ideal world. There are people out there who torture, burn, maim, bomb and enslave others. Mostly because of religion and territory, and they're not going to be dissuaded from their path. Kids should be able to chase butterflies and feed ducks and go to school without fearing a bomb or a bullet. Or worse. And I guess that's why I do what I do.'

'It's as simple as that?'

'As simple and as difficult as that. I've killed people, Erin. That's the reality of me. And not just because it's my job, or because of orders, and sure as hell not for any god or religion. But because sometimes that's the only way to protect the vunerable.'

Her blue eyes held his gaze. 'Does it worry you that you have?'

Did it worry him? The blood on his hands, the responsibility and accountability he'd taken on? He gave her the answer he'd reached after only a few years in the army. 'Yes. The day it stops worrying you is the day you've ceased to value your own and others' humanity.'

She smiled gently. 'Quite the philosopher, aren't you?'

He carried his coffee mug to the microwave to zap some heat back into it. 'Years of arguing with my grandfather. I read a lot of philosophy and theology in high school to gather ammunition against his arguments. Until I realised that it never worked, anyway. He wouldn't listen.'

'So what did you conclude? About religion?'

'I'm not a believer. And I don't think you have to believe in a deity to have a moral and ethical code. So, what about you? Did you have a religious upbringing?' He wasn't the only one who'd never said much about his childhood or family, but he'd never before asked her directly about hers.

'Me? Hell no.' She gave an uncomfortable little laugh and avoided looking at him by going to rinse her mug out in the sink. 'My upbringing was entirely devoid of ethics and morals.'

She turned away before he could come out with another question, and headed to the door, tossing over her shoulder, 'I hope you left plenty of hot water, because I need to get clean.'

For all that she was one of the most together people he knew, something had obviously hurt her in the past, and he'd just trodden on an unhealed wound.

CHAPTER 10

A few washes with shampoo got the stench of smoke out of her hair. Pity she couldn't get the stain off her soul so easily. Joshua Kristos exhorted his 'friends' to lay down the burden of guilt and other negative emotions and embrace purity, but forgiving oneself wasn't so glibly easy – and the feminist in her had always had a deep mistrust of notions of 'purity' in any context. Besides, the dreams she'd had last night of Simon had definitely not been pure.

And that was as much as she'd let her thoughts dwell on *that*.

She found her last clean uniform shirt in the wardrobe and dressed for work. When she returned to the kitchen, Simon was out in the yard, talking on his phone. From the occasional word she caught, she guessed he was beginning the insurance claim process. She heated water for her thermos, packed fruit and muesli bars into her backpack along with drinking water, and repacked the SES gear ready to go.

With Simon still on the phone, she got out her camera and started photographing each page in Hayley's book of drawings. Scanning would be better, but she didn't have a scanner at home. At least with the photos he would have a record of the drawings before handing the book over to the forensic team. Just in case it was damaged or lost.

As she photographed she looked for anything that might indicate if the girl was Simon's. But each drawing proved only that Hayley loved her child, and gave her no other answers.

The hinges of the screen door squeaked and Simon came back inside as she photographed the last drawing.

'Everything okay?' she asked.

'Yep. The insurance company will send out an assessor on Monday. They'll get the police report and I guess it should be straightforward. Fraser called, too. The crime scene people have a few things from the house and will bring some of them back today. Mostly the kit bag and my rifle that I'd dumped inside the door when we first walked in. My laptop's in the bag, and a few clothes. So that's a help. He wants to see Hayley's cards and things, though, so are you almost ready to go?'

'Yes. But can you drop me at the Strathnairn office? I'll take a work truck from there and check the camping grounds on the way to Goodabri, and meet you there later.'

He hesitated but didn't argue. Maybe he craved a little solitude too, even if it was only for the distance between the two towns. She was coping – barely – with what was and wasn't happening between them, but the continued hyperawareness kept her own doubts and insecurities buzzing constantly, not always below the surface.

Yet she almost changed her mind when he dropped her outside the Strathnairn office. She found it hard to give him a brief wave and turn away, even though she'd see him again in an hour or two.

The drive alone on the country roads with the truck window wound down and the fresh air blowing in her face worked to banish some of the fatigue. But still she couldn't quiet her thoughts, and they jumped around as fast and as crazily as a young joey discovering his hopping potential.

She'd downloaded a couple of podcasts from Joshua Kristos's website onto her phone. After her first stop, at a picnic area, where she emptied rubbish bins, cleaned the toilet bowl and stocked up the loo paper, she connected her phone to the truck's audio system and started one of the podcasts. Twenty minutes or more until her next stop. She might as well do something useful with the time.

Kristos's voice was deep, melodic, pleasant enough to listen to – if you enjoyed listening to people speaking without interaction. Erin didn't. She'd daydreamed and doodled through most of her university lectures and had much preferred the fieldwork and lively debates with a couple of tutors who challenged their students' assumptions.

'Concentrate,' she muttered to herself. This guy could provide a clue to what Hayley had been doing and where she'd been for the past fourteen years.

After ten minutes of Joshua's soothing tones, she thought she could understand why his preaching might have appealed to Hayley. Although could you call it preaching if there was no mention of God, just 'the Unknown' and 'the Unknowable'? But it was all very *nice*, she had to admit. He spoke of love and bliss, simplicity and beauty, self-sufficiency and natural living. He didn't thunder against anything but spoke gently of the disconnection and soullessness of the technology- and consumption-driven world and described the value of retreating and being more connected to nature and one's own creativity.

Erin heard little to argue with, yet she found it dissatisfying, lacking in something she couldn't immediately identify. Substance? Reality? Logic? No. She agreed with pretty much everything he said. The planet was going to hell if consumption didn't radically slow, and she wouldn't be a ranger if she didn't believe in the value of the natural environment and encouraging people to discover it, for their own well-being as well as the land's.

She could almost like Joshua. He might even be a genuine and decent man who sincerely believed what he preached. She doubted it, but she'd met plenty of sane and decent people who believed far more radical things.

A few minutes into the second podcast – one on stilling thoughts and finding peace within oneself – she turned it off. She probably needed the advice, but even in just that short time of Joshua talking about peace and stillness she'd felt her alertness slipping, and driving at eighty kilometres an hour on dirt roads needed focused attention. She knew what happened when a vehicle met a tree head-on, and she had no intention of risking her own life.

At the next campground she did the rounds and then stood in the warm sunshine for a few minutes chatting with a couple with young children, taking a short weekend break. A pleasant couple, interested in and full of questions about the park and the area. They were contemplating moving to Strathnairn, and asked about schools, service clubs and community organisations. They believed in getting involved, in contributing. Their kids, barely school age and full of laughter, ran around the grass of the open area and chased butterflies.

Just like Hayley's daughter.

Erin excused herself and returned to the truck to get on the road to Goodabri. The brief conversation with the couple had highlighted for her what was missing from Joshua's philosophy: it was mostly about self, rather than relationships with others. A view of the world framed by the individual's own desires and wants. Nothing about community and society, or about right and wrong and responsibility. Retreating from the problems of the world, not engaging with them.

Had Hayley retreated from the world? Maybe. From the little she now understood about Simon's wife, Erin had gained the impression of a gentle, possibly fragile woman, not emotionally strong. Perhaps not strong enough to deal with the harsh realities of the world that Simon's army service must have constantly reminded her of.

That didn't answer the question of who had killed her, though, or why. Hayley had wanted to save her daughter from a cult, but even if she had been involved with the Simple Bliss people, there was nothing yet to indicate whether that was the cult, or whether her daughter had run off to join another, more dangerous group.

Erin drove through kilometres of sunlit bushland with questions tripping over one another in her mind. Did Joshua's followers all withdraw from the world? The website had mentioned 'communities', plural, but how many people did that involve? Willow's group north of the park had to be one of them, but to what extent were they under Joshua's influence or control?

Joshua's focus on self, on promises of healing, personal happiness, *bliss*, seemed harmless enough on the surface. It was what might lie underneath it that concerned her. She didn't know much about cults, but she knew about scams, and the easiest way of hooking a person in was to promise them something they wanted.

But the whole purpose of establishing a scam was to make money. A couple of books and some podcasts, hundred-and-fifty-dollar-a-night 'visits', and market stalls with handmade clothing hardly qualified as good earning potential.

She could almost hear her father's voice in her ear asking, *Where's the money in it, honey? Where's the money?*

•

Other than some charring on the eaves of Snowy's garage, the RFS had kept the fire contained last night and the only loss was Simon's house. All of it.

Simon didn't cross the police tape that was once again strung across his driveway, now cordoning off the blackened ruins. Beyond it, Fraser spoke with the arson investigator, but their conversation didn't take long. The detective walked back across the front yard and ducked under the tape.

'Arson investigator confirms your statement,' he said. 'Accelerant on and around back and front doors. He thinks you're both damned lucky. Quick thinking saved your lives. Although I guess that's what you're trained for.'

'Yes. Among other things.' Some of them were skills that he hoped he wouldn't ever have to use again.

'Forensics are working on getting fingerprints from the fuel can found last night. They also found a few boot prints in the dust in your yard leading into the back lane. About a size eight.' Fraser made a point of looking down at Simon's boots. 'Obviously not yours.'

'No. Tess and I had a look around the other night. Around the house, though, not to the end of the yard.'

'They're not Tess's,' Fraser said quickly. 'Besides, they end at tyre tracks in the lane. So they're most likely your arsonist's prints.'

Simon nodded but didn't comment. Not much use having fingerprints or boot prints if there wasn't a suspect to match them to. He'd already spent over an hour with Fraser and Aaron this morning, but none of them had any new leads, and they were still waiting on information from the post office in Lismore and Centrelink social services to track down where Hayley had been living.

And most of the time he'd been meeting with the detectives, the coroner's office in Newcastle would have been conducting a post mortem on Hayley. The fact kept catching him, never far from his thoughts.

'You heading back to Strathnairn?' Fraser asked. 'Or is your boss expecting you to work this weekend?'

'No. He's looking after the Goodabri office.' And worrying excessively. Simon had spent a good half-hour assuring Mal that he was fine, Erin was fine, his belongings were insured, he'd be okay. Mal took his staff management responsibilities very seriously. Too seriously, sometimes. As soon as Mal went to deal with a visitor enquiry, Simon had texted Erin: *Mal in G'bri office. Meet me at Niland campground?* She must have been somewhere in range because she'd replied almost immediately.

'I'm not officially on duty,' he told Fraser, 'but I'll go give Erin a hand with some jobs in the park. I'll probably be out of phone range, but I'll call back in later this arvo.'

Goodabri wasn't large enough to support many shops other than a corner store, but across the road from the Parks office was a bakery that made hearty bread rolls. Simon got there just before their midday Saturday closing time, and picked up rolls, slices and soft drinks to take out to the park for himself and Erin.

He reached the camping area before Erin did, but he'd heard her check in on the radio and knew she wasn't far away. One of the few advantages of Malcolm's obsessive concern for safety was his insistence on radio checks whenever they were out and about alone, because so much of the district had no mobile phone coverage.

The campground that had been a rescue staging ground just two nights before had resumed its usual function. Several families gathered around a barbecue at one of the picnic tables, and an older couple relaxed in folding chairs in front of their camper-trailer, birdwatching with binoculars. Simon spent a few minutes talking with them while he waited for Erin.

'We heard there was a tragic incident at the waterfall the other day,' the husband said. 'Do you get that kind of thing often? Someone jumping?'

Simon had attended two suicides in national parks in his career, but he kept his answer circumspect. 'Not here, before this. The police are investigating.'

'So sad,' the woman said. 'It's a beautiful spot. We went up to the lookout earlier. Is there another campground or parking area near it? We saw a young lad up there – just near the track, not to speak to – but there were no other cars here at the time.'

'Some of the land on the other side of the river is state forest,' Simon told her. 'People sometimes hike through from there.' Although not all that often. There wasn't much in the way of tracks in the state forest for any but keen explorers to access the river from the other side. But people on the private property that also abutted the park boundary in that area could easily access the park, if they wanted to.

A figure seen on the night of Sybilla's death, and a young man this morning . . . Simon definitely wanted to find out more about the people on that property.

Erin's truck was coming down the short stretch of winding road to the campground, so he left the couple and walked over to meet her when she parked beside his LandCruiser.

'Another sighting of someone up near the waterfall,' he told her. 'A young lad, apparently. How about we drive in via Harden's Hut and the fire trail? There's still about the same distance to walk, but we can walk along the river.'

'Good thinking. I'll just finish here first.' She was out of the truck and reaching into the back for the cleaning bucket. 'Did you happen to bring lunch? Because I only have muesli bars.'

'I did. Including brownies.'

Her smile flashed at him. 'Intelligent man,' she said, and it was almost like the old, uncomplicated times between them.

They ate lunch at the rough table outside Harden's Hut, an old stockman's hut on a ridge overlooking the river about six kilometres before it plunged down the waterfall. The trail to the hut was locked, with the basic shack not yet open for use by park visitors. The sun shone in a vivid blue sky and he wished he could relax, enjoy the autumn warmth and Erin's company, but tension twisted along his spine and he kept watch on the scenery around them as though he was in Taliban-controlled Afghanistan or extremist territory in Iraq rather than a quiet corner of north-west New South Wales.

They were both fairly quiet, each caught up in their own thoughts, and they quickly finished eating and dusted off the crumbs. Simon spread a detailed map on the table. 'If we drive the fire trail up to here, it's not far to hike down to the river at this point – which is close to the south-east corner of the property. Then we can walk along the river down to the waterfall.'

Erin's arm brushed against his as she reached to point at a place on the trail a few kilometres from where they were. 'The fire trail is blocked by a washout somewhere around here. The SES crew who searched the other night reported it. And it's pretty overgrown – we'll have to clear it soon. But if we go as far as this high point here, we might have a view down over some of the property.'

As usual, it was a practical suggestion. They'd always worked comfortably together and he'd missed that during his absence. But although he didn't expect any danger this afternoon, he wished she wasn't caught up in this situation, that she was safe at home and uninvolved. Still, he knew better than to try to talk her out of it.

They went together in the service truck. While Erin drove, he compared his GPS data to the survey map to work out the exact location of the property.

'The real estate agent told Fraser that the Harcourt Downs property is two thousand hectares,' he said to Erin, and translated that because he still thought in acres rather than metric. 'That's five thousand acres. Plus the company that bought it is also leasing an adjoining five hundred hectares of Pete Molloy's land.'

Erin whistled. 'That's a hell of a lot more than a hobby farm. That's a working property. Not a big one, for around here, but big enough. And some serious money.'

'Yeah.' He'd thought the same himself. 'Sold for close on two million.'

'Are you sure it's the right place? It doesn't make a lot of sense. A group of women selling handmade dresses for sixty bucks and taking in visitors for a few hundred dollars aren't going to finance a two-million-dollar property deal.'

'Definitely the same place Fraser went to last night. Maybe one of them is independently wealthy.'

Erin frowned as she hauled the steering wheel around for a steep, sharp bend. 'No. There's something screwy somewhere. Remind me to tell Steve to follow the money.'

'Follow the money? I don't think Hayley had much.' She could have asked him for money anytime if she'd needed it.

Or just taken it from their bank account. Maybe he was a fool, but he'd never taken her name off it. He wasn't that much of a fool that he'd left all his savings in it, but there had always been a reasonable sum. Yet after a few withdrawals in the first year or so, she'd never touched it again.

'Not Hayley's,' Erin said. 'Although it would be worth finding out if she has any. The company that bought the land. And Joshua Kristos.'

'Maybe he's a philanthropist.'

'Oh, I doubt that,' she said, with a darkness he rarely saw in her. 'Call it a hunch.'

The few times he'd seen that shadow in Erin's expression was when she made some passing comment about her family. *An upbringing entirely devoid of ethics and morals . . .* She was open about everything but her past, and out of respect for her privacy – and because it wasn't his business – he'd never asked. He was hardly the poster boy for full disclosure about his own. Perhaps some day she'd tell him.

She slowed the truck and changed down to first gear. They'd reached the place where erosion on the hillside had washed a chunk of the fire trail away, the gouge in the track too deep to easily cross. From here they'd get out and walk. Kilometres from anywhere, just the two of them in the wilderness.

He'd had no legitimate reason to bring with him the rifle the police had returned, so he'd left it in the lockbox in his vehicle back at the hut. No reason except the uneasiness prickling his skin. He had a knife in his backpack and one in his boot, that was all. A couple of knives, and his bare hands. Lethal enough, if a threat came close.

He didn't plan on letting any threats come close to Erin.

•

From the top of the hill – a low one, but the highest point in the area – there was a reasonable view to the undulating land beyond the river. Erin could make out parts of Millers Road, and a few buildings among the trees.

'There's a fair bit of timber,' she remarked. A lot, for a working property. From an environmental point of view she appreciated that, but it didn't represent the usual grazing or cropping pattern in the region.

Simon had his binoculars to his eyes. 'Yes. The top half fronting the road is mostly cleared into paddocks but there's a large area of uncleared land along the river. A few hundred acres, at a guess.'

She took her own binoculars out of her backpack and focused in for more detail. She could see the main homestead, a large single-storey house not far off the road, and some outbuildings a short distance from it. One of the paddocks fronting the road wore the green of a late-season crop – perhaps winter feed for stock. Most of the other paddocks were the dry brown of drought, with a glisten here and there of water in a dam. The dark reddish-brown scar of earthworks marked a new dam being built.

As well as the road into the homestead, a few other tracks crossed the land, one straight down from the road to stockyards and a woolshed, one from the homestead to the woolshed, meandering beside a dry creek bed before crossing it, and another leading from the woolshed to the area of scrubby timber. The land wasn't flat, though, and a low rise as well as the trees obscured her view of the area between the river and the woolshed area.

'Is that another building in the scrub?' she asked. 'I think I can see the corner of a roof, to the right of the woolshed.'

Simon shifted his binoculars slightly. 'Could be shearers' quarters. Or workers' cottages. They're often some distance from the homestead on these old properties. Harcourt Downs used to have even more land, a hundred or more years ago. Harden's Hut was part of it.'

'Gone are the days,' Erin commented. A century ago the large properties had employed many people – stockmen, domestic staff, an overseer and manager. Now most of them were run by just a married couple, with maybe one or two casual or seasonal workers during peak times.

She found the top of the waterfall through the lenses and then looked around the area for any sign of a track. Her eye caught a flicker of colour in the scrub. 'Something's moving,' she said.

'Where?'

She tried to focus, find it again. 'East of the falls. There's a rocky outcrop and it's to the right of that. It could be stock, but . . .'

Simon's binoculars were better quality than hers. 'It's not stock. A person. Maybe two.' He lowered the glasses. 'You right to go down to the river now? We might just *happen* to meet up with the neighbours.'

They were less than a kilometre from the river, and made quick time down the slope, hiking in a diagonal line towards the waterfall, the scrub not too thick or rugged. Simon led, choosing the best path, holding branches back so they didn't slap in her face. They were concealed among the edge of the trees but she could hear the waterfall when he stopped abruptly, a hand up in warning. He glanced back, a finger to his lips, and dropped to a crouch.

She hunkered down beside him, where she could see. They were about one hundred metres from the top of the falls. Four people stood on the other side of the river, near where the water flowed in narrow channels between the flat rocks. A woman, holding the hand of a child, a girl of maybe five or six. A youth in a shirt and faded jeans. And another slight figure, a little shorter than the youth, in a long top over blue pants, hair and face hidden by a hat.

Simon had his binoculars out again and had inched forward although she hadn't been aware of him moving. A commando. He'd have done this kind of surveillance for years.

She leaned forward. 'I'll go say hello,' she whispered.

He shook his head, signalled that he'd go.

To meet a woman and a few kids in the wilderness? She vetoed that idea by holding up an emphatic palm. 'I'm in uniform and harmless. You're neither.' In jeans and a dark t-shirt, his face grim, he was all soldier, alert and dangerous, and he would have scared *her* off if she didn't already know how his eyes crinkled when he smiled.

He conceded eventually with a bare nod. 'I'll be watching,' he muttered. 'Signal if you need me.'

She'd brought her small camera, and she took it from her pack before she moved quietly through the trees. She made her way forward a short distance from Simon before she came out into the open, using a rough goat track along the edge of the river.

With the water low, the woman and smaller child easily rock-hopped across the river, following the two teenagers, who slowed to give the child a hand across one of the wider channels. None of them saw Erin approaching.

The route from the lookout to the waterfall had been so well trodden and cleared by the police and SES two nights before that it was no longer overgrown, and the teenagers headed down it, into the trees and out of sight. The woman paused with the child at the falls, trying to see down without going too close to the edge. She gripped the girl's hand. When she turned, about to follow the teenagers, she saw Erin and stopped.

Erin waved a hand and gave her a broad smile. 'Hello! Beautiful day, isn't it?'

The woman gave a slight nod, as if she wasn't certain whether it was a beautiful day or not. Or whether she should be talking to National Parks rangers who strolled up out of the bush.

Erin approached them, maintaining a comfortable, relaxed pace. As she came closer, she thought she recognised the woman as the one she'd seen returning to the pop-up shop yesterday afternoon. Slim, dark-haired, similar age to herself. She certainly recognised the signs of stress and worry in her eyes. If she was one of the Simple Bliss people, she'd missed out on the bliss. So had the child, who chewed her thumb and eyed Erin as though she was an alien with four arms. They had to be part of the group – their clothes were similar to the ones Erin had seen at the shop. Plain fabrics and basic cuts with simple decorative bands.

'I'm Erin,' she said, with her friendliest smile. 'I'm one of the rangers. I've just been upriver checking on some fencing. Are you staying at the campground?'

'No,' the woman said. 'No, we're not. We . . . we live nearby.'

'Oh, you must be from Harcourt Downs, then. Our neighbours.' One of the advantages of being a natural blue-eyed blonde was that when she chose to pretend to be dumber than her actual IQ, people tended to believe it.

'Um . . . yes. But we call the land Serenity Hill now.'

'Serenity Hill? That's a lovely name.' Damn but her facial muscles were going to ache tomorrow from all this smiling. 'Much nicer than Harcourt. Hey, I met this girl, Willow, yesterday. She said she lives up this way. Is she your sister or something?'

'Willow? Willow . . . yes, she's a . . . sister. We live in . . . a small community. At Serenity Hill.'

Although Erin assumed the woman to be in her mid-thirties, apprehension or lack of confidence clearly made her nervous and uncertain.

'Are those your kids that went down the track there?' she persisted. 'We'd better catch up with them because some of the fencing went in a landslide. The boss wants me to keep it closed but people keep ignoring the signs and leaving the gate open.'

Erin kept up the easy chatter as they walked together along the track. 'You said you live in a community? That's great. I'm a big believer in escaping the rat race and getting closer to nature. That's why I do this job. Although the bureaucracy and government red tape drives me mad at times, you know? *So* much reporting and paperwork we have to do. It's mental.'

'That's terrible,' the woman said, and although she sounded genuine her words were hesitant, as if she wasn't sure how to respond. 'It sounds very stressful.'

'Yeah, it is. Sometimes I think about chucking the job in.' And there was a big lie, but she was making up her role as she went along and it was going to have to stray from the truth to be convincing for what she had in mind. 'Money's not everything, is it?'

'No, it isn't. Money doesn't heal the spirit.' The woman spoke quietly, the words heartfelt but without Willow's passion and enthusiasm.

They were getting close to the place where Erin had belayed down the cliff two nights ago, and she could see the teenagers ahead, standing a good distance back from the edge. She needed to mention the idea of visiting the community before they reached the kids.

'Willow gave me a flyer about visiting a community, retreating for a few days. That's your place, is it?'

'Yes.' Despite the opening, the woman didn't move in for the hard sell.

Erin had to push the point. 'Is it worth it? Because I'm due for some days off and, I don't know, I've been so restless lately. I want something, something to be different in my life, but I don't know what. So I was thinking about it all last night.'

The woman stopped walking and told the child to go ahead to join the others. She watched while the teenagers each took one of the girl's hands, keeping her between them as they sat down on the rock, metres away from the edge. Only then did she turn to Erin.

'Forgive me, please, for not being more welcoming. I'm a little distracted. One of my friends was the woman who . . . who . . . fell here two nights ago.'

Interesting that the woman at the house last night had denied knowing either of the women, but Sybilla was this woman's friend.

'I'm so sorry about your friend,' Erin said, glad she could speak with total honesty about that.

But the woman gave a slight shake of her head and tried to smile. 'I shouldn't be sad, as she has found pure bliss. But it was a . . . a shock.'

Breaking one's neck smashing into rocks forty metres down a cliff came nowhere near bliss, in Erin's opinion. But if she was going to visit the community, she didn't want any of them to know she'd seen either Hayley or Sybilla. More lies and half-truths. 'I heard about it, of course. The police have set up just next door to our office in Goodabri. I wasn't working yesterday, but I gather it was an accident? That she maybe slipped on a wet rock?'

'Is that what the police are saying?'

'I don't know. That's what my boss reckoned. He was furious because he thought we'd let people up there. Health and safety nut, he is.' *Forgive me that slight on your character, Mal,* she said silently. Health and safety nut, yes. Furious? Never. Although he might be if he found out what she planned. And he would be wounded if he found out how easily she could lie. 'But you being her friend, you could ask the police. I've met the detective – he seems reasonable enough. For a cop, anyway. Detective Sergeant Fraser. Steve Fraser.'

The woman stilled and all colour drained from her face. 'Steve Fraser?' she repeated, in barely more than a whisper.

Just what the hell had Steve – or his namesake – done to her? Erin couldn't imagine him mistreating anyone. Annoying them, yes. Mistreating? She doubted it. 'It's a common enough name,' she said. 'Maybe not the Steve you're thinking of?'

218

'Perhaps.' The woman didn't seem convinced but she shook herself out of her dazed state. She glanced over at the kids and called out, 'Tristan! Jasmine! Lily! Time to go!'

The kids scrambled to their feet immediately. The woman held out her hand to Erin with a strained smile. 'It's good to meet you, Erin. I hope we'll meet again.'

No mention of the community, no encouragement to visit, but Erin was grateful for the breakthrough in friendliness. Erin took her hand to shake it and then clasped her other hand over it. 'I hope we will meet again, too,' she said, holding the woman's gaze to emphasise her sincerity. 'And I am sorry about your friend. Be gentle with yourself.'

She wanted to ask her name but the kids reached them then, the youngest one tugging at the woman's top to get her attention. The woman lifted the girl onto her hip, and with a simple 'Goodbye,' began to walk back the way they'd come.

Erin got her first proper look at the two teenagers as they passed her on the track. The lad in jeans gave her a hard stare as he went by. The other one followed him, turning her head to smile shyly at Erin. A girl's face, under the cloth hat. A girl's face with wisps of brown hair framing her cheeks. No longer a child, not yet a woman.

A girl's face that looked just like Hayley's drawings of her daughter.

CHAPTER 11

He waited until the woman and kids were back across the river and out of sight before he joined Erin on the track in the scrub. Watching from out of earshot had strained his patience. Given Erin's animated face and speech, the woman's evident reticence raised questions and he itched to know what had been said. He also wanted to both hug Erin and shake her for standing near a cliff with four strangers, when the lad in particular had been casting unfriendly sideways looks at her; he could easily have rushed her and pushed her over, or struck her with a rock and rolled her over, or tried any one of fifty other ways of harming her.

On an intellectual level he knew she worked in isolated places like this alone most days and was perfectly capable of facing down drunkards, arseholes and illegal shooters. On a gut level, though, he couldn't be entirely complacent about it, when two women had died and someone had torched his house. On an emotional level . . . On an emotional level he was screwed, well and truly.

'The bliss group is definitely at Harcourt, and Sybilla was a friend of the woman's,' Erin summarised as they began the hike back to the truck. 'She's not happy, and I don't think it's just grief for her friend. She was nervous, and even though I asked about visiting, she didn't try to persuade me at all.'

'I saw she was edgy. Frightened, I'd have said. Although not of you.'

'Just how close were you?'

'Twenty metres. If that.' More like ten, some of the time.

She laughed, not quite comfortably. 'Remind me never to play hide and seek with you.'

'You'd lose,' he said, to keep it light. The afternoon was wearing on, they still had a kilometre or more to hike, and his spine prickled between his shoulder blades as though someone had a laser pointing right at him.

'Did you see the girl?' she asked, after they'd walked in silence for several minutes.

'The older one? Yes.' He'd been taking photos of the lad when she'd looked directly his way. With the powerful zoom on his compact camera, he'd looked straight into her eyes. Hayley's eyes.

He took the camera from the pocket on his pack and, slowing his pace, flicked through to one of the photos he'd taken. He passed the camera to Erin. She stopped to look at it properly. 'It is her, isn't it?' she said. 'Hayley's daughter.'

Hayley's child. Pretty and lively and *real*, so much more real now he'd seen her than in the drawings he'd never quite convinced his mind to accept as truth. Real and smiling and showing no evidence of grief despite being at the place where Sybilla had died, someone she must have known. And despite her mother's murder.

'I'm trying to look on the bright side,' Erin said. 'At least we know where she is, and she doesn't look unhappy or as though she's being mistreated.'

'No.' They started walking again. 'Do you think it's possible she doesn't know? About Hayley?'

'That they haven't told her? I don't know. The woman didn't mention Hayley at all, and I couldn't ask. I didn't want her to know that I'd seen either of them.'

'Why?' She didn't answer immediately and there was only one reason he could think of. 'Shit, Erin, you're not thinking about going in there?'

Her shrug answered the question. 'The person Steve spoke to last night denied knowing Hayley or her child. It might be a way to find out more about the girl and her situation. But let's just see what Steve's found, okay? Maybe he's solved the whole thing this afternoon.'

Simon hoped, but didn't believe it. Unless any of the fingerprints matched a known criminal who happened to be walking around free in the district, or a witness who'd seen everything came forward, then the police so far had more dead ends than leads.

Not much point in trying to talk Erin out of her crazy idea right now, though. He wouldn't give her time to come up with arguments and reasons or to talk herself into a corner. And he'd use the time himself to come up with a barrage of logic and facts that didn't involve his own cold fear for her safety.

•

Erin parked the work truck behind the National Parks building in Goodabri and transferred her pack and SES bag into her own ute, left there last night, before she pushed open the unlocked back door of the office. She'd followed Simon back from the park, and heard him make a brief comment to Mal in the office before the front door buzzer signalled his exit.

'He's gone next door,' Mal told her when she walked into the main office. 'Is everything okay?'

'As much as it can be, in the circumstances,' she told him. 'We went for a hike up around Harden's Hut. I figured he needed to get away from things for a few hours.'

'I hope it helped. Must be tough on him. Listen, you should take next week off. You've got heaps of time off in lieu owing and now Jo's back we can cope.'

As if he'd let Jo go out on her own or work anything like a full load. But Jo could fight her own battles. 'I might take a few days, thanks, Mal. How about I give you a call Tuesday afternoon or Wednesday, see how things are going?'

Tuesday should give her plenty of time. If she went to Serenity Hill tomorrow, it surely wouldn't take more than a day or so to suss out the situation. She just needed to find out about Hayley's daughter – Jasmine or Lily – and then the police could do whatever was necessary. Maybe they were worried over nothing. Maybe the girl's father was there and was a perfectly decent man who loved his daughter, and Hayley's murder was a random crime, and Sybilla really had just slipped on rocks . . . and maybe pigs flew north for the winter.

In the police room, Simon straddled a chair beside Steve's makeshift desk, the two of them deep in conversation. Aaron, Tess and Matt all worked at laptops. Aaron leapt to his feet when he saw her and took a chair over to Steve's table for her. Both men acknowledged her with a nod and Simon signalled to Steve to continue talking.

'We've only got preliminary post-mortem results in,' Steve said. 'The official report will take a while, after blood tests and such are done. Likely cause of death – well, we knew that. Not a lot of internal bleeding, so it was fairly quick. A small mercy, I guess.'

Simon nodded, his face carefully expressionless.

'They've also confirmed that she, well, she had at least one vaginal birth. So that confirms a baby. But the thing is, I've had Aaron chasing records and social security. There's nothing under Hayley's name or Medicare number. She's claimed no benefits of any sort under her name for more than thirteen years. No doctor's visits, no baby added to her card, no family benefit supplement, no back-to-school allowance, nothing. And the child's not registered under Hayley's name – or yours.'

Simon swallowed. 'She must have been using another name.'

She had to have, surely. Erin couldn't imagine a woman with a history of miscarriage not consulting a doctor at least once during her pregnancy. And few women did a home birth without at least a midwife. The Medicare benefits applied to all citizens, regardless of income, so there should be a claim somewhere, for something.

'Yeah, that's what we figure. We'll run fingerprints and Leah's going to ask the specialists for facial recognition scanning. We'll also check interstate, but the Medicare and social security stuff is federal, so it doesn't matter which state she was in, activity would still show. If it was there.'

'We saw the girl,' Simon said abruptly. 'We were up at the waterfall this afternoon and a woman and kids came down from Harcourt. Erin spoke with them.'

Erin quickly described the gist of her conversation with the woman. 'I didn't get her name, I'm sorry. But she definitely said that the woman who'd fallen was a friend of hers, although she didn't refer to Sybilla by name, either. She did call the kids, though – Tristan, Jasmine and Lily. I'm not sure which of the girls was which.'

Simon pulled his camera out of his jeans pocket. 'I've got some photographs. A few close-ups with the zoom. They're reasonable.'

'That little thing has a decent zoom?' Steve asked. 'What is it – special military issue?'

A trace of amusement briefly softened the hard lines of Simon's face as he removed the memory card from the camera. 'No. Just top-of-the-range commercially available. And I wasn't all that far away from the subjects. Do you want copies of these?'

Erin hated having people lean over her shoulder when she was working on the computer, so while Steve inserted the card into his laptop and they started going through the images, she stood up from the hard plastic chair and stretched her stiffening muscles.

Hayley's bag and its contents were laid out on a table nearby – the book of drawings, an envelope addressed to Hayley in Simon's handwriting, a half-finished embroidery of butterflies, and a small fabric-covered object about the size of her palm. The book, the letter and the bag itself were in evidence bags, but the embroidery and the fabric-covered object weren't.

Steve saw the direction of her gaze. 'Forensics weren't sure they'd get anything from those and they're swamped so they're prioritising. You're the sewing expert. Is there anything noteworthy or significant about them?'

She picked up the last. A needle book, handmade. Inside the reinforced cloth covers were pockets with a needle threader, lengths of embroidery thread, and a small pair of scissors. The four felt 'pages' of the book held several needles and a dozen or so pins. A practical, pretty sewing accessory.

As she flipped to the back, she noticed a slight, squarish bulge beneath the fabric of the cover. She rubbed her thumb over it to feel the shape. A couple of centimetres in size. What and why? Why insert something inside the cover? She could see no purpose for it. The stiffening inside the cover, whatever it was, was sturdy enough and without any bends or holes.

As she felt over it again, she recognised the size – about the same size as the camera memory card that Steve had just put into his laptop.

She turned the needle book over in her hands, studying the decorative stitching around the edge that disguised the seams. There it was – a three-centimetre section where the thread didn't quite match the rest.

She held the needle book out to Steve. 'I might have found something.'

'Where?'

'In here. There's something under the fabric, and the stitching's been re-done. I think it's a memory card.' She showed him the bulge and he ran a blunt-nailed finger over it.

'Jeez. It is an SD card. Feel the shape of it.' He outlined it with his finger. 'See the cut-off corner?' He passed it to Simon. 'What do you reckon?'

'It has to be. She hid it in there, where no one would think to look.'

'Can you undo it?' Steve asked Erin. 'Can you get it out without ripping the thing apart?'

She took the scissors and snipped the first thread, gently drawing it out. A computer memory card. In a needle book. That had been hidden in a bean bag. And whoever had murdered Hayley had searched and trashed Simon's computers.

It only took a minute to unpick the short section of stitches, and she manoeuvred the card towards the opening without putting her own fingerprints on it. 'You can get it out now,' she told Steve, handing the needle book back to him.

He pulled on a latex glove to remove the card and then paused, holding it in the air in front of his laptop screen, which still displayed an image of Hayley's daughter. 'Dammit. I just want to stick this into the laptop and find out what's on it. But it better go to Forensics so they can take a binary copy of it first and preserve everything on it. Including prints. Shit.'

'How long is that going to take?' Simon asked.

Steve reached across to a nearby table for an evidence bag and dropped the card inside. 'Crime scene officers have gone back to Inverell. I'll get someone to drive it over there now. If we're lucky, we might find out what's on it tomorrow.'

Tomorrow. Erin's spirits sank. But it was already almost six o'clock and Inverell was over an hour away. 'If we're not lucky?'

'They might have to send it to Tamworth or Sydney. I don't know. Aaron, get on to Sandy Cunningham and find out where he wants this. Then get it there, pronto.'

Steve's mobile buzzed and he glanced at the screen before answering. 'Hello, Leah.' He wandered out of the room to take the call, but only paced down the short passage towards the back door, nowhere near out of hearing.

His side of the conversation was mostly monosyllabic at first, punctuated with a few curses. 'We've just found a data card. No, I'll have to send it to be processed. Okay, I'll keep you posted.'

He came back and slumped into his chair. 'She's been called up to another homicide, north of Coffs Harbour. A woman in her thirties. Daughter of a prominent local businessman.'

'Any connection to this case?' Simon asked.

Steve dragged a hand through his hair. 'Who knows? No white dress, but she was stabbed. Leah's on her way there now. We might know more tomorrow, but it's a few hours from here and most likely unconnected. Listen, guys, go. Go to the pub for a meal. Go home or wherever you're staying and get some sleep. I'll let you know if there's any news.'

•

In the process of closing up the office, Malcolm apologised for having to dash off for a family dinner. But he didn't go until he'd reissued an invitation, yet again, for Simon to stay with him and Susan.

'Thanks, but I'll be fine,' Simon said.

'You know you're welcome to stay in my spare room again,' Erin said quietly after Mal had left. She'd been quiet since the phone call from Haddad. And since she'd found the memory card. They'd had a long day and it showed in the strain around her eyes.

He hoped he wasn't about to hurt or offend her now. 'I know that, Erin. You know that I appreciate it. But I'm just going to go bush tonight. There's a lot to think about and perhaps I'll have a clearer head out alone in the starlight.'

'I understand,' she said, and he thought she probably did. She didn't attempt to talk him out of it or insist that he stay with her. 'You've got your sat phone and your radio? Good. Give me a call in the morning.' She smiled, not her full grin but enough to make her eyes shine a little. 'Preferably not to tell me how beautiful the sunrise is. I think I'll be sleeping through it rather than watching it tomorrow.'

He saw her off in her ute without succumbing to the temptation to kiss her soundly. The setting sun cast its last glow and he watched her taillights diminish along the road until she turned a corner. He longed to go with her, to go to her cottage and shut out the world and spend the night, all the nights, with her. His body burned with unsated need and desire but if he gave in . . . He blew out a long, slow breath. Wasn't going to happen. He had work to do tonight and he needed her safely out of the way to do it.

He borrowed some camping equipment from the storeroom and loaded it into his vehicle. Might as well make Harden's Hut a tad more comfortable. Not that he planned to spend much time in it.

Before he left Goodabri and phone reception he dialled a number he hadn't called for a year or more. He thought it might ring out but a gruff voice finally answered.

'Gabe. It's Simon.'

'You okay? Cops called me the other night.'

'Yeah. Thanks.' They'd served alongside each other for more than a decade so he didn't beat around the bush. 'I need a favour. A big one.'

Gabe never bothered with niceties. 'Ask.'

'I need your help for a few days.'

'You still in Strathnairn?'

'Goodabri. East of Strath.'

'Yeah, can do. When?'

'As soon as possible.' Tomorrow, Simon hoped. Tomorrow so Gabe could keep an eye on Harcourt and the girl while he dissuaded Erin from going out there.

Silence for a moment before Gabe said, 'Give me three hours.'

Simon's tension levels shifted down a notch. 'Thanks. Can you bring some gear with you? My place burned down and I don't have much.'

'Tell me what we're doing and what you need and I'll bring it.'

'Surveillance,' Simon answered. 'Large rural property, buildings spread out over hectares. I need to know who's there and what's going on. And I need to ensure protection for a thirteen-year-old girl who's with the group living there.' And for a woman who was likely going to go there tomorrow to infiltrate the group to find Hayley's daughter. He still planned on trying to talk Erin out of going. But if she went,

Gabe's presence would mean they could cover the entire place twenty-four hours a day. Of all the guys he'd served with, he trusted Gabe the most.

'This got something to do with your missus?' Gabe asked.

'Yeah. Someone murdered her. In my house.'

'So that's why the cops asked where you'd been. Who's the kid?'

'Her daughter. Possibly mine.'

When he disconnected the call he mentally corrected the statement. *Probably* his. He'd watched her out there at the falls. There was nothing he could see of himself in her face, but her tall, lean physique bore little resemblance to Hayley's petite, almost fragile figure. It didn't mean Hayley hadn't had a lover, but it narrowed the odds.

In any case, it didn't matter who the girl's father was. Simon had tried to protect Hayley when she was still a teenager. He'd protect her daughter if she needed it, too, whatever the girl's genetic inheritance.

•

Simon had remade the guest bed, neater than it had been before, hung his towel in the bathroom and washed and put away their few dishes from breakfast. He'd left almost no sign that he'd slept under her roof, eaten across the kitchen table from her, held her tightly in his arms for far too brief a time.

And if Erin spent much time remembering that, she'd never get anything done.

She stripped off her uniform in the bathroom and stepped under the low-pressure spluttering of the shower. Hot water to ease her tired body, or cool to energise her? She went for cool and made it quick, washing off the sweat and dust of the day's hike. The energising she'd hoped for didn't happen, but at least it wasn't soporific.

After she'd towel-dried her hair and pulled on jeans and a t-shirt, she returned to the kitchen. She'd made it to Strathnairn's supermarket before it closed for the day, so her fridge and cupboards weren't quite as bare as they'd been. With too much on her mind to cook from scratch, she put a pre-packaged lasagne into the microwave and tore up some lettuce leaves to go with it. Lettuce made it healthy. Almost. But there'd been more salad than chicken in the bread roll Simon had brought her for lunch, and she wouldn't eat the entire block of chocolate she'd picked up at the supermarket this evening.

'Balanced diet,' she muttered to the silent kitchen. 'Something healthy, something unhealthy.' Talking to an empty room probably didn't rank high on the healthy side.

She ate at the kitchen table with her laptop in front of her and the Simple Bliss flyer beside it. The flyer had a web address on it and she typed it into her browser. Saturday night in Strathnairn and it seemed everyone was downloading movies or playing online games, because the browser icon spun for minutes before the page began to load. Rural living meant overloaded network access and no broadband. She'd eaten half the large serve of lasagne before the page appeared fully on the screen.

The site was basic, with a few attractive images of the landscape, the house, vegetable gardens and food. *At Serenity Hill you'll be embraced by the beauty and rhythms of nature, and discover the truths of your spirit . . . In this sanctuary of peace and tranquillity you will find healing for the wounds of the soul and reconnect with your deepest bliss . . .*

'Promises, promises,' Erin murmured. Yet for an instant it truly did appeal. Healing for the wounds of the soul? Oh, she had some great black scars she wished could be healed. If someone could just wave a magic wand, make her past fade to nothing, make her clean and whole and honourable . . . Yep, there went the flying pigs again.

They were serious about encouraging visitors, with online bookings available, and she clicked through to the form. Payment options included credit and debit cards, direct deposit, and – 'for those who prefer' – cash payment on arrival. Nice untraceable cash. That option did little to enhance Erin's faith in the group, but it did mean she didn't have to book and pay now. No, she'd wait until morning, see what news there was, and she could withdraw cash from the ATM in Strathnairn if she decided to go through with it.

After she'd washed her dinner dishes she packed a bag with clothes and toiletries, just in case.

•

While he waited for Gabe, Simon went up to the pub for a meal, running the gauntlet of concerned queries and commiserations as he carried his drink and table number out to the dimly lit far corner of the beer garden. Everyone in Goodabri knew – about Hayley, about the fire. But other than expressing their sympathies and offering support, they left him to himself, exactly the way he wanted it.

He sat with his back to the brick wall of the beer garden, with a clear view through the glass doors back into the dining area. When Fraser arrived, he didn't appear to see him in the shadows, and Simon watched the detective lean on the bar and use that relaxed charm to pump the waitress for information. Fraser was clearly familiar with small towns, understood how they worked and that people who worked in pubs often had the best information. Simon couldn't hear him, but he could imagine: *The hippy mob from up on Millers Road – know anything about them? Do they ever come in here?*

He'd thought Fraser hadn't spotted him, but once he'd paid for his meal order and finished talking with the waitress he came straight outside.

'Carrie says you're not looking for company. Thought I'd ask if you wanted an update.'

Simon pointed at the chair opposite. 'Sit.'

Fraser put his Coke and a packet of crisps on the table and dragged out the chair. 'Nothing linking the vic at Coffs with our case, but her daddy's well connected and demanding a five-star investigation and the media's all over it, so Haddad's there, for who knows how long.'

Simon stayed silent while Fraser took several mouthfuls of his drink.

'The only conclusive thing from Sybilla's post mortem,' he continued, 'is that she fell from a height and died from those injuries. Which we knew already.'

'What about the girl? Can't you just go back out to Harcourt and ask again? We know that she's there.'

'Look, mate, the woman we spoke to last night has already filed a complaint about being disturbed late at night and harassed. And I've got no indisputable evidence that Hayley has a child or was even there, and neither you nor Erin saw any evidence that the girl was abused or in danger. Your unauthorised surveillance photos are of a happy girl in a nice family group. She looks a little like the girl in a sketchbook Hayley had, but it's not proof. So just at the moment my hands are tied.' He tore open the packet of crisps and took one, then pushed the packet towards Simon in invitation.

Simon ignored it. 'You're doing *nothing*?'

'No.' Fraser remained calm, taking no offence. 'Aaron, Tess and I are digging up everything we can find on the company that owns the place, and on Joshua Kristos, and we're combing the records for any trace of Hayley or Sybilla. We've not found much yet. Carrie's given me a name for one of the women up there, though. Mary Saint, she thinks it was. Bought a meal on a credit card a few days ago and Carrie chatted with her. Probably the woman I spoke with. I'll see what I can find on her.'

'How long is it going to take to have enough to go in there?'

Fraser leaned back in his chair and took his time answering. 'Mate, it's more than forty-eight hours since Hayley was found. We don't have a suspect. We don't have a motive. We don't have a witness, and we hardly know anything about the victim. Be prepared for it to take some time.'

'Erin's planning to go there tomorrow.'

'Is she? I did wonder about that.'

Carrie brought over their meals – plates loaded with steak, chunky chips and vegetables. Fraser exchanged some quips with her but she was busy and didn't loiter. Simon waited until she was almost back inside before resuming the discussion as if it hadn't been interrupted.

'Can you stop Erin from going?' he asked.

'Can you stop Erin from doing anything she's decided on?' Fraser countered, and Simon's fist itched to punch the man's grin from his face.

Trouble was, he was right. 'I'm not the law,' Simon pointed out coolly. 'Can't you warn her against interfering in a police investigation or something?'

'I could. Maybe I will. But to be honest, Nick and I have discussed putting someone in there. If things drag out, we'll do it. I can't put anyone local in. They already know Tess is a cop, and they'd spot any other local cops quickly enough. It takes time to get someone in from the undercover squad, brief them, create a persona and get all the backup in place.'

'You're not seriously thinking of encouraging Erin?'

'No, I'm not.' There was no laughter in Fraser's face now. 'But if she's determined to do it, get her to call me first. If I can't dissuade her, I'll ask her to come to a briefing on Monday morning. That way she'll only be there tomorrow night.' He started carving into his steak, but with a telling, sideways glance he added, 'I do want to know how many people are there, how the place is set up, that kind of thing.'

'And if someone else could get that information for you?'

'Well, I couldn't possibly encourage anyone to trespass, let alone invade people's privacy by engaging in unauthorised surveillance, could I?' Fraser said, choirboy innocence positively shining in his face. Until he grinned.

Although he wasn't hungry, Simon tucked into his meal, knowing his body needed the fuel. He'd get that information for Fraser by morning. Erin had said she planned to sleep in, take it easy after the last few days. Simon intended to be back in Goodabri well before she was up and about, and between Fraser's investigation and his own, they should have enough information so that she wouldn't need to go.

CHAPTER 12

Two days past full, the moon still gave good light over the land – and also deep shadows for concealment. On the shadow side of a large machinery shed, Simon checked around both corners, and then signalled Gabe over from the cover of the scrub. He crossed the ten metres of open space, a silent, dark-clothed figure. In the pre-dawn darkness, nothing else moved.

In addition to the machinery shed, Simon counted four other structures on this part of the property. An old timber woolshed; the long shearers' quarters with eight individual rooms opening onto a veranda and a larger room at the end; and two farm workers' cottages. He could see no dogs and no vehicles by the cottages, and the windows were dark. An old truck the size of a removalists' van was parked beside the machinery shed, but the two sets of large double doors on the shed were closed and locked with chains and padlocks.

He signalled Gabe to go to the right, to the two cottages, and watched while he crossed to the first one. With Gabe in place, he used the truck for cover to make his way to the back of the shearers' quarters.

Each room had a casement window in the back wall, three of them propped open a few inches. He flipped down his compact night-vision goggles and risked a glance through one of the closed windows. A double bed took up most of the small room. No heat sources.

A loud rasp broke the silence. And again, gurgling into a snore. Simon hunkered down against the wall as the guttural masculine snore two rooms along settled into a rhythm. But then a drowsy voice mumbled, 'Turn over,' and with a squeak of bedsprings, the snoring stopped.

That made two people in room three. He checked the other rooms. Two more empty ones, but the remaining four each had two people. Ten, total.

He made his way to the woolshed and ducked into the sheep pens beneath it. The earthy smell of dust and old manure filled his nostrils. He remained motionless as small sounds came through the timber floor. Soft footsteps crossed above him. A whimper, winding to a little cry. Whispered, soothing words he couldn't quite make out. The footsteps moved away, barely audible, and quiet settled again.

He moved out of the pens, then stepped out from underneath the shed. The only access to the interior of the shed was up a flight of timber stairs, old, probably full of creaks, and bathed in moonlight. The few corrugated-iron window shutters were a good three metres up, too high to reach. No way to easily see inside.

Grey light seeped into the darkness from the east. Not much time left. He could just see Gabe crouching under one of the cottage windows, and he gestured to him to return to the scrub.

They met at the edge of the tree line and moved fifty metres into their cover, well away from the buildings.

'At least eight in each of the cottages,' Gabe reported.

'Ten in the shearers' quarters. I don't know how many in the woolshed, but there are people in there. Maybe a kid.'

'Dawn's coming. D'you want me to hang around, see what happens?'

'Yeah. I'll go up to the homestead. Meet you back at the river thirty after sunrise.'

Simon moved off, keeping to the tree cover to loop around to the main house without crossing too much open ground. Low in the western sky, the moonlight dimly flickered among a thousand mottled tree shadows. He used the night-vision goggles so he could keep his speed up in the darkness.

On either side of the single-storey homestead were large, open paddocks, but immediately around the house a well-established landscaped garden provided a couple of potential vantage points. If he could get to them, unseen. Two men patrolled around the house, each with his own loop around back, front, and then a figure-of-eight around the garage to one side and the garden sheds on the other. Amateurs, using easily discernible patterns. Foolish amateurs, using patterns that had them meet up on each round, where they stopped for a chat.

Simon used that weak spot in their surveillance to slip past the garden shed to an adjacent cluster of callistemon bushes that provided him with excellent cover, overlooking the garden to the house.

The dawn light was silver now, the darkness receding and stars fading. The two guards did another loop. Not young men, maybe in their late forties or early fifties, but thin and reasonably fit in appearance. Neither of them carried a firearm that he could see. One held a baton, the other balanced a metre-long staff on his shoulder.

Simon wanted to know what they protected, but he could see no easy way to get to the house, and the light increased with every minute.

At the end of their next round, the two men consulted, looking to the east. Neither of them glanced at a watch, or a phone. But one then walked across to the back of the garage to where a large bell hung from a frame jutting off the roof. He pulled the bell rope six slow times, each pull sending a clear sonorous ring across the landscape.

A wake-up bell? It would have been quite audible down at the woolshed. In the east, a pink-gold glow edged the sky. Before the sun's rays broke over the horizon, the French doors facing onto the veranda opened. Six women, all dressed in sleeveless white dresses like Hayley's and Sybilla's, proceeded in single file down the veranda steps, followed by two younger girls, teenagers, in similar dresses, though blue, and two youths in blue trousers and sleeveless tops. The two guards fell into step behind the lads.

With minimal movement, Simon drew out his camera and zoomed in on the faces. The woman who'd spoken with Erin at the waterfall yesterday was third in the line. The second of the two girls was Hayley's daughter, with the lad from yesterday immediately behind her. Simon set the video function on the camera running, kneeling awkwardly to get a clear view through the foliage and hold it steady.

The silent procession crossed to the centre of the lawn, then spiralled around and joined hands to form two circles – an inner circle of the four males, enclosed by the circle of eight women. The leading woman, who appeared to be the oldest – perhaps in her forties – faced due east, and as the first rays of sunlight beamed across the paddock, she began to sing. An ethereal, wordless song with a fluid melody that glided over notes that never seemed expected. When she began the second repetition, the other women joined in, and the men began a lower harmony that wove through the women's voices. On the third repetition, they began a slow dance, the women moving anticlockwise with graceful dipping and swaying steps, the men clockwise.

It was beautiful. It was unusual. And they sang and moved with such total focus and concentration, such precision, that every nerve in Simon's neck prickled.

It wasn't so much that they chanted and danced to the rising sun that unsettled him. Plenty of cultures performed similar rituals, and although he'd ceased believing in any form of religion or mysticism decades ago, when out in the wilderness alone even he'd been tempted to formally greet the sun and acknowledge the beginning of the day. All faiths and cultures had rituals: the singing of hymns, the rite of communion, farewelling the dead. But in none of those rituals – even the solemn ramp ceremony for a fallen comrade – had he witnessed this total unity of voice and movement. That perfect unison had to be the result of commitment, practice and discipline.

As the sun rose above the horizon, their steps slowed and stilled, the notes died away, and only the birds twittering in the trees impinged on the silence. After several heartbeats, the singers broke into smiles. The men's circle dropped hands first. The two older men approached each woman in turn, and kissed them on both cheeks with some deference before kissing each of the two girls the same way. The young lads did the same before they joined the older men, laughing with them as they all traipsed inside, just a bunch of guys together. The eight women hugged, laughed, chatted, then wandered inside as well.

As the last one went through the door, Simon slipped behind the shed and made a dash across the open ground to the trees, hoping the group was too focused on whatever they did immediately after their ritual to be looking out windows. No one shouted or raised an alarm, and he made quick time working his way back through the scrub towards the river. He was almost there when he saw a change in the foliage ahead – not the muted browns and greens of the bush, but a denser green.

The plants grew taller than him, leafy and healthy. There were a couple of acres under cultivation, and he walked around the plot, mapping the coordinates on his GPS. Two varieties, almost ready for harvest. He snapped a few photos before jogging on to meet Gabe.

'At least fifteen kids plus a couple of women in the woolshed,' Gabe reported when he arrived at the rendezvous point in a rocky overhang by the river. 'Eight men in one cottage, ten women in the other, plus ten people from the shearers' quarters. That's how many I counted coming out and doing a chanting thing at sunrise. They were all still at it when I left. Chanting, dancing in circles. They all knew the ceremony – it seemed automatic.'

Simon whistled low under his breath. 'More than forty there all up?'

'Yeah. Kids ranged from tots to maybe teens. Two girls looking after them, maybe only sixteen, seventeen years old. How many people did you see at the main house?'

From where they hunkered under the overhang Simon could see up and down the river, and he kept scanning for movement while they talked. 'Six women, two men. Four teens – two girls and two youths.'

'Was Hayley's kid one of them?'

His throat rasped with dryness. 'Yeah. I'm pretty sure. The two men were patrolling the house. No firearms that I could see, but batons, maybe knives.'

'Guards?'

'They deferred to the women so protection, not prison guards. Probably sensible since two women have died. They all did the chanting up there too. What kind of clothes did you see? What colours?'

'Mostly browns, different shades. Some blue, some green. Trousers, tops, long caftan things. The young girls with the kids both had light blue dresses. Knee-length.'

'So did the two girls up at the house. The women were in white.'

'Some kind of uniform?'

'Possibly.' Ceremony, symbolism, regulation, hierarchy – this mob had it all. He just had to work out the codes. He took a swig from his water bottle and then slipped it back into its carrier on his pack. 'I have to head into town. I'll be back this afternoon. Look out for a sheltered spot. I want to keep watch tonight, but they're forecasting storms.'

•

Erin groaned and pulled the pillow over her head. Early morning wake-up in the bush – if it wasn't the kookaburras chortling, it was the damn possum tap-dancing on the roof. This morning the rosellas skittered back and forth on the corrugated iron directly above her bedroom, picking up seeds from a nearby tree. They might as well have been wearing hobnail boots.

Squinting one eye open, Erin looked at the window. Gold light angled in through the gap in the curtains. Sunrise. She rolled over to check the time on her phone. Too many dreams and not nearly enough sleep.

The rosellas did another sortie up and down the roof. And then the kookaburras decided to celebrate the new day. When the magpies began their carolling, she gave up, pushed back the blanket and dragged on a robe. Morning had definitely broken. Anyone who reckoned the bush was quiet had never lived in it.

She didn't rush, getting showered and dressing in a summer dress she rarely wore, but she still made it to Goodabri before eight o'clock. The Sunday streets were quiet, with hardly anyone up and about. She waved at Des Holder, out walking his fox terrier. Des Holder, who'd retired from building fences and now drove the school bus.

The school bus that picked up kids from Millers Road.

She parked in front of the bakery – closed on Sundays – and crossed the empty main street to the office building.

Mal wouldn't be in until ten to open the visitor centre for Sunday's short hours.

Movement behind the window blinds of the police rooms showed that someone was already at work. Tess opened the door to Erin's knock. Tess, neat and proper in uniform as always, as if she carried a spray can of starch with her. If she smiled more often they'd probably put her on recruitment posters. Erin hadn't found her unfriendly, just reserved. A woman who regarded her job seriously and who took time to relax her guard to make friends.

'I had a thought,' Erin said as Tess invited her in. 'Has anyone asked Des Holder what kids he picks up in the school bus on Millers Road?'

'I did last night. He doesn't pick up any. Well, not in that part of Millers Road.' Tess had a plunger of coffee on her desk, and she collected mugs from a tray and poured out two cups while she spoke. 'I checked with the Goodabri teachers, too, and showed them the photo of the girls, but they don't know them.'

With less than fifty kids at the school, the teachers would know them all. 'Strathnairn High?' Erin suggested, accepting the offered coffee with gratitude. 'The older girl would go there.'

Resuming her place behind her laptop Tess indicated the opposite chair for Erin. 'I've left a message for the principal. I hope she'll get back to me today. But I spoke with Emily Trasker, who teaches English, and she doesn't know the girl.'

'So they must be home-schooled.'

'Or at boarding school. A lot of rural kids board Monday to Friday. If we don't turn up anything today, I'll get on to the boarding schools in Armidale and Tamworth tomorrow.' She gestured to a notepad beside her computer with a long list of tasks, some ticked off. 'I've been on to community services, too. We're working on it, Erin.'

Erin gave her an apologetic smile. 'I should just let you do your job, hey?'

Tess's mouth almost curved into a smile. 'Yes. But if you happen to know anything about holding companies, that could be useful.'

'Can't say I do. Why?'

'From what I can find, the Harcourt Downs property is owned by Serenity Hill Proprietary Limited, which is owned by a holding company that's owned by another holding company registered in the Cayman Islands. Tax minimisation, by the looks of it. But trying to find the actual humans who own the companies is proving impossible. The few names I've found keep drawing blanks.'

'Is Joshua Kristos one of them?'

'No, he's not. But Aaron's been searching for him, and other than his website and books, he doesn't appear to exist either.'

'It's a pen name, then.'

'Yep. But even with pen names, it's not usually hard to find out the real identity. I can tell you the real names of most of my favourite authors. But we've found nothing for Joshua. Not even a photo.'

The mug was warm in Erin's hands and she took a sip of the too-strong black coffee. Tess didn't believe in weak, apparently. Or milk, or sugar.

Erin cautiously broached the topic that had been on her mind since yesterday. 'You know they invite visitors?'

Tess gave her all of her attention. 'Yes.'

'Joshua will be there today. What if I went there for a few days' retreat?'

She expected an instant objection. Tess stilled and said carefully, 'Two women who were probably part of that group have died in recent days.'

'And one of them wanted help to get her daughter out of a cult.'

In a rare sign of vulnerability, Tess briefly closed her eyes before saying, 'Yes.'

Erin had rehearsed her arguments, but she'd expected to use them with Simon or Steve. Not Tess, who wasn't telling her straight out that she shouldn't go. 'I've read some of Joshua's writings. I even downloaded one of the books last night. It all sounds reasonable on the surface, and it won't be hard to pretend to be enthusiastic.'

'Do you know how cults work?' Tess asked, a hard edge to her voice.

'I'm not an expert, but they're scams, right? Suck people in with friendliness, convince them you have what they want, and take their money.'

'And control their lives. Love bombing is just the start of it. Money is only part of it. They separate people from the outside world and use mind-control and brainwashing techniques. Obedience becomes everything. Service to the cult leader and to the cult is required. Deviation is punished by exclusion and loss of the promised love and salvation.' Tess stopped short, gulping in a breath, blowing it out deliberately as if to regain some equilibrium. She clearly had her own demons, possibly more haunting even than Erin's guilt.

'You know about cults.'

'Oh yeah, I know about cults.' Tess let her head fall back for a moment, evidently still trying to regain her composure. 'I've seen what some of them do to kids, too. Girls *and* boys. Believe me, if I could go in there today, find the kids and get them out, I would. But we've got no legal evidence yet, we don't even know for sure if the kids are in danger, and the women at the house have already complained about me, so I can't go in to find out.'

'I can,' Erin said. 'I've already made contact with two of the women, told them how interested I am in visiting the community. I've set the groundwork for running the story that I'm tired and disillusioned and pissed off with the job.'

'It could be dangerous,' Tess stressed. 'At the very least, they'll use all their tactics to convert you.'

'I know about scams. I know those tactics.' Now Erin needed courage to confess. Her heart thumped so loudly she thought Tess could surely hear it. 'My father was a con artist.

A thief, a fraud. Until I was sixteen I helped him run cons. We sold things like fake gemstones and diet pills in shopping centres and online. I sold them to my classmates at school. I know the business, all the tricks, all the manipulations. Tess, I can play roles and lie through my teeth and have people eating out of my hand. If Joshua or his followers are frauds, I'll know it.'

Tess got up and paced back and forth, hands thrust in her pockets. 'I should tell you not to do it,' she said at last, stopping in front of Erin. 'I should remind you that it could be dangerous and that the group is currently subject to a police investigation.'

'You just did. I'll consider myself warned.'

'Listen, I think we'll be in there by tomorrow, if not later today. I know Steve's as suspicious as I am and wants a reason to raid the place to find answers. We're digging as hard as we can, every angle. And we should have the contents of Hayley's memory card by lunchtime today.'

Erin set down her mug on the table and stood to face Tess. 'Then I'll go this morning, start finding out what's going on. I'll phone or come back tonight, or at the latest by tomorrow morning, to let you know what I've discovered. That'll help you plan what you need to do.'

Tess gave her a wan smile that revealed her misgivings. 'Be careful. And get out of here now before I regain my sanity or Steve comes in and talks you out of it.'

Erin had her hand on the door when Tess said her name. She looked back. The young policewoman still stood, hands in pockets, shoulders tense.

'Erin, kids who've been in cults – they won't trust easily. They don't know "normal". They believe that all outsiders are evil and they'll follow the cult leader whatever he says. They're damaged in ways you can't comprehend.'

Apprehension coiled in Erin's stomach and she didn't know whether it was because of the pain in Tess's harsh voice, or fear for the children she'd briefly met.

She swallowed against the tightness in her throat. 'I'll let you know what I find out. You and the specialists can get them out and deal with the issues.'

•

Simon hiked the couple of kilometres through the scrub back to their base camp at Harden's Hut. A fox crossed his path, a young rabbit in its jaws. A few wallabies hopped away from his approach, and an echidna curled into a tree stump, pretending it wasn't there. The sun lit a brilliant blue sky, with only wisps of cloud, but the air hung thicker, the humidity building towards the forecast storms.

Despite being out all night, he didn't stop at the hut to sleep. Sleep could come later. He'd seen no violence at Harcourt, no indication of abuse or fear, but the ceremonial rituals had troubled him. Maybe they only performed the chant and danced slowly in the circle on Sundays. Maybe it was nothing more than greeting the sun and marking the start of the new day. But Hayley had run from them, and someone had murdered her, and her daughter, who was not much more than a child, was under the influence of a group of women who dressed in white and had guards protecting them during the night.

He drove into Goodabri shortly after nine and parked behind the office building. Fraser's car was out the front, beside the local police four-wheel drive and another car.

After shooting a quick text to Erin, he rapped on the back door of the police rooms and Aaron opened it, a slice of toast in his hand. Chewing on a mouthful, he waved Simon through to the kitchen. The scent of burnt toast clogged the air, but underneath it he caught the aroma of ground coffee. He could go months without the stuff if he had to, but that only made him appreciate it more when he had it. Especially after a night out scouting a large property and observing its residents.

In the kitchen, Fraser poured a large mug of coffee from a plunger and handed it to him in greeting. 'That'll get a brain cell functioning,' he said. 'Or blow it to smithereens.'

Simon gripped the mug in his hand and inhaled. Strong, hot, black, and with a caffeine hit that would keep him going for hours.

'American cops get donuts,' Fraser continued in mock complaint as he dropped a couple of slices of bread into an ageing toaster. 'Out here in the bush, we get toast and Vegemite.

Although Tess said there's some yoghurt in the fridge, if you want to, you know, be *healthy*.'

'Toast is good,' Simon responded. Carbs for energy, and he needed energy. Maybe a loaf of it. 'Any news?'

'Not a lot to report. But the good news is I'll have the contents of that memory card within the hour. Assuming I can download it on the prehistoric wires out here. What about you?'

'Good news and bad news.'

'Give me the bad first.'

'There are more than forty people out there. Six women, two men and some teens at the homestead, the rest in the old woolshed and outbuildings at the back of the property. Including fifteen children.'

Fraser whistled. 'What kind of conditions?'

'Pretty good, from what we could see. But they all did a ceremony at sunrise, chanting and stuff. I read signs of a hierarchy – particularly with the separation of the women at the house and the others, but also clothing. Light blue dresses on at least four of the adolescent girls. And the women from the house were all in white.'

Fraser's eyebrows shot up. 'Same as Hayley and Sybilla?'

'As far as I can tell, yes. It's pretty open up there and I couldn't get as close as I wanted. They also had two guards on patrol around the house.'

That made Fraser stop stock still. 'Armed?'

'No guns. Batons. Maybe knives. We didn't see any evidence of weaponry other than that. Certainly no stockpiles of military weapons.'

Fraser visibly relaxed and turned to rescue the toast. 'Good. "We?"' he queried.

Simon grabbed a knife and buttered the slices of toast Fraser passed him while they were hot. 'My old army mate,' he explained. 'Gabe McCallum. I asked him to come up for a few days.'

'So now I've got commandos running around out there, too.' Fraser's tone was only half joking. 'Assure me that neither of you is going to go berserk.'

'He's solid. You needn't be concerned. And he won't touch firearms anymore. So, no guns.'

'I'm relying on your judgement. Make sure he knows not to get in the way.' An order, not a request. Simon respected it, because Fraser had charge of the operation and, despite his frequent levity, shouldered his responsibilities with commitment and professionalism.

'You want the good news now?'

'That wasn't the good news?'

'There's better.' Simon didn't hold back his grin. 'Nice big cannabis crop hidden in the scrub. Two varieties on at least two acres. One's possibly low-THC industrial hemp, but the other certainly isn't.'

Fraser's hoot of delight brought Tess and Aaron to the

kitchen door. 'Oh, you beauty. Best news I've heard all year. You've got the exact location, I presume?'

'Full GPS coordinates of the crop. They've got an irrigation system pumping water from the river. I'm betting they don't have a licence for the industrial hemp crop, the way it's hidden away.'

'That crop's a reason to raid, sarge,' Tess said.

'Yeah, you bet. If we don't find another reason in the computer data, we can use it. Aaron, get on to the drug squad. But tell them not to go rushing in there straightaway. We need to coordinate.'

Simon wolfed down his toast and checked his phone while the three officers discussed possible strategies. No message from Erin. No email, either.

'Anyone heard from Erin?' he asked when there was a break in the discussion.

Aaron looked blank and Fraser shook his head. 'Not yet.'

Tess stood ramrod straight, as if she was on parade. Or facing a firing squad. 'I saw her over an hour ago. She's gone to Harcourt Downs, to visit the community.'

CHAPTER 13

The gates of Serenity Hill stood open. Erin drove past them and pulled up a hundred metres down the road. Bathed in sunlight, the homestead was the image of a dream home – attractive, inviting, surrounded by beautiful gardens and golden paddocks with the bush and low hills for a backdrop.

Her father had 'sold' a property not unlike this in South Australia to an unsuspecting overseas investor. At age twelve, Erin had posed for the happy-family-home photos, taken in the garden while the owners were away, and he'd taken her to Movie World on the Gold Coast with the proceeds. The police never caught up with her father for that one. Perhaps karma did, eventually, when he crossed the wrong mob and ended up in prison.

She blew out a slow breath. Time to go in. Time to become a slightly foolish, disenchanted, thirty-something single girl just looking for love and acceptance and easy answers. She'd spent half the night lying awake, going through ways to alleviate suspicion. If any of the community talked to the locals, they might have heard about her friendship with Simon, perhaps even about her being with him when he found Hayley, although few knew she'd seen the body. The Goodabri locals were also somewhat tight-lipped when it came to strangers, and that might work in her favour. But if not, the incident on the dance floor at the ball now seemed a blessing. So, too, did his silence while watching the fire, and them leaving in separate cars. A rift between her and Simon? Her doubts about his innocence in relation to Hayley's murder? She could make it believable. She'd just have to ensure she didn't choke on every lie.

Act. Perform. Make contact with the girl, Hayley's daughter, find out what she could about the situation, and leave during the night.

Her email to Serenity Hill this morning had been answered within the hour by someone called Mary. Presumably the same Mary who had spoken to Steve Fraser on Friday night. Erin was very welcome to come, any time today.

'Any time' was going to be now, mid-morning, before she lost her nerve.

She did a U-turn and drove through the gates, down the elm-lined drive to the wide turning circle in front of the house. The place had been Harcourt Downs for over a hundred years before it became Serenity Hill, and the well-kept homestead reflected a gracious history.

As she parked, the leadlight front door opened and a woman came down the steps of the wide veranda to greet her. Tall, perhaps in her early forties, she wore her long hair piled in a loose knot at the back of her head. Erin took a moment to switch off the ignition, keeping her face averted to set her expression to reveal no surprise at the woman's white dress.

The moment she stepped out of the ute, the woman greeted her. 'Hello! You must be Erin. I'm Mary. I'm so glad you could come.'

'Thank you. What a beautiful place this is.'

Erin found her hands clasped gently, warm green eyes gazing into hers. 'We're so looking forward to welcoming you. Please, come inside. I believe you've met Willow already? She's just taking some cakes from the oven and will join us in a moment.'

Mary ushered her in, carrying the heavier of her bags for her, inviting her to leave her things in an alcove off the central hallway 'for now'. In an inviting sitting room with wicker furniture and low pine tables overlooking the garden behind the house, Willow joined them, coming straight across to hug her. Willow in a white dress. Maybe it was just a uniform, like women in day spas and hairdressers wore.

'I'm so excited that you came!' Willow exclaimed, her eyes sparkling. 'We're going to have a wonderful time, aren't we, Mary?'

The young woman's pleasure made it easy for Erin to smile in return. 'I'm looking forward to it, I *so* need the break. I told the boss last night that I was too stressed and was taking a week off. You've just got to do that sometimes, you know? You've got to look after yourself, because no one else will.'

'We'll look after you,' Willow assured her, squeezing her hand. 'Now sit down and relax. I've made honey cakes and a pot of peppermint tea. I'll just be a minute.'

'Are there any other visitors at the moment?' Erin asked Mary as she made herself comfortable on the lounge.

'We're only getting established here at Serenity Hill,' Mary explained. 'We're expecting a couple of other visitors, but they aren't arriving until this evening. So you'll be spoilt with attention this afternoon.'

'Sounds great.'

Three more women in the white dresses came into view, walking across the grass towards the house, their steps light and faces animated with laughter. They stepped up onto the long back veranda further down and must have entered the house through the kitchen, as within minutes they came into the sitting room with Willow, bearing trays with glasses, white teacups and a matching white china teapot.

Mary introduced Erin to the three newcomers, Tamara, Callie and Rebecca. Tamara was around Erin's age, but the other two were much younger, perhaps only in their late teens. Young, fresh-faced and pretty, their long hair loosely arranged in fine braids woven together like a peasant girl's crown. Nothing like Erin's own hurried ponytail.

Rebecca placed a small table beside her while Willow knelt at a larger low table and poured herbal tea. 'This is our own organic peppermint,' she said, bringing Erin a china cup. 'Freshly picked just minutes ago. It's refreshing and relaxing for both body and soul. It helps to clear toxins and bring harmony to your body and your mind. And it tastes great,' she added with a smile, before glancing at Mary as if for approval.

Mary nodded at her. Willow then poured for Mary and for Tamara before Callie and Rebecca. If Erin read the dynamics right, Mary was at the head of the hierarchy, like a Mother Superior in a convent, and the younger women at the bottom. Whether intentionally or not, Mary and Tamara sat in two of the three chairs, while the younger ones used the large cushions on the floor, quite relaxed.

Willow brought Erin a small cake on a white plate; a golden-brown cake, smaller than a cupcake, with a sliced strawberry beside it. 'These are honey cakes, made with almond meal and our own organic butter and eggs. We bartered for the honey but we hope to have our own hives soon.'

'Is your community self-sufficient?' Erin directed the question at Mary as Willow was serving cake to the others.

'We aim to be, as much as possible,' Mary answered, her enthusiasm only slightly more tempered than Willow's. 'We grow most of our food, and we make the majority of our clothing, furniture and tools. We practise the principles of reducing and re-using even more than recycling. We also barter with our sister communities and others. But that's enough about us.' Her smile was full of warmth and interest, almost maternal. 'We'd love to get to know you.'

Convincing lies stick to the truth as much as possible. Lesson one in Cam Taylor's school for young scammers. 'There's not much to tell, really. My mum died when I was just a baby. I lived with my dad, and he was a lazy sod, always changing jobs, so we moved around a lot. He got a new girlfriend when I was about sixteen and she hated me, so I had to leave. It was a bit tough for a while but I got by.' All true, in one way or another.

The younger girls in particular oozed sympathy. 'You poor thing,' Callie said, patting her on the hand.

Rebecca seemed awed. 'You're so brave, doing that.'

'But you work in the national park now, don't you?' Willow asked. 'That's awesome, working with the animals. Did you always want to do that?'

Working with the animals . . . Yep, dealing with feral pests, being stung by insects, swooped by magpies, and constantly on the alert for spiders and snakes. Not the kind of cute furry animals Willow – and half the population – had in mind. But the question put her on alert, because she hadn't told Willow on Friday where she worked, and she hadn't been in uniform. The woman she'd spoken to yesterday must have told them. The woman who wasn't here now.

'I love it,' Erin said, truthfully. 'I wanted to do something honest, you know, and good for the planet.' That was also true, although it wasn't the way she'd usually express it. Appearing impressionable mattered here, more than the environmental and ethical reasons she'd chosen her career. 'All the reports and paperwork are a pain, though. All just so the politicians can cherry-pick the figures and pretend they're doing something useful.' Not too much risk in that tactic. Neither Hayley nor Sybilla had left records in the usual databases – social security, tax, licensing or health. All the evidence suggested that the group avoided participation in society, and Joshua's writings prioritised community over society's laws. If they saw the world as 'us' and 'them', she had to align herself with 'us'. 'I really just want to be out there, you know, with nature.'

She took a bite of the little honey cake and the delicately sweet, spicy morsel melted in her mouth. Not hard to let her face light up. 'This is wonderful, Willow! So light and delicious.'

Willow beamed like a child. All three of the younger ones had a kind of youthful innocence that made Erin think of them as girls rather than women. Except . . . the way they reclined on the big cushions. Relaxed, but not with the casual sprawl of teenagers. Not quite provocative, but suggestive. Bare feet and long limbs gracefully curled. A dress artfully slipping off a naked shoulder. The wrap front of a bodice draping just loosely enough to frame the swell of firm, round breasts. Mary and Tamara were more subtle in their manner, but they both had the slightly languid air and elegant sensuality that made Erin imagine courtesans of kings.

Joshua Kristos had written about the beauty of the body, the bliss of sensuality and the gift of ecstasy between two people. Nothing Erin disagreed with, although the ecstasy thing was generally overrated in her experience. Yet other than the young lad yesterday, she'd not seen any men. Maybe they were a happy lesbian ménage. Nothing wrong with that, as far as she was concerned. Perhaps that's why Hayley had left Simon, yet still sent him affectionate cards – she'd discovered she loved a woman more than him. Maybe she and Sybilla had been lovers, partners. Perhaps Sybilla had purposely stepped off the cliff, in grief or guilt.

Erin finished the honey cake, drank some tea and accepted another cake pressed on her by Willow, all the while answering the gently probing questions and talking more about herself than she had for years. She didn't have to resort to many lies, but even still the honey cake sat heavily in her stomach.

When she'd finished her tea and set down her cup, Mary leaned forward. 'Erin, we'd love to help you find the joy and bliss within you. You've chosen to come to our community and we hope that during these few days at least you'll embrace the spirit of simplicity that we believe in.'

'Oh, I do want to. After I met Willow the other day and she told me about Joshua Kristos, I downloaded some of his podcasts, and I bought one of his books last night. I haven't finished it yet, but it all just resonates with me.'

Was that a little sparkle of amusement in Mary's eyes? Perhaps she was overplaying her ready-to-be-converted role.

'Wonderful. It's an important aspect of our lives that we free the body of tensions and toxins so that our energy isn't wasted fighting them. So our suggested program starts with a cleansing, relaxing bath that will begin the process of releasing the built-up tension in your muscles. If you're ready, we'll begin?'

Relieved that there was nothing too mystical to start with, Erin agreed readily, and while Callie and Rebecca went to prepare the bath, Willow showed her to her room, down a passageway to one end of the house. Not a large room, but light and attractive, with simplicity the decorating principle. White walls and a white bedspread contrasted with the warm tones of a small pine table and chair and the colourful view of the garden through the window. Other than the bed, table and chair, there was no other furniture in the room.

Willow clasped her hands loosely in front of her. 'We'll provide everything you need during your stay so that you can disconnect from the toxins and distractions of the outside world. Mary will store your belongings in a locker in the office. She'll give you a key, in case there's anything that you really need. But most people discover they don't need any of the "stuff" that consumerism makes them think they must have.'

Isolation from the world – first step. For all Willow's genuine, considerate eagerness to help her, they were separating her from the familiar.

'My clothes?' Erin queried. She didn't ask about her phone, her wallet, her car keys. Yet. Her phone was no use to her here anyway, and presumably Mary or one of the others would ask for her cash payment sooner or later.

'We'll provide you with clothes made from organic, natural fabrics. You'll love how beautiful they feel on your skin. No poisonous chemicals or plastic fibres. You wouldn't believe what goes into commercial fabrics these days.' Willow stepped out into the passage again. She opened a cupboard they'd passed on the way, and returned with a folded robe. 'Why don't you change into this now, and I'll take you to the bathroom. I'll just be out here, so come out when you're ready.'

Willow pulled the door closed, and Erin stood in the middle of the room for several moments, thinking. She'd made it through, so far – she hoped. The women seemed friendly, interested, compassionate. Their questions had been politely probing but not suspicious.

Love bombing, Tess had said. Separation from the outside world.

Two boxes ticked.

Erin unzipped her dress and stepped out of it, then laid it on the bed. The robe was a standard kimono style, similar to those found in any up-market hotel, except this one was made of a densely woven cotton, or maybe hemp. She unclipped her bra and took it off – stupid to go for a bath in a bra – but after a moment's indecision she left her briefs on.

The robe did feel good against her skin. She tied the belt and went out to meet Willow.

The bathroom was six times the size of her draughty add-on bathroom in the cottage, with a deep sunken bath in the middle, already filled with water. The room had the same simple decorating scheme as the bedroom – white walls, timber finishing and furnishings around a double white vanity and basins. But there were flowers and candles on numerous shelves around the walls, and the timber venetian blinds on the window were partially closed for privacy, dimming the light.

'I'll put on some music and leave you in peace,' Willow said. 'Relax and enjoy.' The door closed behind her, and the soft strains of gentle instrumental music floated around the room.

Erin undressed and stepped into the warm, scented water, letting it envelop her. Her body began relaxing in the warmth. Her brain didn't, despite the soothing music and aromatic oils.

She'd not yet seen Hayley's daughter, or the woman she'd met yesterday. That woman hadn't worn the white uniform either in Strathnairn on Friday, or yesterday at the river. Erin hadn't heard any noises suggesting that there were other people in the house, but it was a large house. Maybe later she could explore. Maybe later there'd be an opportunity to ask about Hayley and Sybilla, or one of the women would mention them.

So far, the five women presented a caring, unthreatening approach. Even if they ticked some of the boxes for a cult, it was a broad term that could include a wide range of groups, not all of them dangerous.

But she'd only been here an hour or two.

She closed her eyes and tried to consciously relax her limbs and muscles. Even if the body-washing was designed to soften her up for the brainwashing, she could still enjoy the first part. They'd find washing a waterproof brain more of a challenge.

•

'How damn long does it take to get a search warrant?' Simon demanded. Two hours since he'd found out that Erin had gone to Harcourt Downs. Two long, dragging hours in which he'd paced through half his boot soles going back and forth between the Parks office and the police rooms next door and come up with fifteen different strategies to extract Erin if the police didn't move soon.

'The magistrate wants more information,' Fraser said, after finishing another phone call. 'We could get a warrant pretty quickly to search for the cannabis crop, but we can't search the rest of the place unless we have more than hearsay and coincidences to go on. Either about the girl or Hayley's murder.'

The edges of Simon's control frayed a little more. 'Have the files from the memory card finished downloading yet?'

'There are over a hundred files on the card so Forensics sent it as a zip file. It's only fifty per cent done and it's been going for twenty minutes. The wireless network link keeps cutting out. Tess has gone up to the station to try downloading on the wired link.'

Simon ground his teeth. Over a hundred files. They'd still have to go through all of them, try to figure out what was significant. More time. More time while Erin was with a group of bizarre people whom Hayley had called a cult and run from.

Fraser slapped him on the back as he headed to the kitchen. 'Chill, Kennedy. Erin's tough and smart. She deals with all kinds when she's working out there alone in the bush. And Tess told us what she said.'

That her father was a con man. That she'd helped him when she was a kid. Close on twenty years ago. Simon didn't care what her father had persuaded her to do when she was a kid. The Erin he knew was decent, straightforward, hard-working and honest.

Simon followed Fraser to the kitchen, and occupied the doorway. 'I looked him up,' he said. In the interminable hours while he'd waited for the police to take action. 'Her father. Campbell Taylor. Convicted of a multi-million-dollar fraud in South Australia fourteen years ago and jailed for ten.'

'And died in a hostel for homeless men six months after getting out on parole,' Fraser added. 'I looked him up, too.' His phone beeped and he checked the message. 'Tess has the files. She's on her way back.'

Three minutes to walk from the police station, two hundred metres down the adjoining street. Simon eschewed a chair and hunkered on the floor while he waited. He checked his phone for a text from Erin. Again. Uselessly, because Harcourt Downs was in an area with no mobile reception. He refrained from sending her a fourth message. Barely.

He heard footsteps, saw a shadow pass the closed blinds, and pulled the door open for Tess. She carried her laptop, and she went straight to the table she'd been using and opened it.

'Right, it's documents. Lots of documents,' she said. 'PDF files, mostly. A couple of image files.'

Simon and Fraser stood shoulder to shoulder behind her to see the screen. 'Don't open anything yet,' Fraser said. 'Let's just look at those file names.'

The files were sorted in alphabetical order, the first group of file names made up of numbers and letters, followed by another group which had a word-number-word format.

'They're dates,' Simon said at the same time as Tess said, 'I think I know —'

Simon shifted slightly to get a better view of the screen. 'This first group. Six digits, year, month, day. Dates and places, maybe? S-Y-D – that could be Sydney. Bris – that'd be Brisbane. And there's N-Y. New York?'

'They're documents, not image files,' Fraser said. 'Probably not holiday snaps. Tess, you were going to say something?'

Tess indicated the second section of the file list, where Simon could make out a few words, and what looked like years – 1988, 1996, 2014. 'These might be academic journal articles, or resources. It's the same way I label readings for my university course. Main author's surname, year of publication, keywords from the title.'

'Was Hayley a student anywhere, I wonder?' Fraser mused.

'She completed her childcare certificate,' Simon answered, 'but she struggled with the study aspect. Maybe she went back.'

Tess pointed at the screen. 'Look at the titles. The words are run together but there's "charismatic", "deviant", and "hypnosis" there, and "psychiatric". I think that these could be articles about cults.'

Not the kinds of topics Simon expected Hayley would research. 'Find the last opened files,' he suggested. 'If these documents aren't hers, the last opened files may be the reason she took the memory card.'

Tess clicked a few menus, found the names of the most recently viewed files. The filename on top of the list had a date about a week prior and the initials 'CHKH', but Simon's gaze stuck on the date and time the file had last been opened.

'Monday morning.' Fraser's voice sounded loud in the still room.

Simon nodded wordlessly. Monday morning. Just after ten o'clock. And Hayley had fled not long afterwards.

Tess pointed at the screen with a pen. 'There are two files viewed that morning.' Before opening them she reached for the notepad beside her and jotted down the names and dates. The second filename included a date ten days ago and the initials NY.

Simon held his breath as she clicked open the first one.

An article from the online edition of the Coffs Harbour newspaper with the headline 'Local Woman's Cult Warning'. She scrolled past the headline and read aloud from the text. "'A local woman has warned against a group that has recently set up on a property in the area. The group promotes healthy, simple living and self-sufficiency, but the woman, who wishes to remain anonymous, says the group is a cult and its leader, who goes by the name Joshua, is a charlatan." There he is. Did Hayley read that and realise? Or suspect it already?'

Simon squinted to continue reading silently over Tess's shoulder. *The woman joined the group more than ten years ago on the north coast hinterland but left when restrictions on* members became more severe and sexual services were expected of female members. 'Joshua uses mind-control techniques to persuade his followers to do his bidding,' she said.

There was more, but Tess hadn't yet scrolled that far.

'Email me that article,' Fraser told her. He had his phone in his hand and dialled a number. 'Copy it to Leah.'

'And to me,' Simon added.

Fraser took a few steps away, phone to his ear. 'What's the name of the Coffs journo?' he asked Tess.

'Jane Cooper.'

'Leah, did your vic in Coffs talk to a journalist by the name of Jane Cooper about a week ago? Yeah. Article about Kristos in the paper with an anonymous informant, on . . .' Tess gave him the date and he repeated it for Haddad.

Fraser waited, listening, and they all waited, the only sounds the buzzing of a fly at the window and Tess's fingers clicking on her laptop keys as she forwarded the article.

Fraser spoke again. 'Yes . . . Right. Shit. Yep, done. . . Okay, keep in touch.' He ended the call. 'Tess, search the rest of those documents for "Joshua Kristos" or for the names of any of our victims. The one at Coffs is Kirsty Hamilton. Leah's been checking her phone records and had them handy. Kirsty made a forty-eight-minute call to the newspaper three days before that article was published.' He dropped his phone on the table, sat down heavily. 'I'd say "bingo", but this is getting way too nasty to be frivolous. Jane Cooper, the journalist, has been missing since Tuesday.'

Aaron swore, and Tess's fingers stopped still on the keyboard.

Simon went to the window and stared out through the blinds. Hayley, Sybilla and Kirsty. All three connected to Joshua. All three of them dead. He breathed slowly in and out, struggling for clear thought and logic instead of anger.

'I'll check the second article Hayley looked at, sarge,' Tess said after a long moment.

Simon glanced over to see the banner of an American newspaper filling the top half of the screen, with a headline below it: *Expert Warns of Cult's Spread.*

'"At an international conference on new-age religion in New York this week, an Australian psychologist has warned about the spread of a quasi-religious cult which promises its adherents bliss and love,"' Tess read aloud. '"Doctor P.J. Hollywell has been researching the group for more than a decade and says that its leader, who calls himself Joshua Kristos, uses advanced techniques in persuasion, hypnosis and mind control to sexually and financially exploit his followers."'

Simon listened with increasing unease. His training had covered mind-control techniques and how to resist them, but Hayley hadn't had the benefit of that training, or the same level of emotional resilience, and she'd been with this group for years. But she also didn't have much in the way of money. At least as far as he knew. Erin was much stronger than Hayley, physically and emotionally, but despite her background, no way would she be prepared for the kind of mind games a skilled person could subject her to.

They all waited while Tess took a sip of water, her gaze still on the screen. 'I'll skim the rest. He's interviewed people who have left the group. He says there's a hierarchy typical of cults. There's also a sexual hierarchy, who can sleep with who. Sex is equated with bliss but permanent pair bonds are discouraged except for . . . ' Her voice shook. 'Except for the women Joshua chooses as his. Okay, the money. Let's see . . . book sales are a part of it – a million books sold worldwide, he says – but there's stuff here about property and donations of hundreds of thousands of dollars to enter the community. And here he's hinting at drugs.'

Simon gripped the window frame so tightly flakes of old paint speared under his fingernails. Hayley had read those articles. She'd read those articles exposing Joshua as a fraud, and she'd run within hours. She'd been up on the north coast for longer than ten years. If she'd been with Joshua's group then, she'd have known the woman who'd been murdered at Coffs Harbour.

If she'd been with Joshua's group all this time . . . She hadn't had much money, but she was young when she went there. Young, slim, pretty. Young and innocent and sweet and the thought that she might have been manipulated or coerced into a sexual relationship made his gut burn with fury.

Steve's chair creaked as he sat up straighter and leaned his elbows on the desk. 'If there's drugs and fraud involved I'll see if the Feds have got anything on Kristos. But this guy might be a useful source of info – what's his name and where is he?'

Tess continued scrolling through screens. 'There's a bio line at the bottom of the article. Doctor P.J. Hollywell. He has a Doctor of Psychology degree from the University of Melbourne, has been researching cults in Australia and Kristos for some years.'

The name tickled something in Simon's memory. Maybe he'd served with a Hollywell.

Aaron typed quickly on his laptop. 'Hollywell, P. . . . Okay, there's a profile here on a professional networking site for a Peter James Hollywell who's a psychologist. Western Sydney . . . Blue Mountains now, by the looks of it.'

'*Peter* Hollywell?' Fraser frowned.

The memory clicked into place. 'I know of that guy. I think. When we were at Holsworthy, those first couple of years, Hayley battled depression. He's the counsellor she saw. I'm pretty sure that was his name. Peter Hollywell.'

'Shit.' Fraser dragged a hand through his hair, more agitated than Simon had seen him before. 'Hayley knew Peter Hollywell?'

'Yes. I think so. You know him?'

'Yeah. Know of him, anyway. My sister —' He swallowed, visibly shaken. 'My sister was a patient of his.'

'What happened?' Simon probed, because clearly something had. 'What did he do?'

'I don't know that he did anything. He certainly didn't do enough. She committed suicide. At fourteen.'

Simon didn't know what to say. Aaron seemed not to, either.

Tess spoke up. 'I'm sorry, sarge. What a tragedy.'

Fraser shrugged, embarrassed, and picked up his phone. 'Let's hope the Feds have something that can help us.'

Simon leaned back against the wall, fists thrust into his pockets, almost oblivious to the police officers while his brain gnawed through the new information. Fraser's sister and Hayley had seen the same psychologist when they lived in the same area. Had to be just coincidence. Must be. Except that the psychologist knew about Joshua's cult. Maybe Hayley had kept in touch with him. But if he'd known she was there, why hadn't he contacted Simon to warn him? Surely patient confidentiality didn't rule out a warning that she was in danger?

The muscles in his spine tensed, urging him to action, to fight. But he couldn't fight an unknown foe. He needed more information. He needed facts to go on, evidence more solid than the nagging, insistent sense that something about the Hayley–Hollywell–Joshua connection didn't add up.

CHAPTER 14

After enough rotations through the same soothing music track that it was beginning to get on her nerves, Erin pulled the plug out of the bath and dried herself with one of the towels on the rack. It wasn't the usual cotton terry cloth but a waffle weave in a natural linen, and surprisingly absorbent. She was tying the belt on the robe when someone knocked at the door.

The woman she'd spoken with yesterday at the falls stood outside, a short distance back from the doorway, now wearing the same white uniform as the others. She immediately gave a tiny shake of her head and raised her eyes towards the bathroom ceiling.

A warning.

Microphone or camera? Erin didn't look up. The thought of either instantly reversed any relaxing effects of the bath.

'Hello, I'm Madeleine,' the woman said brightly. 'I'm sorry I wasn't here earlier to welcome you, Erin. If you'd like to come this way, I'll give you a massage to deepen your body's relaxation and healing.'

It seemed Madeleine hadn't told the others about their meeting, yet they'd known she was a ranger. The muscles woven around Erin's spine tightened. Madeleine trusted her enough to warn her about the surveillance in the bathroom, and to tell her yesterday about Sybilla. Was Madeleine a potential ally? Or was she only protecting herself, not Erin?

The massage room, next door to the bathroom, overlooked the garden through layers of gauzy curtains that shifted and danced with the wind coming through the open casement window. Madeleine pulled the window closed. 'There's a storm coming,' she said. 'I can feel the shift in the air. I think it's going to be a big one.'

Although she'd read the weather forecast that morning, Erin wasn't entirely sure that Madeleine was talking about the effects of low-pressure cells and cold fronts.

If there was surveillance in the bathroom, there might well be here, too. But now wasn't the time to be prudish and give the game away. She shrugged out of her robe and climbed onto the towel-covered massage table, playing it safe with the usual rural weather chat. 'We sure could do with the rain. It was a very dry summer.' She fitted her face into the cushioned hole in the massage table, narrowing her field of vision to a small patch of floor below her. 'I've lived out in the country so long that I like rain.'

Madeleine began to lay warm towels over her back. 'I do too. And it's wonderful how a storm refreshes everything, isn't it? Washes away all the old dust and death and decay and encourages new growth.'

Old dust, death and decay. Erin had never been good at cryptic crosswords. *If* Madeleine spoke metaphorically, she must be signifying a change coming. Encourages new growth – what did she mean by that? Erin hadn't detected in her voice any indication whether she believed that to be good or bad.

The warm oil and Madeleine's firm, steady hands worked on loosening her newly tense muscles. Usually Erin enjoyed a massage, and Madeleine was skilled. But normally she had little more concerning her than an overload of work.

For the benefit of any observers, she'd better continue to play her role. 'I'd love to find out more about the group here. Everyone is so friendly. Have you been part of the community for long?'

The pressure of the hands on her shoulder blades didn't falter. 'Yes, for a long time. Joshua saved my life when I was young. I owe him everything. His wisdom, his love – they transformed me. I found peace, and joy in working with my hands, and bliss in the abundance of a simple life, shared lovingly with others.'

Erin's thoughts bustled with questions, most of which would give her away if she asked them. If not to Madeleine, then to anyone listening. Madeleine said she had known Joshua for 'a long time', Erin noted. Like Willow, he'd 'changed her life'. That seemed a safe topic to explore further.

'I've downloaded Joshua's book – the first one – and some of the letters on his website. He truly is wise, isn't he? And compassionate. Last night when I was reading, I felt as though he was there, that he knew me and was talking to me.' That was a porky. She'd actually felt like throwing the book at the wall, because it continually repeated the same ideas, but tossing hundreds of dollars' worth of electronic tablet at a solid object wouldn't have been so satisfying.

'Joshua has helped many people find joy and bliss,' said Madeleine. 'Although our group began as a small family, his truth and teachings have spread, and our communities are evolving and growing. He is beloved by thousands, and over a hundred of us have devoted ourselves to living simply within his communities.'

Erin hoped there was no camera in the floor, watching her face. Communities, plural. Over a hundred people in them. Bigger than she'd imagined. 'Can anyone join a community?' she asked.

She felt the towels being shifted and then Madeleine began working on her legs. 'Not everyone is suited to the life. Although there is great joy and bliss in living our way, we must all serve the community in a harmonious and constructive manner. So we have a gradual process in which potentials come to know us, and we come to know them. Visits like this are the first step. Those who wish to pursue the path are invited for a longer visit, to learn more of Joshua's teachings. Some then make their first commitment and join the community.'

'Their first commitment? There are those who make more?'

'Yes. There are different ways to serve the community, using different gifts. Some paths require training for the development of specific knowledge, skills and disciplines.'

'You're certainly skilled at massage,' Erin said. Truthfully, because despite her stress and uneasiness, the woman was working wonders.

'Thank you. It is a joy to share the gift with you.'

'Is that what you do here? Provide massages?'

'It is only a small part of my service. I am one of the sisters. We have devoted our lives to supporting Joshua in his work and providing guidance to the community.'

Sisters. Women in white dresses. Hardly a nun's habit, but the symbolism wasn't so different. Although with the sensuality on display earlier, just what kind of 'support' did they give Joshua?

She grappled for an innocent question to ask. 'How many sisters are there?'

'Six in each community. There are also potentials who are selected for training.'

'It must be an honour to serve Joshua so closely.'

Did she imagine the pause? Perhaps Madeleine was simply contemplating the callus on Erin's heel from boots that had never quite fitted properly. Her voice came softly. 'I am blessed by all he has given me.'

Did she mean the child, the little girl? The older girl was Hayley's daughter, but the boy, Tristan, might have been seventeen or so, and if Madeleine was her own age . . . Either Tristan wasn't hers or she'd had a child very young. She said she'd been with Joshua since she was young. Hayley had been with him for years, too, and she'd worn the white dress of the sisters. Erin's gut did an uneasy somersault.

'What about men?' she asked. 'Are there brothers, too?'

'Yes, but not in quite the same way. There are men who have committed their lives to Joshua and to the community. There are brothers who oversee the training of the young boys, and others who accept a particular responsibility for the security of the community.'

The security of the community. Police and soldiers looked after the security of communities. So did spies. The surveillance in the bathroom and here might not only be for lecherous intent.

Madeleine was massaging her toes. 'You are very fortunate,' she began, and for one crazy heartbeat Erin thought she referred to her crooked toes. But she continued, 'Joshua is coming today. He will be here soon. This evening, the whole community will celebrate his presence with us.' She rested a hand on each of Erin's feet for a moment. 'I am finished here. There is a dress for you on the shelf. Rise when you're ready.'

She didn't leave immediately. Through the hole in the massage table Erin saw the hem of her dress swish towards the window, and the movement of the gauze curtains.

Erin rolled over, and reached for her robe. Madeleine had her back to her, looking out between the curtains.

'There is a huge bank of dark clouds,' Madeleine said. 'The storm is almost here. The wind is getting stronger and gusty and I'm afraid that with all these trees and dead wood around, it could be dangerous.' She turned and gave a weak smile, but there was nothing weak in the depth of her eyes. 'Be careful in the storm, Erin.'

•

Simon checked the time on his watch. Five minutes to go. Five minutes before he rejoined Fraser and the others to pool whatever information they'd managed to find in the last forty minutes. Five minutes to the deadline he'd set for himself. If the police didn't turn up something significant or have a plan in place within that time, he was going out to Harcourt Downs or Serenity Hill or whatever they called the place now to find Erin and the girl himself.

On an intellectual level, he understood the wariness of the police – Haddad, Fraser, even Nick – to move too quickly. The fact that there were multiple communities involved and potential fraud and drugs complicated matters and required consultation with other units in the state police, and with the Feds. While the local cops, like him, wanted to raid the place immediately, they all knew they didn't have enough evidence to justify it. Fraser's hands were tied by the rules of due process and police procedure.

Simon didn't have to follow police procedure. His actions were subject only to the law and his own moral and ethical principles. To ensure the safety of Erin and the girl he'd trespass on the grey areas of the law if he had to.

Three minutes to go. He'd had no luck, so far, finding anything of significance in his internet searching. He'd found plenty of fans of Joshua Kristos, people around the world who claimed their lives had been transformed by reading his books, but none of them had met him or lived in a Simple Bliss community. There were a few critiques, too, of the books but not many. In a market saturated with self-help and new-age philosophy, maybe people just moved on to the next one if Joshua's teachings didn't inspire them.

Searching for more criticism of the guru, he typed Peter Hollywell's name into the search box and skimmed the results. A few references to his recent speech at the international conference. A couple of references to an academic journal article about cults. The profile on the website Aaron had accessed earlier. Simon clicked through to it. The brief resumé listed the counselling practice in western Sydney, then one in the Blue Mountains for two years. But according to the dates, that had ended ten years ago. Since then, Hollywell had, according to his own profile, been engaged in 'private consulting'. Very vague, with no current contact details or information about areas of specialty or interest.

Simon went back to the search results and found, down the page, a personal website for Hollywell. It opened on the screen with a few images of coastal scenes, some basic information about Hollywell that repeated mostly what was in the other site, with links to his journal articles and some other resources.

Nothing in the content leapt out at him. But it was the layout and design that struck Simon. Basic, older-style, adequate but not impressive. *Familiar.*

Simon flicked to the Serenity Hill website, still open in another browser tab, and reopened Joshua's website in another tab. Switching between the three in quick succession, he saw similarities in style, in font, in layout. Not identical by any means, but similar enough to raise questions. None of the sites had a designer listed, so he looked at the source code.

He whistled long and low, flicked back and forth between tabs, and scribbled some notes on the writing pad beside him.

The alarm he'd set on his phone beeped a reminder. Time to meet with the others. His thoughts buzzing with unanswered questions, he ripped the page off the writing pad and went back next door.

Fraser was still on the phone but seemed to be finishing up. Tess and Aaron were both back at their laptops, going through the documents on the memory card.

'Hi, Simon,' Aaron said. 'Still working on these. There's a bunch of media reports, mostly boring stuff about Joshua's communities and development applications with local councils, although there's a few about Hollywell and a couple with no mention of either but mention of cults. There are also a dozen or so book reviews. It's basically a press clippings folder. Assuming this is Joshua's, he keeps track of what's being said and what his people are doing. And what Hollywell is doing.'

Tess glanced up from her laptop. 'There's over a hundred academic journal articles. He's gathered a research library about cults, with emphasis on manipulation and hypnosis. There's a couple by Hollywell, one of which refers to Joshua directly, but the others are broader. Nothing that's much help now, though. Did you find anything?'

Simon handed her his notes. 'I don't know. Maybe. It's weird. Peter Hollywell uses the same website designer as Joshua Kristos and Serenity Hill. It could just be a stock template, but I don't think so. There's a reference in the source code of each site to the same company or design business. We need to check that out.'

'Jesus.' Fraser blew out a breath. 'What are the chances of that? Can you get on to that, Tess?'

Tess nodded, and immediately set to work.

'Anything from the Federal police?' Simon asked Fraser.

'They definitely have an interest in Kristos. Nothing firm at this stage though, other than some suspicions. But they're sending me a photo of him. The bloody guy's camera-shy and I couldn't find any online but they've got one.' His phone beeped as he spoke and he picked it up from the table, tapped the screen. And then his expression changed, the way Simon had seen soldiers' faces change sometimes when they faced a living hell. White. No mask of pretence. Just the harsh look of disbelief and dread.

Fraser's chair clattered backwards onto the floor as he stood up. He paced back and forth twice, then leaned his hands up against the wall, his head lowered and his breath coming heavily. 'Oh, Jesus. Oh, fuck.' He slammed his hand against the wall, turned on his heel and walked outside, letting the front door slam closed behind him.

Tess and Aaron were both on their feet, looking uncertain. 'Should we follow him?' Tess asked.

Simon's instinct told him that a man like Fraser didn't need Aaron's innocence right now, or for Tess to see him vulnerable. 'I'll go,' he said.

He caught up with the detective at the end of the block, where Goodabri Primary School's playing fields began and the paddocks stretched beyond, overshadowed by the wide bank of thick, black, angry clouds rolling in from the west. Fraser leaned on the fence, phone in his hand, his head hanging down.

Simon propped beside him. 'You wanna talk about it?'

'Nope. But you want to know.'

'Only if it's relevant to Hayley.'

'Yeah. I guess it is.' A breath shuddered through him. 'My sister was fourteen, having a tough time after our mother died. The sessions with Hollywell seemed to help. She thought he was great, got all starry-eyed about him. But you know alarm bells ring when a teenage girl becomes keen on a guy twenty or more years her senior. I was only seventeen though, didn't know how to raise it with her, and the one time I tried we got into a blazing argument.'

'You were a kid. It's a hard one to deal with even for adults.'

'Yep. But the next afternoon . . . I was supposed to pick her up after school. I was late, and she wasn't there. She'd disappeared. A week later, they found her schoolbag, her clothes and a suicide note near the cliffs at Kurnell. We used to have cousins in Kurnell, used to roam the bush and the cliffs there some weekends. There'd been a wild storm the night she disappeared. The police never found her body.'

'Damn tough on everyone.' Simon couldn't see the relevance yet, but Fraser wasn't the kind of guy to get worked up over nothing.

'Hollywell came to the funeral. Very sympathetic.' Fraser touched the screen of the phone and it lit up with an image of a man. A man in his fifties, with piercing blue eyes, a Hollywood smile, and wavy dark hair brushing his collar. 'That's the photo the Feds sent of Joshua Kristos,' Fraser said. 'But give him glasses, shorter, greyer hair, and he's the image of Peter Hollywell.'

Simon stared at the image, trying to make sense of it all. 'Hollywell *is* Kristos?'

'I'm betting yes.'

'But Hollywell's just spoken at a conference, exposing Joshua.'

'Yeah. I can't work that out.'

Simon's thoughts raced through possibilities. 'They could be twin brothers, I suppose. Or maybe it's one of those multiple personality disorders.'

'Either way, one of them hates the other. If it's that.'

But they still used the same website designer. And the documents on the memory card were just as relevant to Hollywell as to Kristos.

Fraser's phone beeped with a message. 'From Tess,' he said, and read aloud, ' "Same holding company registered all domains and owns company that bought Serenity Hill. Batch of new domains registered last week." Jesus. Hollywell is Kristos, and this week three women connected with him are dead.'

Simon's thoughts raced through all the small pieces of information, linking them, searching for their meaning. 'He's got something planned with those new domains. Has to have. Some kind of mad game he's been playing for years. He outed Kristos as a fraud last week but he can't build on that if anyone knows who he really is.'

Hayley and Sybilla, who'd been with him for years, and the woman in Coffs, who'd known him ten or more years ago. Simon gripped Fraser's arm.

'Hayley knew the truth. That he's both Joshua and Hollywell. Probably Sybilla and the other woman knew, too.'

Fraser had already reached the same conclusion. 'And there may be others who know. He may think Erin knows. Come on.'

They set off at a run back to the incident room as thunder cracked overhead and the first heavy raindrops began to fall.

CHAPTER 15

The weather forecast Erin had read that morning had mentioned scattered storms. The solid black sky to the west appeared to have gathered up every rain cloud in the country and combined them into one enormous, ominous storm front. The wind had turned gusty. A few heavy drops of rain fell, splattering on her skin.

Willow looked up at the cloud again. 'We might have to run for it.'

Halfway between one of the cottages and the woolshed, they quickened their pace. A few metres on, they both started to run.

Her sandals slippery on the still-dusty ground, Erin nonetheless kept pace with Willow, and they ran up the wooden stairs of the woolshed as the intermittent raindrops became a sheet of solid rain. Willow dragged open the door and they dashed inside. The young woman laughed aloud, shaking water from her hair like an exuberant puppy, and Erin couldn't help but join in, the exhilaration of the mad run temporarily overriding her wariness. She liked Willow. In the family she used to imagine as a kid – the family with her mother, as well as a dependable father, and a house they lived in for years – there'd also been a little sister to play with and boss around. That imaginary kid might have grown up to be like Willow.

People milled around inside the woolshed, and a young girl hastened towards them, offering towels, even though they'd escaped the worst of the downpour. The rain pounding on the corrugated-iron roof made conversation almost impossible, but Erin thanked her with a smile. While she wiped her face dry and blotted her hair and shoulders, she surveyed her surroundings.

It was a decent-sized woolshed which might have had twelve or more stands in the days when graziers out here ran sheep. The old stands and pens were now gone, and foldable wooden screens divided the open space into several smaller areas. Some little kids played in a netted-off corner, and around fifteen people were clearing space, stacking fold-up beds and cots behind a screen at one end of the shed.

Willow had already shown Erin the 'women's house', one of the old farm cottages that was now fitted with bunk beds, dormitory-style, and they'd passed the 'men's house', similarly fitted out. The community wasn't entirely segregated: the small rooms of the shearers' quarters were available when a couple wanted privacy. For 'bliss', Willow had said.

Willow handed her towel back to the waiting girl. 'We're going to build another house for the children but at the moment all the children sleep and learn in here,' she explained to Erin. 'The whole community shares responsibility for raising our little ones. But this space is also one of our work rooms and a gathering place.' She clasped Erin's hand. 'Come! I'll show you the looms like I promised.'

Willow had told her about the spinning and weaving workshop before their late-afternoon tour of the community. Erin was particularly interested in the textile production, intrigued by the notion of the self-sufficient lifestyle being taken to such an extreme. The community processed wool all the way through from sheep to garment, and also grew and processed flax into fabric. They bartered for hemp yarn and wove it, then dyed and sewed it. The fact that almost all the garments she'd seen so far, in addition to the ones in the shop on Friday, were entirely handmade astounded her.

Willow showed her to a large enclosed space off to the side of the main shearing floor that would once have been the wool classing and baling area. Behind partitions, weavers sat at five looms of various sizes, the rhythmic wooden clatter of treadles going up and down adding to the rain's percussion on the roof. Two women and two girls sat at spinning wheels and an older man tinkered with a machine, spanner in hand.

'That's the spinning machine,' Willow explained. 'It has ten spindles so it will mean our spinners don't have to spend such long hours at the wheels. We're hoping to get it fully operational soon. We want to be able to have a third shift each day on the looms, but we can't produce enough yarn yet.'

Erin held her tongue and didn't ask how long the long hours were. She already knew no one received pay – everyone had their service to contribute for the good of the community. Willow took evident pride in the community's achievements but seemed oblivious to the issues that might arise. Erin already had the impression that some people's work was valued more highly than others'. Like most ideologies, communism had its strengths as a theory, but given human nature the practice never lived up to the ideals.

One of the young girls at the spinning wheels paused in her treadling and lifted her head to yawn. On catching sight of Willow, she looked horrified and hurriedly restarted her wheel.

Erin turned away and asked another question to draw Willow with her. Those working didn't need one of the sisters watching them. It seemed that in the hierarchy, the sisters ranked only one step lower than Joshua himself.

In the main part of the shed a large space was now clear and a few people, soaked to the skin, carried in bench seats from outside and began to set them up along the sides. The people Erin had seen ranged in age from babies through to men and women in their fifties and sixties. More women than men, but Willow had explained that most of the men were busy with the heavy work of developing the property for the necessary gardens, livestock and cropping.

There was a slight flurry at the door, people getting out of the way as a figure draped in an oilcloth cape entered. A woman rushed to help her take off the dripping cape. Madeleine. Erin followed Willow to greet her.

'Everything's in hand here, Madeleine,' Willow reported. 'We should be finished with the setting up soon.'

Not that 'we' had actually done anything yet, Erin noted to herself.

'Excellent. Joshua has arrived safely. He has asked to see you, Willow, and Rebecca and our new trainees, before the celebration.'

Willow gasped, hand over her mouth, her eyes wide with incredulity. 'Oh, I must go.'

Madeleine's hand on her arm stopped her from running off immediately. 'Christopher has the car outside because of the rain. Go and get the girls and he will drive you back to the house.'

Willow quickly crossed the floor to the netted-off corner and spoke to the two teenage girls in pale blue dresses supervising the children. Erin hadn't had a chance to look at them properly before. The girls instantly rose to their feet and followed her, brushing dust from their dresses, jittery and nervous. They didn't give any attention to Erin as they passed but one paused by Madeleine. Hayley's daughter. Madeleine kissed her forehead, brushed her cheek and watched her go.

'Joshua will welcome Willow and Rebecca as our new sisters tonight, and Jasmine and Fleur as trainees. It's a significant day for them.' She smiled as a mourner smiles at a funeral, and standing beside her Erin saw the disquiet in her eyes.

Thankful to know at last the name of Hayley's child, Erin nevertheless was worried by Madeleine's unease. 'What are they being trained as?' she asked quietly.

'Joshua has chosen them to be trained as sisters. If they prove suitable, they will support Joshua in his work and provide leadership to the community.'

'They will serve Joshua?' She didn't succeed entirely in hiding the distaste from her voice. The girls were both slim, attractive – and young. So young.

'Not yet,' Madeleine said, her voice low. 'They must learn how to best be of service to him, and develop their skills and knowledge. But he has chosen them, and they are dedicated to him now.'

A hands-off signal to the other males in the group? Erin suppressed a shudder. The thought of Jasmine learning to be 'of service' to the man made her stomach churn.

They were still standing near the main doorway and people bustled around them, asking pardon when they needed them to step aside so that the long benches could be carried past. Not quite the tugging of forelocks, but they treated Madeleine with an almost formal respect that Erin found uncomfortable. No sign of the usual cheeky, teasing Australian informality that she was used to with SES training activities or other community efforts.

'I would like to help,' she said to Madeleine, touching her on the arm and choosing her words with care. 'Is there something I can do? Some way I can help the community prepare for tonight?'

Madeleine clasped her hand and her direct gaze held many questions, although she asked only one, in not much more than a murmur. 'Did you come here to help us?'

'Yes, I did. Just tell me what you need me to do.'

'Come with me.'

Madeleine draped the dripping rain cloak over both of them. Huddled together under it, they went out into the teeming rain and down the woolshed steps. Muddy water ran in rivulets everywhere, the soil washing away under the torrent, huge dark puddles in low ground fast becoming small lakes.

'Don't drink the water tonight.'

Erin could have sworn that was what Madeleine had said, in a low voice right beside her ear, but the wind whipped the oilcloth cloak around them and the heavy rain beat down incessantly, making it hard to distinguish individual sounds.

They splashed through puddles and ankle-deep water, clutching the cloak around them as best they could. Madeleine steered her towards the long building of the shearers' quarters. They ran up onto the veranda, but the winds sheeted the rain almost sideways. Madeleine tugged open a door; when she slammed it shut behind them they were finally out of the wet, save for the water dripping off them and pooling at their feet on the stone floor.

They were in the shearers' kitchen, seemingly scarcely changed since its early days a century ago. At one end was a large stone fireplace with a wood-fired stove and a bread oven inside it, pots and pans hanging on hooks above them. A wooden slab table with bench seats long enough to accommodate a dozen or more occupied the centre of the room. Under a window facing west, water dripped from a leaking tap into a double concrete sink. The south wall, between the kitchen and the sleeping quarters, was floor-to-ceiling storage cupboards.

The wood stove burned, pumping out heat, and the kitchen appeared to have been recently used, with dish towels hanging on the edge of the sink and a stack of plates and cutlery on the end of the table.

Madeleine draped the cloak over a hook on the back of the door. Despite the words they'd just exchanged, she now chatted as if she had no concerns at all. 'This is the community's main kitchen. But today is a fast day, so it's quiet. The children will have a small meal, however. Will you help me prepare it? I can answer some of your questions about our community while we work.'

A fast day explained why Erin had been offered no food since this morning's honey cakes. She'd assumed there'd be food at the celebration. Her stomach rumbled in protest.

Madeleine was taking loaves of bread from a cupboard and must have heard. 'As a guest, you're not expected to fast if you don't want to. We're used to it so it isn't hard for us. Could you pass me that breadboard, please?'

As she sliced bread and Erin spread it with soft butter and honey from the cupboard, Madeleine said, 'You asked about whether people come and go from the community.'

Erin hadn't. She kept buttering bread and focused on Madeleine's words.

'Of course people are free to leave, any time they want.' Madeleine answered the question she hadn't asked with the formality of a teacher explaining something critical to a student. 'But on the very rare occasion that someone who has made a commitment to us chooses to return to the artificiality of the world, they've betrayed their promise and chosen lies over truth. We no longer speak their name and they become nothing to us, as if they never existed, because we are that to them.'

Which explained why, other than Madeleine's oblique reference at the waterfall, not one of the sisters had mentioned Hayley and Sybilla. Two new sisters to make six again, and no one had said why. Hayley had certainly left, of her own volition. But if Sybilla had tried to leave she hadn't made it far.

'What do you believe,' Erin asked carefully, 'about what happens when life ends? I haven't finished all of Joshua's book yet, I'm sorry.'

'When someone passes, we also don't speak their name. Their path on earth has ended. The souls of those who have lived a pure life and found bliss will continue in an even purer form of bliss. But if the soul is not pure, there is no chance of bliss, ever.'

Erin assumed from Madeleine's very careful, formal way of imparting the group's doctrine that the kitchen might also be under surveillance.

'That sounds like a kind of hell,' she said.

Madeleine wrapped the remains of the bread in a cloth. 'Losing the hope of bliss? Knowing that you'll never find it again?' Her fingers tightened on the cloth. 'Yes, it's a form of hell.'

Over the drumming of the rain on the roof they both heard the brisk, heavy footsteps on the veranda. The door swung open and two men in stockmen's oilskin coats barged in. A man well into his fifties, tall and beefy with a face so hard and cold that Erin couldn't imagine it ever softening in bliss. And a boy, maybe eighteen, such confidence in his grin that it bordered on arrogance.

Madeleine greeted them without surprise, as if she hadn't been speaking about hell a moment ago. 'Tom, David, I'm glad you've come. We've just finished making the sandwiches for the children. Fleur and Jasmine are with Joshua so I'm doing this for them. I'll put the sandwiches in boxes, and then if you could take them across, I'd be very grateful.'

'I guess we can.' The older man spoke slowly, twisting defiance through the words.

'Thank you.' Madeleine took two cardboard boxes from a cupboard and arranged the plates of sandwiches in them. 'I still have to knead the loaves for tomorrow but I'll be back across there soon. Have you met Erin yet? She's visiting us for a retreat.'

The man barely nodded at her but the youth gave her a smile that contained more triumph than pleasantness. She acknowledged both men with a smile, then picked up the knives she'd used for the sandwiches and went to the sink to wash them.

'Road's closed because of flooding,' the man said. 'No one can get in now.' He glanced at Erin. 'Or out.'

She should have thought of that already. Millers Road only had a causeway across the river. With such a heavy downpour it would have quickly become impassable. And it turned due north from here, not meeting another road until it joined the highway at the Queensland border, more than a hundred kilometres from Strathnairn. There'd be no police raid tonight, no way for Simon to reach her, and no way for her to leave, other than cross-country in the storm.

In the reflection in the window she watched Madeleine close the lids on the boxes and hand one to the older man. 'I'm sure you'll keep us safe here, Tom. I'll see you across there shortly.'

The men stomped out, Tom throwing a backward glance as though the two women might already be doing something he could catch them out at.

'Tom's the safety coordinator for our community,' Madeleine said evenly when they'd gone. 'He's training David as his deputy. They're very dedicated to protecting Joshua and his people.'

And there was another warning.

Madeleine went to the end cupboard, the largest of them. It was a small walk-in pantry, and Madeleine stepped inside it, out of view. 'Have you ever kneaded bread dough?'

Madeleine asked. 'The dough for tomorrow's loaves has finished the first rise, and we just need to punch them down and knead them again quickly for their second rise.' She emerged holding in both hands a heavy earthenware bowl covered in a cloth. 'Can you grab the other bowl, please? On the shelf on the right.'

In the pantry, Erin saw that the shelf on the right received light from the western window. Beside another earthenware bowl, flour had been spilled – no, dusted – on the shelf. And written in the flour were the words: *Bugs everywhere*.

Erin quickly brushed her hand over the flour to obscure the words, and wrote with her fingertip, *Trust me*. Then she carried the second bowl out to the table and received instructions on how to punch down the risen dough.

'Now we turn it out onto the table to knead it,' Madeleine said. 'I'll just grab some flour to stop it sticking.'

When she returned with the crock of flour, she focused on the dough and scarcely looked at Erin, until they'd finished the five minutes of kneading and she asked Erin to fetch the bread tins from the pantry.

This time the words in the flour read: *Pls save Lily Jas Tris*.

'Oh, I spilled some flour on the shelf, Erin,' Madeleine called. 'Could you wipe it up, please?'

No more messages in spilled flour, then. Maybe that was too risky as well.

I am finished here, Madeleine had said at the end of the massage earlier. Afraid, hounded by the community's watchful security, and begging for help to save her children and Hayley's child.

Erin went to the sink for a damp cloth. 'Of course, Madeleine. Flour's always so sticky but I'll do my best.'

She just had to work out what exactly she would be saving them from, and how to do it.

•

Simon drove as far as possible along the fire trail before he left his vehicle at a washout. The deluge showed no signs of abating, and in his t-shirt and jeans he was soaked to the skin within seconds. Being wet didn't concern him. His disassembled rifle and other gear were secure inside the waterproof liner of his backpack. He jogged where he could, watching the flow of runoff water down the hillside towards the river. He headed towards a place where the riverbed was wide and sandy.

Usually little more than a creek, sometimes dry, the river had already risen by a metre, spreading here across the width of the riverbed. In the narrower channels at the falls downstream it would be roaring through, and the low-level crossing on Millers Road would already be impassable.

In the grey of the rain on the other bank, Gabe moved to the water's edge. 'You're mad,' his voice said in Simon's earpiece.

'It's not that deep,' Simon retorted. It'd be chest deep in the middle, he reckoned. Maximum of twenty metres wide at present. Do-able. Probably.

He threw a line across to Gabe and they secured each end before Simon pulled on gloves and stepped into the water.

The force of the flow pummelled his legs but he kept moving, gripping the rope, one step at a time, hand over hand. Hip deep. Waist deep. Water kept splashing up into his face and a piece of debris hit his thigh, hard. Chest deep. The water dragged at his backpack, dragged at him, powerful and relentless. Sand gave way to rock and he almost lost his footing, but he dragged himself forward, kept dragging forward, hand over hand over hand, to Gabe, to Erin, to Hayley's child.

Waist deep. His legs shaky with the effort, he made it another metre, then another. Hip deep. Gabe waded in and grabbed his arm, hauling him forward. Simon staggered out of the water and collapsed to his knees in the mud.

'Lunatic,' Gabe said, and gave him a hand up.

Simon gasped for breath, his chest burning. 'Road's blocked. No way around it. Dark soon.' As if it wasn't already dark enough with the rain and clouds.

'They're gathering at the woolshed,' Gabe reported. 'Something big's going on. They're scurrying around in the rain and carting benches inside.'

'Have you seen the girl?'

'They took her in a car with some others up to the house. That was a while ago.'

'Did she go willingly?'

'Eagerly.'

'What security is there now?'

'Bit hard to tell. A few guys wandering around looking thuggish and giving orders. No one obviously standing guard though. Not in this rain, anyway.'

Targets split across two different locations made a silent, non-violent extraction one hell of a challenge. Plus they were outnumbered, two to who knew how many? They'd have to come up with a plan and wait for the right opportunity.

Simon resettled his pack on his shoulders. 'Let's move.'

•

The rain slowed and gradually stopped as Erin returned with Madeleine to the woolshed. More people had gathered, the bench seats around the walls filling. She counted forty people, including children, but the other sisters and the trainees hadn't arrived. Nor Joshua.

No one wore dressy clothes, there were no decorations other than strings of white bulbs to light the space, and there was no food, but a palpable sense of excitement and celebration pulsed in the air.

'Perhaps you'd like to sit with the children?' Madeleine suggested. 'I have services to perform so I'll be busy.'

Under the circumstances, Erin would take any suggestion of Madeleine's.

The looms had been pushed back to make room for a few mattresses and cushions, and most of the children sat there, out of the way of the main area but still part of it and able to see. Fifteen children, from toddlers to almost teens, with two older boys with unbroken voices trying to keep the more restless ones entertained with games.

Madeleine introduced her to the group. 'This is Erin. She's our guest, so will you all look after her? Robbie, you might like to explain the ceremony to her.'

Even after the introduction, the children looked at Erin warily. Suspicious of outsiders, as Tess had predicted. Erin sat on a mattress on the edge of the group, near the small girl she'd seen with Madeleine yesterday. Lily. The child gave her a long, grave stare but said nothing, returning her attention to the scrap of blue cloth in her lap that she inexpertly stitched the edge of with thick yellow yarn. Erin considered offering a compliment, or asking what she was making, but a hush fell over the crowd. Robbie scooted over to sit beside her.

The six sisters stood in a circle in the centre of the space, with Jasmine, Fleur and two other young girls in light blue dresses. Mary began to sing, alone, a short wordless floating melody that she repeated once more.

'Focus on the voices,' Robbie whispered to Erin, taking his responsibility seriously. 'Clear your mind and focus on the sound.'

Despite several attempts at meditation at university she'd never got the hang of it. Tonight she didn't even attempt it. Her mind was crowded with concerns and questions and no way would she try to empty it, or reduce her alertness.

The other sisters and the young girls joined in with Mary on the second repetition of the melody, their voices clear and sweet, singing as one. Jasmine kept her gaze on Madeleine, as if she looked to her for guidance, her young face taut with concentration and trepidation.

As the chant progressed, other voices joined in. Men's voices, weaving an alternate harmony through the women's song. Some of the men moved into place, circling the women. Other women formed a circle around the men, contributing another harmony, and the rest of the men around them, so that all the adults were on the floor, singing, swaying with the tranquil, fluid cadence.

Even most of the children stood and sang, and Erin stood, too, glad that their childish voices were never quite in tune with the music, the scratchy edges of their singing holding her back from slipping into the soothing river of sound and floating there languidly.

And then Joshua was there. It had to be Joshua weaving through the circles, touching a shoulder here, kissing a forehead there, embracing a few, clasping hands fleetingly with others, and all the while the singing continued, until he came to the middle of the circle and held out his arms and turned unhurriedly on the spot, there in the centre of them all, rotating slowly again and again as the song wound down and voices became silent and then there was only Mary singing, one pure voice with the last repetition of notes, holding the very last note until it faded into stillness.

Theatrics, the cynic in Erin whispered. Theatrics and stage management and manipulation. And yet the elation infused her body, as if her nerves and muscles and skin had become the music itself, and she wanted to close her eyes, hold on to the perfect pleasure.

It was science, she told herself. Alteration of perception and mood through the manipulation of sensory stimulation, therefore influencing the body's biochemical responses. Whole fields of psychology, psychiatry, neuroscience and marketing studied the intricacies of neurotransmitters and their effects. Musicians and composers and film directors and writers had used an instinctual awareness of these effects for centuries.

Yet none of the rational logic and knowledge changed the fact that a whole lot of endorphins were lighting up her nervous system and her body hummed with a flood of its own natural happy chemicals.

'Beloved friends!' Joshua began, projecting his voice like an accomplished actor on a large stage. 'You cannot imagine how overjoyed I am to be with you once again.'

Erin only caught glimpses of him among the others. Not quite as tall as some of the other men, he nevertheless held a commanding presence.

A hand touched her thigh. Lily, trying to balance on tiptoe to see. The girl was maybe five or six but small for her age. Erin bent down and picked her up, and Lily wrapped her arm around her, settling on her hip with her gaze still focused intently on Joshua, so transfixed that she seemed oblivious to who was holding her.

Erin could have slipped away with Lily now, out the door behind the looms, while everyone was captivated by Joshua.

But even if Lily didn't raise a ruckus, what good would it do? Jasmine was still somewhere in the centre of the group. Tristan was there, too. She could just see him, standing beside David.

And how could she save any of them when she didn't yet know exactly what she was saving them from?

'To be greeted with such love humbles me,' Joshua continued.

Humble? Erin's cynicism punched out a few more of the happy endorphins.

'I am honoured and blessed, so truly blessed to have your love and friendship. You sustain me in the dark places I must walk. You are my lifeline to hope and joy.' He did one slow revolution on the spot, arms held out. 'Each and every one of you is precious to me.' He smiled and clapped his hands lightly. 'Please, please be comfortable. You've all worked too hard serving the community to stand all the time. Rest yourselves.'

The people drifted away, some to the benches, some sitting on the floor. David and Tristan and two other men in dark blue clothes carried benches across for the six sisters and they sat like nuns at the front of a church service, the four young girls in pale blue at their feet. Except nuns didn't wear sleeveless dresses short enough to showcase smooth calves and elegant feet.

Few of the loose-fitting clothes the others wore could be described as a uniform, but as Erin sat down with Lily on her lap she scanned the room and realised that colour was significant. A few people wore a similar drab brown to the dress the sisters had given her. Others wore muted greens or reds. But the six men and youths standing behind the sisters, and the ones on either side of the main doorway, wore dark blue clothing. She recognised Tom standing by the door, without his oilskin coat. His Nehru-style buttoned jacket with a mandarin collar over loose trousers probably didn't conceal much in the way of weapons or communications technology, and she saw no sign of an earpiece, but his solid, alert stance could have belonged beside a US president.

David had a similar stance of controlled power, but he stood right behind Madeleine where she sat with the other sisters, and a smile played around his mouth. Tristan was beside him; although the boy stood straight, worry creased his young face and he stared at Joshua without rapture.

The man himself remained standing in the centre of the floor. He wore white – a natural white like the sisters, not a blinding, commercially bleached white. His clothes might have belonged in Central Asia or the Middle East – a long-sleeved tunic over trousers, and leather shoes that might have been handcrafted.

Joshua's eloquent and passionate message for his beloved friends was about the further deterioration of the world outside. He held them spellbound as he spoke about the spreading of Ebola and other deadly diseases by people flying across the world; the disruption of the jet stream and the warm, ice-melting air blowing across the Arctic; the continuing spread of hatred and violence across the globe; the poisoning of lakes and rivers by industrial processes and chemical spills.

Again, Erin couldn't disagree with most of it. He was fairly right on essential facts if somewhat thin on science and reason.

She'd barely passed some of her science subjects at uni yet she could have made more convincing, research-supported arguments than he did. But his beloved followers weren't interested in science and reason. They wanted to believe, and Joshua gave them something to believe in. They were safe, here, from the terrors of the world beyond.

'My friends, you have chosen the right path. You tread lightly on the earth without demanding more than it can give. You love each other with generosity and loyalty and you abhor violence and greed. You nurture and care for your children and mine with constancy and devotion.'

His children. Lily's dark hair, curls teasing around her temple, rested against Erin's breast. Despite his short haircut, Tristan's dark hair refused to lie flat and tried to curl.

Joshua's wavy black hair framed his head like a halo.

I am blessed by all he has given me, Madeleine had said.

Jasmine had straight brown hair like her mother. Not dark and wavy, like Joshua's. Not dark and straight, like Simon's.

Fervour gripped Joshua and his voice rose, intense and passionate. 'Out there, in the world, greed reigns, but it never satisfies the emptiness. They will eat hamburgers washed in chemicals and never be sated. They buy more and more clothes made by slave labour from cloth coated in poisons so that they don't have to spend a few minutes ironing them. They live in concrete mansions where there is no grass, no earth to connect to, and that will crumble and shatter around them and crush them to dust when the earth, angry with its mistreatment, tries to shrug off the leeches.'

Oh, he was good. A master of the art. Her father had done okay one-on-one, scamming his targets, but Joshua captivated the whole room, kept them mesmerised and spellbound, affirmed and righteous in their choices and beliefs.

'But you, my beloved friends, you have chosen to embrace simplicity, to know yourselves and to give of yourselves. And in choosing that path, you find joy in honest work, in loving others, in the sweet natural tastes of the food that you grow and the water that you drink. You do not gorge yourselves on emptiness and lust for things you do not need and that can never make you happy. You fast to preserve the earth's precious resources and use only what you need.'

There was still nothing *wrong* or evil in what he said. But restraint and fasting were also, Erin's cynicism noted, a pretty handy philosophy if you had dozens of people and wanted to keep costs down.

She still couldn't work out the money angle. There was definitely money. Millions to buy this property, and – if Madeleine was to be believed – install high-tech surveillance. Perhaps making 'a commitment' involved donating to the cause. She studied the people listening so avidly to Joshua. A few couples, some old enough to have accrued reasonable finances, maybe even a home. Perhaps they'd sold everything to join. But four or five couples donating two hundred thousand each barely made a million dollars.

The younger ones couldn't have contributed that much. Tristan and Jasmine must have grown up in the group; David too, perhaps, and Fleur, sitting at Tamara's feet. Erin thought she could see a slight resemblance between the three of them. Fleur gazed at Joshua, rapt, but Tamara and David seemed more fascinated than enthralled.

The three younger sisters – Callie, Willow and Rebecca – where had they come from? Their innocent trust in Joshua and the community suggested they must have been in the group for years. But if they'd been born into it, then it had been going for more than two decades. A long time to run a scam without significant financial return.

Joshua had moved on to praising 'the brothers who keep us safe from those outside who would hurt us, who would deny us the right to live a simple life as we choose'. Then he praised the sisters. 'Like Mother Earth herself they nourish and cherish us, providing succour and tenderness. They support and guide you on your path and are the light we aspire to. They are bliss, and they give bliss, and I love them as they love us all.' The women rose, and he embraced them in turn, holding them close against his body, and kissing each one on the mouth.

Courtesans of kings, she'd thought earlier. Six women in one house with the same lover? That had to be a recipe for trouble.

The eldest, Mary, smiled as she kissed him, as though they shared some intimate joke. Tamara cupped his face in her hands and kissed him with an open mouth, seductive and inviting. Madeleine stepped forward with head bowed, but he curved

313

one hand around the nape of her neck and tipped her chin up with the other and kissed her despite her reserve. And then he rested his forehead against hers and murmured something, and she went so still that time might have ceased to exist around her.

He moved to Callie and said something that made her laugh, and she kissed him joyfully, and Willow gazed at him in awe and accepted his kiss with a blush reddening her cheeks. Rebecca, the last and perhaps youngest, all shining eyes and beatific smile, almost hyperventilated with the caresses of his gentle mouth.

Erin steeled herself to witness him kissing the trainees, the young teenage girls, but he merely enfolded them in his arms and bestowed a chaste kiss on each cheek. Then he faced the group, raised his arms and cried, 'Let's celebrate! Celebrate our joys, our love, our bliss! Music! Singing! Dancing! Joy and love from within us!'

Several drumbeats sounded and a man stepped into the centre of the room with a long drum slung on a leather cord over his body, his hands building the rhythm steadily. Another man pulled across a stool and sat to play a set of African drums, and a young woman with a wooden flute stood near them, inserting intermittent flutters of notes like birdsong into the rhythmic patterns. People clapped hands, began dancing, and a woman ululated, her long, wavering high-pitched tongue-trill darting in and around the bird-calling flute.

Lily had fallen asleep on Erin's lap, and didn't stir despite the shaking of the timber floor under the dancing feet. But some of the dancers came close in their exuberance. Concerned Lily might be trampled or kicked, Erin carefully picked up the sleeping child and carried her to a mattress in the dim light further back where a couple of little ones already slept under a blanket. She laid her down, tucked the end of the blanket over her.

'So sweet, isn't she?' Joshua said behind her. 'And she already works so hard to serve.'

Erin made herself smile before she faced him. His eyes were blue. The bright, intense blue of the ocean on a summer day. No longer young, perhaps fifty, he still looked youthful, and energy and vitality radiated from him.

'Hello, Erin. Welcome to our community. I'm so pleased that you have come to meet us.' He held out his hand to her. 'Please, dance with me.'

A potential disciple refusing his offered hand? She couldn't decline, or all would be over. He closed his hand over hers and drew her into the mass of dancers.

In the centre of the room he crossed hands with her, his grip firm and warm. 'Put your right foot beside mine,' he said.

Hands joined, he began to turn, and she had no choice but to spin with him, her back foot driving the movement, their right feet keeping the centre. He leaned back, hands strongly gripping hers, and the speed and the force made her lean out too.

As the drums beat their rhythm and the flute and voices soared, they whirled, faster and faster, around and around, and she couldn't stop it or miss a step because the centrifugal force would have sent her flying. She couldn't look at anything but him, because otherwise the spinning would make her too dizzy, and those too-blue eyes held hers and he controlled it with his strength and his will and she knew that he toyed with her as confidently as a cat with a mouse.

He eventually slowed, and the drumming slowed, and with several more revolutions they came to a stop. He let go of one hand, but holding the other firmly he twirled her under his raised arm and pulled her in close to him so that her back was against his chest. Her head still spun and she closed her eyes so that the room didn't keep moving around her, and she needed that support behind her lest she fall.

'Oh, you are beautiful, Erin,' he said, and it was no intimate compliment but projected in the voice he used to speak to everyone. 'Friends, this is Erin. She is searching for the truth and has come to us to find it.'

The drumbeat continued, but soft, muted, marking time.

Her head no longer spinning quite as fast, Erin opened her eyes. They were all around her. All of them. Around her and Joshua, and his arms circled her waist holding her tight against him, so tight she couldn't twist her head far enough to see him.

'We have to be careful, Erin. There are forces in the world outside that want to destroy what we have. We have to protect what is ours, don't we, friends?'

The voices of agreement swelled, strong and determined.

'Will you prove your integrity to us, Erin?' he asked.

'Prove it,' someone said. Another picked up the call, and another: 'Yes, prove it.'

They moved in closer, dozens of people, breathless and wired and euphoric from the dancing and the music and Joshua's electrifying presence. If they turned on her, Erin knew there were plenty of places in the bush to hide a body. The constant beating of the drum kicked up a notch, matching her fluttering heartbeat.

'Yes, yes, of course,' she lied. 'I just want to find happiness, to serve the community and be happy.'

'Would you do what I ask of you, Erin?'

'Yes. Yes, I would. I want to love you, Joshua, to serve you.'

'Are you sure, Erin?'

'Yes. Yes.'

His right hand cupped her breast, his left flexed against her abdomen, his fingers dipping suggestively low. She closed her eyes, trying to make her expression ecstatic, and hoped she'd succeed in not throwing up.

He kissed her neck, his breath hot against her ear, and murmured just for her, 'Would you step off a cliff for me, Erin? Would you plunge a knife into your belly for me?'

Her body froze and although her brain screamed at her to fight, run, escape, she could not even think to make a muscle move. Her pulse throbbed in her head louder and harder than the ever-present drumbeat. He knew who she was and why she was there.

He laughed out loud, a rumbling in his chest that reverberated through her body, and although he still held her, his hands no longer caressed her so sexually. 'Oh, Erin, beautiful Erin,' he said loudly, 'I shouldn't tease you so. Later, sweet Erin. Later.'

Later – she couldn't be around for what happened later. She had to get away. But he was strong and she couldn't fight him off and run through a mob of people who'd be only too happy to stop her and punish her for her betrayal.

She tried to step away from him and he released her so suddenly that she staggered on her feet. He caught her hand to steady her and slid his arm around her shoulders. 'You've been dancing too hard. David, some water for Erin.'

She was supposed to want to love him, not wrench herself away from him. 'No. Thank you. I'm just dizzy. I'll be fine.'

'Drink,' he said, holding the cup to her lips.

Don't drink the water tonight.

Panic switched her brain into overdrive. 'I can't. I didn't fast this morning. I didn't know. But I'm fasting now. A total fast.'

'We fast to preserve resources, Erin. But we have an abundance of water today and the tanks are overflowing. You must be thirsty. Please quench your thirst.'

He held her throat and chin tight in one hand, tipped the cup and she could do nothing but take two mouthfuls. She put up her hand to stop him but he tipped a little further and the water rushed her throat so that she spluttered and coughed. He snatched his hand and the cup away, laughing. She'd sprayed water over his hand.

She caught a glimpse of Willow in the group, looking horrified, and she made herself become that, an appalled, ashamed devotee.

'I'm sorry! Oh, I'm so *sorry.*' The tears that welled were genuine. But of dread, not shame. She backed away from him. 'I didn't mean it,' she said. 'I'm so sorry.'

She turned and ran from the woolshed, past Tom, out into the night and down the stairs, around the corner of the building. She fell on her knees in the mud, stuck her fingers down her throat and forced herself to throw up the water he'd made her drink.

CHAPTER 16

Simon watched from sixty metres away as she coughed and retched and sobbed and he couldn't do a damn thing about it because one of the two outside guards was standing near her.

The drumming started up again and through the still-open door he could see them resuming their dancing. The guards had put something into the barrel of water they'd carried up the stairs and it worried the hell out of him, but that had been well over an hour ago. Everyone was still on their feet dancing around like maniacs and no one seemed the worse for wear.

Except Erin.

When he'd seen that door burst open and she came flying out and down the stairs he'd jumped to his feet, ready to run to her. But she'd dropped to her hands and knees and no one had come after her except the burly inside guard who'd casually looked down at her over the railings, and the outside guard who'd leaned over her for a moment as if asking if she was okay and then retreated a few metres away.

She sat back on her heels, wiping her forearm across her mouth, then used her skirt to clean her hands of mud.

The woman from the falls came out the wide door and quickly down the stairs to Erin, the white of her dress a bright flare through his night-vision goggles. Her arm around Erin, she helped her to her feet, and after a brief challenge from the guard – he backed down when the woman in white asserted her authority sharply – they made their way towards the cottages.

The storm had passed, the sky now clear, and moonlight filled the open spaces where the single bulbs on the outside of each cottage didn't reach.

Gabe had gone up to check the house, find out if anyone was still there. That was a while ago. Even with the encrypted radio, Simon and Gabe were on comms silence because they were too close in and he couldn't be sure none of the guards had radios. The encryption only masked the words, not the fact of the signal.

The woman had her arm around Erin as they walked, and Erin's head rested on her shoulder. What the hell had distressed Erin so much? He'd never seen her break down. Even faced with drama and death in their work, she'd sniff back tears and soldier on. But she must trust the woman to show that vulnerability.

The guard patrolling the buildings stopped them but again the woman used her authority and he stepped aside and didn't follow, turning to rejoin his mate by the woolshed. Erin and her companion went up the steps of the first cottage. The women's cottage, Gabe had reported this morning.

Simon checked the location of the guards, planned his route, and set off towards the cottage, looping around behind the machinery shed and using the second cottage as his cover to get to the first. He planned to get Erin out the same way, even if he had to knock out the other woman to do so.

•

For the short walk to the cottage, away from walls that listened and spied, Erin pretended to be distraught, with her head on Madeleine's shoulder so they could talk. The distress was real, but she couldn't afford to be weakened by it. Madeleine seemed closer to breaking point than she was.

'He's planning something. Something big,' Madeleine whispered. 'Tonight. Mary knows, I'm sure. She joined us three years ago, and everything changed.' Her distress almost overwhelmed her. 'In town on Friday – I heard that a woman was murdered. Hayley's dead, isn't she?'

Evidently she hadn't known for certain. Erin squeezed Madeleine's hand. 'Yes. I'm sorry.'

'Was it her husband, Simon Kennedy? Or Joshua?'

Would you plunge a knife into your belly for me? A shudder jarred through her again. Could Hayley have . . . ? No, surely it wasn't physically possible. Once, maybe, but not multiple times. Not cutting your own throat.

'It wasn't Simon,' Erin said quickly. 'Trust him, Madeleine.'

They didn't have much time and Madeleine spoke in a rush. 'She found something, cleaning Mary's office. She wouldn't tell me and Syb but she said it was all a lie. That he'd used us, the whole time, that the children weren't safe. She went to get help. Then Tris saw Joshua at the falls. With Sybilla. He held her hand, and he kissed her, and he stood back and she . . . stepped off.'

The watcher on the cliff top. Had he hoped that Sybilla was still alive? Was that why he'd waited? An inexperienced lad couldn't have easily made his way down to her in the dark.

'I should have left yesterday. That's why we were there. Tris had seen the path on the park side. I thought we could go that way. I didn't tell them I planned it. But then you said – about the detective. I . . . I know him. Steve Fraser. I'm a coward and I couldn't face him. And then David saw us going back.'

They were almost at the cottage. So many questions, not enough time.

'What did Joshua say tonight, when he kissed you?'

'He said, "You're next, Maddie."'

'Why? Why the three of you?'

'We know who he is. Who Joshua really is. And we believed in him.'

•

Simon let himself into the cottage through the unlocked laundry door. The bug scanner Gabe had lent him detected only weak signals here. The bastards had bugged the bathroom and the bedrooms but not the laundry.

The cottage was small and he could hear Erin and the other woman on the veranda, and the creak of the opening front door.

'I'll find some clothes,' the woman said. 'You go and clean up. There are towels in the laundry cupboard. Leave the dress in the sink, and I'll wash it out.'

He breathed a fraction more easily. A piece of luck. He hadn't had much of it up until now. He flipped up the night-vision goggles to let his eyes adjust to the room's darkness.

The corridor light went on, Erin's footsteps approached, and then she was there in the doorway. She started when she saw him move in the shadows.

'Shhh,' he said, a finger to his lips. She didn't say anything. She just walked into his arms and hugged him, hard, and he felt her body shake as if she sobbed silently.

But when he reached with one hand to turn on the tap in the laundry sink, she lifted her head and waited until the water splashed loudly against the metal before she whispered, 'You have to get help. He's mad. He's planning something.'

'It's okay. I'll get you out.' He nodded at the laundry door. 'We can go now.'

'I can't. I have to help Madeleine, and we have to get her kids and Jasmine.'

Jasmine. The girl's name was Jasmine; Lily the little one's name. Jasmine, who might be his daughter.

The woman – Madeleine – came out of one of the bedrooms. 'I've got trousers and a tunic for you . . .'

Erin stood just back from the doorway, signalling her to come in. The water still poured into the sink, making a racket. When Madeleine saw him, fear and hope alternated on her face, but she gathered herself hastily. As she closed the door, she continued her conversation with Erin for the benefit of the bugs. 'Kat's about your size, and she won't mind.'

The door clicked into place, the three of them in the small space together.

'Simon, this is Madeleine,' Erin whispered. 'Please tell us the police are coming.'

'They're not. Not yet. The rivers are up and they can't get through.'

'They have to,' Erin insisted. 'Can you contact Steve? Tell him he has to find a way to come. Joshua's got them all fired up. We don't have much time. I've got to change.' The water still ran into the sink and she pulled her dress over her head and dampened it under the tap, standing in her bra and briefs while she used the cleaner parts of the wet dress to wipe the mud from her legs.

Simon handed her a towel from the cupboard and averted his eyes. 'Joshua is a psychologist. His name's Peter Hollywell. He's been playing some weird game for years, and last week in

New York he outed "Joshua" as a fraud, using mind control, hypnosis and drugs to manipulate his followers.'

Too late, he remembered that Madeleine was one of them. Her face was ashen in pain. 'That's what Hayley discovered?' she whispered. 'That he used us? That it really is all lies?'

'Yes. I'm sorry.'

'We always knew who he was. But we believed him. We believed Joshua was real, and Peter his worldly mask. Then she said she'd discovered it was all lies, and the changes . . . the changes began to seem frightening. Moving here, the secrecy, the spying – he said it was to keep us safe.'

More likely to keep his identity safe, his adherents under control. 'Who else knows he's Hollywell?' Simon asked. He tried to gentle his voice. 'It's important, Madeleine. People who know may not be safe. Whatever he's got planned, he can't do it if people know.'

'Only a few of us, from when it all began. We kept the secret. Me, Hayley, Sybilla, a couple of others who have left. Tamara knows, too, but she – I don't think she believes in him like we did. Maybe she knows it's all lies.'

Her hands shaking, Madeleine tried to rub soap onto the mud on the dress but kept dropping the soap into the tub. Simon closed his hands over hers and took it from her. If they were only meant to be here long enough for Erin to get changed, someone would come looking for them soon.

Erin finished dressing. 'Have you got the sat phone?' she asked. 'Tell Steve there's some kind of drug in the water.

And Joshua as good as told me he murdered Hayley and Sybilla.'

'I'll get on to him.' There had to be a way for the police to come. He and Gabe couldn't deal with the situation alone. Not without risking too many lives. He'd call Steve and Nick and harass them and insist until they found some way to get a show of force in here.

Madeleine touched him on the arm. 'This Steve – Steve Fraser? He's about thirty-six? Brown eyes? His father was also a police officer?'

Simon hadn't really noticed Fraser's eye colour and couldn't see how the hell it mattered, but Erin said, 'Yes. That's him. Why?'

'Then tell him . . . If something happens to me, tell him I beg him to look after my children. They have no one else but him. He's their uncle.'

He stared at her, fitting it all together. 'You're his sister?'

'His *sister*?' Erin echoed.

'Yes.'

He remembered Fraser's face earlier, the pain still raw almost twenty years after the event. 'He thinks you're dead.' He spoke more harshly than he meant to.

Her face as white as her dress, she whispered, 'Yes. Please tell him I'm sorry. More sorry than he can know.'

Boots drummed on the veranda, a hard knock sounded on the front door of the cottage.

Madeleine reached for the laundry door. 'We must go. Or they'll come looking for us.' She'd opened it and was gone before he could object. He could take on a couple of guards, still get them out – but Erin and Madeleine couldn't leave without the children, and their guards were civilians, not enemy combatants, so his hands were ethically and legally tied.

Erin rested her hand on his chest and gave him a crooked smile. 'Watch my back, Kennedy. And if I happen to throw a little girl your way, catch her, okay?' Then she lifted her head and kissed him on the mouth, before she walked out the door, back to Joshua, back into danger, with no weapons but her courage and her heart and her wits.

•

She had no idea what Joshua had planned, but her instincts screamed that he stood on the brink of some dramatic action. His taunting of her, and of Madeleine, the amusement he'd shared with Mary when he'd kissed her, the celebratory gathering of everyone in the woolshed: it was risky, dangerous behaviour, so he had to be confident that he would escape the consequences.

In the woolshed the drumming and the dancing continued unabated and Joshua was in the middle of it all, whipping it up like a ringmaster, encouraging the frenzy. Erin had never been into drugs and didn't know what he'd laced the water with but euphoria and hyper-energy had infected everyone. Even some of the older kids. The woolshed floor vibrated with the pounding of feet and the ceaseless unstoppable drumming. Voices sang and whooped and women ululated while Joshua held a small cask of water under his arm and dispensed it to his beloved followers.

'Water is life! Such beautiful water! Precious gift! Quench your thirst! Tonight we have an abundance!'

They echoed him, celebrating water, cheering and shouting and singing and drinking. The young sisters and the trainees whirled and danced with the others.

'Party drugs,' Madeleine whispered in her ear as they skirted the dancers and made their way towards the dimness of the children's corner. 'He's done it before. He says it's harmless, a path to bliss. But they don't remember, afterwards.'

Three of the littlest ones still slept under the blanket but Lily was stirring, screwing up her eyes in protest at the noise. Madeleine picked her up and held her on her hip and Lily snuggled into her shoulder, her eyes still closed. Tired? Or drugged? Would Joshua have given sedatives to small children?

Erin caught sight of Jasmine on the edge of the dancers, whirling with David, and she had more than one reason to want to drag the young girl away from his groping hands and the lascivious gloating on his face. David had seen Madeleine and the children with her at the waterfall yesterday, and presumably reported it. David couldn't be trusted. She couldn't see Tristan, who could perhaps be trusted, because he'd witnessed Sybilla's death and now doubted Joshua.

She dodged cavorting people and hands reaching out to draw her in, but then a man grabbed her from behind, lifting her bodily and spinning her around, laughing and chanting with the music.

'Water!' Joshua cried, his voice rising above the drums. 'River of water! Come to the river of water!'

'The river! The river!'

'Everyone come to the river! Bring the little ones! All of us to the river's blessings!'

The river. Alarm gave Erin strength to break away from her captor, who spun off obliviously and caught someone else's hands.

The river – swollen by the storm's deluge, it would be a deadly torrent of water and mud and debris.

The first ones were already going, heading out into the night. Joshua called, 'Light! Take the light into the dark! Light the path to the river!' and Mary was there, at the door, with the rushlights they'd made for the outside bonfire before the storm changed the plans and moved the celebration inside. David whisked Jasmine towards the door with him, and before Erin could reach them they were gone.

Soon there were only a few stragglers left. A woman picking up a toddler. An entwined, half-undressed couple making slow progress to the door. Tom, gripping Madeleine's arm as she held Lily. And one more child still sleeping on the mattress on the floor.

Two of them against Tom.

He caught Erin's arm in a vice-like grip before her strike fell. 'Get the child,' he ordered her, and when she didn't move immediately he growled again, 'Get the frigging baby,' and there was a note in his voice that was desperation, not aggression.

She wrapped the blanket quickly around the slumbering toddler, a little boy, and lifted him in her arms.

'Move,' Tom ordered again, and now he had a knife in his hand, held at Madeleine's neck, and he pushed her towards the door.

As they left the woolshed, she caught a strong whiff of smoke. Fire. Its floorboards soaked with a century of lanolin, the woolshed would burn fiercely.

In the night, the ragged line of rushlights twisted and danced past the shearers' quarters and the cottages.

'Keep moving,' Tom ordered, pressing the tip of the knife into Madeleine's neck. 'Erin in front. We're going to the river. All of us are going. I'll kill her if you do anything stupid.'

Her arms full of the dead weight of the sleeping child, Erin's only choice was to follow his orders. Somewhere there would be a chance. And Simon was watching her back.

Away from the shed, she slowed as they passed the women's cottage, but Tom ordered again, 'Keep moving.' Then he dropped his voice. 'She'll still be watching. We have to follow the others. I'm supposed to make sure you don't come back but this isn't right. What he's doing isn't right. We're the only ones who can stop him.'

•

One man and one knife. Just one man, and they were fifty metres behind the rest of the group. No one followed them. The woman in white who'd torched the woolshed was already halfway to the house.

One man and one knife. Easy. Kindergarten easy.

He ended his whispered call to Nick on the sat phone, signalled Gabe and they moved quickly through the trees to intercept the small group. The roar of the river as it surged over the falls and through the gorge made a constant rolling background thunder, and the women and their captor made enough noise on the rough ground to mask his and Gabe's footfalls.

When Gabe stepped out of the trees in front of Erin, Simon fell in behind the man and in one quick move put a throttlehold around his neck and wrenched the knife from his hand.

'Don't!' said Erin. 'Don't hurt him!'

He hadn't been planning to. Much. Not a war zone. Not an enemy combatant.

The man didn't struggle. 'I won't fight you,' he said.

'Tom helped us,' Erin said.

'We have to get to the river,' the man said. 'To the waterfall. He's going to make them go in. He'll make them all go into the water. Madeleine and I might be able to stop them.'

Into the water, where the force of it would suck them under and wash them over the cliff into the seething, churning whirlpools below. Simon dropped his chokehold but kept the knife.

'Please, take Lily to safety,' Madeleine begged him. 'I have to try to save them.'

Upwards of fifty people, men, women and children, standing by that death trap with the twisted man who'd played with their minds for years.

'Gabe, take the kids and Erin somewhere safe. Now.'

Gabe objected but Simon spoke over him. 'Not this time. It's not your fight. Get those kids and Erin off this property and to the police. I need you to do that. I'm trusting you on that.'

In the filtered moonlight among the trees he thought he saw terror on Gabe's face. Giving him kids to save? Exactly what he needed. And Simon had to keep him away from what might happen at the waterfall.

Madeleine thrust her daughter at Gabe. He took the child rather than letting her fall, and shot a pleading look at Simon. Erin stepped forward. 'Take this one, too. You can manage both. You're a strong guy, whoever you are. Use the blanket as a sling, if you like.'

Simon put a hand on her shoulder. 'Erin, go with Gabe. He's a mate of mine.'

She looked him straight in the eye, firm and determined. 'I'm going to the river. We have to hurry.' She grabbed Madeleine's hand and they set off at a run.

Tom began to follow them but then turned and said to Gabe, 'Watch out for Mary. Avoid her. She's in on this. Planned it with Joshua. I believed in him for a long time, but her . . .' He shook his head and followed the others.

'Police should be coming through from the west soon,' Simon told Gabe. 'They crossed the river at the bridge on the main Derringvale road and are borrowing quad bikes from a farmer to cross the paddocks. Meet them and brief them.' He left his friend holding the two sleeping children as awkwardly as if they were live bombs and caught up with Tom, then Erin and Madeleine within fifty paces.

They came out of the trees on a rise overlooking the waterfall. The moonlight shone unimpeded and bright over the open area around the falls. The river powered over the rocks, all the small channels swallowed up into one immensely powerful rush of water, metres deep.

And Joshua stood on a rock overhanging the torrent, arms wide, his followers swaying and chanting on the flat rocks in front of him, their rushlights held high. The gear his goons had carried to the falls earlier this evening had to be a portable speaker system, because the bastard's voice carried even above the thunder of the water.

Madeleine, Erin and Tom scrambled down the slope and Simon almost followed. He stopped, two choices tearing at him. Protecting Erin down there, stopping the carnage . . . but there might be only one way to stop it. Only one way to stop Joshua.

The bastard had no intention of dying out there with his lambs. The road closure had barely put a dent in his plans, and the flooding river was aiding him. He had to be stopped.

Simon slid off his backpack, dropped to the ground, and drew out the waterproof satchel with his disassembled rifle.

'Water is life! Water is bliss!' Joshua proclaimed. 'We are made of water, we crave water! Will you embrace the water?'

Stock. Barrel. Scope.

'Will you embrace bliss? Who will become water?'

Madeleine and Erin had reached the edge of the group.

Ammunition.

'Who will become pure? Who will become one with water?'

'I will!' a woman cried. 'I will!'

'No!' Erin screamed, trying to push her way between the gathered, swaying people. 'No!'

The woman twirled on a rock at the edge of the river, her white dress floating out around her. 'I will!' she cried again, and stepped off the rock into the surging torrent. She disappeared from view in seconds, swept over the edge of the falls.

Unable to do anything to save her, Simon swore aloud but his words were drowned out by cries of joy, of exultation from the group.

'Bliss!' Joshua shouted. 'Such bliss! Who will join us in bliss? Beautiful, beautiful bliss! Eternal bliss!'

They moved closer, all of them, to the water, singing, dancing, captivated by the delusions.

Simon crawled forward, flat on his stomach. Out of the corner of his eye, he saw movement in the trees, between him and the people below.

'Bliss!' a woman cried, and Erin reached her and wrapped her arms around her, struggling to hold her back from the edge. On the far edge of the crowd a young man with his arm around Jasmine pushed through the others, towards the water.

Joshua still stood high on his rock above them, arms held out, his white clothes pale against the sky.

Simon lifted his rifle to his shoulder. They'd go into the water, all of them, within moments, if Joshua wasn't silenced. All of them, willing or not. Madeleine. Jasmine. Erin.

Simon sighted his target through the scope. A civilian. In Australia. A man who was cajoling fifty others to jump to their deaths.

'Bliss!' voices shouted.

Just as the trigger of his rifle fully depressed, Simon heard the double retort of two other shots, blending with the explosion of sound of his own.

Joshua jerked, brought his hands to his chest. For a long moment he stood motionless, before he toppled backwards, falling several metres into the rushing water and then over the edge, out of sight.

His followers shouted, surged forward, perilously close to the water, when a woman's voice cried out, loud and powerfully, 'Stop!'

Madeleine strode between them, a slight figure in white, hair whipping around in the breeze. But when she stood before them on the edge of the rock, hands raised, there was nothing slight about her. She was majestic. Compelling.

'Joshua has ascended to bliss,' she cried, her voice bouncing off rocks and carrying higher than the river's roar. 'But you are not ready. Your work is not done. None of you are ready. None of *us* are ready. Go. Go home and sleep. Tomorrow we will meet to discuss what is next. Go and sleep now. Go and sleep. Take the children with you and sleep.'

She had them. Maybe not in the palm of her hand, but she'd arrested the headlong drive to oblivion.

The youth holding Jasmine pulled her another step forward, and Simon kept the scope on him, trigger finger poised, but someone stepped in – Tom – and with a throttlehold on the lad's neck, dragged him back.

The girl seemed dazed, uncertain, and Erin went to her, took her in her arms, and steered her well away from the water.

And Madeleine kept repeating her message, speaking with love and compassion, and no one challenged her. The urgent, frantic energy of the group dissipated, and they began to drift backwards, away from the water's edge.

Simon took the ammunition from his rifle, slid off the scope, made it secure, and returned it to his backpack. The armour of logic and concentration with which he'd acted began to dissolve and his pulse thudded in his head. More people could have died. Erin could have died. He would play that moment of decision, his hands taking that shot, over and over again. And he'd do it, every time.

At the bottom of the rise he found Steve and Tess, standing back, watching Joshua's disciples from a distance. Steve still held his service pistol loosely clasped by his side. Tess had sheathed hers again, but her hand rested on it.

'Thought it would be you up there,' Steve said, but although he attempted a grin it didn't succeed, and he returned to watching the group, his face pale.

'You both fired,' Simon said, and it wasn't a question.

Tess answered in a flat voice. 'Yes.'

Steve didn't take his eyes off the group and the woman moving slowly through it. 'They'll find his body in a day or two. Then we'll know.'

Which of them had shot him. Perhaps. Depending on bullets and angle and whether they'd lodged or passed through.

In a sense it didn't matter. The other two were serving police officers. Simon wasn't. But on the hill he'd known a murder charge and life in prison was a better alternative to the nightmare of collecting bodies downstream. He slid his backpack off his shoulder and held it out to Steve. 'My rifle's in there. You'll have my statement in the morning. If you want to arrest me now, I understand.'

Steve didn't move. 'We'll talk tomorrow,' he said.

Madeleine continued to move among the group, speaking with them, touching them gently. As a woman who'd spent over half her life under Joshua's influence, her intuition, or her inherent wisdom, recognised what they needed now. It wasn't the truth. If she'd stood in front of them and proclaimed Joshua a fraud, it would have been a disaster.

Steve had to have recognised her, but he made no move to go to her. In the semi-darkness, she wouldn't know he was there.

Erin knew they were there. Simon had watched her, too. She'd taken Jasmine back from the water's edge, far back to safety. And she'd held her while she struggled and cried and eventually quietened. And then they searched together through the group, finding another young woman bereft on her knees, and took her to Madeleine, who embraced them all.

And still neither Simon nor Steve moved.

Smoke drifted over them. The woolshed would have collapsed by now. With everything sodden from the rain, the fire might not have spread to other buildings. If they were lucky. From the things he'd found in the rubbish drums behind the shed, Simon suspected the locked doors concealed a meth lab. That might explain some of the money and the security paranoia, but the highly flammable chemicals made the place potentially explosive. He'd warned Nick on the phone.

'What are we going to do with these people?' Simon asked. The flooded roads wouldn't be reopened until the morning, at least. And they had more than fifty people who would be traumatised and homeless.

Tess had turned away to use the sat phone but she heard his question and broke off her conversation to answer. 'Nick's putting some contingency plans in place. RFS and SES trucks to get them through to the community hall at Derringvale. There'll be paramedics there and he's calling in counsellors. Strathnairn Hospital and the rescue helicopter are on standby.'

It would be a long way around to Strathnairn from here via Derringvale, but accessible. These people would be looked after. But there was a long, rocky road ahead for all of them.

CHAPTER 17

Erin finally found Simon again when she arrived back with Willow and the last of Joshua's people at the cottages. He'd guided others back through the bush ahead of her. The flashing lights of RFS and SES trucks strobed in the pre-dawn light, one more surreal image in an unreal night.

Physical and emotional exhaustion dragged at her but she kept putting one foot in front of the other until the last of her bewildered charges had been reassured by Madeleine and helped aboard a truck.

She could see Simon standing by the shearers' quarters with Steve, and she steered her exhausted body that way and walked the fifteen metres into Simon's arms. He held her tightly, so tightly she could have let him take her weight but she didn't, quite.

'We're on the next truck,' he said. 'Then I'll get you home.'

'Did you see her?' she asked.

He didn't ask who she meant. 'Yes. She doesn't know who I am, of course. She'll be in Derringvale by now. They may take the kids to hospital for assessment.'

Erin lifted her head from the sanctuary of Simon's shoulder. She hadn't seen Steve since the immediate aftermath at the waterfall, and then only from a distance. Now he was there, and Madeleine had put the last of Joshua's people on a truck to safety. 'Go to her,' she told him. 'She thinks you hate her for what she did. For what he made her do.'

Steve hesitated for one long breath. Then he walked across to where his sister waited, watching him, afraid, and he put his arms around her, and the man who pretended to treat life lightly laid his face on her hair and cried.

Erin could hear Simon's heartbeat, feel it under her palm, strong and real and honest. 'Take me home,' she said. 'Take me home and hold me and love me and sleep with me.'

He tensed, his breathing shallow. 'I'll take you home, and I'll always love you. But I . . . They may arrest me for murder tomorrow, Erin.'

She stepped back within the circle of his arms. 'Then I'll fight it and I'll give evidence and keep giving it until they understand that you saved many lives. Callie walked into that water, believing him. Willow would have done it too. And Rebecca. So many others. You saved those lives. All of them.'

'You saved that girl yourself. The one you held back. You saved her.'

'Only because Joshua had gone. If he'd still been there, I couldn't have held her.'

And if Joshua had been there, if he'd asked, Willow would have dragged her into the water as well.

She hoped that when the drugs wore off, Willow wouldn't remember. But Erin would. She'd remember the roar of the water and the smell of mud, and a young girl's dilated eyes and her ecstatic face, desperate to embrace death in her belief of Joshua and his lies.

•

'You are admitting that you fired at an unarmed man?' In the relative privacy of the small area behind the stage of the Derringvale community hall, Leah Haddad shot the question at him.

Simon nodded with more patience than he felt. 'Yes. As I explained to Nick, I considered dozens of lives to be imminently at risk. I'm prepared to give a full statement, and to cooperate with the investigation. You'll want to take the rifle for examination. It's in here.' He handed over his backpack and Haddad took it reluctantly.

'Jesus, what a mess,' she said under her breath, showing some emotion for the first time in Simon's limited experience of her. 'Look, Kennedy, I've already called in Internal Affairs for a full investigation, since two police officers also fired their weapons. They'll be here in a few hours. They'll probably want to talk with you —' she glanced at her watch, 'later today.'

He'd expected to be arrested, but she gave no indication of wanting to. Everything had changed in the few days since she'd arrested him for Hayley's murder.

'I'll be around,' Simon promised. 'I can call down to the Strathnairn station in the afternoon.'

'Good. We'll be in touch.' She handed his pack back to him and dismissed him with a nod.

In the main part of the hall, district services had already swung into action under Nick's direction. The SES squad had brought in camp stretchers and gym mats from the Strathnairn Police Youth Club, but with that done the crew waited at a distance outside, giving Joshua's people privacy.

Dazed, confused, Joshua's followers huddled at one end of the hall, a few asleep, others whispering among themselves, mistrustful of the 'outsiders' and particularly wary of the small group of police officers. The girl, Jasmine, slept on a mat in the corner, her arm protectively around a sleeping child.

Catherine, the community nurse, and one of her colleagues had already spoken with each of the adults and assessed the sleeping ones and the children for responsiveness, while two kindly women from the Country Women's Association moved among the group with sandwiches and cups of tea, gathering names from those prepared to give them. Erin was still in the kitchen at the other end of the hall, briefing Nick and the small team of counsellors and child protection officers he'd assembled.

Simon skirted the group and went outside to wait for her on the veranda of the hall. At a picnic table under a tree nearby, Fraser and his sister, Madeleine, spoke quietly together around the occasional awkward silence. But eventually Madeleine rose and, after a brief hug, left her brother to return inside.

She paused beside Simon, shy but brave. 'I've heard a lot about you over the years,' she said. 'We were only a small group – just a household – when Hayley joined us. She and I became close friends. Steve just asked me about her, and said you need to know. She was already pregnant when she came to us, but she was very frightened of losing the baby. I already had Tristan then, and I helped when Jasmine was born.' Her composure faltering, she sniffed, and wiped damp eyes with her hand. 'Hayley always said you were Jasmine's father, and she felt guilty about not telling you. But she was afraid you'd take Jasmine from her, that she didn't deserve her, because she'd left you.'

The rock-like lump in Simon's throat made words difficult. 'I wouldn't have done that.'

'We were . . . persuaded to believe a lot of things. I don't know anymore what was right, and what was lies.'

'You were very young. And Hayley didn't have a lot of reasons to believe that the world would treat her well.' He said it gently, because the last thing this woman needed was his anger, although the truth was that he wanted to punch a fist through a wall, or into Joshua's face instead of the clean quick kill. But regrets and self-accusation rang even louder in his mind than his anger at Joshua. If he'd looked for Hayley instead of convincing himself she needed to 'fly free', if he'd tried harder to save their marriage, if, if, if . . .

'Steve says you're a good man. Hayley always said that, too. I'll tell Jasmine that she can trust you and believe in you.'

Believe in him? When he'd stuffed up so fatally with Hayley? He swallowed with difficulty. Put his daughter and her needs first. That's what he had to do. 'Does she know? About her mother's death?'

Madeleine shook her head. 'Not yet. After Hayley left, Joshua told her not to worry, that she'd see her mother again soon. Erin said there are counsellors and they will work out the best way to tell her the truth.'

Maybe they'd tell him where to start, too. How to establish a relationship with a daughter he didn't know.

Madeleine put a hand on his arm, looked up earnestly into his face. 'Steve keeps asking me if I was happy. It seems important to him. I *was* happy, Simon. Hayley was happy. Not telling you about Jasmine was the only thing that worried her. Our lives were rich and full of love. It was only when Mary came that it started changing. That Joshua started changing. Mary . . . I think she was like him. That they acted together. And I think they grew tired of us, and wanted something bigger. But all those years before that . . . I did know, then, what bliss meant. And we had it, Hayley and I and the others.'

She left him and went inside, and only then did he see Erin standing in the doorway.

'I heard,' she said, after Madeleine had passed her with a brave smile. She came to him and took his hand and he gripped it, the connection grounding him because she was strong and constant, a rock in his rapidly shifting world.

'Hayley was happy,' she said. 'Maybe it was based on lies and maybe it was because she couldn't cope with the world, but she was happy all that time. Hold on to that. Hold on to me. You're going to make a damn fine father.'

•

From the Derringvale hall they hitched a ride back to Strathnairn on one of the SES trucks. Erin dozed against his shoulder for some of the way but woke when the driver – one of their regular squad – pulled up at her place on the outskirts of town.

The peach-gold light of the rising sun reflected off her front windows as they jumped down from the truck. She found her spare key in its hiding place – her wallet, keys, phone and ute were still back at the main house at Serenity Hill.

He followed her inside but paused in the living room, his backpack still on his shoulder. He hadn't actually been invited to stay. And it was hours since their embrace in the emotion of the scene at Serenity Hill. 'I just assumed,' he began, 'that I could stay in your spare room for a day or two.'

She turned at the kitchen door, and despite everything she'd been through her smile teased him gently. 'You assumed correctly. Except about the spare room. I seem to recall saying something not long ago about holding and loving and sleeping. Consider that an invitation.'

She didn't wait to hear his response. He heard the kettle flick on in the kitchen, the sound of running water in the bathroom.

He had a long list of reasons why he should turn right around and walk back out the door. He had a hunger and a need and a craving that he'd carried for so long that he'd come to believe this half-emptiness was the way it always had been, always had to be.

He'd coped.

Erin coped. No, that wasn't the right word. She tackled challenges, came to grips with problems, found solutions, and if something didn't work and she fell down, she got up, dusted herself off and tackled the problem again.

All the skills and resilience he used to meet the demands of his work, she applied to everything.

His backpack thunked softly to the floor.

She came out of the bathroom wearing an old t-shirt and not much else and kissed him fleetingly and with a taste of peppermint as she passed on her way to the laundry with a bundle of clothes. 'Glad you decided to stay. You can have first shower if you promise not to use all the hot water. Sadly there's not room for two in there. Toss your clothes out to me and I'll put them in the washing machine.'

'Are you sure, Erin?'

She raised an amused eyebrow. 'About the washing machine?'

'About us. I've got a pretty lousy track record in relationships. I failed Hayley.'

She came back the few steps to stand in front of him. 'Don't you dare say that, Simon Kennedy,' she said quietly, and she wasn't teasing now. 'Don't you dare believe that of yourself. You were both young and maybe it was an unequal partnership and a mistake, but you know what? The fact that even after all the time apart she came to you when she needed help – that speaks volumes about the kind of man you are and the type of marriage you had.'

An unequal partnership. With just three words she'd put her finger on the gist of the differences between him and Hayley and the weakness in the foundation of their marriage.

'I guess I married her to protect her.'

'Yep, and you have a caring, compassionate heart under that tough-guy exterior. But I don't need protecting, Simon. I'm not a fragile china doll who needs to be looked after. I won't say no to chocolates or cups of coffee in bed or to having you at my back if there are ever any more homicidal maniacs out there, but I'll be doing the same for you.' She gave him a friendly push. 'Now go. Shower off that mud while I put clean sheets on the bed.'

He showered off mud and sweat and a load of doubts. But he still felt like a teenager on a first date as he wrapped a towel around his hips and emerged from the bathroom. Until she grinned in pure appreciation and slipped past him to the bathroom and he had to wait for her for five long, interminable minutes, during which time he vowed to find a place to live that had a shower big enough for two.

With only a towel around her she walked to him and stopped inches from him, a smile playing on her lips and her blue eyes, so often full of humour and liveliness, shining up at him. He traced the line of her cheek with his finger. Strong, soft, beautiful.

She cupped his face with her hands and the light in her eyes danced in pleasure. 'I've waited a long time for this, Kennedy.'

'Me too,' he murmured. Fourteen years. The physical frustrations he'd dealt with himself, but he'd missed the emotional connection, the intimacy of trusting and sharing, of giving and receiving. Yet he already knew Erin would share more of herself, that he'd share more of himself, than in his past. He trusted her, with his body, with his heart, with all that he was and wanted to be.

Her mouth played against his, teasing and tempting, and her hands slid over the skin of his shoulders, biceps, chest, and he drew her close against his body and returned her kisses, trying to rein in the hunger and need that drove him.

'Don't hold back,' she murmured against his mouth. 'I'm not going to break. We need this now. Affirmation. Catharsis. Love. We both need it.' He felt the vibration of her laughter in her body. 'We can do sweet and tender for dessert, okay?'

Her laughter, her confidence, freed him from his hesitation, from his past. She met his hunger with her own, pulling his head down to hers, tearing away his towel and then her own, setting fire to his body with her touch, skin to skin, exploring him and guiding his hands on her and showing him what she wanted. He carried her to the bedroom with her legs around his waist and they tumbled to the cool sheets together.

He paused then, for a second, to drink in the sight of her, naked, breathless, stunning. Smooth skin over lithe limbs, the curve of abdomen, of breasts, the aroused nipples he planned to tease again, very soon. But her face captured his gaze, and her eyes, and as she drew him down to her, beyond the pleasure and the laughter and the arousal he saw love and trust and peace.

He didn't lose himself in her. He lost his reserve. He lost the concerns that had always held him back. He lost his loneliness. Her beauty and her passion and their trust in each other filled him with joy, and an intimacy of mind and heart he'd never known. And when she cried out in release and gripped his shoulders with strong hands, he let go of thought and found himself in her, together and equal and powerful with it.

•

The sun was setting in a burst of colour as they walked down to the hospital to see Jasmine and her case worker. Tomorrow they'd retrieve their vehicles from the park and Serenity Hill, but this evening Erin was content to walk by Simon's side, savouring the slight chill in the autumn air and the fresh smell of earth still damp from last night's storm. Peaceful. Peace out here in the town, peace in herself, and a new peace between her and Simon, brimming with energy, promise and strength.

There were plenty of challenges ahead – Jasmine, the investigation into Joshua's death, and deciding on and planning the future. They'd both got through worse. They'd deal with it together.

Outside the hospital, Steve sat on one of the bench seats in the small grassed area as though waiting for someone. Sometime during the day he'd shaved and changed but he looked drained and Erin doubted he'd slept at all. They stopped to greet him and to learn any news.

'My father's about to arrive,' he said. 'Aaron picked him up at the airport. I phoned him this morning with the news.'

Erin remembered Steve's comments the first night at the waterfall. Assistant Commissioner Fraser, who had a rocky relationship with his son. And a daughter he'd believed dead for many years.

As if trying to avoid thinking about his father, Steve switched to official mode. 'The critical incident team arrived earlier – they'll conduct an investigation into the two deaths at the falls,' he told them. 'Nick will be in touch because they've asked to interview both of you. But that won't be before tomorrow. They haven't found the bodies yet and I don't know what they'll decide about Joshua's death, but I'm not stressing about it at this point. I know that if the circumstances were repeated, I'd do exactly the same again.'

'So would I,' said Simon. 'If I'd known you were there, I mightn't have. But I didn't know, and people were about to die. I'd make that same decision again.'

And come what may, Erin was glad that he had. If Joshua had lived, she would have battled against impossible odds to save some of his people and might have died doing so. She had way too much to live for, and no intention of dying for at least sixty years.

'I'm off the case now,' Steve said. 'Personal connection and all that. I'll stick around town for a few days though until we sort some things out and Maddie works out what she wants to do. She's helping the police. There's no sign of Mary, or of Tamara. Mary at least knew Joshua's plans and she and Tamara had a long-running dislike of each other.'

Erin thought back to the scene by the river. 'I didn't see either of them at the falls. The last time I saw Mary was at the woolshed.'

Simon nodded agreement. 'Mary's the leader of the women? I saw her leaving the woolshed. But then I had to follow Erin and Madeleine. I'm fairly sure Mary torched the woolshed.'

'Yeah, well, Forensics are still waiting for the ruins to be declared safe, but the bad news is they think there's a body. I haven't told Maddie yet.'

'You think it's Tamara?' Erin probed. 'She knew Joshua was Hollywell. If he was silencing those who knew . . .'

'We'll find out, eventually,' Fraser said. 'There are a few others missing. One or two who went bush before we took the rest to Derringvale. Another couple who scarpered this morning. We've got people out looking for them. They won't get far on foot.'

Erin recognised his frustration. With so much unknown, and a group of wary, scared, distrustful witnesses, it might be days, weeks, maybe even longer before all the truth came out.

Madeleine had said that things had changed when Mary came. But Erin wondered if for Peter Hollywell they had already been changing, if he'd grown bored with the game of his Joshua cult and wanted new games, new power. The notoriety of exposing a cult might have given him that, if there was no one left who could blow his lies. The man could certainly manipulate an audience. The web domains he'd registered suggested he planned new games, maybe new cults that generated more wealth than Joshua's brand of simple bliss could.

'Did you find out anything about his finances?' she asked Steve.

'They're tracking it all down now. But from what he said in that conference speech, many people gave everything they owned to join the communities, and it wasn't just the three here – his followers have established a few communities in the US as well, and elsewhere. People made donations through his website, too – often big ones. And then there's the meth lab. The Feds had been watching him because of that, and suspect his groups have been major suppliers up and down the coast for a while. And Mary Saint . . .' he stopped, became a little cautious. 'Let's just say she is alleged to be a skilled laundress – of the financial variety – and to have *connections* that the Feds are particularly interested in. So if I was a betting man I'd say that what money they made is nicely put away somewhere that she can get to. Oh, and we've also had someone come forward with a description of a woman who could have been her and a youth in a vehicle behind your place on Friday night, Simon.'

'She torched my place?'

Steve shook his head. 'No hard evidence of that. At this stage. And I've probably said way too much already.'

Grateful for his candour, Erin asked, 'You'll keep us informed?'

'Of what I can. But it could all take a while. I'm not officially involved now. Which is a bugger, but I guess we've all got other things to deal with, hey?' He glanced down the road at a police car, heading towards them.

'Simon, just before I go – I'm sure you'll want to do a DNA test and confirm things properly, but you should know that Maddie has told the police and the staff here that you're Jasmine's father.'

Simon's hand gripped Erin's just a little tighter.

Steve was right. The rest was out of their hands, and Jasmine had become their priority now.

They'd talked about her, curled together in bed this afternoon after the hospital called to say that they'd admitted Jasmine for observation and assessment. They both expected there'd be meetings with authorities and health checks, evaluations and ongoing support for Jasmine. There'd also be DNA testing, custody procedures and possibly temporary foster care while it was all sorted out. But at the heart of it was a thirteen-year-old girl who'd need love and support and emotional safety.

Sometime in the last day, seeing Joshua's influence, his control over his followers, Erin had found a new perspective on her father and her own childhood. He hadn't been in the same league, he hadn't been so extreme, but the manipulation, the lies were similar. She'd been only a child who'd wanted to please him, to be loved and appreciated, and he'd used that selfishly. Jasmine bore no responsibility for what had been done to her, how she'd been taught to view the world. And neither did the girl Erin had been, her childhood self.

They farewelled Steve and left him to greet his father.

After a brief meeting with the sympathetic case worker who outlined the issues they expected, she walked them through the wards to Jasmine's room and stopped in front of the closed door.

Erin slipped her hand into Simon's again. 'Are you ready?'

'No.' He stood tall and strong and frowning and serious, and a little scary.

'Relax, soldier,' she told him. 'Different kind of battle. To start with, we're not battling each other and we're all going to win. So smile. Show her your dimples. The ones on your face, anyway.' She kissed one of those dimples lightly. 'You can do this. We can do this. We're in it together, and we make a damn fine team.'

He managed a grin, and then kissed her firmly on the mouth.

'Okay,' he said to the case worker. 'We're ready now.'

ACKNOWLEDGEMENTS

This book is the result of about a year's work, and there are many people who have helped it see the light of day.

I'm fortunate to be part of a close family. My mother, Gladys, my sisters Andrea and Margaret and my niece Lauren have variously critiqued, cajoled, brainstormed, encouraged – and have all believed in me.

My publisher at Hachette, Bernadette Foley, has not only provided her expert guidance on this book, but has supported and encouraged me through all five books with patience, professionalism, good humour and friendship. Likewise my agent, Clare Forster, whose experience, calmness and publishing wisdom I value.

I'm grateful to the editorial team at Hachette, especially editors Karen, Clara and Chris, for all their work and suggestions to make *Storm Clouds* a stronger book.

Once again, police Sergeant Gemma Gallagher has generously provided invaluable advice about police procedure and the realities and challenges of rural policing.

Writing can be a lonely business, because no one can do it for you. I'm deeply appreciative of my circle of writing friends, near and far, who continue to cheer, support and encourage me through all the ups and downs of the writing life.

A special thank you to my readers. Without you, there would be no books. Your emails, Facebook comments, reviews, and your enthusiasm at events always brighten my days and make the long hours of staring at a screen worthwhile.

Finally, as ever, this book would not have been possible without Gordon. His understanding and patience with my distracted writer's brain, my muttering and odd questions when I'm stuck, my late-night writing and my neglect of housework, are legendary. He is truly a hero.

Read on for a taste of another gripping thriller by
bestselling romantic suspense author Bronwyn Parry

DEAD HEAT

ONE

Vermin.

They had to be the worst thing about her job. The feral dogs, pigs, cats, goats and horses did enough damage, but the vermin Jo really disliked – the ones responsible for the vandalised camping ground in front of her – were the two-legged, hoon variety.

Five days since the State Minister and her entourage of hangers-on and media had, at this very spot, declared the new National Park open, and already the vermin had left their mark. Not only had they hauled down the information board – the one she'd dug the post-holes for herself because they couldn't get the mechanical digger repaired in time for the Minister's media event – they'd cut the posts into pieces with a chainsaw.

The door to the loo hung crookedly on a single hinge, the watertank beside the covered cooking area was riddled with bullet holes, and, judging by the copious amounts of broken glass around the campfire remains, they'd also smashed – or perhaps shot – a fair number of beer bottles. Presumably after drinking the contents.

They sure hadn't come out here to appreciate the natural environment.

But they weren't here now. She could see the whole camping area – no cars, no tents, no people.

She reached into the cab of the vehicle for the radio mike and rattled off her boss's call sign. 'Are you there, Mal?'

'Yeah, Jo.'

'Can you give the police a call? A mob of *Homo idiota* has been rampaging. The tank's full of bullet holes, the loo door is cactus and the info board's down – they took to it with a chainsaw.'

'Damn it. Are you all right? How many of them are there?'

'I'm fine, Mal. They're gone.'

'Are you sure?'

'Yes. Brazen louts aren't likely to be skulking in the bush, afraid of a lone woman.' Being out in the wilderness by herself was a normal part of her job, and if she spooked easily she wouldn't have lasted a week, let alone ten years.

'Okay. Can you wait until either the cops or I get there? I might be an hour. And even if there are police available, they'll probably be at least that long.'

Jo stifled a sigh. She would just have to hang around and wait for the police to take whatever evidence they needed before she would be able to start clearing up the mess.

'No worries. I'll photograph and document the wreckage.'

Photograph and document – a standard procedure she'd completed too many times, although she'd hoped such deliberate vandalism would be less frequent out here in the north-west of New South Wales than in the parks she'd worked in further east, closer to cities and city hoons.

It would take all of thirty minutes, if that. Then maybe she could map the track to the lookout while she waited, so the morning wouldn't be a total waste. Checking and updating the maps they'd inherited from State Forests was only one task on the long list of jobs to be done now that the area had officially become a National Park.

The sun's heat already warm on her back, she retrieved her camera from her day pack in the rear of the vehicle. Taking a moment to scan the large camping area, she watched, listened, alert for anything that didn't belong. The typical morning birdlife filled the air with sound. A flock of corellas, white on the dark branches of a eucalypt near the river, squabbled among themselves. A young magpie, fatter than its parents, squawked on the grass, demanding more food, and a treecreeper hopped up the bark of an iron gum, foraging for insects. At one end of the car park some of the local mob of kangaroos sprawled lazily in the shade, their morning grazing completed.

Nothing out of the ordinary, nothing disturbing the peace. Other than the wildlife, she was alone out here. Exactly the way she liked it: peaceful, without distractions, just her and the natural beauty of the wilderness. A different beauty from the parks she'd worked in for most of her career, on the eastern fall of the Great Dividing Range, but this dry, scrubby landscape of the western slopes and plains brought her almost full circle, back to the kind of landscape where she'd grown up.

She drew in a deep breath of warm, dust-dry air. A good decision, moving here, away from the constant reminders of loss and grief, as well as an enjoyable professional challenge, establishing the new park. Definitely plenty to keep her busy.

This vandalism added a few more tasks to her list for the day. Nate Harrison, the lone constable based in Goodabri, might come the twenty or more kilometres out if he was in the area, but the chance of any other police driving the fifty-plus kilometres from Strathnairn, let alone bringing a crime-scene officer, was close to zilch. Yet, just in case, she took care to disturb as little as possible as she photographed the destruction and recorded the details in a notebook.

On the edge of the camping ground, among the under-growth, a family of fairy wrens flittered in the bushes. Two young males, just coming into their adult plumage, chased each other, the half-grown tufts of blue feathers on their heads punk-like.

'At least *you* don't go around wrecking camp sites, boys,' she murmured, zooming the camera on them.

From this distance her voice didn't disturb them, but as she snapped a few shots they flew off, startled. She turned the camera to the dingo emerging from the low bushes, breakfast in its mouth. She caught its face close-up in the frame, the eyes watching her warily, ears upright, jaws clenched tightly around . . .

The image in the viewfinder began to shake violently but she snapped the photo, and another. Five fingers. A tattoo winding past the knuckles, up to the stump of the wrist, blood dark against the pale skin.

The dingo turned away and she yelled at it, desperate for it to drop its find, but it disappeared back into the undergrowth.

'Shit, shit, shit, shit.' Indecision held her motionless while she ran through her options, her heart racing as quickly as her thoughts. Follow it and see what she could find, or radio Mal to report it? She flicked the camera back to the two images she'd taken. No, it wasn't a joke artificial limb left over from a Halloween prank. Real flesh, mostly whole, so it had not been lying on the ground for days. Whatever had happened, it had to be recent. Not a minor injury. So where, and in what condition, was the person the hand belonged to?

She jogged back to her vehicle. With insufficient mobile phone reception for a call, she radioed her boss again. First things first: find out if there was still reason to worry. 'Mal, have you heard anything about someone being injured out here? Calling an ambulance, yesterday or overnight?'

'Nothing I know of, Jo. Why?'

She hesitated. No, not information she wanted to broadcast on an open radio channel, with farmers, truckies and others potentially listening in. 'There's some signs of a major injury,' she explained briefly. 'I haven't heard anything about an ambulance call-out last night, but maybe they left here by car. If you hear anything, let me know.'

Still on edge, she surveyed the camping area and surrounds, the key questions ringing in her mind: How the hell had someone lost a hand out here? Where were they now, and in what state?

The hoons had felled the posts with a chainsaw, but it would be pretty damned hard to accidentally cut off your own hand with one. Likewise with an axe or a hunting knife. Fingers, easily enough, or a chunk out of a leg or foot, but not your own hand.

That meant a much higher probability of foul play than of accident.

If the injured man was out here, the sooner she found him, the better. Aware of the isolation, kilometres from anywhere and anyone, while she checked her backpack for first-aid kit, satellite phone and portable radio she listened again for any indication of company.

Nothing but bird calls, insects and the breeze stirring the leaves.

Not far from where the dingo had trotted back into the scrub, she found drag marks, half a metre or so wide, and a few ants still gathered, here and there, around dark smears in the gravel. Pairs of footprints flanked the drag marks.

Boot prints, not wild pig or dog tracks.

She stared at them, the skin on her arms prickling despite the heat of the sun. No, there couldn't be any sort of innocent explanation for this.

Wary, making herself breathe slowly and evenly, she followed the drag marks and tracks over the rough, rocky ground among the trees.

Less than forty metres in, she found a pile of broken branches under a tree, glimpses of denim visible through the thin, dry foliage.

She'd done her share of search and rescue over the years, and dealt with more than her share of injury and death. And she could do it again.

She steeled herself and pulled aside one of the branches to check what lay beneath . . . and then jerked away, gagging, her mind reeling in horror. Not an accident. No way an accident. The man whose body lay semi-hidden had been coldly, brutally, tortured and murdered.

•

The cow stood in the middle of the narrow dirt road and stared at him. Nick stared back and inched the car forward. The cow didn't budge.

A second blast from the horn finally had it ambling to the verge, and he pressed down on the accelerator as soon as he was past.

'Turn left in one hundred metres,' the female voice of the sat nav intoned.

Down a rough track with a locked gate across it, and an 'Authorised Vehicles Only' sign?

'That'd be another "no", honey,' he muttered and turned off the useless system.

An hour since the call had come in and he still had to travel at least ten kilometres to get there. Assuming his constable's directions for the 'shortcut' route between Strathnairn and the National Park were correct. Assuming he hadn't taken the wrong road. Both the map and the sat nav had proved useless – the scale of the map not large enough to show the minor roads, the sat nav thinking every farm track and fire trail was a public road.

He mentally added *decent maps* to the list of resources he would request. Only three days into the job and his list was already long. His predecessor in the senior detective position at Strathnairn might have been content to work without adequate resources, but Nick wasn't. Although, given the large number of open cases Nick had inherited, he wondered if the word *work* had been in the man's vocabulary. That made his own posting to the almost-outback command not just a banishment but a poisoned chalice as well. Detective Garry Coulter, killed in a car accident over a month ago, had apparently been held in high regard by the locals, so raising questions about the man's competence or integrity would not make Nick popular with his new colleagues.

He would worry about that later. Right now, he had a murder to investigate – once he reached the crime scene. At least the body that had been reported wouldn't get any deader. Just – he flicked the airconditioning up a notch – just riper, in this heat.

The road joined another at a T-junction, and a National Parks sign helpfully pointed to Ghost Gums Camping Ground.

After another ten minutes of winding road through dry, rocky bush he descended to the camping ground on the river flats, the parking area already busy with three police cars, an ambulance and two National Parks utilities.

The two paramedics stood beside their ambulance, idly talking, but as Nick got out of his unmarked car, one strolled across.

'Are you the new detective?'

'Yes. Nick Matheson.' He shook hands, unblinkingly meeting the man's frankly curious and not entirely trusting gaze. So, the gossip had gone beyond his new colleagues in the Local Area Command to other emergency services. So be it. He had a job to do, and he'd do it.

'Where's the victim?'

The paramedic nodded towards the police cars at the other end of the camping ground. 'In the bush over there. He definitely doesn't need us.'

'But you're hanging around anyway?'

The guy shrugged. 'It's pretty gruesome. Someone might faint or suffer from shock.'

'Who found him?'

'Jo did.' He waved a hand towards two people in khaki shirts and trousers, leaning against the bonnet of a National Parks vehicle. 'Jo Lockwood. She's a bit shook up but she doesn't need us, either. Jo's tougher than she looks.'

Jo would be the slim one with the light brown hair held back in a ponytail. Nick couldn't see the woman's face, but from her hands-in-pockets, straight-backed stance, Jo Lockwood clearly wasn't falling apart in hysterics. That would make his job of interviewing her a hell of a lot easier.

'Thanks. I'll talk to her after I've seen what she found.'

What she'd found, he discovered when he followed the local constable through the scrub to the scene, was enough to give most people nightmares for months.

The smells of death – piss, shit and blood – turned Nick's stomach, but he quelled the response automatically. *Never show weakness.* That had been life's first lesson growing up on the docks of Newcastle, and kids who didn't learn it early suffered constant beatings and degradation.

The constable stayed to one side, staring intently at the body. 'Must be a sick bloody psycho, to have done that,' he said.

Nick crouched and, without touching a thing, surveyed the body. Facts. Evidence. That's what he needed to focus on. A rope tied tightly as a ligature above the amputated hand; another above a mangled and bloody foot. A major wound to the other knee, covered in blood, dirt and grit. The gunshot to the head probably the final of many other cuts and injuries.

The sustained violence and torture of this death – the patterns of blood flow suggested that the injuries were ante-mortem – were among the worst of the innumerable violent crimes he'd seen.

'No,' he mused, as much to himself as to the constable. 'Not *a* psycho. This guy's big, and he fought. It would have taken more than one man to restrain him.'

'From the looks of the camping-ground damage there were a few crims here last night,' the constable said. 'And he's got some unusual tattoos. Haven't seen anything like them before. Must be some sort of gang thing. You'd know about that, wouldn't you, Sarge?'

Another one who'd heard the rumours. The question might have been asked out of curiosity, but the sly grin suggested insolence.

Nick kept his expression carefully neutral and muttered a noncommittal 'Hmm.' Yes, he knew about gangs. Street gangs, bikie gangs, criminal mobs. The possibility of a gang connection in this youth's death was on his rapidly growing list but, far more than most cops, he knew there was no such simplistic crime as a 'gang thing'. He knew the complexities, the constantly shifting dynamics of power and personalities, of opportunity and risk, of adrenaline and testosterone and fear.

No, tattoos on the man's arms – which weren't any gang tattoos he was familiar with – didn't amount to evidence of an organised gang. If there were even any such thing out here in the north-west of New South Wales.

He stood and glanced at the constable's name tag. Harrison. A senior constable. Young, confident to the point of cocksure; the know-it-all type who probably didn't like taking orders. Too bad, because Nick would be giving plenty of them.

'This area needs to be taped off, Harrison. From the grassed area to past here. I called Forensic Services when you first reported in and the Crime Scene Officers are on their way from Inverell. They're contacting the forensic pathologist.'

'Don't expect one to come in person, Sarge. We're too far from Newcastle.'

Eight or more hours' drive, Nick knew. Too far from city resources . . . but not far enough from his memories. Not that Newcastle had a monopoly on bad memories. He'd collected more than enough of them from all over the map during his career. The poor dead bastard in front of him was just another drop in the ocean. Just one more crime that might, or might not, be solved.

'Have you got an ID on him? Or found his car?' he asked Harrison.

'No. None of us know him. He's not local. CSOs will search his pockets for ID.'

Nick nodded but he doubted they'd find anything useful. And judging by the burns on the remaining hand, identifiable fingerprints might be almost impossible to obtain.

He also doubted they'd find a car. If the guy had driven his own car, the assailants had probably taken it, could be a few hundred kilometres away by now.

He couldn't learn much more from the victim until after the crime-scene officers arrived, so he would have to start with the nearest thing he had to a witness.

'The National Parks officer who found him – do you know her?' he asked.

'Jo? She's a newcomer to Goodabri. Setting up things for the new park. She's the quiet type, doesn't socialise much. Seems to work hard enough though.'

Nick had taken a detour through Goodabri on his way to Strathnairn on Sunday, scoping a fraction of the large region covered by the police command. The town was thirty kilometres off the main road and consisted of fifty or so scattered houses, a police cottage, a small primary school, a row of empty shop buildings in the main street and a run-down pub. Not a thriving community, and presumably reliant on the larger Strathnairn, seventy kilometres away.

A woman who kept to herself in a small community . . . He mentally filed that piece of information. Jo Lockwood turned as he walked towards her across the grass, assessing him in the same kind of way he instinctively assessed her during those few moments.

She's the quiet type . . . Her emotions tightly leashed behind her pale face and closed expression, she shook his hand with a firm grasp when he introduced himself, and the constable's description underwent a swift revision in Nick's mind: Quiet perhaps, but from reserve, not shyness.

The calloused hand briefly in his, her lean, fit frame and her lightly tanned skin confirmed the 'seems to work hard' part of Harrison's description.

Despite her control, the haunting determination in her hazel eyes held his attention. Shock, yes – she still fought to keep it from overwhelming her. But she knew she could. He'd seen that same determination in the eyes of too many colleagues over the years – people who'd seen incomprehensible death, and survived it.

He guessed she'd be in her early thirties, but those eyes were older. No makeup, no artifice, nothing *pretty* in her face, only a stunning, stark beauty he found compelling.

Her colleague stepped forward and extended his hand. 'I'm Malcolm Stewart, senior ranger for the Strathnairn National Parks division. Do you really need to interview Jo now? She's had a tough morning.'

Before Nick could answer, Jo threw her boss a glance that mixed affection with slight exasperation. 'I don't need mollycoddling, Mal. The sooner we get this done, the sooner we can all get on with our jobs. I presume you'll want this part of the park closed, at least for today, Detective?'

'Yes. Perhaps you could liaise with the uniformed police, Mr Stewart, while I ask Ms Lockwood a few questions?'

'It's Doctor Lockwood,' Stewart corrected him. 'Doctor Joanna Lockwood. She has a PhD.'

With a gentle hand on Stewart's arm, Jo said, 'It's just a piece of paper, Mal. The title is irrelevant.'

Irrelevant? Not in Nick's estimation. He added intelligence and perseverance to his impressions of capability and control.

For all the cool calmness of her manner, the late morning was already hot, and she'd been standing around waiting for a couple of hours. Nick dragged his gaze away from a trickle of sweat running down her neck and disappearing below her open collar.

'Can we find somewhere in the shade to talk?' he asked her.

She nodded. 'There's a table down by the river. I don't think we'd be disturbing any evidence there.'

She slung a small backpack over her shoulder and led the way, skirting around the edge of the camping ground, along a thick line of trees and rough undergrowth that obscured the river from view. He could hear it – water running over rocks – but only caught glimpses now and then. So he looked, instead, at the open area of the camping ground. He would go over it closely later, but for now he concentrated on getting the general layout, the context in which the crimes had occurred. Even from this distance, the damage was obvious.

'They sure made a mess. I don't suppose you collect names, addresses or car registrations from visitors?'

'Names and postcodes sometimes – when they fill in a form. But that's hit and miss.' She turned on to a path through a break in the trees, into a clearing beside the water's edge. 'However, I can tell you that there were at least two vehicles here. And two dogs.'

Hope sparked in him. 'You saw them?'

'No. I was only here yesterday morning, and it was after that. The tyre tracks are there, though, and dog tracks and faeces beside where they were parked.' She rested her backpack on the wooden picnic table and drew out a camera. 'I have photos. I was compiling evidence for a long list of offences – criminal damage, bringing dogs and chainsaws into a National Park, lighting a campfire during a total fire ban – but I guess . . .' She sat down abruptly on the bench seat, her bitter, somewhat shaky laugh a small crack in her control. 'Murder pretty much trumps all of those.'

'It would. *If* the people who did the vandalism committed the murder.' Avoiding a lump of bird shit on the seat, he sat opposite her, taking the camera she offered and flicking through the images while keeping half his attention on her.

It was incongruous, sitting in such a cool, restful spot under the trees, the river winding its way over rocks less than ten metres away, when thirty metres behind him havoc had reigned in the night.

She stared at the table, circling a knot in the timber with her fingertip. Short, unpainted fingernails, he noticed. And tanned wrists and hands that, although small, were corded with lean muscle.

After a few moments of silence, she looked up at him and said, 'If it wasn't them, then the timing would have had to be close.'

'Why do you say that?'

'When I arrived this morning, the dog faeces were still moist. Only a few hours old. And the . . .' she steadied her voice and continued, 'the victim – there was no sign of rigor. And few insects.'

She had all his attention now. He considered her argument, and explored possible holes in it. 'The dogs might belong to the murderer.'

'The vehicle the dogs were tied up beside is the same one that rammed down the information board. There's a distinctive tyre track.'

'You're very observant.'

'I'm a scientist.'

She said it simply, as though it explained everything. Which, he supposed, it did. Scientists relied on logical processes and evidence – just as he did.